# Mary Raymond Shipman Andrews, best novels

**In this book:**
**The Perfect Tribute**
**The Lifted Bandage**
**The Courage of the Commonplace**
**Through the Ivory Gate**
**Joy in the Morning**
**A Good Samaritan**
**The Militants**

Mary Raymond Shipman Andrews (1860 - 1936) was an American writer. She is best known for a widely read short story about US President Abraham Lincoln, "The Perfect Tribute", which was adapted for film twice and sold 600,000 copies when published as a standalone volume.

Andrews primarily was known for sentimental and melodramatic magazine fiction. Many of her works were published in Scribner's Magazine, including her first published story, "Crowned with Glory and Honor", in 1902. She also wrote The Marshal, a Napoleonic historical novel, Crosses of War, a collection of World War I poetry, A Lost Commander, a biography of Florence Nightingale, and The Eternal Feminine, a collection of stories about women.

Andrews also wrote the chapter "The School Boy" in The Whole Family, a collaborative novel featuring chapters written by different authors, including Henry James and William Dean Howells. Andrews was asked to contribute the chapter about the boy Billy Talbert after Mark Twain declined.

## In this book:

**The Perfect Tribute…………………………Pag. 3**
**A Good Samaritan………………………Pag. 14**
**The Lifted Bandage……………………..Pag. 27**
**The Courage of the Commonplace……..Pag. 36**
**Through the Ivory Gate……………..…….Pag. 53**
**Joy in the Morning………..……..………Pag. 67**
**The Militants…………………………..Pag. 165**

# The Perfect Tribute

On the morning of November 18, 1863, a special train drew out from Washington, carrying a distinguished company. The presence with them of the Marine Band from the Navy Yard spoke a public occasion to come, and among the travellers there were those who might be gathered only for an occasion of importance. There were judges of the Supreme Court of the United States; there were heads of departments; the general-in-chief of the army and his staff; members of the cabinet. In their midst, as they stood about the car before settling for the journey, towered a man sad, preoccupied, unassuming; a man awkward and ill-dressed; a man, as he leaned slouchingly against the wall, of no grace of look or manner, in whose haggard face seemed to be the suffering of the sins of the world. Abraham Lincoln, President of the United States, journeyed with his party to assist at the consecration, the next day, of the national cemetery at Gettysburg. The quiet November landscape slipped past the rattling train, and the President's deep-set eyes stared out at it gravely, a bit listlessly. From time to time he talked with those who were about him; from time to time there were flashes of that quaint wit which is linked, as his greatness, with his name, but his mind was to-day dispirited, unhopeful. The weight on his shoulders seemed pressing more heavily than he had courage to press back against it, the responsibility of one almost a dictator in a wide, war-torn country came near to crushing, at times, the mere human soul and body. There was, moreover, a speech to be made to-morrow to thousands who would expect their President to say something to them worth the listening of a people who were making history; something brilliant, eloquent, strong. The melancholy gaze glittered with a grim smile. He—Abraham Lincoln—the lad bred in a cabin, tutored in rough schools here and there, fighting for, snatching at crumbs of learning that fell from rich tables, struggling to a hard knowledge which well knew its own limitations—it was he of whom this was expected. He glanced across the car. Edward Everett sat there, the orator of the following day, the finished gentleman, the careful student, the heir of traditions of learning and breeding, of scholarly instincts and resources. The self-made President gazed at him wistfully. From him the people might expect and would get a balanced and polished oration. For that end he had been born, and inheritance and opportunity and inclination had worked together for that end's perfection. While Lincoln had wrested from a scanty schooling a command of English clear and forcible always, but, he feared, rough-hewn, lacking, he feared, in finish and in breadth—of what use was it for such a one to try to fashion a speech fit to take a place by the side of Everett's silver sentences? He sighed. Yet the people had a right to the best he could give, and he would give them his best; at least he could see to it that the words were real and were short; at least he would not, so, exhaust their patience. And the work might as well be done now in the leisure of the journey. He put a hand, big, powerful, labor-knotted, into first one sagging pocket and then another, in search of a pencil, and drew out one broken across the end. He glanced about inquiringly—there was nothing to write upon. Across the car the Secretary of State had just opened a package of books and their wrapping of brown paper lay on the floor, torn carelessly in a zigzag. The President stretched a long arm.

"Mr. Seward, may I have this to do a little writing?" he asked, and the Secretary protested, insisting on finding better material.

But Lincoln, with few words, had his way, and soon the untidy stump of a pencil was at work and the great head, the deep-lined face, bent over Seward's bit of brown paper, the whole man absorbed in his task.

Earnestly, with that "capacity for taking infinite pains" which has been defined as genius, he labored as the hours flew, building together close-fitted word on word, sentence on sentence. As the sculptor must dream the statue prisoned in the marble, as the artist must dream the picture to come from the brilliant unmeaning of his palette, as the musician dreams a song, so he who writes must have a vision of his finished work before he touches, to begin it, a medium more elastic, more vivid, more powerful than any other—words—prismatic bits of humanity, old as the Pharaohs, new as the Arabs of the street, broken, sparkling, alive, from the age-long life of the race. Abraham Lincoln, with the clear thought in his mind of what he would say, found the sentences that came to him colorless, wooden. A wonder flashed over him once or twice of Everett's skill with these symbols which, it seemed to him, were to the Bostonian a key-board facile to make music, to Lincoln tools to do his labor. He put the idea aside, for it hindered him. As he found the sword fitted to his hand he must fight with it; it might be that he, as well as Everett, could say that which should go straight from him to his people, to the nation who struggled at his back towards a goal. At least each syllable he said should be chiselled from the rock of his sincerity. So he cut here and there an adjective, here and there a phrase, baring the heart of his thought, leaving no ribbon or flower of rhetoric to flutter in the eyes of those with whom he would be utterly honest. And when he had done he read the speech and dropped it from his hand to the floor and stared again from the window. It was the best he could do, and it was a failure. So, with the pang of the workman who believes his work done wrong, he lifted and folded the torn bit of paper and put it in his pocket, and put aside the thought of it, as of a bad thing which he might not better, and turned and talked cheerfully with his friends.

At eleven o'clock on the morning of the day following, on November 19, 1863, a vast, silent multitude billowed, like waves of the sea, over what had been not long before the battle-field of Gettysburg. There were wounded soldiers there who had beaten their way four months before through a singing fire across these quiet fields, who had seen the men die who were buried here; there were troops, grave and responsible, who must soon go again into battle; there were the rank and file of an everyday American gathering in surging thousands; and above them all, on the open-air platform, there were the leaders of the land, the pilots who to-day lifted a hand from the wheel of the ship of state to salute the memory of those gone down in the storm. Most of the men in that group of honor are now passed over to the majority, but their names are not dead in American history—great ghosts who walk still in the annals of their country, their flesh-and-blood faces were turned attentively that bright, still November afternoon towards the orator of the day, whose voice held the audience.

For two hours Everett spoke and the throng listened untired, fascinated by the dignity of his high-bred look and manner almost as much, perhaps, as by the speech which has taken a place in literature. As he had been expected to speak he spoke, of the great battle, of the causes of the war, of the results to come after. It was an oration which missed no shade of expression, no reach of grasp. Yet there were those in the multitude, sympathetic to a unit as it was with the Northern cause, who grew restless when this man who had been crowned with so thick a laurel wreath by Americans spoke of Americans as rebels, of a cause for which honest Americans were giving their lives as a crime. The days were war days, and men's passions were inflamed, yet there were men who listened to Edward Everett who believed that his great speech would have been greater unenforced with bitterness.

As the clear, cultivated voice fell into silence, the mass of people burst into a long storm of applause, for they knew that they had heard an oration which was an event. They clapped and cheered him again and again and again, as good citizens acclaim a man worthy of honor whom they have delighted to honor. At last, as the ex-Governor of Massachusetts, the ex-ambassador to England, the ex-Secretary of State, the ex-Senator of the United States—handsome, distinguished, graceful, sure of voice and of movement—took his seat, a tall, gaunt figure detached itself from the group on the platform and slouched slowly across the open space and stood facing the audience. A stir and a whisper brushed over the field of humanity, as if a breeze had rippled a monstrous bed of poppies. This was the President. A quivering silence settled down and every eye was wide to watch this strange, disappointing appearance, every ear alert to catch the first sound of his voice. Suddenly the voice came, in a queer, squeaking falsetto. The effect on the audience was irrepressible, ghastly. After Everett's deep tones, after the strain of expectancy, this extraordinary, gaunt apparition, this high, thin sound from the huge body, were too much for the American crowd's sense of humor, always stronger than its sense of reverence. A suppressed yet unmistakable titter caught the throng, ran through it, and was gone. Yet no one who knew the President's face could doubt that he had heard it and had understood. Calmly enough, after a pause almost too slight to be recognized, he went on, and in a dozen words his tones had gathered volume, he had come to his power and dignity. There was no smile now on any face of those who listened. People stopped breathing rather, as if they feared to miss an inflection. A loose-hung figure, six feet four inches high, he towered above them, conscious of and quietly ignoring the bad first impression, unconscious of a charm of personality which reversed that impression within a sentence. That these were his people was his only thought. He had something to say to them; what did it matter about him or his voice?

"Fourscore and seven years ago," spoke the President, "our fathers brought forth on this continent a new nation, conceived in liberty and dedicated to the proposition that all men are created equal. Now we are engaged in a great civil war, testing whether that nation, or any nation, so conceived and so dedicated, can long endure. We are met on a great battle-field of that war. We have come to dedicate a portion of it as a final resting-place for those who here gave their lives that that nation might live. It is altogether fitting and proper that we should do this.

"But in a larger sense we cannot dedicate, we cannot consecrate, we cannot hallow, this ground. The brave men, living and dead, who struggled here, have consecrated it far above our poor power to add or to detract. The world will little note nor long remember what we say here, but it can never forget what they did here. It is for us, the living, rather, to be dedicated here to the unfinished work which they who fought here have thus far so nobly advanced. It is rather for us to be here dedicated to the great task remaining before us—that from these honored dead we take increased devotion to that cause for which they here gave the last full measure of devotion—that we here highly resolve that these dead shall not have died in vain, that this nation, under God, shall have a new birth of freedom, and that government of the people, by the people, for the people shall not perish from the earth."

There was no sound from the silent, vast assembly. The President's large figure stood before them, at first inspired, glorified with the thrill and swing of his words, lapsing slowly in the stillness into lax, ungraceful lines. He stared at them a moment with sad eyes full of gentleness, of resignation, and in the deep quiet they stared at him. Not a hand was lifted in applause. Slowly the big, awkward man slouched back across the platform and sank into his seat, and yet there was no sound of approval, of recognition from the audience; only a long sigh ran like a ripple on an ocean through rank after rank. In Lincoln's heart a throb of pain answered it. His speech had been, as he feared it would be, a failure. As he gazed steadily at these his countrymen who would not give him even a little perfunctory applause for his best effort, he knew that the disappointment of it cut into his soul. And then he was aware that there was music, the choir was singing a dirge; his part was done, and his part had failed.

When the ceremonies were over Everett at once found the President. "Mr. President," he began, "your speech—" but Lincoln had interrupted, flashing a kindly smile down at him, laying a hand on his shoulder.

"We'll manage not to talk about my speech, Mr. Everett," he said. "This isn't the first time I've felt that my dignity ought not to permit me to be a public speaker."

He went on in a few cordial sentences to pay tribute to the orator of the occasion. Everett listened thoughtfully and when the chief had done, "Mr. President," he said simply, "I should be glad if I could flatter myself that I came as near the central idea of the occasion in two hours as you did in two minutes."

But Lincoln shook his head and laughed and turned to speak to a newcomer with no change of opinion—he was apt to trust his own judgments.

The special train which left Gettysburg immediately after the solemnities on the battle-field cemetery brought the President's party into Washington during the night. There was no rest for the man at the wheel of the nation next day, but rather added work until, at about four in the afternoon, he felt sorely the need of air and went out from the White House alone, for a walk. His mind still ran on the events of the day before—the impressive, quiet multitude, the serene sky of November arched, in the hushed interregnum of the year, between the joy of summer and the war of winter, over those who had gone from earthly war to heavenly joy. The picture was deeply engraved in his memory; it haunted him. And with it came a soreness, a discomfort of mind which had haunted him as well in the hours between—the chagrin of the failure of his speech. During the day he had gently but decisively put aside all reference to it from those about him; he had glanced at the head-lines in the newspapers with a sarcastic smile; the Chief Executive must he flattered, of course; newspaper notices meant nothing. He knew well that he had made many successful speeches; no man of his shrewdness could be ignorant that again and again he had carried an audience by storm; yet he had no high idea of his own speech-making, and yesterday's affair had shaken his confidence more. He remembered sadly that, even for the President, no hand, no voice had been lifted in applause.

"It must have been pretty poor stuff," he said half aloud; "yet I thought it was a fair little composition. I meant to do well by them."

His long strides had carried him into the outskirts of the city, and suddenly, at a corner, from behind a hedge, a young boy of fifteen years or so came rushing toward him and tripped and stumbled against him, and Lincoln kept him from falling with a quick, vigorous arm. The lad righted himself and tossed back his thick, light hair and stared haughtily, and the President, regarding him, saw that his blue eyes were blind with tears.

"Do you want all of the public highway? Can't a gentleman from the South even walk in the streets without—without—" and the broken sentence ended in a sob.

The anger and the insolence of the lad were nothing to the man who towered above him—to that broad mind this was but a child in trouble. "My boy, the fellow that's interfering with your walking is down inside of you," he said gently, and with that the astonished youngster opened his wet eyes wide and laughed—a choking, childish laugh that pulled at the older man's heart-strings. "That's better, sonny," he said, and patted the slim shoulder. "Now tell me what's wrong with the world. Maybe I might help straighten it."

"Wrong, wrong!" the child raved; "everything's wrong," and launched into a mad tirade against the government from the President down.

Lincoln listened patiently, and when the lad paused for breath, "Go ahead," he said good-naturedly. "Every little helps."

With that the youngster was silent and drew himself up with stiff dignity, offended yet fascinated; unable to tear himself away from this strange giant who was so insultingly kind under his abuse, who yet inspired him with such a sense of trust and of hope.

"I want a lawyer," he said impulsively, looking up anxiously into the deep-lined face inches above him. "I don't know where to find a lawyer in this horrible city, and I must have one—I can't wait—it may be too late—I want a lawyer *now*" and once more he was in a fever of excitement.

"What do you want with a lawyer?" Again the calm, friendly tone quieted him.

"I want him to draw a will. My brother is—" he caught his breath with a gasp in a desperate effort for self-control. "They say he's—dying." He finished the sentence with a quiver in his voice, and the brave front and the trembling, childish tone went to the man's heart. "I don't believe it—he can't be dying," the boy talked on, gathering courage. "But anyway, he wants to make a will, and—and I reckon—it may be that he—he must."

"I see," the other answered gravely, and the young, torn soul felt an unreasoning confidence that he had found a friend. "Where is your brother?"

"He's in the prison hospital there—in that big building," he pointed down the street. "He's captain in our army—in the Confederate army. He was wounded at Gettysburg."

"Oh!" The deep-set eyes gazed down at the fresh face, its muscles straining under grief and responsibility, with the gentlest, most fatherly pity. "I think I can manage your job, my boy," he said. "I used to practise law in a small way myself, and I'll be glad to draw the will for you."

The young fellow had whirled him around before he had finished the sentence. "Come," he said. "Don't waste time talking—why didn't you tell me before?" and then he glanced up. He saw the ill-fitting clothes, the crag-like, rough-modelled head, the awkward carriage of the man; he was too young to know that what he felt beyond these was greatness. There was a tone of patronage in his voice and in the cock of his aristocratic young head as he spoke. "We can pay you, you know—we're not paupers." He fixed his eyes on Lincoln's face to watch the impression as he added, "My brother is Carter Hampton Blair, of Georgia. I'm Warrington Blair. The Hampton Court Blairs, you know."

"Oh!" said the President.

The lad went on:

"It would have been all right if Nellie hadn't left Washington to-day—my sister, Miss Eleanor Hampton Blair. Carter was better this morning, and so she went with the Senator. She's secretary to Senator Warrington, you know. He's on the Yankee side"—the tone was full of contempt—"but yet he's our cousin, and when he offered Nellie the position she would take it in spite of Carter and me. We were so poor"—the lad's pride was off its guard for the moment, melted in the soothing trust with which this stranger thrilled his soul. It was a relief to him to talk, and the large hand which rested on his shoulder as they walked seemed an assurance that his words were accorded respect and understanding. "Of course, if Nellie had been here she would have known how to get a lawyer, but Carter had a bad turn half an hour ago, and the doctor said he might get better or he might die any minute, and Carter remembered about the money, and got so excited that they said it was hurting him, so I said I'd get a lawyer, and I rushed out, and the first thing I ran against you. I'm afraid I wasn't very polite." The smile on the gaunt face above him was all the answer he needed. "I'm sorry. I apologize. It certainly was good of you to come right back with me." The child's manner was full of the assured graciousness of a high-born gentleman; there was a lovable quality in his very patronage, and the suffering and the sweetness and the pride combined held Lincoln by his sense of humor as well as by his soft heart. "You sha'n't lose anything by it," the youngster went on. "We may be poor, but we have more than plenty to pay you, I'm sure. Nellie has some jewels, you see—oh, I think several things yet. Is it very expensive to draw a will?" he asked wistfully.

"No, sonny; it's one of the cheapest things a man can do," was the hurried answer, and the child's tone showed a lighter heart.

"I'm glad of that, for, of course, Carter wants to leave—to leave as much as he can. You see, that's what the will is about—Carter is engaged to marry Miss Sally Maxfield, and they would have been married now if he hadn't been wounded and taken prisoner. So, of course, like any gentleman that's engaged, he wants to give her everything that he has. Hampton Court has to come to me after Carter, but there's some money—quite a lot—only we can't get it now. And that ought to go to Carter's wife, which is what she is—just about—and if he doesn't make a will it won't. It will come to Nellie and me if—if anything should happen to Carter."

"So you're worrying for fear you'll inherit some money?" Lincoln asked meditatively.

"Of course," the boy threw back impatiently. "Of course, it would be a shame if it came to Nellie and me, for we couldn't ever make her take it. We don't need it—I can look after Nellie and myself," he said proudly, with a quick, tossing motion of his fair head that was like the motion of a spirited, thoroughbred horse. They had arrived at the prison. "I can get you through all right. They all know me here," he spoke over his shoulder reassuringly to the President with a friendly glance. Dashing down the corridors in front, he did not see the guards salute the tall figure which followed him; too preoccupied to wonder at the ease of their entrance, he flew along through the big building, and behind him in large strides came his friend.

A young man—almost a boy, too—of twenty-three or twenty-four, his handsome face a white shadow, lay propped against the pillows, watching the door eagerly as they entered.

"Good boy, Warry," he greeted the little fellow; "you've got me a lawyer," and the pale features lighted with a smile of such radiance as seemed incongruous in this gruesome place. He held out his hand to the man who swung toward him, looming mountainous behind his brother's slight figure. "Thank you for coming," he said cordially, and in his tone was the same air of a *grand seigneur* as in the lad's. Suddenly a spasm of pain caught him, his head fell into the pillows, his muscles twisted, his arm about the neck of the kneeling boy tightened convulsively. Yet while the agony still held him he was smiling again with gay courage. "It nearly blew me away," he whispered, his voice shaking, but his eyes bright with amusement. "We'd better get to work before one of those little breezes carries me too far. There's pen and ink on the table, Mr.—my brother did not tell me your name."

"Your brother and I met informally," the other answered, setting the materials in order for writing. "He charged into me like a young steer," and the boy, out of his deep trouble, laughed delightedly. "My name is Lincoln."

The young officer regarded him. "That's a good name from your standpoint—you are, I take it, a Northerner?"

The deep eyes smiled whimsically. "I'm on that side of the fence. You may call me a Yankee if you'd like."

"There's something about you, Mr. Lincoln," the young Georgian answered gravely, with a kindly and unconscious condescension, "which makes me wish to call you, if I may, a friend."

He had that happy instinct which shapes a sentence to fall on its smoothest surface, and the President, in whom the same instinct was strong, felt a quick comradeship with this enemy who, about to die, saluted him. He put out his great fist swiftly. "Shake hands," he said. "Friends it is."

"'Till death us do part,'" said the officer slowly, and smiled, and then threw back his head with a gesture like the boy's. "We must do the will," he said peremptorily.

"Yes, now we'll fix this will business, Captain Blair," the big man answered cheerfully. "When your mind's relieved about your plunder you can rest easier and get well faster."

The sweet, brilliant smile of the Southerner shone out, his arm drew the boy's shoulder closer, and the President, with a pang, knew that his friend knew that he must die.

With direct, condensed question and clear answer the simple will was shortly drawn and the impromptu lawyer rose to take his leave. But the wounded man put out his hand.

"Don't go yet," he pleaded, with the imperious, winning accent which was characteristic of both brothers. The sudden, radiant smile broke again over the face, young, drawn with suffering, prophetic of close death. "I like you," he brought out frankly. "I've never liked a stranger as much in such short order before."

His head, fair as the boy's, lay back on the pillows, locks of hair damp against the whiteness, the blue eyes shone like jewels from the colorless face, a weak arm stretched protectingly about the young brother who pressed against him. There was so much courage, so much helplessness, so much pathos in the picture that the President's great heart throbbed with a desire to comfort them.

"I want to talk to you about that man Lincoln, your namesake," the prisoner's deep, uncertain voice went on, trying pathetically to make conversation which might interest, might hold his guest. The man who stood hesitating controlled a startled movement. "I'm Southern to the core of me, and I believe with my soul in the cause I've fought for, the cause I'm—" he stopped, and his hand caressed the boy's shoulder. "But that President of yours is a remarkable man. He's regarded as a red devil by most of us down home, you know," and he laughed, "but I've admired him all along. He's inspired by principle, not by animosity, in this fight; he's real and he's powerful and"—he lifted his head impetuously and his eyes flashed—"and, by Jove, have you read his speech of yesterday in the papers?"

Lincoln gave him an odd look. "No," he said, "I haven't."

"Sit down," Blair commanded. "Don't grudge a few minutes to a man in hard luck. I want to tell you about that speech. You're not so busy but that you ought to know."

"Well, yes," said Lincoln, "perhaps I ought." He took out his watch and made a quick mental calculation. "It's only a question of going without my dinner, and the boy is dying," he thought. "If I can give him a little pleasure the dinner is a small matter." He spoke again. "It's the soldiers who are the busy men, not the lawyers, nowadays," he said. "I'll be delighted to spend a half hour with you, Captain Blair, if I won't tire you."

"That's good of you," the young officer said, and a king on his throne could not have been gracious in a more lordly yet unconscious way. "By the way, this great man isn't any relation of yours, is he, Mr. Lincoln?"

"He's a kind of connection—through my grandfather," Lincoln acknowledged. "But I know just the sort of fellow he is—you can say what you want."

"What I want to say first is this: that he yesterday made one of the great speeches of history."

"What?" demanded Lincoln, staring.

"I know what I'm talking about." The young fellow brought his thin fist down on the bedclothes. "My father was a speaker—all my uncles and my grandfather were speakers. I've been brought up on oratory. I've studied and read the best models since I was a lad in knee-breeches. And I know a great speech when I see it. And when Nellie—my sister—brought in the paper this morning and read that to me I told her at once that not six times since history began has a speech been made which was its equal. That was before she told me what the Senator said."

"What did the Senator say?" asked the quiet man who listened.

"It was Senator Warrington, to whom my sister is—is acting as secretary." The explanation was distasteful, but he went on, carried past the jog by the interest of his story. "He was at Gettysburg yesterday, with the President's party. He told my sister that the speech so went home to the hearts of all those thousands of people that when it was ended it was as if the whole audience held its breath—there was not a hand lifted to applaud. One might as well applaud the Lord's Prayer—it would have been sacrilege. And they all felt it—down to the lowest. There was a long minute of reverent silence, no sound from all that great throng—it seems to me, an enemy, that it was the most perfect tribute that has ever been paid by any people to any orator."

The boy, lifting his hand from his brother's shoulder to mark the effect of his brother's words, saw with surprise that in the strange lawyer's eyes were tears. But the wounded man did not notice.

"It will live, that speech. Fifty years from now American schoolboys will be learning it as part of their education. It is not merely my opinion," he went on. "Warrington says the whole country is ringing with it. And you haven't read it? And your name's Lincoln? Warry, boy, where's the paper Nellie left? I'll read the speech to Mr. Lincoln myself."

The boy had sprung to his feet and across the room, and had lifted a folded newspaper from the table. "Let me read it, Carter—it might tire you."

The giant figure which had crouched, elbows on knees, in the shadows by the narrow hospital cot, heaved itself slowly upward till it loomed at its full height in air. Lincoln turned his face toward the boy standing under the flickering gas-jet and reading with soft, sliding inflections the words which had for twenty-four hours been gall and wormwood to his memory. And as the sentences slipped from the lad's mouth, behold, a miracle happened, for the man who had written them knew that they were great. He knew then, as many a lesser one has known, that out of a little loving-kindness had come great joy; that he had wrested with gentleness a blessing from his enemy.

"'Fourscore and seven years ago,'" the fresh voice began, and the face of the dying man stood out white in the white pillows, sharp with eagerness, and the face of the President shone as he listened as if to new words. The field of yesterday, the speech, the deep silence which followed it, all were illuminated, as his mind went back, with new meaning. With the realization that the stillness had meant, not indifference, but perhaps, as this generous enemy had said, "The most perfect tribute ever paid by any people to any orator," there came to him a rush of glad strength to bear the burdens of the nation. The boy's tones ended clearly, deliberately:

"'We here highly resolve that these dead shall not have died in vain, that this nation, under God, shall have a new birth of freedom, and that government of the people, by the people, for the people shall not perish from the earth.'"

There was deep stillness in the hospital ward as there had been stillness on the field of Gettysburg. The soldier's voice broke it. "It's a wonderful speech," he said. "There's nothing finer. Other men have spoken stirring words, for the North and for the South, but never before, I think, with the love of both breathing through them. It is only the greatest who can be a partisan without bitterness, and only such to-day may call himself not Northern or Southern, but American. To feel that your enemy can fight you to death without malice, with charity—it lifts country, it lifts humanity to something worth dying for. They are beautiful, broad words and the sting of war would be drawn if the soul of Lincoln could be breathed into the armies. Do you agree with me?" he demanded abruptly, and Lincoln answered slowly, from a happy heart.

"I believe it is a good speech," he said.

The impetuous Southerner went on: "Of course, it's all wrong from my point of view," and the gentleness of his look made the words charming. "The thought which underlies it is warped, inverted, as I look at it, yet that doesn't alter my admiration of the man and of his words. I'd like to put my hand in his before I die," he said, and the sudden, brilliant, sweet smile lit the transparency of his face like a lamp; "and I'd like to tell him that I know that what we're all fighting for, the best of us, is the right of our country as it is given us to see it." He was laboring a bit with the words now as if he were tired, but he hushed the boy imperiously. "When a man gets so close to death's door that he feels the wind through it from a larger atmosphere, then the small things are blown away. The bitterness of the fight has faded for me. I only feel the love of country, the satisfaction of giving my life for it. The speech—that speech—has made it look higher and simpler—your side as well as ours. I would like to put my hand in Abraham Lincoln's—"

The clear, deep voice, with its hesitations, its catch of weakness, stopped short. Convulsively the hand shot out and caught at the great fingers that hung near him, pulling the President, with the strength of agony, to his knees by the cot. The prisoner was writhing in an attack of mortal pain, while he held, unknowing that he held it, the hand of his new friend in a torturing grip. The door of death had opened wide and a stormy wind was carrying the bright, conquered spirit into that larger atmosphere of which he had spoken. Suddenly the struggle ceased, the unconscious head rested in the boy's arms, and the hand of the Southern soldier lay quiet, where he had wished to place it, in the hand of Abraham Lincoln.

# A Good Samaritan

The little District Telegraph boy, with a dirty face, stood at the edge of the desk, and, rubbing his sleeve across his cheek, made it unnecessarily dirtier.

"Answer, sir?"

"No—yes—wait a minute." Reed tore the yellow envelope and spread the telegram. It read:

"Do I meet you at your office or at Martin's and what time?"

"The devil!" Reed commented, and the boy blinked indifferently. He was used to stronger. "The casual Rex all over! Yes, boy, there's an answer." He scribbled rapidly, and the two lines of writing said this:

"Waiting for you at office now. Hurry up. C. Reed."

He fumbled in his pocket and gave the youngster a coin. "See that it's sent instantly—like lightning. Run!" and the sharp little son of New York was off before the last word was well out.

Half an hour later, to Reed waiting at his office in Broadway impatiently, there strolled in a good-looking and leisurely young man with black clothes on his back and peace and good-will on his face. "Hope I haven't kept you waiting, Carty," he remarked in friendly tones. "Plenty of time, isn't there?"

"No, there isn't," his cousin answered, and there was a touch of snap in the accent. "Really, Rex, you ought to grow up and be responsible. It was distinctly arranged that you should call here for me at six, and now it's a quarter before seven."

"Couldn't remember the hour or the place to save my life," the younger man asserted earnestly. "I'm just as sorry as I can be, Carty. You see I did remember we were to dine at Martin's. So much I got all right—and that was something, wasn't it, Carty?" he inquired with an air of wistful pride, and the frown on the face of the other dissolved in laughter.

"Rex, there's no making you over—worse luck. Come along. I've got to go home to dress after dinner you see, before we make our call. You'll do, on the strength of being a theological student."

The situation was this: Reginald Fairfax, in his last year at the Theological Seminary, in this month of May, and lately ordained, had been seriously spoken of as assistant to the Rector of the great church of St. Eric's. It was a remarkable position to come the way of an undergraduate, and his brilliant record at the seminary was one of the two things which made it possible. The other was the friendship and interest of his cousin, Carter Reed, head clerk in the law firm of Rush, Walden, Lee and Lee, whose leading member, Judge Rush, was also senior warden at St. Eric's. Reed had called Judge Rush's attention to his young cousin's career, and, after some inquiry, the vestryman had asked that the young man should be brought to see him, to discuss certain questions bearing on the work. It was almost equivalent to a call coming from such a man, and Reed was delighted; but here his troubles began. In vain did he hopefully fix date after date with the slippery Rex—something always interfered. Twice, to his knowledge, it had been the chance of seeing a girl from Orange which had thrown over the chance of seeing the man of influence and power. Once the evening had been definitely arranged with Judge Rush himself, and Reed was obliged to go alone and report that the candidate had disappeared into a tenement district and no one knew where to find him. The effect of that was fortunately good—Judge Rush was rather pleased than otherwise that a young clergyman should be so taken up with his work as to forget his interests. But Reed was most anxious that this evening's appointment should go off successfully, while Rex was as light-hearted as a bird. Any one would have thought it was Reed's own future he was laboring over instead of that of the youngster who had a gift of making men care for him and work for him without effort on his own part.

The two walked down Broadway toward the elevated road, Rex's dark eyes gathering amusement here and there in the crowded way as they went.

"Look at Billy Strong—why there's Billy Strong across the street. Come over and I'll present you, Carty. Just the chap you want to meet. He's a great athlete—on the water-polo team of the New York Athletic Club, you know—as much of an old sport as you are." And Reed found himself swung across and standing before a powerful, big figure of a man, almost before he could answer. There was another man with the distinguished Billy, and Reed had not regarded the two for more than one second before he discovered that they were both in a distinct state of intoxication. In fact, Strong proclaimed the truth at once, false shame cast to the winds. He threw his arm about Rex's neck with a force of affection which almost knocked down the quartette.

*"Recky," he bubbled, "good old Recky—bes' fren' ev' had"*

"Recky," he bubbled, "good old Recky—bes' fren' ev' had—I'm drunk, Recky—too bad. We're both drunk. Take's home." Rex glanced at his cousin in dismay, and Strong repeated his invitation cordially. "Take's home, Recky," he insisted, with the easy air of a man who confers an honor. "'S up to you, Recky."

Rex looked at his frowning cousin doubtfully, pleadingly.

"It almost seems as if it was, doesn't it, Carty?" he said. "We can't leave them like this."

"I don't see why we can't—I can," Reed asserted. "It's none of our business, Rex, and we really haven't time to palaver. Come along."

The gentle soul of Rex Fairfax was surprisingly firm. "Carty, they'd be arrested in five minutes," he reasoned. "It's a wonder they haven't been already. And Billy's people—it would break their hearts. I know some of them well, you see. I was with him only last week over in Orange."

"Oh!" Reed groaned. "That Girl from Orange again." He opened his lips once more to launch nervous English against this quixotism, but Strong interposed.

"'S all true," he solemnly stated, fixing his eyes rollingly on Reed. "Got Orange-colored cousin what break Recky's heart if don't take's home. Y'see—y'see—" The President of these United States in a cabinet council would have stopped to listen to him, so freighted with great facts coming was his confidential manner. "Y'see—wouldn't tell ev'body—only you," and he laid a mighty hand on Reed's shoulder. "I'm so drunk. Awful pity—too bad," and he sighed deeply. "Now, Recky, ol' man, take's home."

*"Who's your friend, Billy?"*

"Who's your friend, Billy?" Rex inquired, disregarding this appeal.

Billy burst into a shout of laughter which Fairfax promptly clipped by putting his hand over the big man's mouth. "He's bes' joke yet," Strong remarked through Rex's fingers. "He's go'n' kill himself," and he kissed the restraining hand gallantly.

The two sober citizens turned and stared at the gentlemen. He looked it. He looked as if there could be no step deeper into the gloom which enveloped him, except suicide. He nodded darkly as the two regarded him.

"Uh-huh. Life's failure. Lost cuff-button. Won't live to be indecent. Go'n' kill m'self soon's this dizhiness goesh pasht. Billy's drunk, but I'm subject to—to dizhiness."

Rex turned to his cousin with a gesture. "You see, Carty, we can't leave them. I'm just as disappointed as you are, but it would be a beastly thing to do, to let them get pulled in as common drunks. What's your friend's name?" he demanded again of Strong.

"Got lovely name," he averred eagerly. "Good ol' moth-eaten name. Name's Schuyler VanCourtlandt Van de Water—ain't it Schuylie—ain't that your name—or's that mine? I—I f'rget lil' things," he said in an explanatory manner.

But the suicide spoke up for himself. "Tha's my name," he said aggressively. "Knew it in a minute. Tha's my father's name and my grandfath's name, and my great grandfath's name and my great-great——"

"Stop," said Rex tersely, and the man stopped. "Now tell me where you live."

Billy Strong leaned over and punched the man in the ribs. "You lemme tell 'em. Lives nine-thous-n sixt'-four East West Street," he addressed Rex, and chuckled.

"Don't be a donkey, Billy—tell me his right address." Rex spoke with annoyance—this scene was getting tiresome, and although Reed was laughing hopelessly, he was on his mind.

"Oh! F'got!" Billy's tipsy coyness was elephantine. "Lives *six* thous'n *sev*'nty four North S—South Street," and he roared with laughter.

Rex was about to learn how to manage Billy Strong. "Bill," he said, "be decent. You're making me lots of trouble," and Billy burst into tears and sobbed out:

"Wouldn' make Recky trouble for worlds—good ol' Recky—half-witted ol' goat, but bes' fren' ev' had," and the address was captured.

Rex turned to his cousin, his winning, deprecating manner warning Reed but softening him against his will. "Carty," he said, "there's nothing for it, but for you to take one chap and I the other and see 'em home. It's only a little after seven and we ought to be able to meet by half-past eight—at the Hotel Netherland, say—that's near the Rush's. We'll have to give up dinner, but we'll get a sandwich somewhere, and we'll do. I'll take Strong because he's more troublesome—I think I can manage him. It's awfully good of you, and I can tell you I appreciate it. But it wouldn't be civilized to do less, old Carty, would it?" And Reed found himself, grumbling but docile, linked to the suicide's arm, and guiding his shuffling foot-steps in the way they should go.

"Now, we'll both kill ourselves, old Carty, won't we?" Rex heard his cousin's charge mumble cheerfully as they started off, with a visible lengthening of his gloom at the thought of companionship at death.

Strong was marching along with an unearthly decorum that should have made Fairfax suspicious. But instead it cheered his optimistic soul immensely. "Good for you old man," he said encouragingly. "At this rate we'll get you home in no time." And Billy, at that second, thrust out his great shoulder into the crowd, and almost knocked a man down. The man, whirled sidewise in front of them, glared savagely.

"What do you mean by that?" he demanded. Strong, to whom nothing would have given more joy than a tussle, bent down and peered into the other's face.

"Is it a man or a monkey?" he piped, and shrieked with laughter.

The man's strained temper broke suddenly and Rex caught him by the arm as he was about to spring for Strong, and promptly threw himself between the two.

"Look here, Billy," he remonstrated, "if you fight anybody it's got to be me," and he spoke over his shoulder to the stranger. "You see what I'm up against. I'm getting him home—do just go on," and the man went.

But Billy's head was in his guardian's neck and he was spluttering and sobbing. "Fight you? Nev'—s' help me—nev'—Fight poor, ole fool Recky—bes' fren' ev' had? No sir. I wouldn' fight you Recky," and he raised a tear-stained face and gazed mournfully into his eyes. "D'ye think I'd——"

"Oh, shut up!" Rex ejaculated, "and hold your head up, Billy. You make me sick."

The intoxicated heavy freight being under way again, Rex looked about for the rest of the train, but in vain. After a halt of a minute or so he decided that they were lost and would have to stay lost, the situation being too precarious, in this land of policemen, with one hundred and ninety pounds of noisy uncertainty on his hands, to risk any unnecessary movement. Billy kept every breath of time alive and varied. Within two minutes of the first adventure he managed to put his elbow clearly and forcibly into a small man's mouth, and before the other could resent it:

"'S my elbow, sir," he said, haughtily, stopping and staring down.

"Well, why in thunder don't you keep it where it belongs?" snapped the man, and Billy caught him by the sleeve.

"Lil' sir," he said impressively, "if you should bite off my elbow, you saucy baggage"—and the thought was too much for him. Tears filling his eyes he turned to Rex. "Recky, you spank that lil' sir," he pleaded brokenly. "He's too lil' for me—I'd hurt him"—and Rex meditated again. A shock came when they reached the corner of Broadway and Chambers Street. "Up's' daisy," crowed Billy Strong, and swung Fairfax facing uptown with a mighty heave.

"The Elevated station's down a block, old chap," explained the sober contingent. "We have to take the Elevated to Seventy-second you know, and walk across to your place."

Billy looked at him pityingly. "You poor lil' pup," he crooned. "Didn' I keep tellin' you had to go Chris'pher Street ferry meet a girl? Goin' theater with girl." He tipped his derby one-sided and started off on a cakewalk.

Rex had to march beside him willy-nilly. "Look here, Billy," he reasoned, exasperated at this entirely fresh twist in the corkscrew business of getting Strong home. "Look here, Billy, this is tommy-rot. You haven't any date with a girl, and if you had you couldn't keep it. Come along home, man; that's the place for you."

But Billy was suddenly a Gibraltar of firmness. "Got date with lovely blue-eyed girlie—couldn't dish'point her. Unmanly deed—Recky, d'*you* want bes' fren' ev' had to do unmanly deed, and dish'point trustin' female? Nev', Recky—nev', ol' man. Lesh be true to th' ladies till hell runs dry—Oh, 'scuse me Recky—f'got you was parson— till *well* runs dry, meant say. That all right? Come on t' Chris'pher Street." And in spite of desperate attempts, of long argument and appeal on Rex's part, to Christopher Street they went.

The ministering angel had no hankering to risk his charge in a street-car, so, as the distance was not great, they walked.

Fairfax's dread was that, having saved his friend so far, he should attract the attention of a policeman and be arrested. So he kept a sharp lookout for bluecoats and passed them studiously on the other side. What was his horror therefore, turning a corner, to turn squarely into the majestic arm of the law, and what was his greater horror, to hear Billy Strong suavely address him. Billy lifted his hat to the large, fat officer as he might have lifted it to his sweetheart in her box at the Horse Show.

"Would you have the g—goodness to tell me," he inquired, with distinguished courtesy, "if this is"—Billy's articulation was improving, but otherwise he was just as tipsy as ever—"if this is—Chris-to-pher Street—or—or Wednesday?"

"Hey?" inquired the policeman, and stared. Repartee seemed not to be his forte.

*"Thank you—thank you very much—very, very much—old rhinoceros"*

"Thank you—thank you very much"—Billy's gratitude spilled over conventional limits—"very, *very* much—old rhinoceros," he finished, and shot suddenly ahead, dragging Rex with him into the whirlpool of a moving crowd, and it dawned on the policeman five minutes later that the courtly gentleman was drunk.

The anxiety of this game was its unexpectedness. Strong, in the turn of a hand grew playful, after the fashion of a mammoth kitten. He bounded this way and that, knocking into somebody inevitably at every leap, and at each contact he wheeled toward the injured and lifted his hat and bowed low and brought out "I—beg—your—pardon" with a drawl of sarcastic emphasis too insulting to be described.

"Billy," pleaded Rex, taking to pathos, "don't do that again. You'll get arrested, and maybe they'll arrest me too, and you don't want to get me into a hole, do you?"

Billy stopped short with a suddenness which came near to upsetting his guide, and put both large hands on Rex's shoulders, and gazed into his eyes with a world of blurred affection. "Reck, ol'fel'," and his voice broke with a sob, "if I got you into hole, I'd jump in hole after you, and I'd—and I'd—pull hole in after both of us, and then I'd—I'd tell hole you was bes' fren' ev' had, and——"

"Come along and behave," cut in the victim of this devotion shortly. "Don't be a fool."

Strong lifted a fatherly forefinger. "Naughty naughty! Shouldn' call brother fool. Danger hell fire if you call brother fool. Nev' min', Recky—we un'stand each other. Two fools. I'm go'n behave." He knocked his derby in the back so it rested on his nose, stuck his chin up to meet it, and started off in the most unmistakable semblance of a tipsy man to be met anywhere. "See me behavin'?" he remarked sidewise, with a gleam of rollicking deviltry out of his eyes.

*"So tired" he remarked. "Go'n have good nap now"*

Christopher Street ferry was reached safely by a miracle, and inside the ferry-house Strong made a bee line for a truck and threw his great body full length upon it with a loud yawn of joy. "So tired," he remarked. "Go'n have good nap now," and he closed his eyes peacefully.

"See here, Billy, this won't do. You said you had to meet a girl—what about that?"

"Oh, tha's all right," Billy agreed easily. "You meet girl—tell her you got me drunk," and he turned over and prepared for slumber. Strenuous argument was necessary to rouse him even to half a sense of responsibility. "Recky, dear, you—'noy me," he said with severity, coming to a sitting position and contemplating Rex with mild displeasure. "What kin' girl? Why, jes' girly-girl. Lovely blue-eyed girly-girl—kind of girl—colored hair,"—he swept his hand descriptively over his own black locks. "Wears sort of—skirts, you know—you 'member the kind. All of 'em same thing—well, she wears 'em too. Tha's all," and he dropped heavily back to the truck and retired into his coat collar.

Rex shook him. "That won't do, Billy. I can't pick out a girl on that. Will there be a chaperone with her?"

"No!" thundered Billy.

"How is a girl allowed to go to the theater with you without a chaperone?" inquired Rex incredulously. "This is New York."

Strong brought down his fist. "Death to chaperones! *A bas les chaperones!* Don't you think girl's mother trust her to me? Look at me! I'll be chaperone to tha' girl, and father, 'n' mother, 'n' a few uncles and aunts." He threw his arm out with a gesture which comprised the universe. "I'll be all the world to tha' girl. You go meet her 'n' tell her you got me drunk," he concluded with a radiant smile.

Rex considered. There seemed to be enough method in Strong's madness to justify the belief that he had an engagement. If so, he must by all means wait and trust to luck to pick out the "lovely blue-eyed girlie" who was the "party of the other part," and hope for an inspiration as to what to tell her. She might be with or without a chaperone, she might be any variety of the species, but Strong seemed to be quite clear that she had blue eyes.

The crowd from the incoming boat began to unload into the ferry-house, and Rex placed himself anxiously by the entrance. Three or four thin men scurried in advance, then a bunch of stout and middle-aged persons straggled along puffing. Then came a set of young people in theater array, chattering and laughing as they hurried, and another set, and another—the main body of the little army was upon him. Rex scanned them for a girl alone or a girl with her mother. Ah! here she was—this must be Strong's "blue-eyed girlie." She was alone and pretty, a little under-bred and blond. Rex lifted his hat.

"I beg your pardon," he said, in his most winning way; "are you waiting for Mr. Strong?"

The girl threw up her head and looked frightened, and then angry.

"No, I am not," she said, and then, with a haughty look, "I call you pretty saucy," and Rex was left mortified and silent, while a passing man murmured, "Served you right," and a woman laughed scornfully. He stalked across to the tranquil form on the truck.

"Billy," he said, and shook a massive shoulder. "Wake up. Tell me that girl's name."

Strong opened his eyes like a baby waked from dewy sleep. "Wha's that, Recky—dear old Recky—bes' fren'——"

"Cut that out," said Rex, sharply. "Tell me the name of the girl you're waiting here to meet," and he laughed a short bitter laugh. The girl whom "Billy" was waiting to meet! Rex was getting tired and hungry.

Strong smiled a gentle, obstinate, tipsy smile and shook his head. "No, Recky, dear ol' fren'—bes' fren'—well, nev' min'. Can't tell girl's name; tha's her secret."

"Don't be an ass, Billy—quick, now, tell me the name."

"Naughty, naughty!" quoted Billy again, and waggled his forefinger. "Danger hell fire! Couldn' tell girl's name, Recky—be dishon'able. Couldn', no, couldn'. Anythin' else—ask m' anythin' else in all these wide worlds"—and he struck his breast with fervor. "Tell you *anythin'*, Recky, but couldn' betray trustin' girl's secret."

"Billy, can't you give me an idea what the girl's like?" pleaded Rex desperately. Billy smiled up at him drowsily. "Perfectly good girl," he elucidated. "Good eyes, good wind, kind to mother—perfectly good girl in ev—every r-respect," he concluded, emphasizing his sentences by articulating them. He dropped his chin into his chest with a recumbent bow, and his arm described an impressive semicircle. "Present to her 'surances my most disting'shed consider-ration—soon's you find her," and he went flop on his side and was asleep.

Rex had to give it up. He heard the gates rattling open for the next boat-load, and took his stand again, bracing himself for another rebuff. The usual vanguard, the usual quicksilver bunch of humanity, massing, separating, flowing this way and that, and in the midst of them a fair-haired, timid-looking young girl, walking quietly with downcast eyes, as if unused to being in big New York alone at eight o'clock at night. Rex stood in front of her with bared head.

"I beg your pardon," he repeated his formula; "are you looking for Mr. Strong?"

The startled eyes lifted to his a short second, then dropped again. "No, for Mr. Week," she answered softly, and unconscious of witticism, melted into the throng.

This was a heavy boat-load, for it was just theater time—they were still coming. And suddenly his heart bounded and stopped. Of course—he was utterly foolish not to have known—it was she—Billy Strong's bewitching cousin, the girl from Orange. There she stood with her big, brown eyes searching, gazing here and there, as lovely, as incongruous as a wood-nymph strayed into a political meeting. The feather of her hat tossed in the May breeze; the fading light from the window behind her shone through loose hair about her face, turned it into a soft dark aureole; the gray of her tailor gown was crisp and fresh as spring-time. To Rex's eyes no picture had ever been more satisfying.

Suddenly she caught sight of him, and her face lighted as if lamps had shone out of a twilight, and in a second he had her hand in his, and was talking away, with responsibility and worry, and that heavy weight on the truck back there, quite gone out of the world. She was in it, and himself—the world was full. The girl seemed to be as oblivious of outside facts, as he, for it was quite two minutes, and the last straggler from the boat had disappeared into the street before she broke into one of his sentences.

"Why, but—I forgot. You made me forget entirely, Mr. Fairfax. I'm going to the theater with my cousin, Billy Strong. He ought to be here—where is he?"

Rex shivered lest her roving eyes might answer the question, for Billy's truck with Billy slumbering peacefully on it, lay in full view not fifty feet away. But her gaze passed unsuspiciously over the prostrate, huddled form.

"It's very queer—I'm sure this was the right boat." She looked up at his face anxiously, and he almost moaned aloud. What was he going to say to her?

"That's what I'm here for, Miss Margery—to explain about Billy. He—he isn't feeling at all himself to-night, and it's utterly impossible for him to go with you." To his astonishment her face broke into a very satisfied smile. "Oh—well, I'm sorry Billy's ill, but we'll hope for the best, and I won't really object to you as a substitute, you know. Of course it's improper, and mother wouldn't think of letting me go with you—but I'm going. Mother won't mind when I tell her it's done. I've never been alone with a man to anything, except with my cousin—it's like stealing watermelons, isn't it? Don't you think it's rather fun?"

Staggered by the situation, Fairfax thought desperately and murmured something which sounded like "Oochee-Goochee," as he tried to recall it later. The girl's gay voice went on: "It would be wicked to waste the tickets. City people aren't going to the theater as late as this, so we won't see any one we know. I think it's a dispensation of Providence, and I'd be a poor-spirited mouse to waste the chance. I think I'll go with you—don't you?"

*"Could he—couldn't he?"*

19

Could he leave that prostrate form on the truck and snatch at this bit of heaven dangling before him? Could he—Couldn't he? No, he could not. It would be a question of fifteen minutes perhaps before the drowsy Billy would be marching to the police station, and in his entirely casual and fearless state of mind, the big athlete would make history for some policeman, his friend could not doubt, before he got there. Rex had put his hand to this intoxicated plow and he must not look back, even when the prospect backwards was so bewilderingly attractive, so tantalizingly easy. He stammered badly when, at length, the silence which followed the soft voice had to be filled.

"I'm simply—simply—broken up, Miss Margery," and the girl's eyes looked at him with a sweet wideness that made it harder. "I don't know how to tell you, and I don't know how to resign myself to it either, but I—I can't take you to the theater. I—I've got to—got to—well, you see, I've got to be with Billy."

She spoke quickly at that. "Mr. Fairfax, is Billy really ill—is there something more than I understand? Why didn't you tell me? Has their been an accident, perhaps? Why, I must go to him too—come—hurry—I'll go with you, of course."

Rex stumbled again in his effort to quiet her alarm, to prevent this scheme of seeking Billy on his couch of pain. "Oh no, indeed you mustn't do that," he objected strenuously. "I couldn't let you, you know. I don't want you to be bothered. Billy isn't ill at all—there hasn't been any accident, I give you my word. He's all right—Billy's all right." He had quite lost his prospective by now, and did not see the rocks upon which he rushed.

"If Billy's all right, why isn't he here?" demanded Billy's cousin severely.

Rex saw now. "He isn't exactly—that is to say—all right, you know. You see how it is," and he gazed involuntarily at the sleeping giant huddled on the truck.

"I do not see." The brown eyes had never looked at him so coldly before, and their expression cut him.

"I'm glad you don't," he cried, and realized that the words had taken him a step deeper into trouble. "It's just this way, Miss Margery—Billy isn't hurt or ill, but he isn't—isn't feeling quite himself, and—and I've got to—I've got to be with him." His voice sounded as if he were going to cry, but it moved the girl to no pity.

"Oh!" she said, and her bewildered tone was a whole world removed from the bright comradeship with which she had met him. "I see—you and Billy have something else planned." Her face flushed suddenly. "I'm sorry I misunderstood about—about the theater. I wouldn't for worlds have—have seemed to force you to—" She stopped, embarrassed, hurt, but yet with her graceful dignity untouched.

"Oh," the wretched Rex exclaimed impetuously, "if I could only take you to the theater, I'd rather than—" but the girl stopped him.

"Never mind about that, please," she said, with gentle decision. "I must go home—when is the next boat? One is going now—good-night, Mr. Fairfax—no, don't come with me—I don't need you," and she was gone.

Two minutes later Strong's innocent slumbers were dispersed by a vicious shake. "Wake up! wake up!" ordered Fairfax, restraining himself with difficulty from mangling the cause of his sufferings. "I've had enough, and we're going home, straight."

Rex was mistaken about that, but Billy was cordial in agreeing with him. "Good idea, Recky! Howd'y' ever come to think of it? Le's go home straight; tha's a bully good thing to do. Le's do it. Big head on you, ol' boy," and yawning still, but with unperturbed good nature, Strong marched, a bit crookedly, arm in arm with his friend to the street.

*At every station the conductor and Rex had to reason with him*

Rex's memory of the trip uptown on the Elevated was like an evil dream. Strong, after his nap, was as a giant refreshed, and his play of wit knew no contracting limits. There were, luckily, not many passengers going up at this hour, but the dozen or so on the car were regaled. Billy selected a seat on the floor with his broad back planted against the door, and at every station the conductor and Rex had to reason with him at length before the door could be opened. The official threatened as well as he could for laughing to put him off, but he threatened less strenuously for the sight of six feet two of muscle in magnificently fit condition. This lasted for half a dozen stations and then the patient began to play like a mountainous kitten. He took a strap on either side of the car and turned somersaults; he did traveling ring work with them; he gave a standing broad jump that would have been creditable on an athletic field; he had his audience screaming with laughter at an imitation of water polo over the back of a seat. Then, just as the fun was at an almost impossible point, and the conductor, highly entertained but worried, was considering how to get this chap arrested, Billy walked up to him with charming friendliness and shook hands.

"One th' besh track meets I've ever had pleasure attendin', sir," he said genially, and sat down and relapsed into grave dignity.

So he remained for five minutes, to the trembling joy of his exhausted guardian, but it was too good to be true. Suddenly, at Fifty-third Street, he spied a young woman at the other end of the car. There were not more than nine passengers, so that each person might have had a matter of half a dozen seats a piece, but Strong suddenly felt a demand on his politeness, and reason was nothing to him. He rose and marched the forty feet or so between himself and the woman, and, standing in front of her, lifted, with some difficulty, his hat.

"Won't you take my seat, madam?" he inquired, with a smile of perfect courtesy.

The young person was a young person of common-sense and she caught the situation. She flashed a reassuring glance at Rex, hovering distressed in the background, and shook her head at Strong politely. "No—no, thank you," she said; "I think I can find a seat at this end that will do nicely."

"Madam, I insist," Strong addressed her again earnestly.

"No, really," The young woman was embarrassed, for the eyes of the car were on her. "Thank you so much," she said finally; "I think I'd better stay here."

Strong bent over and put a great hand lightly on her arm. "Madam, as gen'leman I cannot, cannot allow it. Madam, you mush take my seat. Pleash, madam, do not make scene. 'S pleasure to me, 'sure you—greates' pleasure," and beneath this courtly urgency the flushed girl walked shamefacedly the length of the almost empty car, and sat down in Strong's seat, while that soul of chivalry put his hand through a strap and so stood till his ministering angel extracted him from the train at Seventy-second Street.

With a sigh of heartfelt relief, Rex put his arm in the big fellow's at the foot of the steps. Freedom must now be at hand, for Billy's home was in a great apartment building not ten minutes' walk away. The culprit himself seemed to realize that his fling was over.

"Raished Cain t'night, didn' we, ol' pal?" he inquired, and squeezed Rex's guiding arm with affection. "I'll shay this for you, Rex—you may be soft-hearted ol' slob, you may be half-witted donkey—I'm not denyin' all that 'n more, but I'll shay thish—you're the bes' man to go on a drunk with in—in—in The'logican Sem'nary. I'm not 'xceptin' th'——"

"Shut up, Billy," remarked Rex, not for the first time that night. "I'd get myself pulled together a bit if I were you," he advised. "You're going to see your family in a minute."

"M' poor fam'ly!" mourned Strong, shaking his head. "M' poor fam'ly! Thish'll be awful blow to m' fam'ly, Recky. They all like so mush to see me sober—always—'s their fad, Recky. Don't blame 'em, Recky, 's natural to 'em. Some peop' born that way. M' poor fam'ly."

They stood in front of the broad driveway which swept under lofty arches into the huge apartment house. Strong stopped and gazed upwards mournfully. "Right up there," he murmured, pointing skywards—"M' fam'ly." The tears were streaming down his face frankly now. "I can't face 'em Recky, 'n this condition you've got me in," he said more in sorrow than in anger. At that second the last inspiration of the evening caught him. Across the street arose the mighty pile of an enormous uptown hotel. Strong jerked his thumb over his shoulder. "Go'n' break it to m' fam'ly by telegraph' 'em," he stated, and bitterly Rex repented of that thoughtless mention of the Strongs to their son and heir.

Good-naturedly as he had done everything, but relentlessly, he dragged his victim over the way, and direct to the Western Union office of the hotel—"Webster's Union" he preferred to call it. His first telegram read:

"Rex Fairfax got me drunk. Don't blame him. It's natural to him."

That one was confiscated, Strong complaining gently that his friend was all "fads." The second message was this:

"Dear Mama: Billy's intoxicated. Awfully sorry. Couldn't be helped. Home soon."

That one went in spite of Fairfax's efforts, with two cents extra to pay, which item was the first event of the evening to ruffle Strong's temper.

"Shame, shame on rich cap'talists like Webster's Union to wring two cents from poor drunk chap, for lil' word like 'soon'," he growled, and appealed to the operator. "Couldn't you let me off that two cents?" he asked winningly. "You're good fellow—good lookin' fellow too"—which was the truth. "Well, then, can I get 'em cheaper 'f I sen 'em by quantity? I'll do that—how many for dollar, hey?"

"Five," said the grinning operator, troubled by the irregularity, but taken by this highly entertaining scheme of telegraphing across the street. And Rex, his arts exhausted in vain, watched hopelessly while, one after another, five telegrams were sent to The Montana, a hundred feet away. The first being short two of the regulation ten words. Strong finished with a cabalistic phrase: "Rectangular parallelopipedon."

"That'll get even Webster's Union for chargin' me two cents for 'soon'," he chuckled. "Don't y' wish y' hadn' charged me that two cents, hey?" he demanded of the operator, laughing joyfully and cocking his hat over one ear, and the operator and two or three men who stood near could do no otherwise than laugh joyfully too. Strong straightened his face into a semblance of deep gravity. "Thish next one's important," he announced, and put the end of the pencil in his mouth and meditated, while his fascinated audience watched him. He was lost in thought for perhaps two minutes, and then scribbled madly, and as he ended the little bunch of men crowded frankly to look at what he had written. He pushed it toward them with charming unreserve, and the bewilderment with which it was read seemed to please him.

"Dear Papa": it ran. "I'm Calymene Blumembachii, a trilobite, one of the crustaceans related to the emtomostracans, but looking more like a tetradecapod, but always your affectionate—Billy."

He pushed it to the operator. "Split that in three," he ordered. "Don't want ruin the wires I'm careful 'bout wires. Big fall snow wouldn't do more damage 'n heavy words like that," he explained to the listening circle. "Think I look like tetradecapod?" he asked of them as one who makes conversation. "Had that in geology lesson when I was fifteen," he went on. "Got lodged in crack in brain and there tish t' thish day! Every now'n then I go 'flip,'"—he appeared to pull a light lever situated in his head—"'n fire it off. See? Always hit something."

It was ten o'clock when, the job lot of telegrams despatched, Fairfax led his volcano from the hotel and headed for the apartment house. He expected another balk at the entrance, for his round of gaiety had come now to seem to him eternal—he could hardly imagine a life in which he was not conducting a tipsy man through a maze of experiences. So that it was one of the surprises of the evening when Strong entered quietly and with perfect deportment took his place in the elevator and got out again, eight floors up, with the mildness of a dove. At the door of the apartment came the last brief but sharp action of the campaign.

"Recky," he said, taking Fairfax's shoulders in his great grasp, "no mother could be t' me what you've been."

"I hope not," Rex responded promptly, but Strong was not to be side-tracked.

"No mother 'n the world—not one—no sir!" he went on. His voice broke with feeling. "I'll nev' forget it—nev'—don't ask me to," he insisted. "Dear Recky—blessed old tomfool—I'm go'n kiss you good-night."

"You bet you're not," said Fairfax with emphasis. "Let go of me, you idiot," and he tried to loosen the hands on his shoulders.

But one of the most powerful men in New York had him in his grip, and Rex found himself suddenly folded in Billy's arms, while a chaste salute was planted full on his mouth. As he emerged a second later, disgusted and furious, from this tender embrace, the clang of the elevator twenty feet away caught his ear and, turning, his eyes met the astonished gaze of two young girls and their scornful, frowning father. At that moment the door of the Strongs' apartment opened, there was a vision of the elder Mr. Strong's distracted face, the yellow gleam of the last telegram in his hands, and Rex fled.

---

Two weeks later, a May breeze rustling through the greenness of the quadrangle, brushed softly the ivy-clad brick walls, and stole, like a runaway child to its playmate, through an open window of the Theological Seminary building at Chelsea Square. Entering so, it flapped suddenly at the white curtains as if astonished. What was this? Two muscular black clad arms were stretched across a table, and between them lay a brown head, inert, hopeless. It seemed strange that on such a May day, with such a May breeze, life could look dark to anything young, yet Reginald Fairfax, at the head of the graduating class, easily first in more than one way—in scholarship, in athletics, in versatility, and, more than all, like George Washington, "first in the hearts of his countrymen," the most popular man of the Seminary—this successful and well beloved young person sat wretched and restless in his room and let the breeze blow over his prostrate head and his idle, nerveless hands. Since the night of the rescue of Billy Strong he had felt himself another and a worse man. He sent a note to his cousin the next day.

"Dear Carty," it read, "For mercy sake let me alone. I know I've lost my chance at St. Eric's and I know you'll say it was my own fault. I don't want to hear either statement, so don't come near me till I hunt you up, which I will do when I'm fit to talk to a white man. I'm grateful, though you may not believe it. Yours—Rex."

But the lost chance at St. Eric's, although it was coming to weigh heavily on his buoyant spirit, was not the worst of his troubles. The girl from Orange—there lay the sting. He had sent her a note as well, but there was little he was free to say without betraying Billy, the note was mostly vague expressions of regret, and Rex knew her clearheaded directness too well to hope that it would count for much. No answer had come, and, day by day, he had grown more dejected, hoping against hope for one.

A knock—the postman's knock—and Rex started and sprang to the door. One letter, but he could hardly believe his glad eyes when he saw the address on it, for it was the handwriting which he had come to know well, had known well, seeing it once—her handwriting. In a moment the jagged-edged envelope, torn in a desperate hurry to get what it held, lay one side, and he was reading.

"Dear Mr. Fairfax": the letter ran; "For two weeks I have been very unjust to you and I want to beg your pardon. Billy was here three days ago, and what I didn't know and what he didn't know we patched together, and the consequence is I want to apologize and to make up to you, if I can, for being so disagreeable. Billy's recollections of that night were disjointed, but he remembered a lot in spots, and I know now just what a friend you were to him and how you saved him. I think he was horrid, but I think you were fine—simply fine. I can't half say it in writing so will you please come out for over Sunday—mother says—and I'll try to show you how splendid I think you were. Will you? Yours sincerely"—and her name.

Would he? Such a radiant smile shone through the little bare room that the May breeze, catching its light at the window, clapped gay applause against the flapping curtain. This was as it should be.

But the breeze and the postman were not to be the only messengers of happiness. Steps sounded down the long, empty hall, stopped at his door, and Rex, a new joy of living pulsing through him, sprang again, almost before the knock sounded, to meet gladly what might be coming. His face looked out of the wide-open doorway with so bright a welcome to the world, that the two men who stood across the threshold smiled an involuntary answer.

"Carty! I'm awfully glad"—and Rex stopped to put his hand out graciously, deferentially, to the gray-haired and distinguished man who stood with Carter Reed.

"Judge Rush, this is my cousin, Mr. Fairfax," Reed presented him, and in a moment Rex's friend, the breeze, was helping hospitality on with gay little refreshing dashes at a warm, silvered head, as Judge Rush sat in the biggest chair at the big open window. He beamed upon the young man with interested, friendly eyes.

"That's all very well about the quadrangle, Mr. Reed. It certainly is beautiful and like the English Universities," he broke into a sentence genially. "But I wish to talk to Mr. Fairfax. I've come to bring you the first news, Mr. Fairfax, of what you will hear officially within a day or two—that the vestry of St. Eric's hope you will consider a call to be our assistant rector." Rex's heart almost stopped beating, and his smile faded as he stared breathless at this portly and beneficent Mercury. Mercury went on "A vestry meeting was held last night in which this was decided upon. Your brilliant record in this seminary and other qualifications which have been mentioned to us by high authorities, were the reasons for this action which appeared upon the surface, but I want you to know the inner workings—I asked your cousin to bring me here that I might have the pleasure of telling you."

It was rather warm, and the old gentleman had climbed stairs, and his conversation had been weighty and steady. He arrested its flow for a moment and took a long breath. "Don't stop," said Rex earnestly, and the others broke into sudden laughter.

"I like that," Judge Rush sputtered, chuckling. "You're ready to let me kill myself, if needs be, to get the facts. All right, young man—I like impetuosity—it means energy. I'll go on. The facts not known to the public, which I wish to tell you, are as follows. After your failure to keep your appointment on the evening of the th, I was about through with you. I considered you careless both of your own interests and ours, and we began to look for another assistant. A man who fitted the place as you did seemed hard to find and the case was *in statu quo* when, two nights ago, my son brought home young William Strong to dinner. Our families are old friends and Billy's father and I were chums in college, so the boy is at home in our house. As you probably know, he has the gift of telling a good story, so when he began on the events of an evening which you will remember——"

Rex's deep laughter broke into the dignified sentences at this point.

"I see you remember." Judge Rush smiled benignly. "Well, Mr. Fairfax, Billy made an amusing story of that evening. Only the family were at the table and he spared himself not at all. He had been in Orange the day before, and the young lady in the case had told him how you had protected him at your own expense—he made that funny too, but I thought it very fine behavior—very fine, indeed, sir." Rex's face flushed under this. "And as I thought the whole affair over afterwards, I not only understood why you had failed me, but I honored you for attempting no explanation, and I made up my mind that you were the man we wanted. Yes, sir, the man we want. A man who knows how to deal with the situations of to-day, with the vices of a great city, that is what we want. I consider tact, and broad-mindedness and self-sacrifice no small qualities for a minister of the gospel; and a combination of those qualities, as in you, I consider exceptional. So I went to this vestry meeting primed, and I told them we had got to have you, sir—and we've got to. You'll come?"

The question was much like an order, but Rex did not mind. "Indeed, I'll come, Judge Rush," he said, and his manner of saying it won the last doubtful bit of the Judge's heart.

The Sunday morning when the new assistant preached his first sermon in St. Eric's, there sat well back in the congregation a dark-eyed girl, and with her a tall and powerful young man, whose deep shoulders and movements, as of a well fitted machine, advertised an athlete in perfect form. The girl's face was rapt as she followed, her soul in her eyes, the clean-cut, short sermon, and when the congregation filtered slowly down the aisles she said not a word. But as the two turned into the street she spoke at last.

"He is a saint, isn't he, Billy?" she asked, and drew a long breath of contentment.

And from six-feet-two in mid-air came Billy Strong's dictum. "Margery," he said, impressively, "Rex may be a parson and all that, but, to my mind, that's not against him; to my mind that suits his style of handling the gloves. There was a chap in the Bible"—Billy swallowed as if embarrassed—"who—who was the spit 'n' image of Rex—the good Samaritan chap, you know. He found a seedy one falling over himself by the wayside, and he called him a beast and set him up, and took him to a hotel or something and told the innkeeper to charge it to him, and—I forget the exact words, but he saw him through, don't you know? And he did it all in a sporty sort of way and there wasn't a word of whining or fussing at him because he was loaded—that was awfully white of the chap. Rex did more than that for me and not a syllable has he peeped since. And, you know, the consequence of that masterly silence is that I've gone on the water-wagon—yes, sir—for a year. And I'm hanged if I'm not going to church every Sunday. He may be a saint as you say, and I suppose there's no doubt but he's horrid intellectual—every man must have his weaknesses. But the man that's a good Samaritan and a good sport all in one, he's my sort, I'm for him," said Billy Strong.

# The Lifted Bandage

The man let himself into his front door and, staggering lightly, like a drunken man, as he closed it, walked to the hall table, and mechanically laid down his hat, but still wearing his overcoat turned and went into his library, and dropped on the edge of a divan and stared out through the leaded panes of glass across the room facing him. The grayish skin of his face seemed to fall in diagonal furrows, from the eyes, from the nose, from the mouth. He sat, still to his finger-tips, staring.

He was sitting so when a servant slipped in and stood motionless a minute, and went to the wide window where the west light glared through leafless branches outside, and drew the shades lower, and went to the fireplace and touched a match. Wood caught and crackled and a cheerful orange flame flew noisily up the chimney, but the man sitting on the divan did not notice. The butler waited a moment, watching, hesitating, and then:

"Have you had lunch, sir?" he asked in a tentative, gentle voice.

The staring eyes moved with an effort and rested on the servant's face. "Lunch?" he repeated, apparently trying to focus on the meaning of the word. "Lunch? I don't know, Miller. But don't bring anything."

With a great anxiety in his face Miller regarded his master. "Would you let me take your overcoat, Judge?—you'll be too warm," he said.

He spoke in a suppressed tone as if waiting for, fearing something, as if longing to show sympathy, and the man stood and let himself be cared for, and then sat down again in the same unrestful, fixed attitude, gazing out again through the glittering panes into the stormy, tawny west sky. Miller came back and stood quiet, patient; in a few minutes the man seemed to become aware of him.

"I forgot, Miller. You'll want to know," he said in a tone which went to show an old bond between the two. "You'll be sorry to hear, Miller," he said—and the dull eyes moved difficultly to the anxious ones, and his voice was uninflected—"you'll be sorry to know that the coroner's jury decided that Master Jack was a murderer."

The word came more horribly because of an air of detachment from the man's mind. It was like a soulless, evil mechanism, running unguided. Miller caught at a chair.

"I don't believe it, sir," he gasped. "No lawyer shall make me. I've known him since he was ten, Judge, and they're mistaken. It's not any mere lawyers can make me believe that awful thing, sir, of our Master Jack." The servant was shaking from head to foot with intense rejection, and the man put up his hand as if to ward off his emotion.

"I wish I could agree with you," he said quietly, and then added, "Thank you, Miller." And the old butler, walking as if struck with a sickness, was gone.

The man sat on the edge of the divan staring out of the window, minute after minute; the November wind tossed the clean, black lines of the branches backward and forward against the copper sky, as if a giant hand moved a fan of sea-weed before a fire. The man sat still and stared. The sky dulled; the delicate, wild branches melted together; the diamond lines in the window blurred; yet, unmoved, unseeing, the eyes stared through them.

The burr of an electric bell sounded; some one came in at the front door and came to the door of the library, but the fixed figure did not stir. The newcomer stood silent a minute, two minutes; a young man in clerical dress, boyish, with gray, serious eyes. At length he spoke.

"May I come in? It's Dick."

The man's head turned slowly and his look rested inquiringly on his nephew. It was a minute before he said, as if recognizing him, "Dick. Yes." And set himself as before to the persistent gazing through the window.

"I lost you at the court-house," the younger man said. "I didn't mean to let you come home alone."

"Thank you, Dick." It seemed as if neither joy nor sorrow would find a way into the quiet voice again.

The wind roared; the boughs rustled against the glass; the fire, soberly settled to work, steamed and crackled; the clock ticked indifferently; there was no other sound in the room; the two men were silent, the one staring always before him, the other sitting with a hand on the older man's hand, waiting. Minutes they sat so, and the wintry sky outside darkened and lay sullenly in bands of gray and orange against the windows; the light of the logs was stronger than the daylight; it flickered carelessly across the ashiness of the emotionless face. The young man, watching the face, bent forward and gripped his other hand on the unresponsive one in his clasp.

"Uncle," he asked, "will it make things worse if I talk to you?"

"No, Dick."

Nothing made a difference, it seemed. Silence or words must simply fall without effect on the rock bottom of despair. The young man halted, as if dismayed, before this overpowering inertia of hopelessness; he drew a quick breath.

"A coroner's jury isn't infallible. I don't believe it of Jack—a lot of people don't believe it," he said.

The older man looked at him heavily. "You'd say that. Jack's friends will. I've been trained to weigh evidence—I must believe it."

"Listen," the young man urged. "Don't shut down the gates like that. I'm not a lawyer, but I've been trained to think, too, and I believe you're not thinking squarely. There's other evidence that counts besides this. There's Jack—his personality."

"It has been taken into consideration."

"It can't be taken into consideration by strangers—it needs years of intimacy to weigh that evidence as I can weigh it—as you—You know best of all," he cried out impulsively, "if you'll let yourself know, how impossible it was. That Jack should have bought that pistol and taken it to Ben Armstrong's rooms to kill him—it was impossible—impossible!" The clinched fist came down on the black broadcloth knee with the conviction of the man behind it. The words rushed like melted metal, hot, stinging, not to be stopped. The judge quivered as if they had stung through the callousness, touched a nerve. A faint color crawled to his cheeks; for the first time he spoke quickly, as if his thoughts connected with something more than gray matter.

"You talk about my not allowing myself to believe in Jack. You seem not to realize that such a belief would—might—stand between me and madness. I've been trying to adjust myself to a possible scheme of living—getting through the years till I go into nothingness. I can't. All I can grasp is the feeling that a man might have if dropped from a balloon and forced to stay gasping in the air, with no place in it, nothing to hold to, no breath to draw, no earth to rest on, no end to hope for. There is nothing beyond."

"Everything is beyond," the young man cried triumphantly. "'The end,' as you call it, is an end to hope for—it is the beginning. The beginning of more than you have ever had—with them, with the people you care about."

The judge turned a ghastly look upon the impetuous, bright face. "If I believed that, I should be even now perfectly happy. I don't see how you Christians can ever be sorry when your friends die—it's childish; anybody ought to be able to wait a few years. But I don't believe it," he said heavily, and went on again as if an inertia of speech were carrying him as an inertia of silence had held him a few minutes before. "When my wife died a year ago it ended my personal life, but I could live Jack's life. I was glad in the success and honor of it. Now the success—" he made a gesture. "And the honor—if I had that, only the honor of Jack's life left, I think I could finish the years with dignity. I've not been a bad man—I've done my part and lived as seemed right. Before I'm old the joy is wiped out and long years left. Why? It's not reasonable—not logical. With one thing to hold to, with Jack's good name, I might live. How can I, now? What can I do? A life must have a *raison d'être*."

"Listen," the clergyman cried again. "You are not judging Jack as fairly as you would judge a common criminal. You know better than I how often juries make mistakes—why should you trust this jury to have made none?"

"I didn't trust the jury. I watched as I have never before known how to watch a case. I felt my mind more clear and alert than common."

"Alert!" he caught at the word. "But alert on the side of terror—abnormally clear to see what you dreaded. Because you are fair-minded, because it has been the habit of your life to correct at once any conscious prejudice in your judgment, you have swayed to the side of unfairness to yourself, to Jack. Uncle," he flashed out, "would it tear your soul to have me state the case as I see it? I might, you know—I might bring out something that would make it look different."

Almost a smile touched the gray lines of his face. "If you wish."

The young man drew himself into his chair and clasped his hands around his knee. "Here it is. Mr. Newbold, on the seventh floor of the Bruzon bachelor apartments, heard a shot at one in the morning, next his bedroom, in Ben Armstrong's room. He hurried into the public hall, saw the door wide open into Ben's apartment, went in and found Ben shot dead. Trying to use the telephone to call help, he found it was out of order. So he rushed again into the hall toward the elevator with the idea of getting Dr. Avery, who lived below on the second floor. The elevator door was open also, and a man's opera-hat lay near it on the floor; he saw, just in time, that the car was at the bottom of the shaft, almost stepping inside, in his excitement, before he noticed this. Then he ran down the stairs with Jack's hat in his hand, and got Dr. Avery, and they found Jack at the foot of the elevator shaft. It was known that Ben Armstrong and Jack had quarrelled the day before; it was known that Jack was quick-tempered; it is known that he bought that evening the pistol which was found on the floor by Ben, loaded, with one empty shell. That's the story."

The steady voice stopped a moment and the young man shivered slightly; his look was strained. Steadily he went on.

"That's the story. From that the coroner's jury have found that Jack killed Ben Armstrong—that he bought the pistol to kill him, and went to his rooms with that purpose; that in his haste to escape, he missed seeing that the elevator was down, as Mr. Newbold all but missed seeing it later, and jumped into the shaft and was killed instantly himself. That's what the jury get from the facts, but it seems to me they're begging the question. There are a hundred hypotheses that would fit the case of Jack's innocence—why is it reasonable to settle on the one that means his guilt? This is my idea. Jack and Ben Armstrong had been friends since boyhood and Jack, quick-tempered as he was, was warm-hearted and loyal. It was like him to decide suddenly to go to Ben and make friends. He had been to a play in the evening which had more or less that *motif*; he was open to such influences. It was like the pair of them, after the reconciliation, to set to work looking at Jack's new toy, the pistol. It was a brand-new sort, and the two have been interested always in guns—I remember how I, as a youngster, was impressed when Ben and Jack bought their first shot-guns together. Jack had got the pistol at Mellingham's that evening, you know—he was likely to be keen about it still, and then—it went off. There are plenty of other cases where a man has shot his friend by accident—why shouldn't poor Jack be given the benefit of the doubt? The telephone wouldn't work; Jack rushed out with the same idea which struck Mr. Newbold later, of getting Dr. Avery—and fell down the shaft.

"For me there is no doubt. I never knew him to hold malice. He was violent sometimes, but that he could have gone about for hours with a pistol in his pocket and murder in his heart; that he could have planned Ben Armstrong's death and carried it out deliberately—it's a contradiction in terms. It's impossible, being Jack. You must know this—you know your son—you know human nature."

The rapid *résumé* was but an impassioned appeal. Its answer came after a minute; to the torrent of eager words, three words:

"Thank you, Dick."

The absolute lack of impression on the man's judgment was plain.

"Ah!" The clergyman sprang to his feet and stood, his eyes blazing, despairing, looking down at the bent, listless figure. How could he let a human being suffer as this one was suffering? Quickly his thoughts shifted their basis. He could not affect the mind of the lawyer; might he reach now, perhaps, the soul of the man? He knew the difficulty, for before this his belief had crossed swords with the agnosticism of his uncle, an agnosticism shared by his father, in which he had been trained, from which he had broken free only five years before. He had faced the batteries of the two older brains at that time, and come out with the brightness of his new-found faith untarnished, but without, he remembered, scratching the armor of their profound doubt in everything. One could see, looking at the slender black figure, at the visionary gaze of the gray wide eyes, at the shape of the face, broad-browed, ovalled, that this man's psychic make-up must lift him like wings into an atmosphere outside a material, outside even an intellectual world. He could breathe freely only in a spiritual air, and things hard to believe to most human beings were, perhaps, his every-day thoughts. He caught a quick breath of excitement as it flashed to his brain that now, possibly, was coming the moment when he might justify his life, might help this man whom he loved, to peace. The breath he caught was a prayer; his strong, nervous fingers trembled. He spoke in a tone whose concentration lifted the eyes below him, that brooded, stared.

"I can't bear it to stand by and see you go under, when there's help close. You said that if you could believe that they were living, that you would have them again, you would be perfectly happy no matter how many years you must wait. They are living as sure as I am here, and as sure as Jack was here, and Jack's mother. They are living still. Perhaps they're close to you now. You've bound a bandage over your eyes, you've covered the vision of your spirit, so that you can't see; but that doesn't make nothingness of God's world. It's there—here—close, maybe. A more real world than this—this little thing." With a boyish gesture he thrust behind him the universe. "What do we know about the earth, except effects upon our consciousness? It's all a matter of inference—you know that better than I. The thing we do know beyond doubt is that we are each of us a something that suffers and is happy. How is that something the same as the body—the body that gets old and dies—how can it be? You can't change thought into matter—not conceivably—everybody acknowledges that. Why should the thinking part die then, because the material part dies? When the organ is broken is the organist dead? The body is the hull, the covering, and when it has grown useless it will fall away and the live seed in it will stand free to sunlight and air—just at the beginning of life, as a plant is when it breaks through earth in the spring. It's the seed in the ground, and it's the flower in the sunlight, but it's the same thing—the same life—it is—it *is*." The boy's intensity of conviction shot like a flame across the quiet room.

"It is the same thing with us too. The same spirit-substance underlies both worlds and there is no separation in space, only in view-point. Life goes on—it's just transfigured. It's as if a bandage should be lifted from our eyes and we should suddenly see things in whose presence we had been always."

The rushing, eager voice stopped. He bent and laid his hand on the older man's and stared at his face, half hidden now in the shadows of the lowering fire. There was no response. The heavy head did not lift and the attitude was unstirred, hopeless. As if struck by a blow he sprang erect and his fingers shut hard. He spoke as if to himself, brokenly.

"He does not believe—a single word—I say. I can't help him—I *can't* help him."

Suddenly the clinched fists flung out as if of a power not their own, and his voice rang across the room.

"God!" The word shot from him as if a thunderbolt fell with it. "God! Lift the bandage!"

A log fell with a crash into the fire; great battling shadows blurred all the air; he was gone.

The man, startled, drew up his bent shoulders, and pushed back a lock of gray hair and stared about, shaking, bewildered. The ringing voice, the word that had flashed as if out of a larger atmosphere—the place was yet full of these, and the shock of it added a keenness to his misery. His figure swung sideways; he fell on the cushions of the sofa and his arms stretched across them, his gray head lying heedless; sobs that tore roots came painfully; it was the last depth. Out of it, without his volition, he spoke aloud.

"God, God, God!" his voice said, not prayerfully, but repeating the sound that had shocked his torture. The word wailed, mocked, reproached, defied—and yet it was a prayer. Out of a soul in mortal stress that word comes sometimes driven by a force of the spirit like the force of the lungs fighting for breath—and it is a prayer.

"God, God, God!" the broken voice repeated, and sobs cut the words. And again. Over and over, and again the sobbing broke it.

As suddenly as if a knife had stopped the life inside the body, all sound stopped. A movement shook the man as he lay face down, arms stretched. Then for a minute, two minutes, he was quiet, with a quiet that meant muscles stretched, nerves alert. Slowly, slowly the tightened muscles of the arms pushed the shoulders backward and upward; the head lifted; the face turned outward, and if an observer had been there he might have seen by the glow of the firelight that the features wet, distorted, wore, more than all at this moment, a look of amazement. Slowly, slowly, moving as if afraid to disturb something—a dream—a presence—the man sat erect as he had been sitting before, only that the rigidity was in some way gone. He sat alert, his eyes wide, filled with astonishment, gazing before him eagerly—a look different from the dull stare of an hour ago by the difference between hope and despair. His hands caught at the stuff of the divan on either side and clutched it.

All the time the look of his face changed; all the time, not at once, but by fast, startling degrees, the gray misery which had bound eyes and mouth and brow in iron dropped as if a cover were being torn off and a light set free. Amazement, doubting, incredulous came first, and with that eagerness, trembling and afraid. And then hope—and then the fear to hope. And hunger. He bent forward, his eyes peered into the quiet emptiness, his fingers gripped the cloth as if to anchor him to a wonder, to an unbelievable something; his body leaned—to something—and his face now was the face of a starved man, of a man dying from thirst, who sees food, water, salvation.

And his face changed; a quality incredible was coming into it—joy. He was transformed. Lines softened by magic; color came, and light in the eyes; the first unbelief, the amazement, shifted surely, swiftly, and in a flash the whole man shone, shook with rapture. He threw out before him his arms, reaching, clasping, and from his radiant look the arms might have held all happiness.

A minute he stayed so with his hands stretched out, with face glowing, then slowly, his eyes straining as if perhaps they followed a vision which faded from them—slowly his arms fell and the expectancy went from his look. Yet not the light, not the joy. His body quivered; his breath came unevenly, as of one just gone through a crisis; every sense seemed still alive to catch a faintest note of something exquisite which vanished; and with that the spell, rapidly as it had come, was gone. And the man sat there quiet, as he had sat an hour before, and the face which had been leaden was brilliant. He stirred and glanced about the room as if trying to adjust himself, and his eyes smiled as they rested on the familiar objects, as if for love of them, for pleasure in them. One might have said that this man had been given back at a blow youth and happiness. Movement seemed beyond him yet—he was yet dazed with the newness of a marvel—but he turned his head and saw the fire and at that put out his hand to it as if to a friend.

The electric bell burred softly again through the house, and the man heard it, and his eyes rested inquiringly on the door of the library. In a moment another man stood there, of his own age, iron-gray, strong-featured.

"Dick told me I might come," he said. "Shall I trouble you? May I stay with you awhile?"

The judge put out his hand friendlily, a little vaguely, much as he had put it out to the fire. "Surely," he said, and the newcomer was all at once aware of his look. He started.

"You're not well," he said. "You must take something—whiskey—Miller——"

The butler moved in the room making lights here and there, and he came quickly.

"No," the judge said. "I don't want anything—I don't need anything. It's not as you think. I'll tell you about it."

Miller was gone; Dick's father waited, his gaze fixed on the judge's face anxiously, and for moments no word was spoken. The judge gazed into the fire with the rapt, smiling look which had so startled his brother-in-law. At length:

"I don't know how to tell you," he said. "There seem no words. Something has happened, yet it's difficult to explain."

"Something happened?" the other repeated, bewildered but guarded. "I don't understand. Has some one been here? Is it about—the trial?"

"No." A slight spasm twisted the smiling lines of the man's mouth, but it was gone and the mouth smiled still.

A horror-struck expression gleamed for a second from the anxious eyes of the brother-in-law, but he controlled it quickly. He spoke gently. "Tell me about it—it will do you good to talk."

The judge turned from the fire, and at sight of his flushed cheeks and lighted eyes the other shrank back, and the judge saw it. "You needn't be alarmed," he said quietly. "Nothing is wrong with me. But something has happened, as I told you, and everything—is changed." His eyes lifted as he spoke and strayed about the room as if considering a change which had come also to the accustomed setting.

A shock of pity flashed from the other, and was mastered at once. "Can you tell me what has happened?" he urged. The judge, his face bright with a brightness that was dreadful to the man who watched him, held his hand to the fire, turning it about as if enjoying the warmth. The other shivered. There was silence for a minute. The judge broke it, speaking thoughtfully:

"Suppose you had been born blind, Ned," he began, "and no one had ever given you a hint of the sense of vision, and your imagination had never presented such a power to your mind. Can you suppose that?"

"I think so—yes," the brother-in-law answered, with careful gentleness, watching always the illumined countenance. "Yes, I can suppose it."

"Then fancy if you will that all at once sight came, and the world flashed before you. Do you think you'd be able to describe such an experience?"

The voice was normal, reflective. Many a time the two had talked together of such things in this very room, and the naturalness of the scene, and of the judge's manner, made the brother-in-law for a second forget the tragedy in which they were living.

"Why, of course," he answered. "If one had never heard of such a power one's vocabulary wouldn't take in the words to describe it."

"Exactly," the judge agreed. "That's the point I'm making. Perhaps now I may tell you what it is that has happened. Or rather, I may make you understand how a definite and concrete event has come to pass, which I can't tell you."

Alarm suddenly expressed itself beyond control in the brother-in-law's face. "John, what do you mean? Do you see that you distress me? Can't you tell clearly if some one has been here—what it is, in plain English, that has happened?"

The judge turned his dreamy, bright look toward the frightened man. "I do see—I do see," he brought out affectionately. "I'll try to tell, as you say, in plain English. But it is like the case I put—it is a question of lack of vocabulary. A remarkable experience has occurred in this room within an hour. I can no more describe it than the man born blind could describe sight. I can only call it by one name, which may startle you. A revelation."

"A revelation!" the tone expressed incredulity, scarcely veiled scorn.

The judge's brilliant gaze rested undisturbed on the speaker. "I understand—none better. A day ago, two hours ago, I should have answered in that tone. We have been trained in the same school, and have thought alike. Dick was here a while ago and said things—you know what Dick would say. You know how you and I have been sorry for the lad—been indulgent to him—with his keen, broad mind and that inspired self-forgetfulness of his—how we've been sorry to have such qualities wasted on a parson, a religion machine. We've thought he'd come around in time, that he was too large a personality to be tied to a treadmill. We've thought that all along, haven't we? Well, Dick was here, and out of the hell where I was I thought that again. When he talked I thought in a way—for I couldn't think much—that after a consistent voyage of agnosticism, I wouldn't be whipped into snivelling belief at the end, by shipwreck. I would at least go down without surrendering. In a dim way I thought that. And all that I thought then, and have thought through my life, is nothing. Reasoning doesn't weigh against experience. Dick is right."

The other man sat before him, bent forward, his hands on his knees, listening, dazed. There was a quality in the speaker's tone which made it necessary to take his words seriously. Yet—the other sighed and relaxed a bit as he waited, watched. The calm voice went on.

"The largest event of my life has happened in the last hour, in this room. It was this way. When Dick went out I—went utterly to pieces. It was the farthest depth. Out of it I called on God, not knowing what I did. And he answered. That's what happened. As if—as if a bandage had been lifted from my eyes, I was—I was in the presence of things—indescribable. There was no change, only that where I was blind before I now saw. I don't mean vision. I haven't words to explain what I mean. But a world was about me as real as this; it had perhaps always been there; in that moment I was first aware of it. I knew, as if a door had been opened, what heaven means—a condition of being. And I knew another thing more personal—that, without question, it was right with those I thought I had lost and that the horror which seemed blackest I have no need to dread. I cannot say that I saw them or heard or touched them, but I was with them. I understand, but I can't make you understand. I told Dick an hour ago that if I could believe they were living, that I should ever have them again, I should be perfectly happy. That's true now. I believe it, and I am—perfectly happy."

The listener groaned uncontrollably.

"I know your thought," the judge answered the sound, and his eyes were like lamps as he turned them toward the man. "But you're wrong—my mind is not unhinged. You'll see. After what I've gone through, after facing eternity without hope, what are mere years? I can wait. I know. I am—perfectly happy."

Then the man who listened rose from his chair and came and put a hand gently on the shoulder of the judge, looking down at him gravely. "I don't understand you very well, John," he said, "but I'm glad of anything—of anything"—his voice went suddenly. "Will you wait for me here a few minutes? I'm going home and I'll be back. I think I'll spend the night with you if you don't object."

"Object! Wait!" The judge looked up in surprise, and with that he smiled. "I see. Surely. I'd like to have you here. Yes, I'll certainly wait."

Outside in the hall one might have heard the brother-in-law say a low word or two to Miller as the man helped him on with his coat; then the front door shut softly, and he was gone, and the judge sat alone, his head thrown back against his chair, his face luminous.

The other man swung down the dark street, rushing, agitated. As he came to the corner an electric light shone full on him and a figure crossing down toward him halted.

"Father! I was coming to find you. Something extraordinary has happened. I was coming to find you."

"Yes, Dick." The older man waited.

"I've just left Charley Owen at the house—you remember Charley Owen?"

"No."

"Oh, yes, you do—he's been here with—Jack. He was in Jack's class in college—in Jack's and Ben Armstrong's. He used to go on shooting trips with them both—often."

"I remember now."

"Yes, I knew you would." The young voice rushed on. "He has been away just now—down in Florida shooting—away from civilization. He got all his mail for a month in one lump—just now—two days ago. In it was a letter from Jack and Ben Armstrong, written that night, written together. Do you see what that means?"

"What!" The word was not a question, but an exclamation. "What—Dick!"

"Yes—yes. There were newspapers, too, which gave an account of the trial—the first he'd heard of it—he was away in the Everglades. He started instantly, and came on here when he had read the papers, and realized the bearing his letter would have on the trial. He has travelled day and night. He hoped to get here in time. Jack and Ben thought he was in New York. They wrote to ask him to go duck-shooting—with them. And, father—here's the most startling point of it all." As the man waited, watching his son's face, he groaned suddenly and made a gesture of despair.

"Don't, father—don't take it that way. It's good—it's glorious—it clears Jack. My uncle will be almost happy. But I wouldn't tell him at once—I'd be careful," he warned the other.

"What was it—the startling point you spoke of?"

"Oh—surely—this. The letter to Charley Owen spoke of Jack's new pistol—that pistol. Jack said they would have target-shooting with it in camp. They were all crack shots, you know. He said he had bought it that evening, and that Ben thought well of it. Ben signed the letter after Jack, and then added a postscript. It clears Jack—it clears him. Doesn't it, father? But I wouldn't tell my uncle just yet. He's not fit to take it in for a few hours—don't you think so?"

"No, I won't tell him—just yet."

The young man's wide glance concentrated with a flash on his father's face. "What is it? You speak queerly. You've just come from there. How is he—how is my uncle?"

There was a letterbox at the corner, a foot from the older man's shoulder. He put out his hand and held to the lid a moment before he answered. His voice was harsh.

"Your uncle is—perfectly happy," he said. "He's gone mad."

# The Courage of the Commonplace

The girl and her chaperon had been deposited early in the desirable second-story window in Durfee, looking down on the tree. Brant was a senior and a "Bones" man, and so had a leading part to play in the afternoon's drama. He must get the girl and the chaperon off his hands, and be at his business. This was "Tap Day." It is perhaps well to explain what "Tap Day" means; there are people who have not been at Yale or had sons or sweethearts there.

In New Haven, on the last Thursday of May, toward five in the afternoon, one becomes aware that the sea of boys which ripples always over the little city has condensed into a river flowing into the campus. There the flood divides and re-divides; the junior class is separating and gathering from all directions into a solid mass about the nucleus of a large, low-hanging oak tree inside the college fence in front of Durfee Hall. The three senior societies of Yale, Skull and Bones, Scroll and Key, and Wolf's Head, choose to-day fifteen members each from the junior class, the fifteen members of the outgoing senior class making the choice. Each senior is allotted his man of the juniors, and must find him in the crowd at the tree and tap him on the shoulder and give him the order to go to his room. Followed by his sponsor he obeys and what happens at the room no one but the men of the society know. With shining face the lad comes back later and is slapped on the shoulder and told, "good work, old man," cordially and whole-heartedly by every friend and acquaintance—by lads who have "made" every honor possible, by lads who have "made" nothing, just as heartily. For that is the spirit of Yale.

Only juniors room in Durfee Hall. On Tap Day an outsider is lucky who has a friend there, for a window is a proscenium box for the play—the play which is a tragedy to all but forty-five of the three hundred and odd juniors. The windows of every story of the gray stone facade are crowded with a deeply interested audience; grizzled heads of old graduates mix with flowery hats of women; every one is watching every detail, every arrival. In front of the Hall is a drive, and room for perhaps a dozen carriages next the fence—the famous fence of Yale—which rails the campus round. Just inside it, at the north-east corner, rises the tree. People stand up in the carriages, women and men; the fence is loaded with people, often standing, too, to see that tree.

All over the campus surges a crowd; students of the other classes, seniors who last year stood in the compact gathering at the tree and left it sore-hearted, not having been "taken"; sophomores who will stand there next year, who already are hoping for and dreading their Tap Day; little freshmen, each one sure that he, at least, will be of the elect; and again the iron-gray heads, the interested faces of old Yale men, and the gay spring hats like bouquets of flowers.

It is, perhaps, the most critical single day of the four years' course at the University. It shows to the world whether or no a boy, after three years of college life, has in the eyes of the student body "made good." It is a crucial test, a heart-rending test for a boy of twenty years.

The girl sitting in the window of Durfee understood thoroughly the character and the chances of the day. The seniors at the tree wear derby hats; the juniors none at all; it is easier by this sign to distinguish the classmen, and to keep track of the tapping. The girl knew of what society was each black-hatted man who twisted through the bareheaded throng; in that sea of tense faces she recognized many; she could find a familiar head almost anywhere in the mass and tell as much as an outsider might what hope was hovering over it. She came of Yale people; Brant, her brother, would graduate this year; she was staying at the house of a Yale professor; she was in the atmosphere.

There, near the edge of the pack, was Bob Floyd, captain of the crew, a fair, square face with quiet blue eyes, whose tranquil gaze was characteristic. To-day it was not tranquil; it flashed anxiously here and there, and the girl smiled. She knew as certainly as if the fifteen seniors had told her that Floyd would be "tapped for Bones." The crew captain and the foot-ball captain are almost inevitably taken for Skull and Bones. Yet five years before Jack Emmett, captain of the crew, had not been taken; only two years back Bert Connolly, captain of the foot-ball team, had not been taken. The girl, watching the big chap's unconscious face, knew well what was in his mind. "What chance have I against all these bully fellows," he was saying to himself in his soul, "even if I do happen to be crew captain? Connolly was a mutt—couldn't take him—but Jack Emmett—there wasn't any reason to be seen for that. And it's just muscles I've got—I'm not clever—I don't hit it off with the crowd—I've done nothing for Yale, but just for the crew. Why the dickens should they take me?" But the girl knew.

The great height and refined, supercilious face of another boy towered near—Lionel Arnold, a born litterateur, and an artist—he looked more confident than most. It seemed to the girl he felt sure of being taken; sure that his name and position and, more than all, his developed, finished personality must count as much as that. And the girl knew that in the direct, unsophisticated judgments of the judges these things did not count at all.

So she gunned over the swarm which gathered to the oak tree as bees to a hive, able to tell often what was to happen. Even to her young eyes all these anxious, upturned faces, watching silently with throbbing pulses for this first vital decision of their lives, was a stirring sight.

"I can't bear it for the ones who aren't taken," she cried out, and the chaperon did not smile.

"I know," she said. "Each year I think I'll never come again— it's too heart-rending. It means so much to them, and only forty-five can go away happy. Numbers are just broken-hearted. I don't like it—it's brutal."

"Yes, but it's an incentive to the under-classmen—it holds them to the mark and gives them ambition, doesn't it?" the girl argued doubtfully.

The older woman agreed. "I suppose on the whole it's a good institution. And it's wonderful what wisdom the boys show. Of course, they make mistakes, but on the whole they pick the best men astonishingly. So many times they hit the ones who come to be distinguished."

"But so many times they don't," the girl followed her words. Her father and Brant were Bones men—why was the girl arguing against senior societies? "So many, Mrs. Anderson. Uncle Ted's friend, the President of Hardrington College, was in Yale in the '80's and made no senior society; Judge Marston of the Supreme Court dined with us the other night—he didn't make anything; Dr. Hamlin, who is certainly one of the great physicians of the country, wasn't taken. I know a lot more. And look at some who've made things. Look at my cousin, Gus Vanderpool—he made Keys twenty years ago and has never done a thing since. And that fat Mr. Hough, who's so rich and dull—he's Bones."

"You've got statistics at your fingers' ends, haven't you?" said Mrs. Anderson. "Anybody might think you had a brother among the juniors who you weren't hopeful about." She looked at the girl curiously. Then: "They must be about all there," she spoke, leaning out. "A full fifty feet square of dear frightened laddies. There's Brant, coming across the campus. He looks as if he was going to make some one president. I suppose he feels so. There's Johnny McLean. I hope he'll be taken—he's the nicest boy in the whole junior class—but I'm afraid. He hasn't done anything in particular."

With that, a thrill caught the most callous of the hundreds of spectators; a stillness fixed the shifting crowd; from the tower of Battell chapel, close by, the college bell clanged the stroke of five; before it stopped striking the first two juniors would be tapped.

The dominating, unhurried note rang, echoed, and began to die away as they saw Brant's hand fall on Bob Floyd's shoulder. The crew captain whirled and leaped, unseeing, through the crowd. A great shout rose; all over the campus the people surged like a wind-driven wave toward the two rushing figures, and everywhere some one cried, "Floyd has gone Bones!" and the exciting business had begun.

One looks at the smooth faces of boys of twenty and wonders what the sculptor Life is going to make of them. Those who have known his work know what sharp tools are in his kit; they know the tragic possibilities as well as the happy ones of those inevitable strokes; they shrink a bit as they look at the smooth faces of the boys and realize how that clay must be moulded in the workshop—how the strong lines which ought to be there some day must come from the cutting of pain and the grinding of care and the push and weight of responsibility. Yet there is service and love, too, and happiness and the slippery bright blade of success in the kit of Life the sculptor; so they stand and watch, a bit pitifully but hopefully, as the work begins, and cannot guide the chisel but a little way, yet would not, if they could, stop it, for the finished job is going to be, they trust, a man, and only the sculptor Life can make such.

The boy called Johnny McLean glanced up at the window in Durfee; he met the girl's eyes, and the girl smiled back and made a gay motion with her hand as if to say, "Keep up your pluck; you'll be taken." And wished she felt sure of it. For, as Mrs. Anderson had said, he had done nothing in particular. His marks were good, he was a fair athlete; good at rowing, good at track work; he had "heeled" the News for a year, but had not made the board. A gift of music, which bubbled without effort, had put him on the Glee Club. Yet that had come to him; it was not a thing he had done; boys are critical of such distinctions. It is said that Skull and Bones aims at setting its seal above all else on character. This boy had sailed buoyantly from term to term delighted with the honors which came to his friends, friends with the men who carried off honors, with the best and strongest men in his class, yet never quite arriving for himself. As the bright, anxious young face looked up at the window where the women sat, the older one thought she could read the future in it, and she sighed. It was a face which attracted, broad-browed, clear-eyed, and honest, but not a strong face—yet. John McLean had only made beginnings; he had accomplished nothing. Mrs. Anderson, out of an older experience, sighed, because she had seen just such winning, lovable boys before, and had seen them grow into saddened, unsuccessful men. Yet he was full of possibility; the girl was hoping against hope that Brant and the fourteen other seniors of Skull and Bones would see it so and take him on that promise. She was not pretending to herself that anything but Johnny McLean's fate in it was the point of this Tap Day to her. She was very young, only twenty also, but there was a maturity in her to which the boy made an appeal. She felt a strength which others missed; she wanted him to find it; she wanted passionately to see him take his place where she felt he belonged, with the men who counted.

The play was in full action. Grave and responsible seniors worked swiftly here and there through the tight mass, searching each one his man; every two or three minutes a man was found and felt that thrilling touch and heard the order, "Go to your room." Each time there was a shout of applause; each time the campus rushed in a wave. And still the three hundred stood packed, waiting— thinning a little, but so little. About thirty had been taken now, and the black senior hats were visibly fewer, but the upturned boy faces seemed exactly the same. Only they grew more anxious minute by minute; minute by minute they turned more nervously this way and that as the seniors worked through the mass. And as another and another crashed from among them blind and solemn and happy with his guardian senior close after, the ones who were left seemed to drop into deeper quiet. And now there were only two black hats in the throng; the girl looking down saw John McLean standing stiffly, his gray eyes fixed, his face pale and set; at that moment the two seniors found their men together. It was all over. He had not been taken.

Slowly the two hundred and fifty odd men who had not been good enough dispersed, pluckily laughing and talking together— all of them, it is safe to say, with heavy hearts; for Tap Day counts as much as that at Yale.

John McLean swung across the diagonal of the campus toward Welch Hall where he lived. He saw the girl and her chaperon come out of Durfee; and he lingered to meet them. Two days ago he had met the girl here with Brant, and she had stopped and shaken hands. It seemed to him it would help if that should happen today. She might say a word; anything at all to show that she was friends all the same with a fellow who wasn't good enough. He longed for that. With a sick chaos of pain pounding at what seemed to be his lungs he met her. Mrs. Anderson was between them, putting out a quick hand; the boy hardly saw her as he took it. He saw the girl, and the girl did not look at him. With her head up and her brown eyes fixed on Phelps gate-way she hurried along—and did not look at him. He could not believe it— that girl—the girl. But she was gone; she had not looked at him. Like a shot animal he suddenly began to run. He got to his rooms; they were empty; Baby Thomas, his "wife," known as Archibald Babington Thomas on the catalogue, but not elsewhere, had been taken for Scroll and Key; he was off with the others who were worth while. This boy went into his tiny bedroom and threw himself down with his face in his pillow and lay still. Men and women learn—sometimes—as they grow older, how to shut the doors against disappointments so that only the vital ones cut through, but at twenty all doors are open; the iron had come into his soul, and the girl had given it a twist which had taken his last ounce of courage. He lay still a long time, enduring— all he could manage at first. It might have been an hour later that he got up and went to his desk and sat down in the fading light, his hands deep in his trousers pockets; his athletic young figure dropped together listlessly; his eyes staring at the desk where had worked away so many cheerful hours. Pictures hung around it; there was a group taken last summer of girls and boys at his home in the country, the girl was in it—he did not look at her. His father's portrait stood on the desk, and a painting of his long-dead mother. He thought to himself hotly that it was good she was dead rather than see him shamed. For the wound was throbbing with a fever, and the boy had not got to a sense of proportion; his future seemed blackened. His father's picture stabbed him; he was a "Bones" man—all of his family—his grandfather, and the older brothers who had graduated four and six years ago—all of them. Except himself. The girl had thought it such a disgrace that she would not look at him! Then he grew angry. It wasn't decent, to hit a man when he was down. A woman ought to be gentle—if his mother had been alive—but then he was glad she wasn't. With that a sob shook him—startled him. Angrily he stood up and glared about the place. This wouldn't do; he must pull himself together. He walked up and down the little living room, bright with boys' belongings, with fraternity shields and flags and fencing foils and paddles and pictures; he walked up and down and he whistled "Dunderbeck," which somehow was in his head. Then he was singing it:

"Oh Dunderbeck, Oh Dunderbeck, how could you be so mean
As even to have thought of such a terrible machine!
For bob-tailed rats and pussy-cats shall never more be seen;
They'll all be ground to sausage-meat in Dunderbeck's machine."

There are times when Camembert cheese is a steadying thing to think of—or golf balls. "Dunderbeck" answered for John McLean. It appeared difficult to sing, however—he harked back to whistling. Then the clear piping broke suddenly. He bit his lower lip and went and sat down before the desk again and turned on the electric reading-lamp. Now he had given in long enough; now he must face the situation; now was the time to find if there was any backbone in him to "buck up." To fool those chaps by amounting to something. There was good stuff in this boy that he applied this caustic and not a salve. His buoyant lightheartedness whispered that the fellows made mistakes; that he was only one of many good chaps left; that Dick Harding had a pull and Jim Stanton had an older brother—excuses came. But the boy checked them.

"That's not the point; I didn't make it; I didn't deserve it; I've been easy on myself; I've got to change; so some day my people won't be ashamed of me—maybe." Slowly, painfully, he fought his way to a tentative self-respect. He might not ever be anything big, a power as his father was, but he could be a hard worker, he could make a place. A few days before a famous speaker had given an address on an ethical subject at Yale. A sentence of it came to the boy's struggling mind. "The courage of the commonplace is greater than the courage of the crisis," the orator had said. That was his chance— "the courage of the commonplace." No fireworks for him, perhaps, ever, but, by Jove, work and will could do a lot, and he could prove himself worthy.

"I'm not through yet, but ginger," he said out loud. "I can do my best anyhow and I'll show if I'm not fit"—the energetic tone trailed off—he was only a boy of twenty—"not fit to be looked at," he finished brokenly.

It came to him in a vague, comforting way that probably the best game a man could play with his life would be to use it as a tool to do work with; to keep it at its brightest, cleanest, most efficient for the sake of the work. This boy, of no phenomenal sort, had one marked quality—when he had made a decision he acted on it. Tonight through the soreness of a bitter disappointment he put his finger on the highest note of his character and resolved. All unknown to himself it was a crisis.

It was long past dinner-time, but he dashed out now and got food, and when Baby Thomas came in he found his room-mate sleepy, but quite himself; quite steady in his congratulations as well as normal in his abuse for "keeping a decent white man awake to this hour."

Three years later the boy graduated from the Boston "Tech." As his class poured from Huntington Hall, he saw his father waiting for him. He noted with pride, as he always did, the tall figure, topped with a wonderful head—a mane of gray hair, a face carved in iron, squared and cut down to the marrow of brains and force—a man to be seen in any crowd. With that, as his own met the keen eyes behind the spectacles, he was aware of a look which startled him. The boy had graduated at the very head of his class; that light in his father's eyes all at once made two years of work a small thing.

"I didn't know you were coming, sir. That's mighty nice of you," he said, as they walked down Boylston Street together, and his father waited a moment and then spoke in his usual incisive tone.

"I wouldn't have liked to miss it, Johnny," he said. "I don't remember that anything in my life has ever made me as satisfied as you have to-day."

With a gasp of astonishment the young man looked at him, looked away, looked at the tops of the houses, and did not find a word anywhere. His father had never spoken to him so; never before, perhaps, had he said anything as intimate to any of his sons. They knew that the cold manner of the great engineer covered depths, but they never expected to see the depths uncovered. But here he was, talking of what he felt, of character, and honor and effort.

"I've appreciated what you've been doing," the even voice went on. "I talk little about personal affairs. But I'm not uninterested; I watch. I was anxious about you. You were a more uncertain quantity than Ted and Harry. Your first three years at Yale were not satisfactory. I was afraid you lacked manliness. Then came—a disappointment. It was a blow to us—to family pride. I watched you more closely, and I saw before that year ended that you were taking your medicine rightly. I wanted to tell you of my contentment, but being slow of speech I—couldn't. So"—the iron face broke for a second into a whimsical grin— "so I offered you a motor. And you wouldn't take it. I knew, though you didn't explain, that you feared it would interfere with your studies. I was right?" Johnny nodded. "Yes. And your last year at college was—was all I could wish. I see now that you needed a blow in the face to wake you up—and you got it. And you waked." The great engineer smiled with clean pleasure. "I have had"—he hesitated—"I have had always a feeling of responsibility to your mother for you—more than for the others. You were so young when she died that you seem more her child. I was afraid I had not treated you well—that it was my fault if you failed." The boy made a gesture—he could not very well speak. His father went on: "So when you refused the motor, when you went into engineer's camp that first summer instead of going abroad, I was pleased. Your course here has been a satisfaction, without a drawback—keener, certainly, because I am an engineer, and could appreciate, step by step, how well you were doing, how much you were giving up to do it, how much power you were gaining by that long sacrifice. I've respected you through these years of commonplace, and I've known how much more courage it meant in a pleasure-loving lad such as you than it would have meant in a serious person such as I am—such as Ted and Harry are, to an extent, also." The older man, proud and strong and reserved, turned on his son such a shining face as the boy had never seen. "That boyish failure isn't wiped out, Johnny, for I shall remember it as the corner-stone of your career, already built over with an honorable record. You've made good. I congratulate you and I honor you."

The boy never knew how he got home. He knocked his shins badly on a quite visible railing and it was out of the question to say a single word. But if he staggered it was with an overload of happiness, and if he was speechless and blind the stricken faculties were paralyzed with joy. His father walked beside him and they understood each other. He reeled up the streets contented.

That night there was a family dinner, and with the coffee his father turned and ordered fresh champagne opened.

"We must have a new explosion to drink to the new superintendent of the Oriel mine," he said. Johnny looked at him surprised, and then at the others, and the faces were bright with the same look of something which they knew and he did not.

"What's up?" asked Johnny. "Who's the superintendent of the Oriel mine? Why do we drink to him? What are you all grinning about, anyway?" The cork flew up to the ceiling, and the butler poured gold bubbles into the glasses, all but his own.

"Can't I drink to the beggar, too, whoever he is?" asked Johnny, and moved his glass and glanced up at Mullins. But his father was beaming at Mullins in a most unusual way and Johnny got no wine. With that Ted, the oldest brother, pushed back his chair and stood and lifted his glass.

"We'll drink," he said, and bowed formally to Johnny, "to the gentleman who is covering us all with glory, to the new superintendent of the Oriel mine, Mr. John Archer McLean," and they stood and drank the toast. Johnny, more or less dizzy, more or less scarlet, crammed his hands in his pockets and started and turned redder, and brought out interrogations in the nervous English which is acquired at our great institutions of learning.

"Gosh! are you all gone dotty?" he asked. And "Is this a merry jape?" And "Why, for cat's sake, can't you tell a fellow what's up your sleeve?" While the family sipped champagne and regarded him.

"Now, if I've squirmed for you enough, I wish you'd explain— father, tell me!" the boy begged.

And the tale was told by the family, in chorus, without politeness, interrupting freely. It seemed that the president of the big mine needed a superintendent, and wishing young blood and the latest ideas had written to the head of the Mining Department in the School of Technology to ask if he would give him the name of the ablest man in the graduating class—a man to be relied on for character as much as brains, he specified, for the rough army of miners needed a general at their head almost more than a scientist. Was there such a combination to be found, he asked, in a youngster of twenty-three or twenty-four, such as would be graduating from the "Tech"? If possible, he wanted a very young man—he wanted the enthusiasm, he wanted the athletic tendency, he wanted the plus-strength, he wanted the unmade reputation which would look for its making to hard work in the mine. The letter was produced and read to the shamefaced Johnny. "Gosh!" he remarked at intervals and remarked practically nothing else. There was no need. They were so proud and so glad that it was almost too much for the boy who had been a failure three years ago.

On the urgent insistence of every one he made a speech. He got to his six-feet-two slowly, and his hands went into his trousers pockets as usual. "Holy mackerel," he began—"I don't call it decent to knock the wind out of a man and then hold him up for remarks. They all said in college that I talked the darnedest hash in the class, anyway. But you will have it, will you? I haven't got anything to say, so's you'd notice it, except that I'll be blamed if I see how this is true. Of course I'm keen for it—Keen! I should say I was! And what makes me keenest, I believe, is that I know it's satisfactory to Henry McLean." He turned his bright face to his father. "Any little plugging I've done seems like thirty cents compared to that. You're all peaches to take such an interest, and I thank you a lot. Me, the superintendent of the Oriel mine! Holy mackerel!" gasped Johnny, and sat down.

The proportion of fighting in the battle of life outweighs the "beer and skittles"; as does the interest. Johnny McLean found interest in masses, in the drab-and-dun village on the prairie. He found pleasure, too, and as far as he could reach he tried to share it; buoyancy and generosity were born in him; strenuousness he had painfully acquired, and like most converts was a fanatic about it. He was splendidly fit; he was the best and last output of the best institution in the country; he went at his work like a joyful locomotive. Yet more goes to explain what he was and what he did. He developed a faculty for leading men. The cold bath of failure, the fire of success had tempered the young steel of him to an excellent quality; bright and sharp, it cut cobwebs in the Oriel mine where cobwebs had been thickening for months. The boy, normal enough, quite unphenomenal, was growing strong by virtue of his one strong quality: he did what he resolved to do. For such a character to make a vital decision rightly is a career. On the night of the Tap Day which had so shaken him, he had struck the key-note. He had resolved to use his life as if it were a tool in his hand to do work, and he had so used it. The habit of bigness, once caught, possesses one as quickly as the habit of drink; Johnny McLean was as unhampered by the net of smallnesses which tangle most of us as a hermit; the freedom gave him a power which was fast making a marked man of him.

There was dissatisfaction among the miners; a strike was probable; the popularity of the new superintendent warded it off from month to month, which counted unto him for righteousness in the mind of the president, of which Johnny himself was unaware. Yet the cobwebs grew; there was an element not reached by, resentful of, the atmosphere of Johnny's friendliness—"Terence O'Hara's gang." By the old road of music he had found his way to the hearts of many. There were good voices among the thousand odd workmen, and Johnny McLean could not well live without music. He heard Dennis Mulligan's lovely baritone and Jack Dennison's rolling bass, as they sang at work in the dim tunnels of the coal-mine, and it seemed quite simple to him that they and he and others should meet when work hours were over and do some singing. Soon it was a club—then a big club; it kept men out of saloons, which Johnny was glad of, but had not planned. A small kindliness seems often to be watered and fertilized by magic. Johnny's music-club grew to be a spell to quiet wild beasts. Yet Terence O'Hara and his gang had a strong hold; there was storm in the air and the distant thunder was heard almost continually.

Johnny, as he swung up the main street of the flat little town, the brick school-house and the two churches at one end, many saloons en route, and the gray rock dump and the chimneys and shaft-towers of the mine at the other, carried a ribbon of brightness through the sordid place. Women came to the doors to smile at the handsome young gentleman who took his hat off as if they were ladies; children ran by his side, and he knocked their caps over their eyes and talked nonsense to them, and swung on whistling. But at night, alone in his room, he was serious. How to keep the men patient; how to use his influence with them; how to advise the president—for young as he was he had to do this because of the hold he had gained on the situation; what concessions were wise—the young face fell into grave lines as he sat, hands deep in his pockets as usual, and considered these questions. Already the sculptor Life was chiselling away the easy curves with the tool of responsibility.

He thought of other things sometimes as he sat before the wood fire in his old Morris chair. His college desk was in the corner by the window, and around it hung photographs ordered much as they had been in New Haven. The portrait of his father on the desk, the painting of his mother, and above them, among the boys' faces, the group of boys and girls of whom she was one, the girl whom he had not forgotten. He had not seen her since that Tap Day. She had written him soon after—an invitation for a week-end at her mother's camp in the woods. But he would not go. He sat in the big chair staring at the fire, this small room in the West, and thought about it. No, he could not have gone to her house party—how could he? He had thought, poor lunatic, that there was an unspoken word between them; that she was different to him from what she was to the others. Then she had failed him at the moment of need. He would not be taken back half-way, with the crowd. He could not. So he had civilly ignored the hand which had held out several times, in several ways. Hurt and proud, yet without conceit, he believed that she kept him at a distance, and would not risk coming too near, and so stayed altogether away. It happens at times that a big, attractive, self-possessed man is secretly as shy, as fanciful, as the shyest girl—if he cares. Once and again indeed the idea flashed into the mind of Johnny McLean—that perhaps she had been so sorry that she did not dare look at him. But he flung that aside with a savage half-thought.

"What rot! It's probable that I was important enough for that, isn't it? You fool!" And about then he was likely to get up with a spring and attack a new book on pillar and shaft versus the block system of mining coal.

The busy days went on, and the work grew more absorbing, the atmosphere more charged with an electricity which foretold tempest. The president knew that the personality of the young superintendent almost alone held the electricity in solution that for months he and his little musical club and his large popularity had kept off the strike. Till at last a day came in early May.

We sit at the ends of the earth and sew on buttons and play cards while fate wipes from existence the thing dearest to us. Johnny's father that afternoon mounted his new saddle-horse and rode through the afternoon lights and shadows of spring. The girl, who had not forgotten, either, went to a luncheon and the theatre after. And it was not till next morning that Brant, her brother, called to her, as she went upstairs after breakfast, in a voice which brought her running back. He had a paper in his hand, and he held it to her.

"What is it, Brant? Something bad?"

"Yes," he said, breathing fast. "Awful. It's going to make you feel badly, for you liked him—poor old Johnny McLean."

"Johnny McLean?" she repeated. Brant went on.

"Yesterday—a mine accident. He went down after the entombed men. Not a chance." Brant's mouth worked. "He died—like a hero— you know." The girl stared.

"Died? Is Johnny McLean dead?"

She did fall down, or cry out, but then Brant knew. Swiftly he came up and put his big, brotherly arm around her.

"Wait, my dear," he said. "There's a ray of hope. Not really hope, you know—it was certain death he went to—but yet they haven't found—they don't know, absolutely, that he's dead."

Five minutes later the girl was locked in her room with the paper. His name was in large letters in the head-lines. She read the account over many times, with painstaking effort to understand that this meant Johnny McLean. That he was down there now, while she breathed pure air. Many times she read it, dazed. Suddenly she flashed to the window and threw it open and beat on the stone sill and dragged her hands across it. Then in a turn she felt this to be worse than useless and dropped on her knees and found out what prayer is. She read the paper again, then, and faced things.

It was the oft-repeated, incredible story of men so accustomed to danger that they throw away their lives in sheer carelessness. A fire down in the third level, five hundred feet underground; delay in putting it out; shifting of responsibility of one to another, mistakes and stupidity; then the sudden discovering that they were all but cut off; the panic and the crowding for the shaft, and scenes of terror and selfishness and heroism down in the darkness and smothering smoke.

The newspaper story told how McLean, the young superintendent, had come running down the street, bare-headed, with his light, great pace of an athlete. How, just as he got there, the cage of six men, which had gone to the third level, had been drawn up after vague, wild signalling, filled with six corpses. How, when the crowd had seen that he meant to go down, a storm of appeal had broken that he should not throw his life away; how the very women whose husbands and sons were below had clung to him. Then the paper told of how he had turned at the mouth of the shaft—the girl could see him standing there tall and broad, with the light on his boyish blond head. He had snatched a paper from his pocket and waved it at arm's-length so that everyone could see. The map of the mine. Gallery 57, on the second level, where the men now below had been working, was close to gallery 9, entered from the other shaft a quarter of a mile away. The two galleries did not communicate, but only six feet of earth divided them. The men might chop through to 9 and reach the other shaft and be saved. But the men did not know it. He explained shortly that he must get to them and tell them. He would go to the second level and with an oxygen helmet would reach possible air before he was caught. Quickly, with an unhesitating decision, he talked, and his buoyancy put courage in to the stricken crowd. With that a woman's voice lifted.

"Don't go—don't ye go, darlin'," it screamed. "'Tis no frinds down there. 'Tis Terence O'Hara and his gang—'tis the strike-makers. Don't be throwin' away your sweet young life for thim."

The boy laughed. "That's all right. Terence has a right to his chance." He went on rapidly. "I want five volunteers—quick. A one-man chance isn't enough to take help. Quick—five."

And twenty men pushed to the boy to follow him into hell. Swiftly he picked five; they put on the heavy oxygen helmets; there was a deep silence as the six stepped into the cage and McLean rang the bell that signaled the engineer to let them down. That was all. They were the last rescuers to go down, and the cage had been drawn up empty. That was all, the newspaper said. The girl read it. All! And his father racing across the continent, to stand with the shawled women at the head of the shaft. And she, in the far-off city, going though the motions of living.

The papers told of the crowds gathering, of the Red Cross, of the experts come to consider the situation, of the line of patient women, with shawls over their heads, waiting always, there at the first gray light, there when night fell; the girl, gasping at her window, would have given years of her life to have stood with those women. The second day she read that they had closed the mouth of the shaft; it was considered that the one chance for life below lay in smothering the flames. When the girl read that, a madness came on her. The shawled women felt that same madness; if the inspectors and the company officials had insisted they could not have kept the mine closed long—the people would have opened it by force; it was felt unendurable to seal their men below; the shaft was unsealed in twenty-four hours. But the smoke came out, and then the watchers realized that a wall of flame was worse than a wall of planks and sand, and the shaft was closed again.

For days there was no news; then the first fruitless descent; then men went down and brought up heavy shapes rolled in canvas and bore them to the women; and "each morning the Red Cross president, lifting the curtain of the car where he slept, would see at first light the still rows of those muffled figures waiting in the hopeless daybreak." Not yet had the body of the young superintendent been found; yet one might not hope because of that. But when one afternoon the head-lines of the papers blazed with a huge "Rescued," she could not read it, and she knew that she had hoped.

It was true. Eighteen men had been brought up alive, and Johnny McLean was one. Johnny McLean carried out senseless, with an arm broken, with a gash in his forehead done by a falling beam as he crawled to hail the rescuers—but Johnny McLean alive. He was very ill, yet the girl had not a minute's doubt that he would get well.

And while he lay unconscious, the papers of the country rang with the story of what he had done, and his father sitting by his bed read it, through unashamed tears, but Johnny took no interest. Breathing satisfied him pretty well for a while. There is no need to tell over what the papers told—how he had taken the leadership of the demoralized band; how when he found them cut off from the escape which he had planned he had set them to work building a barrier across a passage where the air was fresher; how behind this barrier they had lived for six days, by the faith and courage of Johnny McLean. How he had kept them busy playing games, telling stories; had taught them music and put heart into them to sing glees, down in their tomb; how he had stood guard over the pitiful supply of water which dripped from the rock walls, and found ways of saving every drop and made each man take his turn; how when Tom Steele went mad and tried to break out of the barrier on the fifth day, it was McLean who fought him and kept him from the act which would have let in the black damp to kill all of them; how it was the fall in the slippery darkness of that struggle which had broken his arm. The eighteen told the story, bit by bit, as the men grew strong enough to talk, and the record rounded out, of life and reason saved by a boy who had risen out of the gray of commonplace into the red light of heroism. The men who came out of that burial spoke afterward of McLean as of an inspired being.

At all events the strike question was settled in that week below, and Johnny McLean held the ringleaders now in the hollow of his hand. Terence O'Hara opened his eyes and delivered a dictum two hours after he was carried home. "Tell thim byes," he growled in weak jerks, "that if any wan of thim says shtrike till that McLean child drops the hat, they'll fight—O'Hara."

Day after day, while the country was in an uproar of enthusiasm, Johnny lay unconscious, breathing, and doing no more. And large engineering affairs were allowed to go and rack and ruin while Henry McLean watched his son.

On a hot morning such as comes in May, a veteran fly of the year before buzzed about the dim window of the sick-room and banged against the half-closed shutters. Half-conscious of the sound the boy's father read near it, when another sound made his pulse jump.

"Chase him out," came from the bed in a weak, cheerful voice. "Don't want any more things shut up for a spell."

An hour later the older man stood over the boy. "Do you know your next job, Johnny?" he said. "You've got to get well in three weeks. Your triennial in New Haven is then."

"Holy—mackerel!" exploded the feeble tones. "All right, Henry, I'll do it."

\* \* \*

Somewhere in the last days of June, New England is at its loveliest and it is commencement time at Yale. Under the tall elms stretch the shady streets, alive eternally with the ever-new youth of ever-coming hundreds of boys. But at commencement the pleasant, drowsy ways take on an astonishing character; it is as if the little city had gone joyfully mad. Hordes of men of all ages, in startling clothes, appear in all quarters. Under Phelps Gate-way one meets pirates with long hair, with ear-rings, with red sashes; crossing the campus comes a band of Highlanders, in front of the New Haven House are stray Dutchmen and Japanese and Punchinellos and other flotsam not expected in a decorous town; down College Street a group of men in gowns of white swing away through the dappled shadows.

The atmosphere is enchanted; it is full of greetings and reunions and new beginnings and of old friendship; with the every-day clothes the boys of old have shed responsibilities and dignities and are once more irresponsibly the boys of old. From California and Florida, even from China and France, they come swarming into the Puritan place, while in and out through the light-hearted kaleidoscopic crowd hurry slim youngsters in floating black gown and scholar's cap—the text of all this celebration, the graduating class. Because of them it is commencement, it is they who step now over the threshold and carry Yale's honor in their young hands into the world. But small attention do they get, the graduating class, at commencement. The classic note of their grave youthfulness is drowned in the joyful uproar; in the clamor of a thousand greetings one does not listen to these voices which say farewell. From the nucleus of these busy, black-clad young fellows, the folds of their gowns billowing about light, strong figures, the stern lines of the Oxford cap graciously at odds with the fresh modelling of their faces—down from these lads in black, the largest class of all, taper the classes,—fewer, grayer, as the date is older, till a placard on a tree in the campus tells that the class of '51, it may be, has its head-quarters at such a place; a handful of men with white hair are lunching together—and that is a reunion.

In the afternoon of commencement day there is a base-ball game at Yale Field. To that the returning classes go in costume, mostly marching out afoot, each with its band of music, through the gay, dusty street, by the side of the gay, dusty street, by the side of the gay, crowded trolley-cars loaded to the last inch of the last step with a holiday crowd, good-natured, sympathetic, full of humor as an American crowd is always. The men march laughing, talking, nodding to friends in the cars, in the motors, in the carriages which fly past them; the bands play; the houses are faced with people come to see the show.

The amphitheatre of Yale Field is packed with more than ten thousand. The seniors are there with their mothers and fathers, their pretty little sisters and their proud little brothers—the flower of the country. One looks about and sees everywhere high-bred faces, strong faces, open-eyed, drinking in this extraordinary scene. For there is nothing just like it elsewhere. Across the field where hundreds of automobiles and carriages are drawn close—beyond that is a gate-way, and through this, at three o'clock or so, comes pouring a rainbow. A gigantic, light-filled, motion-swept rainbow of men. The first rays of vivid color resolve into a hundred Japanese geishas; they come dancing, waving paper umbrellas down Yale Field; on their heels press Dutch kiddie, wooden-shod, in scarlet and white, with wigs of peroxide hair. Then sailors, some of them twirling oars—the famous victorious crew of fifteen years back; with these march a dozen lads from fourteen to eight, the sons of the class, sailor-clad too; up from their midst as they reach the centre of the field drifts a flight of blue balloons of all sizes. Then come the men of twenty years ago stately in white gowns and mortar-boards; then the Triennials, with a class boy of two years, costumed in miniature and trundled in a go-cart by a nervous father. The Highlanders stalk by to the skirl of bagpipes with their contingent of tall boys, the coming sons of Alma Mater. The thirty-five-year graduates, eighty strong, the men who are handling the nation, wear a unanimous sudden growth of rolling gray beard. Class after class they come, till over a thousand men have marched out to the music of bands, down Yale Field and past the great circle of the seats, and have settled in brilliant masses of color on the "bleachers." Then from across the field rise men's voices singing. They sing the college songs which their fathers sang, which their sons and great-grandsons will sing. The rhythm rolls forward steadily in all those deep voices:

"Nor time nor change can aught avail," the words come,

"To break the friendships formed at Yale."

There is many a breath caught in the crowded multitude to hear the men sing that.

Then the game—and Yale wins. The classes pour on the field in a stormy sea of color, and dance quadrilles, and form long lines hand in hand which sway and cross and play fantastically in a dizzying, tremendous jubilation which fills all of Yale Field. The people standing up to go cannot go, but stay and watch them, these thousand children of many ages, this marvellous show of light-heartedness and loyalty. Till at last the costumes drift together in platoons and disappear slowly; and the crowd thins and the last and most stirring act of the commencement-day drama is at hand.

It has come to be an institution that after the game the old graduates should go, class by class, to the house of the president of Yale, to renew allegiance. It has come to be an institution that he, standing on the steps of his house, should make a short speech to each class. The rainbow of men, sweeping gloriously down the city streets with their bands, dissolves into a whirlwind at the sight of that well-known, slight, dignified figure on the doorstep of the modest house—this is a thing which one who has seen it does not forget; the three-minute speeches, each apt to its audience, each pointed with a dart straight to the heart of class pride and sentiment, these are a marvel. Few men living could come out of a such a test creditably; only this master of men and of boys could do it as he does. For each class goes away confident that the president at least shares its conviction that it is the best class ever graduated. Life might well be worth living, it would seem, to a man who should hear every year hundreds of men's voices thundering his name as these men behind the class banners.

Six weeks after the disaster of the Oriel mine it was commencement day in New Haven and Johnny McLean, his broken arm in a sling, a square of adhesive plaster on his forehead, was back for his Triennial. He was mightily astonished at the greeting he got. Classmates came up to him and shook his hand and said half a sentence and stopped, with an arm around his shoulder; people treated him in a remarkable way, as if he had done something unheard of.

It gratified him, after a fashion, yet it more than half annoyed him. He mentioned over and over again in protest that he had done nothing which "every one of you fellows wouldn't have done just the same," but they laughed at that and stood staring in a most embarrassing way.

"Gosh, Johnny McLean," Tim Erwin remarked finally, "wake up and hear the birdies sing. Do you mean to tell me you don't know you're the hero of the whole blamed nation?"

And Johnny McLean turned scarlet and replied that he didn't think it so particularly funny to guy a man who had attended strictly to his business, and walked off. While Erwin and the others regarded him astounded.

"Well, if that isn't too much!" gasped Tim. "He actually doesn't know!"

"He's likely to find out before we get through," Neddy Haines, of Denver, jerked out nasally and they laughed as if at a secret known together.

So Johnny pursued his way through the two or three days before commencement, absorbed in meeting friends, embarrassed at times by their manner, but taking obstinately the modest place in the class which he had filled in college. It did not enter his mind that anything he had done could alter his standing with the "fellows." Moreover, he did not spend time considering that. So he was one of two hundred Buster Browns who marched to Yale Field in white Russian blouses with shiny blue belts, in sailor hats with blue ribbons, and when the Triennials rushed tempestuously down Trumbull Street in the tracks of the gray-beards of thirty-five years before, Johnny found himself carried forward so that he stood close to the iron fence which guards the little yard from the street. There is always an afternoon tea at the president's house after the game, to let people see the classes make their call on the head of the University. The house was full of people; the yard was filled with gay dresses and men gathered to see the parade.

On the high stone steps under the arch of the doorway stood the president and close by him the white, light figure of a little girl, her black hair tied with a big blue bow. Clustered in the shadow behind them were other figures. Johnny McLean saw the little maid and then his gaze was riveted on the president. It surely was good to see him again; this man who knew how to make them all swear by him.

"What will he have to say to us," Johnny wondered. "Something that will please the whole bunch, I'll bet. He always hits it."

"Men of the class of -," the president began, in his deep, characteristic intonations, "I know that there is only one name you want to hear me speak; only one thought in all the minds of your class."

A hoarse murmur which a second's growth would have made into a wild shout started in the throats of the massed men behind the class banner. The president held up his hand.

"Wait a minute. We want that cheer; we'll have it; but I've got a word first. A great speaker who talked to you boys in your college course said a thing that came to my mind to-day. 'The courage of the commonplace,' he said, 'is greater than the courage of the crisis.'"

Again that throaty, threatening growl, and again the president's hand went up—the boys were hard to hold.

"I see a man among you whose life has added a line to that saying, who has shown to the world that it is the courage of the commonplace which trains for the courage of the crisis. And that's all I've got to say, for the nation is saying the rest-except three times three for the glory of the class of -, the newest name on the honor roll of Yale, McLean of the Oriel mine."

It is probably a dizzying thing to be snatched into the seventh heaven. Johnny McLean standing, scarlet, stunned, his eyes glued on the iron fence between him and the president, knew nothing except a whirling of his brain and an earnest prayer that he might not make a fool of himself. With that, even as the thunder of voices began, he felt himself lifted, swung to men's shoulders, carried forward. And there he sat in his foolish Buster Brown costume, with his broken arm in its sling, with the white patch on his forehead, above his roaring classmates. There he sat perspiring and ashamed, and faced the head of the University, who, it must be said, appeared not to miss the humor of the situation, for he laughed consumedly. And still they cheered and still his name rang again and again. Johnny, hot and squirming under the merry presidential eye, wondered if they were going to cheer all night. And suddenly everything—class-mates, president, roaring voices—died away. There was just one thing on earth. In the doorway, in the group behind the president, a girl stood with her head against the wall and cried as if her heart would break. Cried frankly, openly, mopping away tears with a whole-hearted pocket-handkerchief, and cried more to mop away. As if there were no afternoon tea, no mob of Yale men in the streets, no world full of people who might, if they pleased, see those tears and understand. The girl. Herself. Crying. In a flash, by the light of the happiness that was overwhelming, he found this other happiness. He understood. The mad idea which had come back and back to him out there in the West, which he had put down firmly, the idea that she had cared too much and not too little on that Tap Day four years ago—that idea was true. She did care. She cared still. He knew it without a doubt. He sat on the men's shoulders in his ridiculous clothes, and the heavens opened. Then the tumult and the shouting died and they let the hero down, and to the rapid succession of strong emotions came as a relief another emotion—enthusiasm. They were cheering the president, on the point of bursting themselves into fragments to do it, it seemed. There were two hundred men behind the class banner, and each one was converting what was convertible of his being into noise. Johnny McLean turned to with a will and thundered into the volume of tone which sounded over and over the two short syllables of a name which to a Yale man's idea fits a cheer better than most. The president stood quiet, under the heaped-up honors of a brilliant career, smiling and steady under that delirious music of his own name rising, winged with men's hearts, to the skies. Then the band was playing again and they were marching off down the street together, this wonderful class that knew how to turn earth into heaven for a fellow who hadn't done much of a stunt anyhow, this grand, glorious, big-hearted lot of chaps who would have done much more in his place, every soul of them—so Johnny McLean's thoughts leaped in time with his steps as they marched away. And once or twice a terror seized him—for he was weak yet from his illness—that he was going to make "a fool of himself." He remembered how the girl had cried; he thought of the way the boys had loaded him with honor and affection; he heard the president's voice speaking those impossible words about him— about him—and he would have given a large sum of money at one or two junctures to bolt and get behind a locked door alone where he might cry as the girl had. But the unsentimental hilarity all around saved him and brought him through without a stain on his behavior. Only he could not bolt—he could not get a moment to himself for love or money. It was for love he wanted it. He must find her—he could not wait now. But he had to wait. He had to go into the country to dinner with them all and be lionized and made speeches at, and made fun of, and treated as the darling child and the pride and joy and—what was harder to bear—as the hero and the great man of the class. All the time growing madder with restlessness, for who could tell if she might not be leaving town! A remnant of the class ahead crossed them— and there was Brant, her brother. Diplomacy was not for Johnny McLean—he was much too anxious.

"Brant, look here," and he drew him into a comparative corner.

"Where is she?" Brant did not pretend not to understand, but he grinned.

"At the Andersons', of course."

"Now?"

"Yes, I think so."

"Fellows," said Johnny McLean, "I'm sorry, but I've got to sneak. I'm going back to town."

Sentences and scraps of sentences came flying at him from all over. "Hold him down"—"Chain him up"—"Going—tommy-rot—can't go!" "You'll be game for the roundup at eleven—you've got to be." "Our darling boy—he's got to be," and more language.

"All right for eleven," Johnny agreed. "I'll be at head-quarters then—but I'm going now," and he went.

He found her in a garden, which is the best place to make love. Each place is the best. And in some mystical manner all the doubt and unhappiness which had been gone over in labored volumes of thoughts by each alone, melted to nothing, at two or three broken sentences. There seemed to be nothing to say, for everything was said in a wordless, clear mode of understanding, which lovers and saints know. There was little plot to it, yet there was no lack of interest. In fact so light-footed were the swift moments in the rose-scented dark garden that Johnny McLean forgot, as others have forgotten before him, that time was. He forgot that magnificent lot of fellows, his classmates; there was not a circumstance outside of the shadowy garden which he did not whole-heartedly forget. Till a shock brought him to.

The town was alive with bands and cheers and shouts and marching; the distinct noises rose and fell and fused and separated, but kept their distance. When one body of sound, which unnoticed by the lovers had been growing less vague, more compact, broke all at once into loud proximity—men marching, men shouting, men singing. The two, hand tight in hand, started, looked at each other, listened—and then a name came in a dozen sonorous voices, as they used to shout it in college days, across the Berkeley Oval.

"McLean! McLean!" they called.

"Oh, Johnny McLean!" and "Come out there, oh, Johnny McLean!" That was Baby Thomas.

"By Jove, they've trapped me," he said, smiling in the dark and holding the hand tighter as the swinging steps stopped in front of the house of the garden. "Brant must have told."

"They've certainly found you," the girl said. Her arms, lifted slowly, went about his neck swiftly. "You're mine— but you're theirs to-night. I haven't a right to so much of you even. You're theirs. Go." And she held him. But in a second she had pushed him away. "Go," she said. "You're theirs, bless every one of them."

She was standing alone in the dark, sweet garden and there was a roar in the street which meant that he had opened the door and they had seen him. And with that there were shouts of "Put him up"—"Carry him"—"Carry the boy," and laughter and shouting and then again the measured tread of many men retreating down the street, and men's voices singing together. The girl in the dark garden stood laughing, crying, and listened.

"Mother of men!"—

the deep voices sang—

> "Mother of men grown strong in giving—
> Honor to him thy light have led;
> Rich in the toil of thousands living,
> Proud of the deeds of thousands dead!

We who have felt thy power, and known thee,
We in whose lives thy lights avail,
High, in our hearts enshrined, enthrone thee,
Mother of men, old Yale!"

# Through the Ivory Gate

Breeze filtered through shuffling leafage, the June morning sunlight came in at the open window by the boy's bed, under the green shades, across the shadowy, white room, and danced a noiseless dance of youth and freshness and springtime against the wall opposite. The boy's head stirred on his pillow. He spoke a quick word from out of his dream. "The key?" he said inquiringly, and the sound of his own voice awoke him. Dark, drowsy eyes opened, and he stared half-seeing, at the picture that hung facing him. Was it the play of mischievous sunlight, was it the dream that still held his brain? He knew the picture line by line, and there was no such figure in it. It was a large photograph of Fairfield, the southern home of his mother's people, and the boy remembered it always hanging there, opposite his bed, the first sight to meet his eyes every morning since his babyhood. So he was certain there was no figure in it, more than all one so remarkable as this strapping little chap in his queer clothes, his dress of conspicuous plaid with large black velvet squares sewed on it, who stood now in front of the old manor house. Could it be only a dream? Could it be that a little ghost, wandering childlike in dim, heavenly fields, had joined the gay troop of his boyish visions and slipped in with them through the ivory gate of pleasant dreams? The boy put his fists to his eyes and rubbed them and looked again. The little fellow was still there, standing with sturdy legs wide apart as if owning the scene; he laughed as he held toward the boy a key--a small key tied with a scarlet ribbon. There was no doubt in the boy's mind that the key was for him, and out of the dim world of sleep he stretched his young arm for it; to reach it he sat up in bed. Then he was awake and knew himself alone in the peace of his own little room, and laughed shamefacedly at the reality of the vision which had followed him from dreamland into the very boundaries of consciousness, which held him even now with gentle tenacity, which drew him back through the day, from his studies, from his play, into the strong current of its fascination.

The first time Philip Beckwith had this dream he was only twelve years old, and, withheld by the deep reserve of childhood, he told not even his mother about it, though he lived in its atmosphere all day and remembered it vividly days longer. A year after it came again; and again it was a June morning, and as his eyes opened the little boy came once more out of the picture toward him, laughing and holding out the key on its scarlet string. The dream was a pleasant one, and Philip welcomed it eagerly from his sleep as a friend. There seemed something sweet and familiar in the child's presence beyond the one memory of him, as again the boy, with eyes half-open to everyday life, saw him standing, small but masterful, in the garden of that old house where the Fairfields had lived for more than a century. Half-consciously he tried to prolong the vision, tried not to wake entirely for fear of losing it; but the picture faded surely from the curtain of his mind as the tangible world painted there its heavier outlines. It was as if a happy little spirit had tried to follow him, for love of him, from a country lying close, yet separated; it was as if the common childhood of the two made it almost possible for them to meet; as if a message that might not be spoken, were yet almost delivered.

The third time the dream came it was a December morning of the year when Philip was fifteen, and falling snow made wavering light and shadow on the wall where hung the picture. This time, with eyes wide open, yet with the possession of the dream strongly on him, he lay subconsciously alert and gazed, as in the odd unmistakable dress that Philip knew now in detail, the bright--faced child swung toward him, always from the garden of that old place, always trying with loving, merry efforts to reach Philip from out of it--always holding to him the red ribboned key. Like a wary hunter the big boy lay--knowing it unreal, yet living it keenly--and watched his chance. As the little figure glided close to him, he put out his hand suddenly, swiftly for the key--he was awake. As always, the dream was gone; the little ghost was baffled again; the two worlds might not meet.

That day Mrs. Beckwith, puffing in order an old mahogany secretary, showed him a drawer full of photographs, daguerreotypes. The boy and his gay young mother were the best of friends, for, only nineteen when he was born, she had never let the distance widen between them; had held the freshness of her youth sacred against the time when he should share it. Year by year, living in his enthusiasms, drawing him to hers, she had grown young in his childhood, which year by year came closer to her maturity. Until now there was between the tall, athletic lad and the still young and attractive woman, an equal friendship, a common youth, which gave charm and elasticity to the natural tie between them. Yet even to this comrade-mother the boy had not told his dream, for the difficulty of putting into words the atmosphere, the compelling power of it. So that when she opened one of the old-fashioned black cases which held the early sun-pictures, and showed him the portrait within, he startled her by a sudden exclamation. From the frame of red velvet and tarnished gilt there laughed up at him the little boy of his dream. There was no mistaking him, and if there were doubt about the face, there was the peculiar dress--the black and white plaid with large squares of black velvet sewed here and there as decoration. Philip stared in astonishment at the sturdy figure; the childish face with its wide forehead and level, strong brows; its dark eyes straight-gazing and smiling.

"Mother--who is he? Who is he?" he demanded.

"Why, my lamb, don't you know? It's your little uncle Philip--my brother, for whom you were named--Philip Fairfield the sixth. There was always a Philip Fairfield at Fairfield since 1790. This one was the last, poor baby! And he died when he was five. Unless you go back there some day--that's my hope, but it's not likely to come true. You are a Yankee, except for the big half of you that's me. That's southern, every inch." She laughed and kissed his fresh cheek impulsively. "But what made you so excited over this picture, Phil?"

Philip gazed down, serious, a little embarrassed, at the open case in his hand. "Mother," he said after a moment, "you'll laugh at me, but I've seen this chap in a dream three times now."

"Oh!" She did laugh at him. "Oh, Philip! What have you been eating for dinner, I'd like to know? I can't have you seeing visions of your ancestors at fifteen--it's unhealthy."

The boy, reddening, insisted. "But, Mother, really, don't you think it was queer? I saw him as plainly as I do now--and I've never seen this picture before."

"Oh, yes, you have--you must have seen it," his mother threw back lightly. "You've forgotten, but the image of it was tucked away in some dark corner of your mind, and when you were asleep it stole out and played tricks on you. That's the way forgotten ideas do: they get even with you in dreams for having forgotten them."

"Mother, only listen---" But Mrs. Beckwith, her eyes lighting with a swift turn of thought, interrupted him--laid her finger on his lips.

"No--you listen, boy dear--quick, before I forget it! I've never told you about this, and it's very interesting."

And the youngster, used to these willful ways-of his sistermother, laughed and put his fair head against her shoulder and listened.

"It's quite a romance," she began, "only there isn't any end to it; it's all unfinished and disappointing. It's about this little Philip here, whose name you have--my brother. He died when he was five, as I said, but even then he had a bit of dramatic history in his life. He was born just before wartime in 1859, and he was a beautiful and wonderful baby; I can remember all about it, for I was six years older. He was incarnate sunshine, the happiest child that ever lived, but far too quick and clever for his years. The servants used to ask him, 'Who is you, Marse Philip, sah?' to hear him answer, before he could speak it plainly, 'I'm Philip Fairfield of Fairfield'; he seemed to realize that, and his responsibility to them and to the place, as soon as he could breathe. He wouldn't have a darky scolded in his presence, and every morning my father put him in front of him in the saddle, and they rode together about the plantation. My father adored him, and little Philip's sunshiny way of taking possession of the slaves and the property pleased him more deeply, I think, than anything in his life. But the war came before this time, when the child was about a year old, and my father went off, of course, as every southern man went who could walk, and for a year we did not see him. Then he was badly wounded at the battle of Malvern Hill; and came home to get well. However, it was more serious than he knew, and he did not get well. Twice he went off again to join our army, and each time he was sent back within a month, too ill to be of any use. He chafed constantly, of course, because he must stay at home and farm, when his whole soul ached to be fighting for his flag; but finally in December 1863, he thought he was well enough at last for service. He was to join General John Morgan, who had just made his wonderful escape from prison at Columbus, and it was planned that my mother should take lithe Philip and me to England to live there till the war was over and we could all be together at Fairfield again. With that in view my father drew all of his ready money--it was ten thousand dollars in gold--from the banks in Lexington, for my mother's use in the years they might be separated. When suddenly, the day before he was to have gone, the old wound broke out again, and he was helplessly ill in bed at the hour when he should have been on his horse riding toward Tennessee. We were fifteen miles out from Lexington, yet it might be rumored that father had drawn a large sum of money, and, of course, he was well known as a Southern officer. Because of the Northern soldiers, who held the city, he feared very much to have the money in the house, yet he hoped still to join Morgan a lithe later, and then it would be needed as he had planned. Christmas morning my father was so much better that my mother went to church, taking me, and leaving lithe Philip, then four years old, to amuse him. What happened that morning was the point of all this rambling; so now listen hard, my precious thing."

The boy, sitting erect now, caught his mother's hand silently, and his eyes stared into hers as he drank in every word:

"Mammy, who was, of course, little Philip's nurse, told my mother afterward that she was sent away before my father and the boy went into the garden, but she saw them go and saw that my father had a tin box--a box about twelve inches long, which seemed very heavy--in his arms, and on his finger swung a long red ribbon with a little key strung on it. Mother knew it as the key of the box, and she had tied the ribbon on it herself.

"It was a bright, crisp Christmas day, pleasant in the garden--the box hedges were green and fragrant, aromatic in the sunshine. You don't even know the smell of box in sunshine, you poor child! But I remember that day, for I was ten years old, a right big girl, and it was a beautiful morning for an invalid to take the air. Mammy said she was proud to see how her 'handsome boy' kept step with his father, and she watched the two until they got away down by the rose garden, and then she couldn't see little Philip behind the three-foot hedge, so she turned away. But somewhere in that big garden, or under the trees beside it, my father buried the box that held the money--ten thousand dollars. It shows how he trusted that baby, that he took him with him, and you'll see how his trust was only too well justified. For that evening, Christmas night, very suddenly my father died--before he had time to tell my mother where he had hidden the box. He tried; when consciousness came a few minutes before the end he gasped out, 'I buried the money'--and then he choked. Once again he whispered just two words: 'Philip knows.' And my mother said, 'Yes, dearest--Philip and I will find it--don't worry, dearest,' and that quieted him. She told me about it so many times.

"After the funeral she took little Philip and explained to him as well as she could that he must tell Mother where he and Father had put the box, and--this is the point of it all, Philip--he wouldn't tell. She went over and over it all, again and again, but it was no use. He had given his word to my father never to tell, and he was too much of a baby to understand how death had dissolved that promise. My mother tried every way, of course, explanations and reasoning first, then pleading, and finally severity; she even punished the poor lithe martyr, for it was awfully important to us all. But the four-year-old baby was absolutely incorruptible. He cried bitterly and sobbed out:

"'Farver said I mustn't never tell anybody--never! Farver said Philip Fairfield of Fairfield mustn't never bweak his words,' and that was all.

"Nothing could induce him to give the least hint. Of course there was great search for it, but it was well hidden and it was never found. Finally, Mother took her obdurate son and me and came to New York with us, and we lived on the little income which she had of her own. Her hope was that as soon as Philip was old enough she could make him understand, and go back with him and get that large sum lying underground--lying there yet, perhaps. But in less than a year the little boy was dead and the secret was gone with him."

Philip Beckwith's eyes were intense and wide. The Fairfield eyes, brown and brilliant, their young fire was concentrated on his mother's face.

"Do you mean that money is buried down there, yet, mother?" he asked solemnly.

Mrs. Beckwith caught at the big fellow's sleeve with slim fingers. "Don't go today, Phil--wait till after lunch, anyway!"

"Please don't make fun, Mother--I want to know about it. Think of it lying there in the ground!"

"Greedy boy! We don't need money now, Phil. And the old place will be yours when I am dead--" The lad's arm went about his mother's shoulders. "Oh, but I'm not going to die for ages! Not till I'm a toothless old person with side curls, hobbling along on a stick. Like this!"--she sprang to her feet and the boy laughed a great peal at the haglike effect as his young mother threw herself into the part. She dropped on the divan again at his side.

"What I meant to tell you was that your father thinks it very unlikely that the money is there yet, and almost impossible that we could find it in any case. But some day when the place is yours you can have it put through a sieve if you choose. I wish I could think you would ever live there, Phil; but I can't imagine any chance by which you should. I should hate to have you sell it--it has belonged to a Philip Fairfield so many years."

A week later the boy left his childhood by the side of his mother's grave. His history for the next seven years may go in a few lines. School days, vacations, the four years at college, outwardly the commonplace of an even and prosperous development, inwardly the infinite variety of experience by which each soul is a person; the result of the two so wholesome a product of young manhood that no one realized under the frank and open manner a deep reticence, an intensity, a sensitiveness to impressions, a tendency toward mysticism which made the fiber of his being as delicate as it was strong.

Suddenly, in a turn of the wheel, all the externals of his life changed. His rich father died penniless and he found himself on his own hands, and within a month the boy who had owned five polo ponies was a hard-working reporter on a great daily. The same quick-wittedness and energy which had made him a good polo player made him a good reporter. Promotion came fast and, as those who are busiest have the most time to spare, he fell to writing stories. When the editor of a large magazine took one, Philip first lost respect for that dignified person, then felt ashamed to have imposed on him, then rejoiced utterly over the check. After that editors fell into the habit; the people he ran against knew about his books; the checks grew better reading all the time; a point came where it was more profitable to stay at home and imagine events than to go out and report them. He had been too busy as the days marched to generalize; but suddenly he knew that he was a successful writer, that if he kept his head and worked, a future was before him. So he soberly put his own English by the side of that of a master or two from his bookshelves, to keep his perspective clear, and then he worked harder. And it came to be five years after his father's death.

At the end of those years three things happened at once. The young man suddenly was very tired and knew that he needed the vacation he had gone without; a check came in large enough to make a vacation easy; and he had his old dream. His fagged brain had found it but another worry to decide where he should go to rest, but the dream settled the vexed question offhand--he would go to Kentucky. The very thought of it brought rest to him, for like a memory of childhood, like a bit of his own soul, he knew the country--the "God's Country" of its people--which he had never seen. He caught his breath as he thought of warm, sweet air that held no hurry or nerve strain; of lingering sunny days whose hours are longer than in other places; of the soft speech, the serene and kindly ways of the people; of the royal welcome waiting for him as for everyone, heartfelt and heart-warming; he knew it all from a daughter of Kentucky--his mother. It was May now, and he remembered she had told him that the land was filled with roses at the end of May--he would go then. He owned the old place, Fairfield, and he had never seen it. Perhaps it had fallen to pieces; perhaps his mother had painted it in colors too bright; but it was his, the bit of the earth that belonged to him. The Anglo-Saxon joy of landowning stirred for the first time within him--he would go to his own place. Buoyant with the new thought, he sat down and wrote a letter. A cousin of the family, of a younger branch, a certain John Fairfield, lived yet upon the land. Not in the great house, for that had been closed many years, but in a small house almost as old, called Westerly. Philip had corresponded with him once or twice about affairs of the estate, and each letter of the older man's had brought a simple and urgent invitation to come South and visit him. So, pleased as a child with the plan, he wrote that he was coming on a certain Thursday, late in May. The letter sent, he went about in a dream of the South, and when its answer, delighted and hospitable, came simultaneously with one of those bleak and windy turns of weather which make New York, even in May, a marvelously fitting place to leave, he could not wait. Almost a week ahead of his time he packed his bag and took the Southwestern Limited, and on a bright Sunday morning he awoke in the old Phoenix Hotel in Lexington. He had arrived too late the night before to make the fifteen miles to Fairfield, but he had looked over the horses in the livery stable and chosen the one he wanted, for he meant to go on horseback, as a southern gentleman should, to his domain. That he meant to go alone, that no one, not even John Fairfield, knew of his coming, was not the least of his satisfactions, for the sight of the place of his forefathers, so long neglected, was becoming suddenly a sacred thing to him. The old house and its young owner should meet each other like sweethearts, with no eyes to watch their greeting, their slow and sweet acquainting; with no living voices to drown the sound of the ghostly voices that must greet his homecoming from those walls-- voices of his people who had lived there, voices gone long since into eternal silence.

A little crowd of loungers stared with frank admiration at the young fellow who came out smiling from the door of the Phoenix Hotel, big and handsome in his riding clothes, his eyes taking in the details of girths and bits and straps with the keenness of a horseman.

Philip laughed as he swung into the saddle and looked down at the friendly faces, most of them black faces, below. "Goodbye, " he said. "Wish me good luck, won't you?" and a willing chorus of "Good luck, boss," came flying after him as the horse's hoofs clattered down the street.

Through the bright drowsiness of the little city he rode in the early Sunday morning, and his heart sang for joy to feel himself again across a horse, and for the love of the place that warmed him already. The sun shone hotly, but he liked it; he felt his whole being slipping into place, fitting to its environment; surely, in spite of birth and breeding, he was southern born and bred, for this felt like home more than any home he had known!

As he drew away from the city, every little while, through stately woodlands, a dignified sturdy mansion peeped down its long vista of trees at the passing cavalier, and, enchanted with its beautiful setting, with its air of proud unconsciousness, he hoped each time that Fairfield would look like that. If he might live here--and go to New York, to be sure, two or three times a year to keep the edge of his brain sharpened--but if he might live his life as these people lived, in this unhurried atmosphere, in this perfect climate, with the best things in his reach for everyday use; with horses and dogs, with out-of-doors and a great, lovely country to breathe in; with--he smiled vaguely--with sometime perhaps a wife who loved it as he did--he would ask from earth no better life than that. He could write, he felt certain, better and larger things in such surroundings.

But he pulled himself up sharply as he thought how idle a daydream it was. As a fact, he was a struggling young author, he had come South for two weeks' vacation, and on the first morning he was planning to live here--he must be lightheaded. With a touch of his heel and a word and a quick pull on the curb, his good horse broke into a canter, and then, under the loosened rein, into a rousing gallop, and Philip went dashing down the country road, past the soft, rolling landscape, and under cool caves of foliage, vivid with emerald greens of May, thoughts and dreams all dissolved in exhilaration of the glorious movement, the nearest thing to flying that the wingless animal, man, may achieve.

He opened his coat as the blood rushed faster through him, and a paper fluttered from his pocket. He caught it, and as he pulled the horse to a trot, he saw that it was his cousin's letter. So, walking now along the brown shadows and golden sunlight of the long white pike, he fell to wondering about the family he was going to visit. He opened the folded letter and read:

"My dear Cousin," it said--the kinship was the first thought in John Fairfield's mind--"I received your welcome letter on the 14th. I am delighted that you are coming at last to Kentucky, and I consider that it is high time you paid Fairfield, which has been the cradle of your stock for many generations, the compliment of looking at it. We closed our house in Lexington three weeks ago, and are settled out here now for the summer, and find it lovelier than ever. My family consists only of myself and Shelby, my one child, who is now twenty-two years of age. We are both ready to give you an old-time Kentucky welcome, and Westerly is ready to receive you at any moment you wish to come."

The rest was merely arrangements for meeting the traveler, all of which were done away with by his earlier arrival.

"A prim old party, with an exalted idea of the family," commented Philip mentally. "Well-to-do, apparently, or he wouldn't be having a winter house in the city. I wonder what the boy Shelby is like. At twenty-two he should be doing something more profitable than spending an entire summer out here, I should say."

The questions faded into the general content of his mind at the glimpse of another stately old pillared homestead, white and deep down its avenue of locusts. At length he stopped his horse to wait for a ragged Negro trudging cheerfully down the road.

"Do you know a place around here called Fairfield?" he asked.

"Yessah. I does that, sah. It's that ar' place right hyeh, sah, by yo' hoss. That ar's Fahfiel'. Shall I open the gate fo' you, boss?" and Philip turned to see a hingeless ruin of boards held together by the persuasion of rusty wire.

"The home of my fathers looks down in the mouth," he reflected aloud.

The old Negro's eyes, gleaming from under shaggy sheds of eyebrows, watched him, and he caught the words.

"Is you a Fahfiel', boss?" he asked eagerly. "Is you my young marse?" He jumped at the conclusion promptly. "You favors de fam'ly mightily, sah. I heerd you was comin"; the rag of a hat went off and he bowed low. "Hit's cert'nly good news fo' Fahfiel', Marse Philip, hit's mighty good news fo' us niggers, sah. I'se btlonged to the Fahfiel' fam'ly a hundred years, Marse--me and my folks, and I wishes yo' a welcome home, sah--welcome home, Marse Philip."

Philip bent with a quick movement from his horse and gripped the twisted old black hand, speechless. This humble welcome on the highway caught at his heart deep down, and the appeal of the colored people to southerners, who know them, the thrilling appeal of a gentle, loyal race, doomed to live forever behind a veil and hopeless without bitterness, stirred for the first time his manhood. It touched him to be taken for granted as the child of his people; it pleased him that he should be "Marse Philip" as a matter of course, because there had always been a Marse Philip at the place. It was bred deeper in the bone of him than he knew, to understand the soul of the black man; the stuff he was made of had been southern two hundred years.

The old man went off down the white limestone road singing to himself, and Philip rode slowly under the locusts and beeches up the long drive, grass-grown and lost in places, that wound through the woodland three-quarters of a mile to his house. And as he moved through the park, through sunlight and shadow of these great trees that were his, he felt like a knight of King Arthur, like some young knight long exiled, at last coming to his own. He longed with an unreasonable seizure of desire to come here to live, to take care of it, beautify it, fill it with life and prosperity as it had once been filled, surround it with cheerful faces of colored people whom he might make happy and comfortable. If only he had money to pay off the mortgage, to put the place once in order, it would be the ideal setting for the life that seemed marked out for him--the life of a writer.

The horse turned a corner and broke into a canter up the slope, and as the shoulder of the hill fell away there stood before him the picture of his childhood come to life, smiling drowsily in the morning sunlight with shuttered windows that were its sleeping eyes--the great white house of Fairfield. Its high pillars reached to the roof; its big wings stretched away at either side; the flicker of the shadow of the leaves played over it tenderly and hid broken bits of woodwork, patches of paint cracked away, windowpanes gone here and there. It stood as if too proud to apologize or to look sad for such small matters, as serene, as stately as in its prime. And its master, looking at it for the first time, loved it.

He rode around to the side and tied his mount to an old horse-rack, and then walked up the wide front steps as if each lift were an event. He turned the handle of the big door without much hope that it would yield, but it opened willingly, and he stood inside. A broom lay in a corner, windows were open--his cousin had been making ready for him. There was the huge mahogany sofa, horsehair-covered, in the window under the stairs, where his mother had read Ivanhoe and The Talisman. Philip stepped softly across the wide hall and laid his head where must have rested the brown hair of the little girl who had come to be, first all of his life, and then its dearest memory. Half an hour he spent in the old house, and its walls echoed to his footsteps as if in ready homage, and each empty room whose door he opened met him with a sweet half-familiarity. The whole place was filled with the presence of the child who had loved it and left it, and for whom this tall man, her child, longed now as if for a little sister who should be here, and whom he missed. With her memory came the thought of the five-year-old uncle who had made history for the family so disastrously. He must see the garden where that other Philip had gone with his father to hide the money on the fated Christmas morning. He closed the house door behind him carefully, as if he would not disturb a little girl reading in the window, a little boy sleeping perhaps in the nursery above. Then he walked down the broad sweep of the driveway, the gravel crunching under the grass, and across what had been a bit of velvet lawn, and stood for a moment with his hand on a broken vase, weed-filled, which capped the stone post of a gateway.

All the garden was misty with memories. Where a tall golden flower nodded alone from out of the tangled thicket of an old flowerbed a bright-haired child might have laughed with just that air of starred, gay naughtiness, from the forbidden center of the blossoms. In the molded tan-bark of the path was a vague print, like the ghost of a footprint that had passed down the way a lifetime ago. The box, half-dead, half-sprouted into high unkept growth, still stood stiffly against the riotous overflow of weeds as if it yet held loyally to its business of guarding the borders. Philip shifted his gaze slowly, lingering over the dim contours, the shadowy shape of what the garden had been. Suddenly his eyes opened wide. How was this? There was a hedge as neat, as clipped, as any of Southampton in midseason, and over it a glory of roses, red and white and pink and yellow, waved gay banners to him in trim luxuriance. He swung toward them, and the breeze brought him for the first time in his life the fragrance of box in sunshine.

Three feet tall, shaven and thick and shining, the old hedge stood, and the garnered sweetness of a hundred years' slow growth breathed delicately from it toward the great-great-grandson of the man who planted it. A box hedge takes as long in the making as a gentleman, and when they are done the two are much of a sort. No plant in all the garden has so subtle an air of breeding, so gentle a reserve, yet so gracious a message of sweetness for all of the world who will stop to learn it. It keeps a firm dignity under the stress of tempest when lighter growths are tossed and torn; it shines bright through the snow; it has a well-bred willingness to be background, with the well-bred gift of presence, whether as background or foreground. The soul of the box tree is an aristocrat, and the sap that runs through it is the blue blood of vegetation.

Saluting him bravely in the hot sunshine with its myriad shining sword points, the old hedge sent out to Philip on the May breeze its ancient welcome of aromatic fragrance, and the tall roses crowded gaily to look over its edge at the new master. Slowly, a little dazed at this oasis of shining order in the neglected garden, he walked to the opening and stepped inside the hedge. The rose garden! The famous rose garden of Fairfield, and as his mother had described it, in full splendor of cared-for, orderly bloom. Across the paths he stepped swiftly till he stood amid the roses, giant bushes of Jacqueminot and Marechal Niel; of pink and white and red and yellow blooms in thick array. The glory of them intoxicated him. That he should own all of this beauty seemed too good to be true, and instantly he wanted to taste his ownership. The thought came to him that he would enter into his heritage with strong hands here in the rose garden; he caught a deep-red Jacqueminot almost roughly by its gorgeous head and broke off the stem. He would gather a bunch, a huge, unreasonable bunch of his own flowers. Hungrily he broke one after another; his shoulders bent over them, he was deep in the bushes.

"I reckon I shall have to ask you not to pick any more of those roses," a voice said.

Philip threw up his head as if he had been shot; he turned sharply with a great thrill, for he thought his mother spoke to him. Perhaps it was only the southern inflection so long unheard, perhaps the sunlight that shone in his eyes dazzled him, but, as he stared, the white figure before him seemed to him to look exactly as his mother had looked long ago. Stumbling over his words, he caught at the first that came.

"I--I think it's all right," he said.

The girl smiled frankly, yet with a dignity in her puzzled air. "I'm afraid I shall have to be right decided," she said. "These roses are private property and I mustn't let you have them."

"Oh!" Philip dropped the great bunch of gorgeous color guiltily by his side, but still held tightly the prickly mass of stems, knowing his right, yet half-wondering if he could have made a mistake. He stammered:

"I thought--to whom do they belong?"

"They belong to my cousin, Mr. Philip Fairfield Beckwith"--the sound of his own name was pleasant as the falling voice strayed through it. "He is coming home in a few days, so I want them to look their prettiest for him--for his first sight of them. I take care of this rose garden," she said, and laid a motherly hand on the nearest flower. Then she smiled. "It doesn't seem right hospitable to stop you, but if you will come over to Westerly, to our house, Father will be glad to see you, and I will certainly give you all the flowers you want." The sweet and masterful apparition looked with a gracious certainty of obedience straight into Philip's bewildered eyes.

"The boy Shelby!" Many a time in the months after, Philip Beckwith smiled to himself reminiscently, tenderly, as he thought of "the boy Shelby" whom he had read into John Fairfield's letter; "the boy Shelby" who was twenty-two years old and the only child; "the boy Shelby" whom he had blamed with such easy severity for idling at Fairfield; "the boy Shelby" who was no boy at all, but this white flower of girlhood, called--after the quaint and reasonable southern way--as a boy is called, by the surname of her mother's people.

Toward Westerly, out of the garden of the old time, out of the dimness of a forgotten past, the two took their radiant youth and the brightness of today. But a breeze blew across the tangle of weeds and flowers as they wandered away, and whispered a hope, perhaps a promise; for as it touched them each tall stalk nodded gaily and the box hedges rustled delicately an answering undertone. And just at the edge of the woodland, before they were out of sight, the girl turned and threw a kiss back to the roses and the box.

"I always do that," she said. "I love them so!"

Two weeks later a great train rolled into the Grand Central Station of New York at half-past six at night, and from it stepped a monstrosity--a young man without a heart. He had left all of it, more than he had thought he owned, in Kentucky. But he had brought back with him a store of memories which gave him more joy than ever the heart had done, to his best knowledge, in all the years. They were memories of long and sunshiny days; of afternoons spent in the saddle, rushing through grassy lanes where trumpet flowers flamed over gray farm fences, or trotting slowly down white roads; of whole mornings only an hour long, passed in the enchanted stillness of an old garden; of gay, desultory searches through its length and breadth, and in the park that held it, for buried treasure; of moonlit nights; of roses and June and Kentucky--and always, through all the memories, the presence that made them what they were, that of a girl he loved.

No word of love had been spoken, but the two weeks had made over his life; and he went back to his work with a definite object, a hope stronger than ambition, and, set to it as music to words, came insistently another hope, a dream that he did not let himself dwell on--a longing to make enough money to pay off the mortgage and put Fairfield in order, and live and work there all his life--with Shelby. That was where the thrill of the thought came in, but the place was very dear to him in itself.

The months went, and the point of living now was the mail from the South, and the feast days were the days that brought letters from Fairfield. He had promised to go back for a week at Christmas, and he worked and hoarded all the months between with a thought which he did not formulate, but which ruled his down-sitting and his up-rising, the thought that if he did well and his bank account grew enough to justify it he might, when he saw her at Christmas, tell her what he hoped; ask her--he finished the thought with a jump of his heart. He never worked harder or better, and each check that came in meant a step toward the promised land; and each seemed for the joy that was in it to quicken his pace, to lengthen his stride, to strengthen his touch. Early in November he found one night when he came to his rooms two letters waiting for him with the welcome Kentucky postmark. They were in John Fairfield's handwriting and in his daughter's, and "place aux dames" ruled rather than respect to age, for he opened Shelby's first. His eyes smiling, he read it.

"I am knitting you a diamond necklace for Christmas," she wrote. "Will you like that? Or be sure to write me if you'd rather have me hunt in the garden and dig you up a box of money. I'll tell you--there ought to be luck in the day, for it was hidden on Christmas and it should be found on Christmas; so on Christmas morning we'll have another look, and if you find it I'll catch you 'Christmas gif' as the darkies do, and you'll have to give it to me, and if I find it I'll give it to you; so that's fair, isn't it? Anyway--" and Philip's eyes jumped from line to line, devouring the clear, running writing. "So bring a little present with you, please--just a tiny something for me," she ended, "for I'm certainly going to catch you 'Christmas gif'."

Philip folded the letter back into its envelope and put it in his pocket, and his heart felt warmer for the scrap of paper over it. Then he cut John Fairfield's open dreamily, his mind still on the words he had read, on the threat--"I'm going to catch you 'Christmas gif.'" What was there good enough to give her? Himself, he thought humbly, very far from good enough for the girl, the lily of the world. With a sigh that was not sad he dismissed the question and began to read the other letter. He stood reading it by the fading light from the window, his hat thrown by him on a chair, his overcoat still on, and, as he read, the smile died from his face. With drawn brows he read on to the end, and then the letter dropped from his fingers to the floor and he did not notice; his eyes stared widely at the high building across the street, the endless rows of windows, the lights flashing into them here and there. But he saw none of it. He saw a stretch of quiet woodland, an old house with great white pillars, a silent, neglected garden, with box hedges sweet and ragged, all waiting for him to come and take care of them--the honor of his fathers, the home he had meant, had expected--he knew it now--would be some day his own, the home he had lost! John Fairfield's letter was to tell him that the mortgage on the place, running now so many years, was suddenly to be foreclosed; that, property not being worth much in the neighborhood, no one would take it up; that on January 2nd Fairfield, the house and land, were to be sold at auction. It was a hard blow to Philip Beckwith, With his hands in his overcoat pockets he began to walk up and down the room, trying to plan, to see if by any chance he might save this place he loved. It would mean eight thousand dollars to pay the mortgage. One or two thousand more would put the estate in order, but that might wait if he could only tide over this danger, save the house and land. An hour he walked so, forgetting dinner, forgetting the heavy coat which he still wore, and then he gave it up. With all he had saved--and it was a fair and promising beginning--he could not much more than half-pay the mortgage, and there was no way, which he would consider, by which he could get the money. Fairfield would have to go, and he set his teeth and clenched his fists as he thought how much he wanted to keep it. A year ago it had meant nothing to him, a year from now if things went his way he could have paid the mortgage. That it should happen just this year--just now! He could not go down at Christmas; it would break his heart to see the place again as his own when it was just slipping from his grasp. He would wait until it was all over, and go, perhaps, in the spring. The great hope of his life was still his own, but Fairfield had been the setting of that hope; he must readjust his world before he saw Shelby again. So he wrote them that he would not come at present, and then tried to dull the ache of his loss with hard work.

But three days before Christmas, out of the unknown forces beyond his reasoning swept a wave of desire to go South, which took him off his feet. Trained to trust his brain and deny his impulse as he was, yet there was a vein of sentiment, almost of superstition, in him which the thought of the old place pricked sharply to life. This longing was something beyond him--he must go--and he had thrown his decisions to the winds and was feverish until he could get away.

As before, he rode out from the Phoenix Hotel, and at ten o'clock in the morning he turned into Fairfield. It was a still, bright Christmas morning, crisp and cool, and the air like wine. The house stood bravely in the sunlight, but the branches above it were bare and no softening leafage hid the marks of time; it looked old and sad and deserted today, and its master gazed at it with a pang in his heart. It was his, and he could not save it. He turned away and walked slowly to the garden, and stood a moment as he had stood last May, with his hand on the stone gateway. It was very silent and lonely here, in the hush of winter; nothing stirred; even the shadows of the interlaced branches above lay almost motionless across the walks.

Something moved to his left, down the pathway--he turned to look. Had his heart stopped, that he felt this strange, cold feeling in his breast? Were his eyes--could he be seeing? Was this insanity? Fifty feet down the path, half in the weaving shadows, half in clear sunlight, stood the little boy of his lifelong vision, in the dress with the black velvet squares, his little uncle, dead forty years ago. As he gazed, his breath stopping, the child smiled and held up to him, as of old, a key on a scarlet string, and turned and flitted as if a flower had taken wing, away between the box hedges. Philip, his feet moving as if without his will, followed him. Again the baby face turned its smiling dark eyes toward him, and Philip knew that the child was calling him, though there was no sound; and again without volition of his own his feet took him where it led. He felt his breath coming difficulty, and suddenly a gasp shook him--there was no footprint on the unfrozen earth where the vision had passed. Yet there before him, moving through the deep sunlit silence of the garden, was the familiar, sturdy little form in its Old-World dress. Philip's eyes were open; he was awake, walking; he saw it. Across the neglected tangle it glided, and into the trim order of Shelby's rose garden; in the opening between the box walls it wheeled again, and the sun shone clear on the bronze hair and fresh face, and the scarlet string flashed and the key glinted at the end of it. Philip's fascinated eyes saw all of that. Then the apparition slipped into the shadow of the beech trees and Philip quickened his step breathlessly, for it seemed that life and death hung on the sight. In and out through the trees it moved; once more the face turned toward him; he caught the quick brightness of a smile. The little chap had disappeared behind the broad tree trunk, and Philip, catching his breath, hurried to see him appear again. He was gone. The little spirit that had strayed from over the border of a world--who can say how far, how near?--unafraid in this earth-corner once its home, had slipped away into eternity through the white gate of ghosts and dreams.

Philip's heart was pumping painfully as he came, dazed and staring, to the place where the apparition had vanished. It was a giant-beech tree, all of two hundred and fifty years old, and around its base ran a broken wooden bench, where pretty girls of Fairfield had listened to their sweethearts, where children destined to be generals and judges had played with their black mammies, where gray-haired judges and generals had come back to think over the fights that were fought out. There were letters carved into the strong bark, the branches swung down whisperingly, the green tent of the forest seemed filled with the memory of those who had camped there and gone on. Philip's feet stumbled over the roots as he circled the veteran; he peered this way and that, but the woodland was hushed and empty; the birds whistled above, the grasses rustled below, unconscious, casual, as if they knew nothing of a child-soul that had wandered back on Christmas day with a Christmas message, perhaps, of goodwill to its own.

As he stood on the farther side of the tree where the little ghost had faded from him, at his feet lay, open and conspicuous, a fresh, deep hole. He looked down absent-mindedly. Some animal--a dog, a rabbit--had scratched far into the earth. A bar of sunlight struck a golden arm through the branches above, and as he gazed at the upturned, brown dirt the rays that were its fingers reached into the hollow and touched a square corner, a rusty edge of tin. In a second the young fellow was down on his knees digging as if for his life, and in less than dive minutes he had loosened the earth which had guarded it so many years, and staggering with it to his feet had lifted to the bench a heavy tin box. In its lock was the key, and dangling from it a long bit of no-colored silk, that yet, as he untwisted it, showed a scarlet thread in the crease. He opened the box with the little key; it turned scrapingly, and the ribbon crumbled in his fingers, its long duty done. Then, as he tilted the heavy weight, the double eagles, packed closely, slipped against each other with a soft clink of sliding metal. The young man stared at the mass of gold pieces as if he could not trust his eyesight; he half thought even then that he dreamed it. With a quick memory of the mortgage he began to count. It was all there--ten thousand dollars in gold! He lifted his head and gazed at the quiet woodland, the open shadowwork of the bare branches, the fields beyond lying in the calm sunlit rest of a southern winter. Then he put his hand deep into the gold pieces, and drew a long breath. It was impossible to believe, but it was true. The lost treasure was found. It meant to him Shelby and home; as he realized what it meant, his heart felt as if it would break with the joy of it. He would give her this for his Christmas gift, this legacy of his people and hers, and then he would give her himself It was all easy now--life seemed not to hold a difficulty. And the two would keep tenderly, always, the thought of a child who had loved his home and his people and who had tried so hard, so long, to bring them together. He knew the dream-child would not visit him again--the little ghost was laid that had followed him all his life. From over the border whence it had come with so many loving efforts it would never come again. Slowly, with the heavy weight in his arms, with the eyes of a man who had seen a solemn thing, he walked back to the garden sleeping in the sunshine, and the box hedges met him with a wave of fragrance, the sweetness of a century ago; and as he passed through their shining door, looking beyond, he saw Shelby. The girl's figure stood by the stone column of the garden entrance. The light shone on her bare head, and she had stopped, surprised, as she saw him. Philip lifted his hat high, and his pace quickened with his heartthrob as he looked at her and thought of the little ghostly hands that had brought theirs together; and as he looked the smile that meant his welcome and his happiness broke over her face, and with the sound of her voice all the shades of this world and the next dissolved in light.

"'Christmas gif',' Marse Philip!" called Shelby.

# Joy in the Morning

*FIRST ACT*

>*The time is a summer day in 1918. The scene is the first-line trench of the Germans—held lately by the Prussian Imperial Guard—half an hour after it had been taken by a charge of men from the Blank th Regiment, United States Army. There has been a mistake and the charge was not preceded by artillery preparation as usual. However, the Americans have taken the trench by the unexpectedness of their attack, and the Prussian Guard has been routed in confusion. But the German artillery has at once opened fire on the Americans, and also a German machine gun has enfiladed the trench. Ninety-nine Americans have been killed in the trench. One is alive, but dying. He speaks, being part of the time delirious.*

**The Boy**

Why can't I stand? What—is it? I'm wounded. The sand-bags roll when I try—to hold to them. I'm—badly wounded. (*Sinks down. Silence.*) How still it is! We—we took the trench. Glory be! We took it! (*Shouts weakly as he lies in the trench.*) (*Sits up and stares, shading his eyes.*) It's horrid still. Why—they're here! Jack—you! What makes you—lie there? You beggar—oh, my God! They're dead. Jack Arnold, and Martin and—Cram and Bennett and Emmet and—Dragamore—Oh—God, God! All the boys! Good American boys. The whole blamed bunch—dead in a ditch. Only me. Dying, in a ditch filled with dead men. What's the sense? (*Silence.*) This damned silly war. This devilish—killing. When we ought to be home, doing man's work—and play. Getting some tennis, maybe, this hot afternoon; coming in sweaty and dirty—and happy—to a tub—and dinner—with mother. (*Groans.*) It begins to hurt—oh, it hurts confoundedly. (*Becomes delirious.*) Canoeing on the river. With little Jim. See that trout jump, Jimmie? Cast now. Under the log at the edge of the trees. That's it! Good—oh! (*Groans.*) It hurts—badly. Why, how can I stand it? How can anybody? I'm badly wounded. Jimmie—tell mother. Oh—good boy—you've hooked him. Now play him; lead him away from the lily-pads. (*Groans.*) Oh, mother! Won't you come? I'm wounded. You never failed me before. I need you—if I die. You went away down—to the gate of life, to bring me inside. Now—it's the gate of death—you won't fail? You'll bring me through to that other life? You and I, mother—and I won't be scared. You're the first—and the last. (*Puts out his arm searching and folds a hand, still warm, of a dead soldier.*) Ah—mother, my dear. I knew—you'd come. Your hand is warm—comforting. You always—are there when I need you. All my life. Things are getting—hazy. (*He laughs.*) When I was a kid and came down in an elevator—I was all right, I didn't mind the drop if I might hang on to your hand. Remember? (*Pats dead soldier's hand, then clutches it again tightly.*) You come with me when I go across and let me—hang on—to your hand. And I won't be scared. (*Silence.*) This damned—damned—silly war! All the good American boys. We charged the Fritzes. How they ran! But—there was a mistake. No artillery preparation. There ought to be crosses and medals going for that charge, for the boys—(*Laughs*.) Why, they're all dead. And me—I'm dying, in a ditch. Twenty years old. Done out of sixty years by— by the silly war. What's it for? Mother, what's it about? I'm ill a bit. I can't think what good it is. Slaughtering boys—all the nations' boys—honest, hard-working boys mostly. Junk. Fine chaps an hour ago. What's the good? I'm dying—for the flag. But—what's the good? It'll go on—wars. Again. Peace sometimes, but nothing gained. And all of us—dead. Cheated out of our lives. Wouldn't the world have done as well if this long ditch of good fellows had been let live? Mother?

**The Boy's Dream of His Mother**

(*Seems to speak.*) My very dearest—no. It takes this great burnt-offering to free the world. The world will be free. This is the crisis of humanity; you are bending the lever that lifts the race. Be glad, dearest life of the world, to be part of that glory. Think back to your school-days, to a sentence you learned. Lincoln spoke it. "These dead shall not have died in vain, and government of the people, by the people, for the people, shall not perish from the earth." *The Boy*. (*Whispers*.) I remember. It's good. "Shall not have died in vain"—"The people—shall not perish"—where's your hand, mother? It's taps for me. The lights are going out. Come with me—mother. (*Dies*.)

---

## *SECOND ACT*

*The scene it the same trench one hundred years later, in the year 2018. It is ten o'clock of a summer morning. Two French children have come to the trench to pick flowers. The little girl of seven is gentle and soft-hearted; her older brother is a man of nearly ten years, and feels his patriotism and his responsibilities.*

**Angélique**

(*The little French girl*.) Here's where they grow, Jean-B'tiste.

**Jean-Baptiste**

(*The little French boy*.) I know. They bloom bigger blooms in the American ditch.

#### Angélique

(*Climbs into the ditch and picks flowers busily.*) Why do people call it the 'Merican ditch, Jean-B'tiste? What's 'Merican?

#### Jean-Baptiste

(*Ripples laughter.*) One's little sister doesn't know much! Never mind. One is so young—three years younger than I am. I'm ten, you know.

#### Angélique

*Tiens*, Jean-B'tiste. Not ten till next month.

#### Jean-Baptiste

Oh, but—but—next month!

#### Angélique

What's 'Merican?

#### Jean-Baptiste

Droll *p'tite*. Why, everybody in all France knows that name. Of American.

#### Angélique

(*Unashamed.*) Do they? What is it?

#### Jean-Baptiste

It's the people that live in the so large country across the ocean. They came over and saved all our lives, and France.

#### Angélique

(*Surprised.*) Did they save my life, Jean-B'tiste?

#### Jean-Baptiste

Little *drôle*. You weren't born.

#### Angélique

Oh! Whose life did they then save? Maman's?

#### Jean-Baptiste

But no. She was not born either.

**Angélique**

Whose life, then—the grandfather's?

**Jean-Baptiste**

But—even he was not born. (*Disconcerted by Angélique's direct tactics.*) One sees they could not save the lives of people who were not here. But—they were brave—but 01yes—and friends to France. And they came across the ocean to fight for France. Big, strong young soldiers in brown uniforms—the grandfather told me about it yesterday. I know it all. His father told him, and he was here. In this field. (*Jean-Baptiste looks about the meadow, where the wind blows flowers and wheat.*) There was a large battle—a fight very immense. It was not like this then. It was digged over with ditches and the soldiers stood in the ditches and shot at the wicked Germans in the other ditches. Lots and lots of soldiers died.

**Angélique**

(*Lips trembling.*) Died—in ditches?

**Jean-Baptiste**

(*Grimly.*) Yes, it is true.

**Angélique**

(*Breaks into sobs.*) I can't bear you to tell me that. I can't bear the soldiers to—die—in ditches.

**Jean-Baptiste**

(*Pats her shoulder.*) I'm sorry I told you if it makes you cry. You are so little. But it was one hundred years ago. They're dead now.

**Angélique**

(*Rubs her eyes with her dress and 01smiles.*) Yes, they're quite dead now. So—tell me some more.

**Jean-Baptiste**

But I don't want to make you cry more, *p'tite*. You're so little.

**Angélique**

I'm not *very* little. I'm bigger than Anne-Marie Dupont, and she's eight.

**Jean-Baptiste**

But no. She's not eight till next month. She told me.

**Angélique**

Oh, well—next month. Me, I want to hear about the brave 'Mericans. Did they make this ditch to stand in and shoot the wicked Germans?

**Jean-Baptiste**

They didn't make it, but they fought the wicked Germans in a brave, wonderful charge, the bravest sort, the grandfather said. And they took the ditch away from the wicked Germans, and then—maybe you'll cry.

**Angélique**

I won't. I promise you I won't.

**Jean-Baptiste**

Then, when the ditch—only they called it a trench—was well full of American soldiers, the wicked Germans got a machine gun at the end of it and fired all the way along—the 0lgrandfather called it enfiladed—and killed every American in the whole long ditch.

**Angélique**

(*Bursts into tears again; buries her face in her skirt.*) I—I'm sorry I cry, but the 'Mericans were so brave and fought—for France—and it was cruel of the wicked Germans to—to shoot them.

**Jean-Baptiste**

The wicked Germans were always cruel. But the grandfather says it's quite right now, and as it should be, for they are now a small and weak nation, and scorned and watched by other nations, so that they shall never be strong again. For the grandfather says they are not such as can be trusted—no, never the wicked Germans. The world will not believe their word again. They speak not the truth. Once they nearly smashed the world, when they had power. So it is looked to by all nations that never again shall Germany be powerful. For they are sly, and cruel as wolves, and only intelligent to be wicked. That is what the grandfather says.

**Angélique**

Me, I'm sorry for the poor wicked 0lGermans that they are so bad. It is not nice to be bad. One is punished.

**Jean-Baptiste**

(*Sternly*.) It is the truth. One is always punished. As long as the world lasts it will be a punishment to be a German. But as long as France lasts there will be a nation to love the name of America, one sees. For the Americans were generous and brave. They left their dear land and came and died for us, to keep us free in France from the wicked Germans.

### Angélique

(*Lip trembles*.) I'm sorry—they died.

### Jean-Baptiste

But, *p'tite!* That was one hundred years ago. It is necessary that they would have been dead by now in every case. It was more glorious to die fighting for freedom and France than just to die—fifty years later. Me, I'd enjoy very much to die fighting. But look! You pulled up the roots. And what is that thing hanging to the roots—not a rock?

### Angélique

No, I think not a rock. (She takes the object in her hands and knocks dirt from it.) But what is it, Jean-B'tiste?

01
### Jean-Baptiste

It's—but never mind. I can't always know everything, don't you see, Angélique? It's just something of one of the Americans who died in the ditch. One is always finding something in these old battle-fields.

### Angélique

(*Rubs the object with her dress. Takes a handful of sand and rubs it on the object. Spits on it and rubs the sand*.) *V'là*, Jean-B'tiste—it shines.

### Jean-Baptiste

(*Loftily*.) Yes. It is nothing, that. One finds such things.

### Angélique

(*Rubbing more*.) And there are letters on it.

### Jean-Baptiste

Yes. It is nothing, that. One has flowers *en masse* now, and it is time to go home. Come then, *p'tite*, drop the dirty bit of brass and pick up your pretty flowers. *Tiens!* Give me your hand. I'll pull you up the side of the ditch. (*Jean-Baptiste turns as they start*.) I forgot the thing which the grandfather told me I must do always. (*He stands at attention.*) *Au revoir*, brave Americans. One salutes your immortal glory. (*Exit Jean-Baptiste and Angélique.*)

---

## THIRD ACT

*The scene is the same trench in the year 2018. It is eleven o'clock of the same summer morning. Four American schoolgirls, of from fifteen to seventeen years, have been brought to see the trench, a relic of the Great War, in charge of their teacher. The teacher, a worn and elderly person, has imagination, and is stirred, as far as her tired nerves may be, by the heroic story of the old ditch. One of the schoolgirls also has imagination and is also stirred. The other three are "young barbarians at play." Two out of five is possibly a large proportion to be blessed with imagination, but the American race has improved in a hundred years.*

**Teacher**

This, girls, is an important bit of our sight-seeing. It is the last of the old trenches of the Great War to remain intact in all northern France. It was left untouched out of the reverence of the people of the country for one hundred Americans of the Blank*th* Regiment, who died here—in this old ditch. The regiment had charged too soon, by a mistaken order, across what was called 01No-Man's Land, from their own front trench, about (*consults guide-book*)—about thirty-five yards away—that would be near where you see the red poppies so thick in the wheat. They took the trench from the Germans, and were then wiped out partly by artillery fire, partly by a German machine gun which was placed, disguised, at the end of the trench and enfiladed the entire length. Three-quarters of the regiment, over two thousand men, were killed in this battle. Since then the regiment has been known as the "Charging Blank*th*."

**First Schoolgirl**

Wouldn't those poppies be lovely on a yellow hat?

**Second Schoolgirl**

Ssh! The Eye is on you. How awful, Miss Hadley! And were they all killed? Quite a tragedy!

**Third Schoolgirl**

Not a yellow hat! Stupid! A corn-colored one—just the shade of the grain with the sun on it. Wouldn't it be lovely! When we get back to Paris—

**Fourth Schoolgirl (the one with imagination)**

You idiots! You poor kittens!

**First Schoolgirl**

If we ever do get back to Paris!

**Teacher**

(*Wearily*.) Please pay attention. This is one of the world's most sacred spots. It is the scene of a great heroism. It is the place where many of our fellow countrymen laid down their lives. How can you stand on this solemn ground and chatter about hats?

**Third Schoolgirl**

Well, you see, Miss Hadley, we're fed up with solemn grounds. You can't expect us to go into raptures at this stage over an old ditch. And, to be serious, wouldn't some of those field flowers make a lovely combination for hats? With the French touch, don't you know? You'd be darling in one—so *ingénue!*—

**Second Schoolgirl**

Ssh! She'll kill you. (*Three girls turn their backs and stifle a giggle.*)

**Teacher**

Girls, you may be past your youth yourselves one day.

**First Schoolgirl**

(*Airily.*) But we're well preserved so far, Miss Hadley.

**Fourth Schoolgirl**

(*Has wandered away a few yards. She bends and picks a flower from the ditch. She speaks to herself.*) The flag floated here. There were shells bursting and guns thundering and groans and blood—here. American boys were dying where I stand safe. That's what they did. They made me safe. They kept America free. They made the "world safe for freedom," (*She bends and speaks into the ditch.*) Boy, you who lay just there in suffering and gave your good life away that long-ago summer day—thank you. You died for us. America remembers. Because of you there will be no more wars, and girls such as we are may wander across battle-fields, and nations are happy and well governed, and kings and masters are gone. You did that, you boys. You lost fifty years of life, but you gained our love forever. Your deaths were not in rain. Good-by, dear, dead boys.

**Teacher**

(*Calls*). Child, come! We must catch the train.

---

## FOURTH ACT

*The scene is the same trench in the year 2018. It is three o'clock of the afternoon, of the same summer day. A newly married couple have come to see the trench. He is journeying as to a shrine; she has allowed impersonal interests, such as history, to lapse under the influence of love and a trousseau. She is, however, amenable to patriotism, and, her husband applying the match, she takes fire—she also, from the story of the trench.*

**He**

This must be the place.

**She**

It is nothing but a ditch filled with flowers.

**He**

The old trench. (*Takes off his hat.*)

**She**

Was it—it was—in the Great War?

**He**

My dear!

**She**

You're horrified. But I really—don't know.

**He**

Don't know? You must.

**She**

You've gone and married a person who hasn't a glimmer of history. What will you do about it?

**He**

I'll be brave and stick to my bargain. Do you mean that you've forgotten the charge of the Blank*th* Americans against the Prussian Guard? The charge that practically ended the war?

**She**

Ended the war? How could one charge end the war?

**He**

There was fighting after. But the last critical battle was here (*looks about*) in these meadows, and for miles along. And it was just here that the Blank*th* United States Regiment made its historic dash. In that ditch—filled with flowers—a hundred of our lads were mown down in three minutes. About two thousand more followed them to death.

**She**

Oh—I do know. It was *that* charge. I learned about it in school; it thrilled me always.

**He**

Certainly. Every American child knows the story. I memorized the list of the one hundred soldiers' names of my own free will when I was ten. I can say them now. "Arnold—Ashe—Bennett—Emmet—Dragmore—"

**She**

Don't say the rest, Ted—tell me about it as it happened. (*She slips her hand into his.*) We two, standing here young and happy, looking forward to a, lifetime together, will do honor, that way, to those soldiers who gave up their happy youth and their lives for America.

**He**

(*Puts his arm around her.*) We will. We'll make a little memorial service and I'll preach a sermon about how gloriously they fell and how, unknowingly, they won the war—and so much more!

**She**

Tell me.

**He**

It was a hundred years ago about now—summer. A critical battle raged along a stretch of many miles. About the centre of the line—here—the Prussian Imperial Guards, the crack soldiers of the German army, held the first trench—this ditch. American forces faced them, but in weeks of fighting had not been able to make much impression. Then, on a day, the order came down the lines that the Blank*th* United States Regiment, opposed to the Guard, was to charge and take the German front trench. Of course the artillery was to prepare for their charge as usual, but there was some mistake. There was no curtain of fire before them, no artillery preparation to help them. And the order to charge came. So, right into the German guns, in the face of those terrible Prussian Guards, our lads went "over the top" with a great shout, and poured like a flame, like a catapult, across the space between them—No-Man's Land, they called it then—it was only thirty-five yards—to the German trench. So fast they rushed, and so unexpected was their coming, with no curtain of artillery to shield them, that the Germans were for a moment taken aback. Not a shot was fired for a space of time almost long enough to let the Americans reach the trench, and then the rifles broke out and the brown uniforms fell like leaves in autumn. But not all. They rushed on pell-mell, cutting wire, pouring irresistibly into the German trench. And the Guards, such as were not mown down, lost courage at the astounding impetus of the dash, and scrambled and ran from their trench. They took it—our boys took that trench—this old ditch. But then the big German guns opened a fire like hail and a machine gun at the end—down there it must have been—enfiladed the trench, and every man in it was killed. But the charge ended the war. Other Americans, mad with the glory of it, poured in a sea after their comrades and held the trench, and poured on and on, and wiped out that day the Prussian Guard. The German morale was broken from then; within four months the war was over.

**She**

(*Turns and hides her face on his shoulder and shakes with sobs.*) I'm not—crying for sorrow—for them. I'm crying—for the glory of it. Because—I'm so proud and glad—that it's too much for me. To belong to such a nation—to such men. I'm crying for knowing, it was my nation—my men. And America is—the same today. I know it.

If she needed you today, Ted, you would fight like that. You would go over the top with the charging Blank *th*, with a shout, if the order came—wouldn't you, my own man?

**He**

(*Looking into the old ditch with his head bent reverently.*) I hope so.

**She**

And I hope I would send you with all my heart. Death like that is more than life.

**He**

I've made you cry.

02
**She**

Not you. What they did—those boys.

**He**

It's fitting that Americans should come here, as they do come, as to a Mecca, a holy place. For it was here that America was saved. That's what they did, the boys who made that charge. They saved America from the most savage and barbarous enemy of all time. As sure as France and England were at the end of their rope—and they were—so surely Germany, the victor, would have invaded America, and Belgium would have happened in our country. A hundred years wouldn't have been enough to free us again, if that had happened. You and I, dearest, owe it to those soldiers that we are here together, free, prosperous citizens of an ever greater country.

**She**

(*Drops on her knees by the ditch.*) It's a shrine. Men of my land, I own my debt. I thank you for all I have and am. God bless you in your heaven. (*Silence.*)

**He**

(*Tears in his eyes. His arm around her neck as he bends to her.*) You'll not forget the story of the Charging Blank *th*?

**She**

Never again. In my life. (*Rising.*) I 02think their spirits must be here often. Perhaps they're happy when Americans are here. It's a holy place, as you said. Come away now. I love to leave it in sunshine and flowers with the dear ghosts of the boys. (*Exit He and She.*)

## FIFTH ACT

*The scene it the same trench in the year 2018. It is five o'clock of the same summer afternoon. An officer of the American Army and an English cabinet member come, together, to visit the old trench. The American has a particular reason for his interest; the Englishman accompanies the distinguished American. The two review the story of the trench and speak of other things connected, and it is hoped that they set forth the far-reaching work of the soldiers who died, not realizing their work, in the great fight of the Charging Blank* th.

**Englishman**

It's a peaceful scene.

**American**

(*Advances to the side of the ditch. Looks down. Takes off his cap.*) I came across the ocean to see it. (*He looks over the fields.*) It's quiet.

**Englishman**

The trenches were filled in all over the invaded territory within twenty-five years after the war. Except a very few kept as a manner of monument. Object-lessons, don't you know, in what the thing meant. Even those 02are getting obliterated. They say this is quite the best specimen in all France.

**American**

It doesn't look warlike. What a lot of flowers!

**Englishman**

Yes. The folk about here have a tradition, don't you know, that poppies mark the places where blood flowed most.

**American**

Ah! (*Gazes into the ditch.*) Poppies there. A hundred of our soldiers died at once down there. Mere lads mostly. Their names and ages are on a tablet in the capitol at

Washington, and underneath is a sentence from Lincoln's Gettysburg speech: "These dead shall not have died in vain, and government of the people, by the people, for the people shall not perish from the earth."

**Englishman**

Those are undying words.

**American**

And undying names—the lads' names.

**Englishman**

What they and the other Americans did can never die. Not while the planet endures. No nation at that time realized how vital was your country's entrance into the war. Three months later it would have been too late. Your young, untried forces lifted worn-out France and England and swept us to-victory. It was America's victory at the last. It is our glory to confess that, for from then on America has been our kin.

**American**

(*Smiles.*) England is our well-beloved elder sister for all time now.

**Englishman**

The soldiers who died there (*gestures to the ditch*) and their like did that also. They tied the nations together with a bond of common gratitude, common suffering, common glory.

**American**

You say well that there was common gratitude. England and France had fought our battle for three years at the time we entered the war. We had nestled behind the English fleet. Those grim gray ships of yours stood between us and the barbarians very literally.

**Englishman**

Without doubt Germany would have been happy to invade the only country on earth rich enough to pay her war debt. And you were astonishingly open to invasion. It is one of the historical facts that a student of history of this twenty-first century finds difficult to realize.

**American**

The Great War made revolutionary changes. That condition of unpreparedness was one. That there will never be another war is the belief of all governments. But if all governments should be mistaken, not again would my country, or yours, be caught unprepared. A general staff built of soldiers and free of civilians hampering is one advantage we have drawn from our ordeal of 1917.

**Englishman**

Your army is magnificently efficient.

**American**

And yours. Heaven grant neither may ever be needed! Our military efficiency is the pride of an unmilitary nation. One Congress, since the Great War and its lessons, has vied with another to keep our high place.

**Englishman**

Ah! Your Congress. That has changed since the old days—since La Follette.

**American**

The name is a shame and a warning to us. Our children are taught to remember it so. The "little group of wilful men," the eleven who came near to shipwrecking the country, were 03equally bad, perhaps, but they are forgotten. La Follette stands for them and bears the curses of his countrymen, which they all earned.

**Englishman**

Their ignominy served America; it roused the country to clean its Augean stables.

**American**

The war purified with fire the legislative soul.

**Englishman**

Exactly. Men are human still, certainly, yet genuine patriotism appears to be a *sine qua non* now, where bombast answered in the old day. Corruption is no longer accepted. Public men then were surprisingly simple, surprisingly cheap and limited in their methods. There were two rules for public and private life. It was thought quixotic, I gather from studying the documents of the time, to expect anything different. And how easily the change came!

**American**

The nation rose and demanded honesty, and honesty was there. The enormous majority of decent people woke from a discontented apathy and took charge. Men sprang into place naturally and served the nation. The old log-rolling, brainless, greedy public officials were 03thrown into the junk-heap. As if by magic the stress of the war wrung out the rinsings and the scourings and left the fabric clean.

**Englishman**

The stress of the war affected more than internal politics. You and I, General, are used to a standard of conduct between responsible nations as high as that taken for granted between responsible persons. But, if one considers, that was far from the case a hundred years ago. It was in 1914, that von Bethmann-Hollweg spoke of "a scrap of paper."

**American**

Ah—Germans!

**Englishman**

Certainly one does not expect honor or sincerity from German psychology. Even the little Teutonic Republic of to-day is tricky, scheming always to get a foothold for power, a beginning for the army they will never again be allowed to have. Even after the Kaiser and the Crown Prince and the other rascals were punished they tried to cheat us, if you remember. Yet it is not that which I had in mind. The point I was making was that today it would be out of drawing for a government even of charlatans, 03like the Prussians, to advance the sort of claims which they did. In commonplace words, it was expected then that governments, as against each other, would be self-seeking. To-day decency demands that they should be, as men must be, unselfish.

**America**

(*Musingly*.) It's odd how long it took the world—governments—human beings—to find the truth of the very old phrase that "he who findeth his life must lose it."

**Englishman**

The simple fact of that phrase before the Great War was not commonly grasped. People thought it purely religious and reserved for saints and church services. As a working hypothesis it was not generally known. The every-day ideals of our generation, the friendships and brotherhoods of nations as we know them would have been thought Utopian.

**American**

Utopian? Perhaps our civilization is better than Utopian. The race has grown with a bound since we all went through hell together. How far the civilization of 1914 stood above that of 1614! The difference between galley-slaves and 03able-bodied seamen, of your and our navy! Greater yet than the change in that three hundred years is the change in the last one hundred. I look at it with a soldier's somewhat direct view. Humanity went helpless and alone into a fiery furnace and came through holding on to God's hand. We have clung closely to that powerful grasp since.

**Englishman**

Certainly the race has emerged from an epoch of intellect to an epoch of spirituality—which comprehends and extends intellect. There have never been inventions such as those of our era. And the inventors have been, as it were, men inspired. Something beyond themselves has worked through them for the world. A force like that was known only sporadically before our time.

**American**

(*Looks into old ditch.*) It would be strange to the lads who charged through horror across this flowery field to hear our talk and to know that to them and their deeds we owe the happiness and the greatness of the world we now live in.

**Englishman**

Their short, Homeric episode of 03life admitted few generalizations, I fancy. To be ready and strong and brave—there was scant time for more than that in those strenuous days. Yet under that simple formula lay a sea of patriotism and self-sacrifice, from which sprang their soldiers' force. "Greater love hath no man than this, that a man lay down his life for his friends." It was their love—love of country, of humanity, of freedom—which silenced in the end the great engine of evil—Prussianism. The motive power of life is proved, through those dead soldiers, to be not hate, as the Prussians taught, but love.

**American**

Do you see something shining among the flowers at the bottom of the ditch?

**Englishman**

Why, yes. Is it—a leaf which catches the light?

**American**

(*Stepping down.*) I'll see. (*He picks up a metal identification disk worn by a soldier. Angélique has rubbed it so that the letters may mostly be read.*) This is rather wonderful. (*He reads aloud.*) "R.V.H. Randolph—Blank*th* Regiment—U.S." I can't make out the rest.

**Englishman**

(*Takes the disk.*) Extraordinary! The name and regiment are plain. The identification disk, evidently, of a soldier who died in the trench here. Your own man, General.

**American**

(*Much stirred.*) And—my own regiment. Two years ago I was the colonel of "The Charging Blank*th*."

## HER COUNTRY TOO

David Lance sat wondering. He was not due at the office till ten this Saturday night and he was putting in a long and thorough wonder. About the service in all its branches; about finance; about the new Liberty Loan. First, how was he to stop being a peaceful reporter on the *Daybreak* and get into uniform; that wonder covered a class including the army, navy and air-service, for he had been refused by all three; he wondered how a small limp from apple-tree acrobatics at ten might be so explained away that he might pass; reluctantly he wondered also about the Y.M.C.A. But he was a fighting man *par excellence*. For him it would feel like slacking to go into any but fighting service. Six feet two and weighing a hundred and ninety, every ounce possible to be muscle was muscle; easy, joyful twenty-four-year-old muscle which knew nothing of fatigue. He was certain he would make a fit 04soldier for Uncle Sam, and how, how he wanted to be Uncle Sam's soldier!

He was getting desperate. Every man he knew in the twenties and many a one under and over, was in uniform; bitterly he envied the proud peace in their eyes when he met them. He could not bear to explain things once more as he had explained today to Tom Arnold and "Beef" Johnson, and "Seraph" Olcott, home on leave before sailing for France. He had suffered while they listened courteously and hurried to say that they understood, that it was a shame, and that: "You'll make it yet, old son." And they had then turned to each other comparing notes of camps. It made little impression that he had toiled and sweated early and late in this struggle to get in somewhere—army, navy, air-service—anything to follow the flag. He wasn't allowed. He was still a reporter on the *Daybreak* while the biggest doings of humanity were getting done, and every young son of America had his chance to help. With a strong, tireless body aching for soldier's work, America, his mother, refused him work. He wasn't allowed.

Lance groaned, sitting in his one big chair in his one small room. There were other problems. A Liberty Loan drive was on, and where could he lay hands on money for bonds? He had plunged on the last loan and there was yet something to pay on the $2 subscription. And there was no one and nothing to fall back on except his salary as reporter for the *Daybreak*. His father had died when he was six, and his mother eight years ago; his small capital had gone for his four years, at Yale. There was no one—except a legend of cousins in the South. Never was any one poorer or more alone. Yet he must take a bond or two. How might he hold up his head not to fight and not to buy bonds. A knock at the door.

"Come in," growled Lance.

The door opened, and a picture out of a storybook stood framed and smiling. One seldom sees today in the North the genuine old-fashioned negro-woman. A sample was here in Lance's doorway. A bandanna of red and yellow made a turban for her head; a clean brownish calico dress stood crisply about a solid and waistless figure, 04and a fresh white apron covered it voluminously in front; a folded white handkerchief lay, fichu-wise, around the creases of a fat black neck; a basket covered with a cloth was on her arm. She stood and smiled as if to give the treat time to have its effect on Lance. "Look who's here!" was in large print all over her. And she radiated peace and good-will.

Lance was on his feet with a shout. "Bless your fat heart, Aunt Basha—I'm glad to see you," he flung at her, and seized the basket and slung it half across the room to a sofa with a casualness, alarming to Aunt Basha—christened Bathsheba seventy-five years ago, but "rightly known," she had so instructed Lance, as "Aunt Basha."

"Young marse, don' you ruinate the washin', please sir," she adjured in liquid tones.

"Never you mind. It's the last one you'll do for me," retorted Lance. "Did I tell you you couldn't have the honor of washing for me anymore, Aunt Basha?"

Aunt Basha was wreathed in smiles.

"Yassir, young marse. You tole me dat mo'n tree times befo', a'ready, sir."

"Well—it's final this time. Can't stand your prices. I *can't* stand your exorbitant prices. Now what do you have the heart to charge for dusting off those three old shirts and two and a half collars? Hey?"

Aunt Basha, entirely serene, was enjoying the game. "What does I charges, sir? Fo' dat wash, which you slung 'round acrost de room, sir? Well, sir, young marse, I charges fo' dollars 'n sev'nty fo' cents, sir, dis week. Fo' dat wash."

Lance let loose a howl and flung himself into his chair as if prostrated, long legs out and arms hanging to the floor. Aunt Basha shook with laughter. This was a splendid joke and she never, never tired of it. "You see!" he threw out, between gasps. "Look at that! *Fo'* dollars 'n sev'nty *fo'* cents." He sat up suddenly and pointed a big finger, "Aunt Basha," he whispered, "somebody's been kidding you. Somebody's lied. This palatial apartment, much as it looks like it, is not the home of John D. Rockefeller." He sprung up, drew 04an imaginary mantle about him, grasped one elbow with the other hand, dropped his head into the free palm and was Cassius or Hamlet or Faust—all one to Aunt Basha. His left eyebrow screwed up and his right down, and he glowered. "List to her," he began, and shot out a hand, immediately to replace it where it was most needed, under his elbow. "But list, ye Heavens and protect the lamb from this ravening wolf. She chargeth—oh high Heavens above!— she expecteth me to pay"—he gulped sobs—"the extortioner, the she-wolf—expecteth me to pay her—*fo'* dollars 'n sev'nty *fo'* cents!"

Aunt Basha, entranced with this drama, quaked silently like a large coffee jelly, and with that there happened a high, rich, protracted sound which was laughter, but laughter not to be imitated of any vocal chords of a white race. The delicious note soared higher, higher it seemed than the scale of humanity, and was riotous velvet and cream, with no effort or uncertainty. Lance dropped his Mephistopheles pose and grinned.

"It's Q sharp!" he commented. "However does she do it!"

"Naw, sir, young marse," Aunt Basha began, descending to speech. "De she-wolf, she don' expecteth you to pay no fo' dollars 'n sev'nty fo' cents, sir. Dat's thes what I *charges*. Dat ain' what you *pay*. You thes pay me sev'nty fo' cents sir. Dat's all."

"Oh!" Lance let it out like a ten-year-old. It was hard to say which enjoyed this weekly interview more, the boy or the old woman. The boy was lonely and the humanity unashamed of her race and personality made an atmosphere which delighted him. "Oh!" gasped Lance. "That's a relief. I thought it was goodbye to my Sunday trousers."

Aunt Basha, comfortable and efficient, was unpacking the basket and putting away the wash in the few bureau drawers which easily held the boy's belongings. "Dey's all mended nice," she announced. "Young marse, sir, you better wa' out dese yer ole' undercloses right now, endurin' de warm weather, 'caze dey ain' gwine do you fo' de col'. You 'bleeged to buy some new ones sir, when it comes off right cool."

Lance smiled, for there was no one but this old black woman to take care of him and advise his haphazard housekeeping, and he liked it. "Can't buy new ones," he made answer. "There you go again, mixing me up with Rockefeller. I'm not even the Duke of Westminster, do you see. I haven't got any money. Only sev'nty fo' cents for the she-wolf."

Aunt Basha chuckled. Long ago there had been a household of young people in the South whose clothes she, a very young woman then, had mended; there had been a boy who talked nonsense to her much as this boy—Marse Pendleton. But trouble had come; everything had broken like a card-house under an ocean wave. "De fambly" was lost, and she and her young husband, old Uncle Jeems of today, had drifted by devious ways to this Northern city. "Ef you ain't got de money handy dis week, young marse, you kin pay me nex' week thes as well," suggested the she-wolf.

Then the big boy was standing over her, and she was being patted on the shoulder with a touch that all but brought tears to the black, dim eyes. "Don't you dare pay attention to my drool, or I'll never talk to you again," Lance ordered. "Your sev'nty fo' cents is all right, and lots more. I've got heaps of cash that size, Aunt Basha. But I want to buy Liberty Bonds, and I don't know how in hell I'm going to get big money." The boy was thinking aloud. "How am I to raise two hundred for a couple of bonds, Aunt Basha? Tell me that?" He scratched into his thatch of hair and made a puzzled face.

"What fo' you want big money, young marse?"

"Bonds. Liberty Bonds. You know what that is?"

"Naw, sir."

"You don't? Well you ought to," said Lance. "There isn't a soul in this country who oughtn't to have a bond. It's this way. You know we're fighting a war?"

"Yassir. Young Ananias Johnson, he's Sist' Amanda's boy, he done tole his Unk Jeems 'bout dat war. And Jeems, he done tole me."

Lance regarded her. Was it possible that the ocean upheaval had stirred even the quietest backwater so little? "Well, anyhow, it's the biggest war that ever was on earth."

Aunt Basha shook her head. "You ain't never seed de War of de Rebullium," she stated with superiority. "You's too young. Well, I reckon dis yer war ain't much on to dat war. Naw, sir! Dat ar was a sure 'nough war—yas, sir!"

Lance considered. He decided not to contest the point. "Anyhow Aunt Basha, this is an awfully big war. And if we don't win it the Germans will come over here and murder the most of us, and make you and Uncle Jeems work in the fields from daylight till dark."

"Dem low down white trash!" commented Aunt Basha.

"Yes, and worse. And Uncle Sam can't beat the Germans unless we all help. He needs money to buy guns for the soldiers, and food and clothes. So he's asking everybody—just everybody—to lend him money—every cent they can raise to buy things to win the war. He gives each person who lends him any, a piece of paper which is a promise to pay it back, and that piece of paper is called a bond—Uncle Sam's promise to pay. Everybody ought to help by giving up every cent they have. The soldiers are giving their lives to save us from the horrible Germans. They're going over there to live in mud and water and sleep in holes of the earth, to be shot and wounded and tortured and killed. They're facing that for our sakes, to save us from worse than death, for you and Uncle Jeems and me, Aunt Basha. Now, oughtn't we to give all we've got to take care of those boys—our soldiers?"

Lance had forgotten his audience, except that he was wording his speech carefully in the simplest English. It went home.

"Oh, my Lawd!" moaned Aunt Basha, sitting down and rocking hard. "Does dey sleep in de col' yeth? Oh, my Lawd have mercy!" It was the first realization she had had of the details of the war. "You ain't gwine over dar, is you young marse, honey?" she asked anxiously.

"I wish to God I was," spoke Lance through set teeth. "No, Aunt Basha, they won't take me. Because I'm lame. I'd give my life to go. And because I can't fight I *must* buy bonds. Do you see? I must. I'd sell my soul to get money for Liberty Bonds. Oh, God!" Lance was as if alone, with only that anxious old black face gazing up at him. "Oh, God—it's my country!"

Suddenly the rich flowing voice spoke. "Young marse, it's my country too, sir," said Aunt Basha.

Lance turned and stared. How much did the words mean to the old woman? In a moment he knew.

"Yas, my young marseter, dis yer America's de ole black 'oman's country, thes like it's fine young white man's, like you, sir. I gwine give my las' cent, like you say. Yas, I gwine do dat. I got two hun'erd dollars, sir; I b'en a-savin' and a-savin' for Jeems 'n me 'ginst when we git ole, but I gwine give dat to my country. I want Unc' Sam to buy good food for dem boys in the muddy water. Bacon 'n hominy, sir—'n corn bread, what's nourishin'. 'N I want you to git de—de Liberty what-je-call-'ems. Yassir. 'Caze you ain't got no ma to he'ep you out, 'n de ole black 'oman's gwine to be de bes' ma she know how to her young marse. I got de money tied up—" she leaned forward and whispered—"in a stockin' in de bottom draw' ob de chist unner Jeem's good coat. Tomorrow I gwine fetch it, 'n you go buy yo' what-je-calls-'ems."

Lance went across and knelt on the floor beside her and put his arms around the stout figure. He had been brought up with a colored mammy and this affection seemed natural and homelike. "Aunt Basha, you're one of the saints," he said. "And I love you for it. But I wouldn't take your blessed two hundred, not for anything on earth. I'd be a hound to take it. If you want some bonds"—it flashed to him that the money would be safer so than in the stocking under Jeem's coat—"why, I'll get them for you. Come into the *Daybreak* office and ask for me, say—Monday. And I'll go with you to the bank and get bonds. Here's my card. Show anybody that at the office." And he gave directions.

Five minutes later the old woman went off down the street talking half aloud to herself in fragments of sentences about "Liberty what-je-call-'ems" and "my country too." In the little shack uptown that was home for her and her husband she began at once to set forth her new light. Jeems, who added to the family income by taking care of furnaces and doing odd jobs, was grizzled and hobbling of body, but argumentative of soul.

"'Oman," he addressed Aunt Basha, "Unc' Sam got lots o' money. What use he gwine have, great big rich man lak Unc' Sam, fo' yo' two hun'erd? But we got mighty lot o' use fo' dat money, we'uns. An' you gwine gib dat away? Thes lak a 'oman!" which, in other forms, is an argument used by male people of many classes.

Aunt Basha suggested that Young Marse David said something about a piece of paper and Uncle Sam paying back, but Jeems pooh-poohed that.

"Naw, sir. When big rich folks goes round collectin' po' folkses money, is dey liable to pay back? What good piece o' paper gwine do you? Is dey aimin' to let you see de color ob dat money again? Naw, sir. Dey am not." He proceeded 05to another branch of the subject. "War ain' gwine las' long, nohow. Young Ananias he gwine to Franch right soon, an' de yether colored brothers. De Germans dey ain't gwine las' long, once ef dey see us Anglo-Saxons in de scrablin'. Naw, sir.

"White man what come hyer yether day, he say how dey ain't gwine 'low de colored sojers to fight," suggested Aunt Basha. German propaganda reaches far and takes strange shapes.

"Don' jer go to b'lieve dat white man, 'oman," thundered Jeems, thumping with his fist. "He dunno nawthin', an' I reckon he's a liar. Unc' Sam he say we kin fight an' we *gwine* fight. An' de war ain't las' long atter we git to fightin' good."

Aunt Basha, her hands folded on the rounded volume of apron considered deeply. After a time she arrived at a decision.

"Jeems," she began, "yo' cert'nly is a strong reasoner. Yassir. But I got it bo'ne in upon me powerful dat I gotter give dese yer savin's to Unc' Sam. It's my country too, Jeems, same as dem sojers what's fightin', dem boys in de mud what 05ain' got a soul to wash fo' 'em. An' lak as not dey mas not dere. Dem boys is fightin', and gittin' wet and hunted up lak young marse say, fo' Aunt Basha and—bress dere hearts"—Aunt Basha broke down, and the upshot was that Jeems washed his hands of an obstinate female and—the savings not being his in any case—gave unwilling consent.

Youth of the sterner set is apt to be casual in making appointments. It had not entered Lance's head to arrange in case he was not at the office. As for Aunt Basha, her theory was that he reigned there over an army of subordinates from morning till evening. So that she was taken aback when told that Mr. Lance was out and no one could say when he would be in. She had risen at dawn and done her housework and much of the fine washing which she "took in," and had then arrayed herself in her best calico dress and newest turban and apron for the great occasion and had reported at the *Daybreak* office at nine-thirty. And young marse wasn't there.

"I'll set and rest ontwell he comes in," she announced, 05and retired to a chair against the wall.

There she folded her hands statelily and sat erect, motionless, an image of fine old dignity. But much thinking was going on inside the calm exterior. What was she going to do if young marse did not come back? She had the $2 with her, carefully pinned and double pinned into a pocket in her purple alpaca petticoat. She did not want to take it home. Jeems had submitted this morning, but with mutterings, and a second time there might be trouble. The savings were indeed hers, but a rebellious husband in high finance is an embarrassment. Deeply Aunt Basha considered, and memory whispered something about a bank. Young marse was going to the bank with her to give her money to Uncle Sam. She had just passed a bank. Why could she not go alone? Somebody certainly would tell her what to do. Possibly Uncle Sam was there himself—for Aunt Basha's conception of our national myth was half mystical, half practical—as a child with Santa Claus. In any case banks were responsible places, and somebody would look after her. She 05crossed to the desk where two or three young men appeared to be doing most of the world's business.

"Marsters!"

The three looked up.

"Good mawnin', young marsters. I'm 'bleeged to go now. I cert'nly thank you-all fo' lettin' me set in de cheer. I won't wait fo' marse David Lance no mo', sir. Good mawnin', marsters."

A smiling courtesy dropped, and she was gone.

"I'll be darned!" remarked reporter number one.

"Where did that blow in from?" added reporter number two.

But reporter number three had imagination. "The dearest old soul I've seen in a blue moon," said he.

Aunt Basha proceeded down the street and more than one in the crowd glanced twice at the erect, stout figure swinging, like a quaint and stately ship in full sail, among the steam-tuggery of up-to-date humanity. There were high steps leading to the bank entrance, impressive and alarming to Aunt Basha. She paused to take breath for this adventure. Was a humble old colored woman permitted to walk freely in at those grand doors, open iron-work and enormous of size? She did not know. She stood a moment, suddenly frightened and helpless, not daring to go on, looking about for a friendly face. And behold! there it was—the friendliest face in the world, it seemed to the lost old soul—a vision of loveliness. It was the face of a beautiful young white lady in beautiful clothes who had stepped from a huge limousine. She was coming up the steps, straight to Aunt Basha. She saw the old woman, saw her anxious hesitation, and halted. The next event was a heavenly smile. Aunt Basha knew the repartee to that, and the smile that shone in answer was as heavenly in its way as the girl's.

"Is there anything I can do for you?" spoke a voice of gentleness.

And the world had turned over and come up right side on top. "Mawnin', Miss. Yas'm, I was fixin' to go in dat big do' yander, but I dunno as I'm 'lowed. Is I 'lowed, young miss, to go in dar an' gib my two hun'erd to Unc' Sam?"

"What?" The tone was kindness itself, but bewildered.

Aunt Basha elucidated. "I got two hun'erd, young miss, and I cert'nly want to gib it to Unc' Sam to buy clo'se for dem boys what's fightin' for us in Franch."

"I wonder," spoke the girl, gazing thoughtfully, "if you want to get a Liberty Bond?"

"Yas'm—yas, miss. Dat's sho' it, a whatjer-ma-call-'em. I know'd 'twas some cu'is name lak dat." The vision nodded her head.

"I'm going in to do that very thing myself," she said. "Come with me. I'll help you get yours."

Aunt Basha followed joyfully in the wake, and behold, everything was easy. Ready attention met them and shortly they sat in a private office carpeted in velvet and upholstered in grandeur. A personage gave grave attention to what the vision was saying.

"I met—I don't know your name," she interrupted herself, turning to the old negro woman.

Aunt Basha rose and curtsied. "Dey christened me Bathsheba Jeptha, young miss," she stated. "But I'se rightly known as Aunt Basha. Jes' Aunt Basha, young miss. And marster."

A surname was disinterred by the efforts of the personage which appeared to startle the vision.

"Why, it's our name, Mr. Davidson," she exclaimed. "She said Cabell."

Aunt Basha turned inquiring, vague eyes. "Is it, honey? Is yo' a Cabell?"

And then the personage, who was, after all, cashier of the Ninth National Bank and very busy, cut in. "Ah, yes! A well known Southern name. Doubtless a large connection. And now Mrs.—ah—Cabell—"

"I'd be 'bleeged ef yo' jis' name me Aunt Basha, marster."

And marster, rather *intrigué* because he, being a New Englander, had never in his life addressed as "aunt" a person who was not sister to his mother or his father, nevertheless became human and smiled. "Well, then, Aunt Basha."

At a point a bit later he was again jolted when he asked the amount which his newly adopted "aunt" wanted to invest. For an answer she hauled high the folds of her frock, unconscious of his gasp or of the vision's repressed laughter, and went on to attack the clean purple alpaca petticoat which was next in rank, Mr. Davidson thought it wise at this point to make an errand across the room. He need not have bothered as far as Aunt Basha was concerned. When he came back she was again *à la mode* and held an ancient beaded purse at which she gazed. Out of a less remote pocket she drew steel spectacles, which were put on. Mr. Davidson repeated his question of how much.

"It's all hyer, marster. It's two hun'erd dollars, sir. I ben savin' up fo' twenty years an' mo', and me'n Jeems, we ben countin' it every mont, so I reckon I knows."

The man and the girl regarded the old woman a moment. "It's a large sum for you to invest," Mr. Davidson said.

"Yassir. Yas, marster. It's right smart money. But I sho' am glad to gib dis hyer to Unc' Sam for dem boys."

The cashier of the Ninth National Bank lifted his eyes from the blank he was filling out and looked at Aunt Basha thoughtfully. "You understand, of course, that the Government—Uncle Sam—is only borrowing your money. That you may have it back any time you wish."

Aunt Basha drew herself up. "I don' wish it, sir. I'm gibin' dis hyer gif,' a free gif' to my country. Yassir. It's de onliest country I got, an' I reckon I got a right to gib dis hyer what I earned doin' fine washin' and i'nin. I gibs it to my country. I don't wan' to hyer any talk 'bout payin' back. Naw, sir."

It took Mr. Davidson and the vision at least ten minutes to make clear to Aunt Basha the character and habits of a Liberty Bond, and then, though gratified with the ownership of what seemed a brand new $2 and a valuable slip of paper—which meandered, shamelessly into the purple alpaca petticoat—yet she was disappointed.

"White folks sho' am cu'is," she reflected, "Now who'd 'a thought 'bout dat way ob raisin' money! Not me—no, Lawd! It do beat me." With that she threw an earnest glance at Mr. Davidson, lean and tall and gray, with a clipped pointed beard. "'Scuse me, marster," said Aunt Basha, "mout I ask a quexshun?"

"Surely," agreed Mr. Davidson blandly.

"Is you'—'scuse de ole 'oman, sir—is you' Unc' Sam?"

The "quexshun" left the personage too staggered to laugh. But the girl filled the staid place with gay peals. Then she leaned over and patted the wrinkled and bony worn black knuckles. "Bless your dear heart," she said; "no, he isn't, Aunt Basha. He's awfully important and good to us all, and he knows everything. But he's not Uncle Sam."

The bewilderment of the old face melted to smiles. "Dar, now," she brought out; "I mout 'a know'd, becaze he didn't have no red striped pants. An' de whiskers is diff'ent, too. 'Scuse me, sir, and thank you kindly, marster. Thank you, young miss. De Lawd bress you fo' helpin' de ole 'oman." She had risen and she dropped her old time curtsey at this point. "Mawnin' to yo', marster and young miss."

But the girl sprang up. "You can't go," she said. "I'm going to take you to my house to see my grandmother. She's Southern, and our name is Cabell, and likely—maybe—she knew your people down South."

"Maybe, young miss. Dar's lots o' Cabells," agreed Aunt Basha, and in three minutes found herself where she had never thought to be, inside a fine private car.

She was dumb with rapture and excitement, and quite unable to answer the girl's friendly words except with smiles and nods. The girl saw how it was and let her be, only patting the calico arm once and again reassuringly. "I wonder if she didn't want to come. I wonder if I've frightened her," thought Eleanor Cabell. When into the silence broke suddenly the rich, high, irresistible music which was Aunt Basha's laugh, and which David Lance had said was pitched on "Q sharp." The girl joined the infectious sound and a moment after that the car stopped.

"This is home," said Eleanor.

Aunt Basha observed, with the liking for magnificence of a servant trained in a large house, the fine façade and the huge size of "home." In a moment she was inside, and "young miss" was carefully escorting her into a sunshiny big room, where a wood fire burned, and a bird sang, and there were books and flowers.

"Wait here, Aunt Basha, dear," Eleanor said, "and I'll get Grandmother." It was exactly like the loveliest of dreams, Aunt Basha told Jeems an hour later. It could not possibly have been true, except that it was. When "Grandmother" came in, slender and white-haired and a bit breathless with this last surprise of a surprising granddaughter, Aunt Basha stood and curtsied her stateliest.

Then suddenly she cried out, "Fo' God! Oh, my Miss Jinny!" and fell on her knees.

Mrs. Cabell gazed down, startled. "Who is it? Oh, whom have you brought me, Eleanor?" She bent to look more closely at Aunt Basha, kneeling, speechless, tears streaming from the brave old eyes, holding up clasped hand imploring. "It isn't—Oh, my dear, I believe it *is* our own old nurse, Basha, who took care of your father!"

"Yas'm. Yas, Miss Jinny," endorsed Aunt Basha, climbing to her feet. "Yas, my Miss Jinny, bress de Lawd. It's Basha." She turned to the girl. "Dis yer chile ain't nebber my young Marse Pendleton's chile!"

But it was; and there was explanation and laughter and tears, too, but tears of happiness. Then it was told how, after that crash of disaster was over; the family had tried in vain to find Basha and Jeems; had tried always. It was told how a great fortune had come to them in the turn of a hand by the discovery of an unsuspected salt mine on the old estate; how "young Marse Pendleton," a famous surgeon now, had by that time made for himself a career and a home in this Northern state; how his wife had died young, and his mother, "Miss Jinny," had come to live with him and take care of his one child, the vision. And then the simple annals of Aunt Basha and Uncle Jeems were also told, the long struggle to keep respectable, only respectable; the years of toil and frugality and saving—saving the two hundred dollars which she had offered this morning as a "free gif" to her country. In these annals loomed large for some time past the figure of a "young marse" who had been good to her and helped her much and often in spite of his own "*res augusta domi*,"—which was not Aunt Basha's expression. The story was told of his oration in the little hall bedroom about Liberty "whatjer-m'-call-'ems," and of how the boy had stirred the soul of the old woman with his picture of the soldiers in the trenches.

"So it come to me, Miss Jinny, how ez me'n Jeems was thes two wuthless ole niggers, an' hadn't fur to trabble on de road anyways, an' de Lawd would pervide, an' ef He didn't we could scratch grabble some ways. An' dat boy, dat young Marse David, he tole me everbody ought to gib dey las' cent fo' Unc' Sam an' de sojers. So"—Aunt Basha's high, inexpressibly sweet laughter of pure glee filled the room—"so I thes up'n handed over my two hun'erd."

"It was the most beautiful and wonderful thing that's been done in all wonderful America," pronounced Eleanor Cabell as one having authority. She went on. "But that young man, your young Marse David, why doesn't he fight if he's such a patriot?"

"Bress gracious, honey," Aunt Basha hurried to explain, "he's a-honin' to fight. But he cayn't. He's lame. He goes a-limpin'. Dey won't took him."

"Oh!" retracted Eleanor. Then: "What's his name? Maybe father could cure him."

"He name Lance. Marse David Lance."

Why should Miss Jinny jump? "David Lance? It can't be, Aunt Basha."

With no words Aunt Basha began hauling up her skirts and Eleanor, remembering Mr. Davidson's face, went into gales of laughter. Aunt Basha baited, looked at her with an inquiring gaze of adoration. "Yas'm, my young miss. He name dat. I done put the cyard in my ridicule. Yas'm, it's here." The antique bead purse was opened and Lance's card was presented to Miss Jinny.

"Eleanor! This is too wonderful—look!"

Eleanor looked, and read: "Mr. David Pendleton Lance." "Why, Grandmother, it's Dad's name—David Pendleton Cabell. And the Lance—"

Mrs. Cabell, stronger on genealogy than the younger generation, took up the wandering thread. "The 'Lance' is my mother's maiden name—Virginia Lance she was. And her brother was David Pendleton Lance. I named your father for him because he was born on the day my young uncle was killed, in the battle of Shiloh."

"Well, then—who's this sailing around with our family name?"

"Who is he? But he must be our close kin, Eleanor. My Uncle David left—that's it. His wife came from California and she went out there again to live with her baby. I hadn't heard of them for years. Why, Eleanor, this boy's father must have been—my first cousin. My young Uncle David's baby. Those years of trouble after we left home wiped out so much. I lost track—but that doesn't matter now. Aunt Basha," spoke 06Miss Jinny in a quick, efficient voice, which suddenly recalled the blooming and businesslike mother of the young brood of years ago, "Aunt Basha, where can I find your young Marse David?"

Aunt Basha smiled radiantly and shook her head. "Cayn't fin' him, honey? I done tried, and he warn't dar."

"Wasn't where?"

"At de orfice, Miss Jinny."

"At what office?"

"Why, de *Daybreak* orfice, cose, Miss Jinny. What yether orfice he gwine be at?"

"Oh!" Miss Jinny followed with ease the windings of the African mind. "He's a reporter on the *Daybreak* then."

"'Cose he is, Miss Jinny, ma'am. Whatjer reckon?"

Miss Jinny reflected. Then: "Eleanor, call up the *Daybreak* office and ask if Mr. Lance is there and if he will speak to me."

But Aunt Basha was right. Mr. Lance was not 07at the *Daybreak* office. Mrs. Cabell was as grieved as a child.

"We'll find him, Grandmother," Eleanor asserted. "Why, of course—it's a morning paper. He's home sleeping. I'll get his number." She caught up the telephone book.

Aunt Basha chuckled musically. "He ain't got no tullaphome, honey chile. No, my Lawd! Whar dat boy gwine git money for tullaphome and contraptions? No, my Lawd!"

"How will we get him?" despaired Mrs. Cabell. The end of the council was a cryptic note in the hand of Jackson, the chauffeur, and orders to bring back the addressee at any cost.

Meanwhile, as Jackson stood in his smart dark livery taking orders with the calmness of efficiency, feeling himself capable of getting that young man, howsoever hidden, the young man himself was wasting valuable hours off in day-dreams. In the one shabby big chair of the hall bedroom he sat and smoked a pipe, and stared at a microscopic fire in a toy grate. It was extravagant of David Lance to have a fire at all, but as long as he gave up meals to do it likely it was his own affair. The luxuries mean more than the necessities to plenty of us. With comfort in this, his small luxury, he watched the play of light and shadow, and the pulsing of the live scarlet and orange in the heart of the coals. He needed comfort today, the lonely boy. Two men of the office force who had gotten their commissions lately at an officer's training-camp had come in last night before leaving for Camp Devens; everybody had crowded about and praised them and envied them. They had been joked about the sweaters, and socks made by mothers and sweethearts, and about the trouble Uncle Sam would have with their mass of mail. The men in the office had joined to give each a goodbye present. Pride in them, the honor of them to all the force was shown at every turn; and beyond it all there was the look of grave contentment in their eyes which is the mark of the men who have counted the cost and given up everything for their country. Most of all soldiers, perhaps, in this great war, the American fights for an ideal. Also he knows it; down to the most ignorant drafted man, that inspiration has lifted the army and given it a star in the East to follow. The American fights for an ideal; the sign of it is in the faces of the men in uniform whom one meets everywhere in the street.

David Lance, splendidly powerful and fit except for the small limp which was his undoing, suffered as he joined, whole-hearted, in the glory of those who were going. Back in his room alone, smoking, staring into his dying fire, he was dreaming how it would feel if he were the one who was to march off in uniform to take his man's share of the hardship and comradeship and adventure and suffering, and of the salvation of the world. With that, he took his pipe from his mouth and grinned broadly into the fire as another phase of the question appeared. How would it feel if he was somebody's special soldier, like both of those boys, sent off by a mother or a sweetheart, by both possibly, overstocked with things knitted for him, with all the necessities and luxuries of a soldier's outfit that could be thought of. He remembered how Jarvis, the artillery captain, had showed them, proud and modest, his field glass.

"It's a good one," he had said. "My mother gave it to me. It has the Mills scale."

And Annesley, the kid, who had made his lieutenant's commission so unexpectedly, had broken in: "That's no shakes to the socks I've got on. If somebody'll pull off my boots I'll show you. Made in Poughkeepsie. A dozen pairs. *Not* my mother."

Lance smiled wistfully. Since his own mother died, eight years ago, he had drifted about unanchored, and though women had inevitably held out hands to the tall and beautiful lad, they were not the sort he cared for, and there had been none of his own sort in his life. Fate might so easily have given him a chance to serve his country, with also, maybe, just the common sweet things added which utmost every fellow had, and a woman or two to give him a sendoff and to write him letters over there sometimes. To be a soldier—and to be somebody's soldier! Why, these two things would mean Heaven! And hundreds of thousands of American boys had these and thought nothing of it. Fate certainly had been a bit stingy with a chap, considered David Lance, smiling into his little fire with a touch of wistful self-pity.

At this moment Fate, in smart, dark livery, knocked at his door. "Come in," shouted Lance cheerfully.

The door opened and he stared. Somebody had lost the way. Chauffeurs in expensive livery did not come to his hall bedroom. "Is dis yer Mr. Lance?" inquired Jackson.

Lance admitted it and got the note and read it while Jackson, knowing his Family intimately, knew that something pleasant and surprising was afoot and assisted with a discreet regard. When he saw that the note was finished, Jackson confidently put in his word. "Cyar's waitin', sir. Orders is I was to tote you to de house."

Lance's eyes glowered as he looked up. "Tell me one thing," he demanded.

"Yes, sir," grinned Jackson, pleased with this young gentleman from a very poor neighborhood, who quite evidently was, all the same, "quality."

"Are you," inquired Lance, "are you any relation to Aunt Basha?"

Jackson, for all his efficiency a friendly soul, forgot the dignity of his livery and broke into chuckles. "Naw, sir; naw, sir. I dunno de lady, sir; I reckon I ain't, sir," answered Jackson.

"All right, then, but it's the mistake of your life not to be. She's the best on earth. Wait till I brush my hair," said Lance, and did it.

Inside three minutes he was in the big Pierce-Arrow, almost as unfamiliar, almost as delightful to him as to Aunt Basha, and speeding gloriously through the streets. The note had said that some kinspeople had just discovered him, and would he come straight to them for lunch.

Mrs. Cabell and Eleanor crowded frankly to the window when the car stopped.

"I can't wait to see David's boy," cried Mrs. Cabell, and Eleanor, wise of her generation, followed with:

"Now, don't expect much; he may be deadly."

And out of the limousine stepped, unconscious, the beautiful David, and handed Jackson a dollar.

"Oh!" gasped Mrs. Cabell.

"It was silly, but I love it," added Eleanor; and David limped swiftly up the steps, and one heard Ebenezer, the butler, opening the door with suspicious promptness. Everyone in the house knew, mysteriously, that uncommon things were doing.

"Pendleton," spoke Mrs. Cabell, lying in wait for her son, the great doctor, as he came from his office at lunch time, "Pen, dear, let me tell you something extraordinary." She told, him, condensing as might be, and ended with; "And oh, Pen, he's the most adorable boy I ever saw. And so lonely and so poor and so plucky. Heartbroken because he's lame and can't serve. You'll cure him. Pen, dear, won't you, for his country?"

The tall, tired man bent down and kissed his mother. "Mummy, I'm not God Almighty. But I'll do my damdest for anything you want. Show me the paragon."

The paragon shot up, with the small unevenness which was his limp, and faced the big doctor on a level. The two pairs of eyes from their uncommon height, looked inquiringly into each other.

"I hear you have my name," spoke Dr. Cabell tersely.

"Yes, sir," said David, "And I'm glad." And the doctor knew that he also liked the paragon.

Lunch was an epic meal above and below stairs. Jeems had been fetched by that black Mercury Jackson, messenger today of the gods of joy. And the two old souls had been told by Mrs. Cabell that never again should they work hard or be anxious or want for anything. The sensation-loving colored servants rejoiced in the events as a personal jubilee, and made much of Aunt Basha and Unc' Jeems till their old heads reeled. Above stairs the scroll unrolled more or loss decorously, yet in magic colors unbelievable. Somehow David had told about Annesley and Jarvis last night.

"Somebody knitted him a whole dozen pairs of socks!" he commented, "Really she did. He said 07so. Think of a girl being as good to a chap as that."

"I'll knit you a dozen," Miss Eleanor Cabell capped his sentence, like the Amen at the end of a High Church prayer. "I'll begin this afternoon."

"And, David," said Mrs. Cabell—for it had got to be "David" and "Cousin Virginia" by now—"David, when you get your commission, I'll have your field glass ready, and a few other things."

Dr. Cabell lifted his eyes from his chop. "You'll spoil that boy," he stated. "And, mother, I pointed out that I'm not the Almighty, even on joints, I haven't looked at that game leg yet. I said it *might* be curable."

"That boy" looked up, smiling, with long years of loneliness and lameness written in the back of his glance. "Please don't make 'em stop, doctor," he begged. "I won't spoil easily. I haven't any start. And this is a fairy-story to me—wonderful people like you letting me—letting me belong. I can't believe I won't wake up. Don't 07you imagine it will go to my head. It won't. I'm just so blamed—grateful."

The deep young voice trailed, and the doctor made haste to answer. "You're all right, my lad," he said, "As soon as lunch is over you come into the surgery and I'll have a glance at the leg." Which was done.

After half an hour David came out, limping, pale and radiant. "I can't believe it," he spoke breathless. "He says—it's a simple—operation. I'll walk—like other men. I'll be right for—the service." He choked.

At that Mrs. Cabell sped across the room and put up hands either side of the young face and drew it down and kissed the lad whom she did not, this morning, know to be in existence. "You blessed boy," she whispered, "you shall fight for America, and you'll be our soldier, and we'll be your people." And David, kissing her again, looked over her head and saw Eleanor glowing like a rose, and with a swift, unphrased shock of happiness felt in his soul the wonder of a heaven that might happen. Then they were all about the fire, 08half-crying, laughing, as people do on top of strong feelings.

"Aunt Basha did it all," said David. "If Aunt Basha hadn't been the most magnificent old black woman who ever carried a snow-white soul, if she hadn't been the truest patriot in all America, if she hadn't given everything for her country—I'd likely never have—found you." His eyes went to the two kind and smiling faces, and his last word was a whisper. It was so much to have found. All he had dreamed, people of his own, a straight leg—and—his heart's desire—service to America.

Mrs. Cabell spoke softly, "I've lived a long time and I've seen over and over that a good deed spreads happiness like a pebble thrown into water, more than a bad one spreads evil, for good is stronger and more contagious. We've gained this dear kinsman today because of the nobility of an old negro woman."

David Lance lifted his head quickly. "It was no small nobility," he said. "As Miss Cabell was saying—"

"I'm your cousin Eleanor," interrupted Miss Cabell.

David lingered over the name. "Thank you, my cousin Eleanor. It's as you said, nothing more beautiful and wonderful has been done in wonderful America than this thing Aunt Basha did. It was as gallant as a soldier at the front, for she offered what meant possibly her life."

"Her little two hundred," Eleanor spoke gently. "And so cross at the idea of being paid back! She wanted to *give* it."

David's face gleamed with a thought as he stared into the firelight, "You see," he worked out his idea, "by the standards of the angels a gift must be big not according to its size but according to what's left. If you have millions and give a few thousand you practically give nothing, for you have millions left. But Aunt Basha had nothing left. The angels must have beaten drums and blown trumpets and raised Cain all over Paradise while you sat in the bank, my cousin Eleanor, for the glory of that record gift. 08No plutocrat in the land has touched what Aunt Basha did for her country."

Eleanor's eyes, sending out not only clear vision but a brown light as of the light of stars, shone on the boy. She bent forward, and her slender arms were about her knee. She gazed at David, marveling. How could it be that a human being might have all that David appeared to her to have—clear brain, crystal simplicity, manliness, charm of personality, and such strength and beauty besides!

"Yes," she said, "Aunt Basha gave the most. She has more right than any of us to say that it's her country." She was silent a moment and then spoke softly a single word. "America!" said Eleanor reverently.

America! Her sound has gone out into all lands and her words into the end of the world. America, who in a year took four million of sons untried, untrained, and made them into a mighty army; who adjusted a nation of a hundred million souls in a turn of the hand to unknown and unheard of conditions. America, whose greatest 08glory yet is not these things. America, of whom scholars and statesmen and generals and multi-millionaires say with throbbing pride today: "This is my country," but of whom the least in the land, having brought what they may, however small, to lay on that flaming altar of the world's safety—of whom the least in the land may say as truly as the greatest, "This is my country, too."

---

## THE SWALLOW

The Château Frontenac at Quebec is a turreted pile of masonry wandering down a cliff over the very cellars of the ancient Castle of St. Louis. A twentieth-century hotel, it simulates well a mediæval fortress and lifts against the cold blue northern sky an atmosphere of history. Old voices whisper about its towers and above the clanging hoofs in its paved court; deathless names are in the wind which blows from the "fleuve," the great St. Lawrence River far below. Jacques Cartier's voice was heard hereabouts away back in 1539, and after him others, Champlain and Frontenac, and Father Jogues and Mother Marie of the Conception and Montcalm—upstanding fighting men and heroic women and hardy discoverers of New France walked about here once, on the "Rock" of Quebec; there is romance here if anywhere on earth. Today a new knighthood hails that past. Uniforms are thick in steep streets; men are wearing them with empty sleeves, on crutches, or maybe whole of body yet with racked faces which register a hell lived through. Canada guards heroism of many vintages, from four hundred years back through the years to Wolfe's time, and now a new harvest. Centuries from now children will be told, with the story of Cartier, the tale of Vimy Ridge, and while the Rock stands the records of Frenchmen in Canada, of Canadians in France will not die.

Always when I go to the Château I get a table, if I can, in the smaller dining-room. There the illusion of antiquity holds through modern luxury; there they have hung about the walls portraits of the worthies of old Quebec; there Samuel Champlain himself, made into bronze and heroic of size, aloft on his pedestal on the terrace outside, lifts his plumed hat and stares in at the narrow windows, turning his back on river and lower city. One disregards waiters in evening clothes and up-to-date table appointments, and one looks at Champlain and the "fleuve," and the Isle d'Orléans lying long and low, and one thinks of little ships, storm-beaten, creeping up to this grim bigness ignorant of continental events trailing in their wake.

I was on my way to camp in a club a hundred miles north of the gray-walled town when I drifted into the little dining-room for dinner one night in early September in 1918. The head-waiter was an old friend; he came to meet me and piloted me past a tableful of military color, four men in service uniforms.

"Some high officers, sir," spoke the head waiter. "In conference here, I believe. There's a French officer, and an English, and our Canadian General Sampson, and one of your generals, sir."

I gave my order and sat back to study the group. The waiter had it straight; there was the horizon blue of France; there was the Englishman tall and lean and ruddy and expressionless and handsome; there was the Canadian, more of our own cut, with a mobile, alert face. The American had his back to me and all I could see was an erect carriage, a brown head going to gray, and the one star of a brigadier-general on his shoulders. The beginnings of my dinner went fast, but after soup there was a lull before greater food, and I paid attention again to my neighbors. They were talking in English.

"A Huron of Lorette—does that mean a full-blooded Indian of the Huron tribe, such as one reads of in Parkman?" It was the Englishman who asked, responding to something I had not heard.

"There's no such animal as a full-blooded Huron," stated the Canadian. "They're all French-Indian half-breeds now. Lorette's an interesting scrap of history, just the same. You know your Parkman? You remember how the Iroquois followed the defeated Hurons as far as the Isle d'Orléans, out there?" He nodded toward where the big island lay in the darkness of the St. Lawrence. "Well, what was left after that chase took refuge fifteen miles north of Quebec, and founded what became and has stayed the village of Indian Lorette. There are now about five or six hundred people, and it's a nation. Under its own laws, dealing by treaty with Canada, not subject to draft, for instance. Queer, isn't it? They guard their identity vigilantly. Every one, man or woman, who marries into the tribe, as they religiously call it, is from then on a Huron.

96

And only those who have Huron blood may own land in Lorette. The Hurons were, as Parkman put it, 'the gentlemen of the savages,' and the tradition lasts. The half-breed of today is a good sort, self-respecting and brave, not progressive, but intelligent, with pride in his inheritance, his courage, and his woodscraft."

The Canadian, facing me, spoke distinctly and much as Americans speak; I caught every word. But I missed what the French general threw back rapidly. I wondered why the Frenchman should be excited. I myself was interested because my guides, due to meet me at the club station tomorrow, were all half-breed Hurons. But why the French officer? What should a Frenchman of France know about backwaters of Canadian history? And with that he suddenly spoke slowly, and I caught several sentences of incisive if halting English.

"Zey are to astonish, ze Indian Hurong. For ze sort of work special-ment, as like scouting on a stomach. Qu-vick, ver' qu-vick, and ver' quiet. By dark places of danger. One sees zat nozzing at all af-frightens zose Hurong. Also zey are alike snakes, one cannot catch zem—zey slide; zey are slippy. To me it is to admire zat courage most—personnel—selfeesh—because an Hurong safe my life dere is six mont', when ze Boches make ze drive of ze mont' of March."

At this moment food arrived in a flurry, and I lost what came after. But I had forgotten the Château Frontenac; I had forgotten the group of officers, serious and responsible, who sat on at the next table. I had forgotten even the war. A word had sent my mind roaming. "Huron!" Memory and hope at that repeated word rose and flew away with me. Hope first. Tomorrow I was due to drop civilization and its tethers.

"Allah does not count the days spent out of doors." In Walter Pater's story of "Marius the Epicurean" one reads of a Roman country-seat called "Ad Vigilias Albas," "White Nights." A sense of dreamless sleep distils from the name. One remembers such nights, and the fresh world of the awakening in the morning. There are such days. There are days which ripple past as a night of sleep and leave a worn brain at the end with the same satisfaction of renewal; white days. Crystal they are, like the water of streams, as musical and eventless; as elusive of description as the ripple over rocks or brown pools foaming.

The days and months and years of a life race with accelerating pace and youth goes and age comes as the days race, but one is not older for the white days. The clock stops, the blood runs faster, furrows in gray matter smooth out, time forgets to put in tiny crow's-feet and the extra gray hair a week, or to withdraw by the hundredth of an ounce the oxygen from the veins; one grows no older for the days spent out of doors. Allah does not count them.

It was days like these which hope held ahead as I paid earnest attention to the good food set before me. And behold, beside the pleasant vision of hope rose a happy-minded sister called memory. She took the word "Huron," this kindly spirit, and played magic with it, and the walls of the Château rolled into rustling trees and running water.

I was sitting, in my vision, in flannel shirt and knickerbockers, on a log by a little river, putting together fishing tackle and casting an eye, off and on, where rapids broke cold over rocks and whirled into foam-flecked, shadowy pools. There should be trout in those shadows.

"Take the butt, Rafael, while I string the line."

Rafael slipped across—still in my vision of memory—and was holding my rod as a rod should be held, not too high or too low, or too far or too near—right. He was an old Huron, a chief of Indian Lorette, and woods craft was to him as breathing.

"A varry light rod," commented Rafael in his low voice which held no tones out of harmony with water in streams or wind in trees. "A varry light, good rod," paying meanwhile strict attention to his job. "M'sieu go haf a luck today. I t'ink M'sieu go catch a beeg fish on dat river. Water high enough—not too high. And cold." He shivered a little. "Cold last night—varry cold nights begin now. Good hun-ting wedder."

"Have you got a moose ready for me on the little lake, Rafael? It's the 1st of September next week and I expect you to give me a shot before the 3d."

Rafael nodded. "Oui, m'sieur. First day." The keen-eyed, aquiline old face was as of a prophet. "We go get moose first day. I show you." With that the laughter-loving Frenchman in him flooded over the Indian hunter; for a second the two inheritances played like colors in shot silk, producing an elusive fabric, Rafael's charm. "If nights get so colder, m'sieur go need moose skin kip him warm."

I was looking over my flies now, the book open before me, its fascinating pages of color more brilliant than an old missal, and maybe as filled with religion—the peace of God, charity which endureth, love to one's neighbor. I chose a Parmachene Belle for hand-fly, always good in Canadian waters. "A moose-skin hasn't much warmth, has it, Rafael?"

The hunter was back, hawk-eyed. "But yes, m'sieu. Moose skin one time safe me so I don' freeze to death. But it hol' me so tight so I nearly don' get loose in de morning."

"What do you mean?" I was only half listening, for a brown hackle and a Montreal were competing for the middle place on my cast, and it was a vital point. But Rafael liked to tell a story, and had come by now to a confidence in my liking to hear him. He flashed a glance to gather up my attention, and cleared his throat and began: "Dat was one time—I go on de woods—hunt wid my fader-in-law—*mon beau-père*. It was mont' of March—and col'—but ver' col' and wet. So it happen we separate, my fador-in-law and me, to hunt on both side of large enough river. And I kill moose. What, m'sieur? What sort of gun? Yes. It was rifle—what one call flint-lock. Large round bore. I cast dat beeg ball myself, what I kill dat moose. Also it was col'. And so it happen my matches got wet, but yes, ev-very one. So I couldn' buil' fire. I was tired, yes, and much col'. I t'ink in my head to hurry and skin dat moose and wrap myself in dat skin and go sleep on de snow because if not I would die, I was so col' and so tired. I do dat. I skin heem—*je le plumait*—de beeg moose—beeg skin. Skin all warm off moose; I wrap all aroun' me and dig hole and lie down on deep snow and draw skin over head and over feet, and fol' arms, so"—Rafael illustrated—"and I hol' it aroun' wid my hands. And I get warm right away, warm, as bread toast. So I been slippy, and heavy wid tired, and I got comfortable in dat moose skin and I go aslip quick. I wake early on morning, and dat skin got froze tight, like box made on wood, and I hol' in dat wid my arms fol' so, and my head down so"—illustrations again—"and I can't move, not one inch. No. What, m'sieur? Yes, I was enough warm, me. But I lie lak dat and can't move, and I t'ink somet'ing. I t'ink I got die lak dat, in moose-skin. If no sun come, I did got die. But dat day sun come and be warm, and moose skin melt lil' bit, slow, and I push lil' bit wid shoulder, and after while I got ice broke, on moose skin, and I crawl out. Yes. I don' die yet."

Rafael's chuckle was an amen to his saga, and at once, with one of his lightning-changes, he was austere.

"M'sieur go need beeg trout tonight; not go need moose skin till nex' wik. Ze rod is ready take feesh, I see feesh jump by ole log. Not much room to cast, but m'sieur can do it. Shall I carry rod down to river for m'sieur?"

In not so many words as I have written, but in clear pictures which comprehended the words, Memory, that temperamental goddess of moods, had, at the prick of the word "Huron," shaken out this soft-colored tapestry of the forest, and held it before my eyes. And as she withdrew this one, others took its place and at length I was musing profoundly, as I put more of something on my plate and tucked it away into my anatomy. I mused about Rafael, the guide of sixty, who had begun a life of continued labor at eight years; I considered the undying Indian in him; how with the father who was "French of Picardy"—the 09white blood being a pride to Rafael—he himself, yes, and the father also, for he had married a "*sauvagess*," a Huron woman—had belonged to the tribe and were accounted Hurons; I considered Rafael's proud carriage, his classic head and carved features, his Indian austerity and his French mirth weaving in and out of each other; I considered the fineness and the fearlessness of his spirit, which long hardship had not blunted; I reflected on the tales he had told me of a youth forced to fight the world. "*On a vu de le misère*," Rafael had said: "One has seen trouble"—shaking his head, with lines of old suffering emerging from the reserve of his face like writing in sympathetic ink under heat. And I marvelled that through such fire, out of such neglect, out of lack of opportunity and bitter pressure, the steel of a character should have been tempered to gentleness and bravery and honor.

For it was a very splendid old boy who was cooking for me and greasing my boots and going off with me after moose; putting his keen ancestral instincts of three thousand years at my service for three dollars a day. With my chances would not Rafael have been a bigger man than I? At least never could I achieve that grand air, that austere repose of manner which he had got with no trouble at all from a line of unwashed but courageous old bucks, thinking highly of themselves for untold generations, and killing everything which thought otherwise. I laughed all but aloud at this spot in my meditations, as a special vision of Rafael rose suddenly, when he had stated, on a day, his views of the great war. He talked plain language about the Germans. He specified why he considered the nation a disgrace to humanity—most people, not German, agree on the thesis and its specifications. Then the fire of his ancient fighting blood blazed through restraint of manner. He drew up his tall figure, slim-waisted, deep-shouldered, every inch sliding muscle. "I am too old to go on first call to army," said Rafael. "Zey will not take me. Yes, and on second call. Maybe zird time. But if time come when army take me—I go. If I may kill four Germans I will be content," stated Rafael concisely. And his warrior forebears would have been proud of him as he stated it.

My reflections were disturbed here by the American general at the next table. He was spoken to by his waiter and shot up and left the room, carrying, however, his napkin in his hand, so that I knew he was due to come back. A half sentence suggested a telephone. I watched the soldierly back with plenty of patriotic pride; this was the sort of warrior my country turned out now by tens of thousands. With that he returned, and as I looked up into his face, behold it was Fitzhugh.

My chair went banging as I sprang toward him. "Jim!"

And the general's calm dignity suddenly was the radiant grin of the boy who had played and gone to school and stolen apples with me for a long bright childhood—the boy lost sight of these last years of his in the army. "Dave!" he cried out. "Old Davy Cram!" And his arm went around my shoulder regardless of the public. "My word, but I'm glad!" he sputtered. And then: "Come and have dinner—finish having it. Come to our table." He slewed me about and presented me to the three others.

In a minute I was installed, to the pride of my friend the head waiter, at military headquarters, next to Fitzhugh and the Frenchman. A campact résumé of personal history between Fitzhugh and myself over, I turned to the blue figure on my left hand, Colonel Raffré, of the French, army. On his broad chest hung thrilling bits of color, not only the bronze war cross, with its green watered ribbon striped with red, but the blood-red ribbon of the "Great Cross" itself—the cross of the Legion of Honor. I spoke to him in French, which happens to be my second mother tongue, and he met the sound with a beaming welcome.

"I don't do English as one should," he explained in beautiful Parisian. "No gift of tongues in my kit, I fear; also I'm a bit embarrassed at practising on my friends. It's a relief to meet some one who speaks perfectly French, as m'sieur."

M'sieur was gratified not to have lost his facility. "But my ear is getting slower," I said. "For instance, I eavesdropped a while ago when you were talking about your Huron soldiers, and I got most of what you said because you spoke English. I doubt if I could if you'd been speaking French."

The colonel shrugged massive shoulders. "My English is defective but distinct," he explained. "One is forced to speak slowly when one speaks badly. Also the Colonel Chichely"—the Britisher—"it is he at whom I talk carefully. The English ear, it is not imaginative. One must make things clear. You know the Hurons, then?"

I specified how.

"Ah!" he breathed out. "The men in my command had been, some of them, what you call guides. They got across to France in charge of troop horses on the ships; then they stayed and enlisted. Fine soldier stuff. Hardy, and of resource and of finesse. Quick and fearless as wildcats. They fit into one niche of the war better than any other material. You heard the story of my rescue?"

I had not. At that point food had interfered, and I asked if it was too much that the colonel should repeat.

"By no means," agreed the polite colonel, ready, moreover, I guessed, for any amount of talk in his native tongue. He launched an epic episode. "I was hit leading, in a charge, two battalions. I need not have done that," another shrug—"but what will you? It was snowing; it was going to be bad work; one could perhaps put courage into the men by being at their head. It is often the duty of an officer to do more than, his duty—*n'est-ce-pas?* So that I was hit in the right knee and the left shoulder *par exemple*, and fell about six yards from the German trenches. A place unhealthy, and one sees I could not run away, being shot on the bias. I shammed dead. An alive French officer would have been too interesting in that scenery. I assure m'sieur that the *entr'actes* are far too long in No Man's Land. I became more and more displeased with the management of that play as I lay, very badly amused with my wounds, and afraid to blink an eye, being a corpse. The Huns demand a high state of immobility in corpses. But I fell happily sidewise, and out of the extreme corner of the left eye I caught a glimpse of our sand-bags. One blessed that twist, though it became enough *ennuyant*, and one would have given a year of good life to turn over. Merely to turn over. Am I fatiguing m'sieur?" the colonel broke in.

I prodded him back eagerly into his tale.

"M'sieur is amiable. The long and short of it is that when it became dark my good lads began to try to rescue my body. Four or five times that one-twentieth of eye saw a wriggling form work through sand-bags and start slowly, flat to the earth, toward me. But the ground was snow-covered and the Germans saw too the dark uniform. Each time a fusillade of shots broke out, and the moving figure dropped hastily behind the sand-bags. And each time—" the colonel stopped to light a cigarette, his face ruddy in the glare of the match. "Each time I was—disappointed. I became disgusted with the management of that theatre, till at last the affair seemed beyond hope, and I had about determined to turn over and draw up my bad leg with my good hand for a bit of easement and be shot comfortably, when I was aware that the surface of the ground near by was heaving—the white, snowy ground heaving. I was close enough to madness between cold and pain, and I regarded the phenomenon as a dream. But with that hands came out of the heaving ground, eyes gleamed. A rope was lashed about my middle and I was drawn toward our trenches." The cigarette puffed vigorously at this point. "M'sieur sees?"

I did not.

The colonel laughed. "One of my Hurons had the inspiration to run to a farmhouse not far away and requisition a sheet. He wrapped himself in it, head and all, and, being Indian, it was a bagatelle to him to crawl out on his stomach. They were pleased enough, my good fellows, when they found they had got not only my body but also me in it."

"I can imagine, knowing Hurons, how that Huron enjoyed his success," I said. "It's in their blood to be swift and silent and adventurous. But they're superstitious; they're afraid of anything supernatural." I hesitated, with a laugh in my mind at a memory. "It's not fitting that I should swap stories with a hero of the Great War, yet—I believe you might be amused with an adventure of one of my guides." The Frenchman, all civil interest, disclaimed his heroism with hands and shoulders, but smiling too—for he had small chance at disclaiming with those two crosses on his breast.

"I shall be enchanted to hear m'sieur's tale of his guide. For the rest I am myself quite mad over the 'sport.' I love to insanity the out of doors and shooting and fishing. It is a regret that the service has given me no opportunity these four years for a breathing spell in the woods. M'sieur will tell me the tale of his guide's superstition?"

A scheme began to form in my brain at that instant too delightful, it seemed, to come true. I put it aside and went on with my story. "I have one guide, a Huron half-breed," I said, "whom I particularly like. He's an old fellow—sixty—but light and quick and powerful as a boy. More interesting than a boy, because he's full of experiences. Two years ago a bear swam across the lake where my camp is, and I went out in a canoe with this Rafael and got him."

Colonel Raffré made of this fact an event larger than—I am sure—he would have made of his winning of the war cross.

"You shame me, colonel," I said, and went on hurriedly. "Rafael, the guide, was pleased about the bear. 'When gentlemens kill t'ings, guides is more happy,' he explained to me, and he proceeded to tell an anecdote. He prefaced it by informing me that one time he hunt bear and he see devil. He had been hunting, it seemed, two or three winters before with his brother-in-law at the headwaters of the St. Maurice River, up north there," I elucidated, pointing through the window toward the "long white street of Beauport," across the St. Lawrence. "It's very lonely country, entirely wild, Indian hunting-ground yet. These two Hurons, Rafael and his brother-in-law, were on a two months' trip to hunt and trap, having their meagre belongings and provisions on sleds which they dragged across the snow. They depended for food mostly on what they could trap or shoot—moose, caribou, beaver, and small animals. But they had bad luck. They set many traps but caught nothing, and they saw no game to shoot. So that in a month they were hard pressed. One cold day they went two miles to visit a beaver trap, where they had seen signs. They hoped to find an animal caught and to feast on beaver tail, which is good eating."

Here I had to stop and explain much about beaver tails, and the rest of beavers, to the Frenchman, who was interested like a boy in this new, almost unheard-of beast. At length:

"Rafael and his brother-in-law were disappointed. A beaver had been close and eaten the bark off a birch stick which the men had left, but nothing was in the trap. They turned and began a weary walk through the desolate country back to their little tent. Small comfort waited for them there, as their provisions were low, only flour and bacon left. And they dared not expend much of that. They were down-hearted, and to add to it a snow-storm came on and they lost their way. Almost a hopeless situation—an uninhabited country, winter, snow, hunger. And they were lost. '*Egaré. Perdu,*' Rafael said. But the Huron was far from giving up. He peered through the falling snow, not thick yet, and spied a mountain across a valley. He knew that mountain. He had worked near it for two years, logging—the '*chantier,*' they call it. He knew there was a good camp on a river near the mountain, and he knew there would be a stove in the camp and, as Rafael said, 'Mebbe we haf a luck and somebody done gone and lef' somet'ing to eat,' Rafael prefers to talk English to me. He told me all this in broken English.

"It was three miles to the hypothetical camp, but the two tired, hungry men in their rather wretched clothes started hopefully. And after a hard tramp through unbroken forest they came in sight of a log shanty and their spirits rose. 'Pretty tired work,' Rafael said it was. When they got close to the shanty they hoard a noise inside. They halted and looked at each other. Rafael knew there were no loggers in these parts now, and you'll remember it was absolutely wild country. Then something came to the window and looked out."

"*Something?*" repeated the Frenchman in italics. His eyes were wide and he was as intent on Rafael's story as heart could desire.

"They couldn't tell what it was," I went on. "A formless apparition, not exactly white or black, and huge and unknown of likeness. The Indians were frightened by a manner of unearthliness about the thing, and the brother-in-law fell on his knees and began to pray. 'It is the devil,' he murmured to Rafael. 'He will eat us, or carry us to hell.' And he prayed more.

"But old Rafael, scared to death, too, because the thing seemed not to be of this world, yet had his courage with him. 'Mebbe it devil,' he said—such was his report to me—'anyhow I'm cold and hungry, me. I want dat camp. I go shoot dat devil.'

"He crept up to the camp alone, the brother still praying in the bush. Rafael was rather convinced, mind you, that he was going to face the powers of darkness, but he had his rifle loaded and was ready for business. The door was open and he stepped inside. Something—'great beeg somet'ing' he put it—rose up and came at him, and he fired. And down fell the devil."

"In the name of a sacred pig, what was it?" demanded my Frenchman.

"That was what I asked. It was a bear. The men who had been logging in the camp two months back had left a keg of maple-syrup and a half barrel of flour, and the bear broke into both—successively—and alternately. He probably thought he was in bear-heaven for a while, but it must have gotten irksome. For his head was eighteen inches wide when they found him, white, with black touches. They soaked him in the river two days, and sold his skin for twenty dollars. 'Pretty good for devil skin,' Rafael said."

The Frenchman stared at me a moment and then leaned back in his chair and shouted laughter. The greedy bear's finish had hit his funny-bone. And the three others stopped talking and demanded the story told over, which I did, condensing.

"I like zat Hurong for my soldier," Colonel Raffré stated heartily. "Ze man what are not afraid of man *or* of devil—zat is ze man to fight ze Boches." He was talking English now because Colonel Chichely was listening. He went on. "Zere is human devils—oh, but plentee—what we fight in France. I haf not heard of ozzers. But I believe well ze man who pull me out in sheet would be as your guide Rafael—he also would crip up wiz his rifle on real devil out of hell. But yes. I haf not told you how my Indian soldier bring in prisoners—no?"

We all agreed no, and put in a request.

"He brings zem in not one by one always—not always." The colonel grinned. He went on to tell this tale, which I shift into the vernacular from his laborious English.

It appears that he had discerned the aptitude of his Hurons for reconnaissance work. If he needed information out of the dangerous country lying in front, if he needed a prisoner to question, these men were eager to go and get either, get anything. The more hazardous the job the better, and for a long time they came out of it untouched. In the group one man—nicknamed by the poilus, his comrades—Hirondelle—the Swallow—supposedly because of his lightness and swiftness, was easily chief. He had a fault, however, his dislike to bring in prisoners alive. Four times he had haled a German corpse before the colonel, seeming not rightly to understand that a dead enemy was useless for information.

"The Boches are good killing," he had elucidated to his officer. And finally: "It is well, m'sieur, the colonel. One failed to understand that the colonel prefers a live Boche to a dead one. Me, I am otherwise. It appears a pity to let live such vermin. Has the colonel, by chance, heard the things these savages did in Belgium? Yes? But then—Yet I will bring to m'sieur, the colonel, all there is to be desired of German prisoners alive—*en vie*; fat ones; *en masse*."

That night Hirondelle was sent out with four of his fellow Hurons to get, if possible, a prisoner. Pretty soon he was separated from the others; all but himself returning empty-handed in a couple of hours. No Germans seemed to be abroad. But Hirondelle did not return.

"He risks too far," grumbled his captain. "He has been captured at last. I always knew they would get him, one night."

But that was not the night. At one o'clock there was suddenly a sound of lamentation in the front trench of the French on that sector. The soldiers who were sleeping crawled out of their holes in the sides of the trench walls, and crowded around the zigzag, narrow way and rubbed their eyes and listened to the laughter of officers and soldiers on duty. There was Hirondelle, solemn as a church, yet with a dancing light in his eyes. There, around him, crowded as sheep to a shepherd, twenty figures in German uniform stood with hands up and wet tears running down pasty cheeks. And they were fat, it was noticeable that all of them were bulging of figure beyond even the German average. They wailed "Kamerad! Gut Kamerad!" in a chorus that was sickening to the plucky poilu make-up. Hirondelle, interrogated of many, kept his lips shut till the first excitement quieted. Then: "I report to my colonel," he stated, and finally he and his twenty were led back to the winding trench and the colonel was waked to receive them. This was what had happened: Hirondelle had wandered about, mostly on his stomach, through the darkness and peril of No Man's Land, enjoying himself heartily; when suddenly he missed his companions and realized that he had had no sign of them for some time. That did not trouble him. He explained to the colonel that he felt "more free." Also that if he pulled off a success he would have "more glory." After two hours of this midnight amusement, in deadly danger every second, Hirondelle heard steps. He froze to the earth, as he had learned from wild things in North American forests. The steps came nearer. A star-shell away down the line lighted the scene so that Hirondelle, motionless on the ground, all keen eyes, saw two Germans coming toward him. Instantly he had a scheme. In a subdued growl, yet distinctly, he threw over his shoulder an order that eight men should go to the right and eight to the left. Then, on his feet, he sent into the darkness a stern "Halt!" Instantly there was a sputter, arms thrown up, the inevitable "Kamerad!" and Hirondelle ordered the first German to pass him, then a second. Out of the darkness emerged a third. Hirondelle waved him on, and with that there was a fourth. And a fifth. Behold a sixth. About then Hirondelle judged it wise to give more orders to his imaginary squad of sixteen. But such a panic had seized this German mob; that little acting was necessary. Dark figure followed dark figure out of the darker night—arms up. They whimpered as they came, and on and on they came out of shadows. Hirondelle stated that he began to think the Crown Prince's army was surrendering to him. At last, when the procession stopped, he—and his mythical sixteen—marched the entire covey, without any objection from them, only abject obedience, to the French trenches.

The colonel, with this whining crowd weeping about him, with Hirondelle's erect figure confronting him, his black eyes regarding the cowards with scorn as he made his report—the colonel simply could not understand the situation. All these men! "What are you—soldiers?" he flung at the wretched group. And one answered, "No, my officer. We are not soldiers, we are the cooks." At that there was a wail. "Ach! Who, then, will the breakfast cook for my general? He will *schrecklich* angry be for his sausage and his sauerkraut."

By degrees the colonel got the story. A number of cooks had combined to protest against new regulations, and the general, to punish this astounding insubordination, had sent them out unarmed, petrified with, terror, into No Man's Land for an hour. They had there encountered Hirondelle. Hirondelle drew the attention of the colonel to the fact that he had promised prisoners, fat ones. "Will my colonel regard the shape of these pigs," suggested Hirondelle. "And also that they are twenty in number. Enough *en masse* for one man to take, is it not, my colonel?"

The little dinner-party at the Frontenac discussed this episode. "Almost too good to be true, colonel," I objected. "You're sure it *is* true? Bring out your Hirondelle. He ought to be home wounded, with a war cross on his breast, by now."

The colonel smiled and shook his head. "It is that which I cannot do—show you my Hirondelle. Not here, and not in France, by *malheur*. For he ventured once too often and too far, as the captain prophesied, and he is dead. God rest the brave! Also a Croix de Guerre is indeed his, but no Hirondelle is there to claim it."

The silence of a moment was a salute to the soul of a warrior passed to the happy hunting-grounds. And then I began on another story of my Rafael's adventures which something in the colonel's tale suggested.

The colonel, his winning face all a smile, interrupted. "Does one believe, then, in this Rafael of m'sieur who caps me each time my tales of my Huron Hirondelle? It appears to me that m'sieur has the brain, of a story-teller and hangs good stories on a figure which he has built and named so—Rafael. Me, I cannot believe there exists this Rafael. I believe there is only one such gallant d'Artagnan of the Hurons, and it is—it was—my Hirondelle. Show me your Rafael, then!" demanded the colonel.

At that challenge the scheme which had flashed into my mind an hour ago gathered shape and power. "I will show him to you, colonel," I took up the challenge, "if you will allow me." I turned to include the others. "Isn't it possible for you all to call a truce and come up tomorrow to my club to be my guests for as long or as short a time as you will? I can't say how much pleasure it would give me, and I believe I could give you something also—great fishing, shooting, a moose, likely, or at least a caribou—and Rafael. I promise Rafael. It's not unlikely, colonel, that he may have known the Hirondelle. The Hurons are few. Do come," I threw at them.

They took it after their kind. The Englishman stared and murmured: "Awfully kind, I'm sure, but quite impossible." The Canadian, our next of kin, smiled, shaking his head like a brother. Fitzhugh put his arm of brawn about me again till that glorious star gleamed almost on my own shoulder, and patted me lovingly as he said: "Old son, I'd give my eyes to go, if I wasn't up to my ears in job."

But the Frenchman's face shone, and he lifted a finger that was a sentence. It embodied reflection and eagerness and suspense. The rest of us gazed at that finger as if it were about to address us. And the colonel spoke. "I t'ink," brought out the colonel emphatically, "I t'ink I damn go."

And I snatched the finger and the hand of steel to which it grew, and wrung both. This was a delightful Frenchman. "Good!" I cried out. "Glorious! I want you all, but I'm mightily pleased to get one. Colonel, you're a sport."

"But, yes," agreed the colonel happily, "I am sport. Why not? I haf four days to wait till my sheep sail. Why not kip—how you say?—kip in my hand for shooting—go kill moose? I may talk immensely of zat moose in France—hein? Much more *chic* as to kill Germans, *n'est çe pas*? Everybody kill Germans."

At one o'clock next day the out-of-breath little train which had gasped up mountains for five hours from Quebec uttered a relieved shriek and stopped at a doll-house club station sitting by itself in the wilderness. Four or five men in worn but clean clothes—they always start clean—waited on the platform, and there was a rapid fire of "*Bon jour*, m'sieur," as we alighted. Then ten quick eyes took in my colonel in his horizon-blue uniform. I was aware of a throb of interest. At once there was a scurry for luggage because the train must be held till it was off, and the guides ran forward to the baggage-car to help. I bundled the colonel down a sharp, short hill to the river, while smiling, observant Hurons, missing not a line of braid or a glitter of button, passed with bags and *pacquetons* as we descended. The blue and black and gold was loaded into a canoe with an Indian at bow and stern for the three-mile paddle to the club-house. He was already a schoolboy on a holiday with unashamed enthusiasm.

"But it is fun—fun, zis," he shouted to me from his canoe. "And *lequel*, m'sieur, which is Rafael?"

Rafael, in the bow of my boat, missed a beat of his paddle. It seemed to me he looked older than two years back, when I last saw him. His shoulders were bent, and his merry and stately personality was less in evidence. He appeared subdued. He did not turn with a smile or a grave glance of inquiry at the question, as I had expected. I nodded toward him.

"*Mais oui*," cried out the colonel. "One has heard of you, *mon ami*. One will talk to you later of shooting."

Rafael, not lifting his head, answered quietly, "*C'est bien, m'sieur.*"

Just then the canoes slipped past a sandy bar decorated with a fresh moose track; the excitement of the colonel set us laughing. This man was certainly a joy! And with that, after a long paddle down the winding river and across two breezy lakes, we were at the club-house. We lunched, and in short order—for we wanted to make camp that night—I dug into my *pacquetons* and transformed my officer into a sportsman, his huge delight in Abernethy & Flitch's creations being a part of the game. Then we were off.

One has small chance for associating with guides while travelling in the woods. One sits in a canoe between two, but if there is a wind and the boat is *chargé* their hands are full with the small craft and its heavy load; when the landing is made and the "messieurs" are *débarqués*, instantly the men are busy lifting canoes on their heads and packs on their backs in bizarre, piled-up masses to be carried from a leather tumpline, a strap of two inches wide going around the forehead. The whole length of the spine helps in the carrying. My colonel watched Delphise, a husky specimen, load. With a grunt he swung up a canvas U.S. mailbag stuffed with *butin*, which includes clothes and books and shoes and tobacco and cartridges and more. With a half-syllable Delphise indicated to Laurent a bag of potatoes weighing eighty pounds, a box of tinned biscuit, a wooden package of cans of condensed milk, a rod case, and a raincoat. These Laurent added to the spine of Delphise.

"How many pounds?" I asked, as the dark head bent forward to equalize the strain.

Delphise shifted weight with another grunt to gauge the pull. "About a hundred and eighty pounds, m'sieur—quite heavy—*assez pesant*." Off he trotted uphill, head bent forward.

The colonel was entranced. "Hardy fellows—the making of fine soldiers," he commented, tossing his cigarette away to stare.

That night after dinner—but it was called supper—the colonel and I went into the big, airy log kitchen with the lake looking in at three windows and the forest at two doors. We gunned over with the men plans for the next day, for the most must be made of every minute of this precious military holiday. I explained how precious it was, and then I spoke a few words about the honor of having as our guest a soldier who had come from the front, and who was going back to the front. For the life of me I could not resist a sentence more about the two crosses they had seen on his uniform that day. The Cross of War, the Legion of Honor! I could not let my men miss that! Rafael had been quiet and colorless, and I was disappointed in the show qualities of my show guide. But the colonel beamed with satisfaction, in everything and everybody, and received my small introduction with a bow and a flourish worthy of Carnegie Hall.

"I am happy to be in this so charming camp, in this forest magnificent, on these ancient mountains," orated the colonel floridly. "I am most pleased of all to have Huron Indians as my guides, because between Hurons and me there are memories." The men were listening spell-bound. "But yes. I had Huron soldiers serving in my regiment, just now at the western front, of whom I thought highly. They were all that there is, those Hurons of mine, of most fearless, most skilful. One among them was pre-eminent. Some of you may have known him. I regret to say that I never knew his real name, but among his comrades he went by the name of l'Hirondelle. From that name one guesses his qualities—swift as a swallow, untamable, gay, brave to foolishness, moving in dashes not to be followed—such was my Hirondelle. And yet this swift bird was in the end shot down."

At this point in the colonel's speech, I happened to look at Rafael, back in the shadows of the half-lighted big room. His eyes glittered out of the dimness like disks of fire, his face was strained, and his figure bent forward. "He must have known this chap, the Swallow," I thought to myself. "Just possibly a son or brother or nephew of his." The colonel was going on, telling in fluent, beautiful French the story of how Hirondelle, wrapped in a sheet, had rescued him. The men drank it in. "When those guides are old, old fellows, they'll talk about this night and the colonel's speech to their great-grandchildren," I considered, and again the colonel went on.

"Have I m'sieur's permission to *raconter* a short story of the most amusing which was the last escapade of my Hirondelle before he was killed?"

M'sieur gave permission eagerly, and the low murmur of the voices of the hypnotized guides, standing in a group before the colonel, added to its force and set him smiling.

"It was like this," he stated. "My Hirondelle was out in No Man's Land of a night, strictly charged to behave in a manner *comme il faut*, for he was of a rashness, and we did not wish to lose him. He was valuable to us, and beyond that the regiment had an affection for him. For such reasons his captain tried—but, yes—to keep him within bounds. As I say, on this night he had received particular orders to be *sage*. So that the first thing the fellow does is to lose his comrades, for which he had a *penchant*, one knows. After that he crawls over that accursed country, in and out of shellholes, rifle in his teeth likely—the good God knows where else, for one need be all hands and feet for such crawling. He crawled in that fashion till at last he lost himself. And then he was concerned to find out where might be our lines till in time he heard a sound of snoring and was well content. Home at last. He tumbled into a dark trench, remarking only that it was filled with men since he left, and so tired he was with his adventure that he pushed away the man next, who was at the end, to gain space, and he rolled over to sleep. But that troublesome man next took too much room. Our Hirondelle planted him a kick in the middle of the back. At which the man half waked and swore at him—in German. And dropped off to sleep again with his leg of a pig slung across Hirondelle's chest. At that second a star-shell lighted up the affair, and Hirondelle, staring with much interest, believe me, saw a trench filled with sleeping Boches. To get out of that as quietly as might be was the game—*n'est-ce-pas, mes amis*? But not for Hirondelle.

"'My colonel has a liking for prisoners,' he reported later. 'My captain's orders were to conduct oneself *très comme il faut*. It is always *comme il faut* to please the colonel. Therefore it seemed *en regle* to take a prisoner. I took him. *Le v'la*.'

"What the fellow did was to wait till the Boche next door was well asleep, then slowly remove his rifle, then fasten on his throat with a grip which Hirondelle understood, and finally to overpower the Boche till he was ready enough to crawl out at the muzzle of Hirondelle's rifle."

There was a stir in the little group of guides, and from the shadows Rafael's voice spoke.

"Mon colonel—pardon!"

The colonel turned sharply. "Who is that?"

"There were two Germans," spoke the voice out of the shadows.

The colonel, too astonished to answer, stared. The voice, trembling, old, went on. "The second man waked and one was obliged to strangle him also. One brought the brace to the captain at the end of the carabine—rifle."

"In heaven's name who are you?" demanded the colonel.

From where old Rafael had been, bowed and limp in his humble, worn clothes, stepped at a stride a soldier, head up, shoulders squared, glittering eyes forward, and stood at attention. It was like magic. One hand snapped up in a smart salute.

"Who are you?" whispered the colonel.

"If the colonel pleases—l'Hirondelle."

I heard the colonel's breath come and go as he peered, leaning forward to the soldierly figure. "*Nom de Ciel*," he murmured, "I believe it is." Then in sharp sentences: "You were reported killed. Are you a deserter?"

The steady image of a soldier dropped back a step.

"My colonel—no."

"Explain this."

Rafael—l'Hirondelle—explained. He had not been killed, but captured and sent to a German prison-camp.

"You escaped?" the colonel threw in.

"But yes, my colonel."

The colonel laughed. "One would know it. The clumsy Boches could not hold the Swallow."

"But no, my colonel."

"Go on."

"One went to work before light, my colonel, in that accursed prison-camp. One was out of sight from the guard for a moment, turning a corner, so that on a morning I slipped into some bushes and hid in a dugout—for it was an old camp—all day. That night I walked. I walked for seven nights and lay hid for seven days, eating, my colonel, very little. Then, *v'la*, I was in front of the French lines."

"You ran across to our lines?"

"But not exactly. One sees that I was yet in dirty German prison clothes, and looked like an infantryman of the Boches, so that a poilu rushed at me with a bayonet. I believed, then, that I had come upon a German patrol. Each thought the other a Hun. I managed to wrest from the poilu his rifle with the bayonet, but as we fought another shot me—in the side."

"You were wounded?"

"Yes, my colonel."

"In hospital?"

"Yes, my colonel."

"How long?"

"Three months, my colonel."

"Why are you not again in the army?"

The face of the erect soldier, Hirondelle, the dare-devil, was suddenly the face of a man grown old, ill, and broken-hearted. He stared at the stalwart French officer, gathering himself with an effort. "I—was discharged, my colonel, as—unfit." His head in its old felt hat dropped into his hands suddenly, and he broke beyond control into sobs that shook not only him but every man there.

The colonel stepped forward and put an arm around the bent shoulders. "*Mon héros!*" said the colonel.

With that Rafael found words, never a hard task for him. Yet they came with gasps between. "To be cast out as an old horse—at the moment of glory! I had dreamed all my life—of fighting. And I had it—oh, my colonel—I had it! The glory came when I was old and knew how to be happy in it. Not as a boy who laughs and takes all as his right. I was old, yes, but I was good to kill the vermin. I avenged the children and the women whom those savages—My people, the savages of the wood, knew no better, yet they have not done things as bad as these vile ones who were educated, who knew. Therefore I killed them. I was old, but I was strong, my colonel knows. Not for nothing have I lived a hard life. *On a vu de la misère.* I have hunted moose and bear and kept my muscles of steel and my eyes of a hawk. It is in my blood to be a fighting man. I fought with pleasure, and I was troubled with no fear. I was old, but I could have killed many devils more. And so I was shot down by my own friend after seven days of hard life. And the young soldier doctor discharged me as unfit to fight. And so I am come home very fast to hide myself, for I am ashamed. I am finished. The fighting and the glory are for me no more."

The colonel stepped back a bit and his face flamed. "Glory!" he whispered. "Glory no more for the Hirondelle? What of the Croix de Guerre?"

Rafael shook his head. "I haf heard my colonel who said they would have given me—me, the Hirondelle—the war cross. That now is lost too."

"Lost!" The colonel's deep tone was full of the vibration which only a French voice carries. With a quick movement he unfastened the catch that held the green ribbon, red-striped, of his own cross of war. He turned and pinned the thing which men die for on the shabby coat of the guide. Then he kissed him on either cheek. "My comrade," he said, "your glory will never be old."

There was deep silence in the camp kitchen. The crackling of wood that fell apart, the splashing of the waves of the lake on the pebbles by the shore were the only sounds on earth. For a long minute the men stood as if rooted; the colonel, poised and dramatic, and, I stirred to the depths of my soul by this great ceremony which had come out of the skies to its humble setting in the forest—the men and the colonel and I, we all watched Rafael.

And Rafael slowly, yet with the iron tenacity of his race, got back his control. "My colonel," he began, and then failed. The Swallow did not dare trust his broken wings. It could not be done—to speak his thanks. He looked up with black eyes shining through tears which spoke everything.

"Tomorrow," he stated brokenly, "if we haf a luck, my colonel and I go kill a moose."

They had a luck.

## ONLY ONE OF THEM

It was noon on a Saturday. Out of the many buildings of the great electrical manufacturing plant at Schenectady poured employees by hundreds. Thirty trolley-cars were run on special tracks to the place and stood ready to receive the sea streaming towards them. Massed motor-cars waited beyond the trolleys for their owners, officials of the works. The girl in blue serge, standing at a special door of a special building counted, keeping watch meantime of the crowd, the cars. A hundred and twenty-five she made it; it came to her mind that State Street in Albany on a day of some giant parade was not unlike this, not less a throng. The girl, who was secretary to an assistant manager, was used to the sight, but it was an impressive sight and she was impressionable and found each Saturday's pageant a wonder. The pageant was more interesting it may be because it focussed always on one figure—and here he was.

"Did you wait, long?" he asked as he came up, broad-shouldered and athletic of build, boyish and honest of face, as good looking a young American as one may see in any crowd.

"I was early." She smiled up at him as they swung off towards the trolleys; her eyes flashed a glance which said frankly that she found him satisfactory to look upon.

They sped past others, many others, and made a trolley car and a seat together, which was the goal. They always made it, every Saturday, yet it was always a game. Exhilarated by the winning of the game they settled into the seat for the three-quarters of an hour run; it was quite a worth-while world, the smiling glances said one to the other.

The girl gazed, not seeing them particularly, at the slower people filling the seats and the passage of the car. Then: "Oh," she spoke, "what was it you were going to tell me?"

The man's face grew sober, a bit troubled. "Well," he said, "I've decided. I'm going to enlist."

She was still for a second. Then: "I think that's splendid," she brought out. "Splendid. Of course, I knew you'd do it. It's the only thing that could be. I'm glad."

"Yes," the man spoke slowly. "It's the only thing that could be. There's nothing to keep me. My mother's dead. My father's husky and not old and my sisters are with him. There's nobody to suffer by my going."

"N-no," the girl agreed. "But—it's the fine thing to do just the same. You're thirty-two you see, and couldn't be drafted. That makes it rather great of you to go."

"Well," the man answered, "not so very great, I suppose, as it's what all young Americans are doing. I rather think it's one of those things, like spelling, which are no particular credit if you do them, but a disgrace if you don't."

"What a gray way of looking at it!" the girl objected. "As if all the country wasn't glorying in the boys who go! As if we didn't all stand back of you and crowd the side lines to watch you, bursting with pride. You know we all love you."

"Do you love me, Mary? Enough to marry me before I go?" His voice was low, but the girl missed no syllable. She had heard those words or some like them in his voice before.

"Oh, Jim," she begged, "don't ask me now. I'm not certain—yet. I—I couldn't get along very well without you. I care a lot. But—I'm not just sure it's—the way I ought to care to marry you."

110

As alone in the packed car as in a wood, the little drama went on and no one noticed. "I'm sorry, Mary." The tone was dispirited. "I could go with a lot lighter heart if we belonged to each other."

"Don't say that, Jim," she pleaded. "You make me out—a slacker. You don't want me to marry you as a duty?"

"Good Lord, no!"

"I know that. And I—do care. There's nobody like you. I admire you so for going—but you're not afraid of anything. It's easy for you, that part. I suppose a good many are really—afraid. Of the guns and the horror—all that. You're lucky, Jim. You don't give that a thought."

The man flashed an odd look, and then regarded his hands joined on his knee.

"I do appreciate your courage. I admire that a lot. But somehow Jim there's a doubt that holds me back. I can't be sure I—love you enough; that it's the right way—for that."

The man sighed. "Yes," he said. "I see. Maybe some time. Heavens knows I wouldn't want you unless it was whole-hearted. I wouldn't risk your regretting it, not if I wanted you ten times more. Which is impossible." He put out his big hand with a swift touch on hers. "Maybe some time. Don't worry," he said. "I'm yours." And went on in a commonplace tone, "I think I'll show up at the recruiting office this afternoon, and I'll come to your house in the evening as usual. Is that all right?"

The car sped into Albany and the man went to her door with the girl and left her with few words more and those about commonplace subjects. As he swung down the street he went over the episode in his mind, and dissected it and dwelt on words and phrases and glances, and drew conclusions as lovers have done before, each detail, each conclusion mightily important, outweighing weeks of conversation of the rest of the world together. At last he shook his head and set his lips.

"It's not honest." He formed the words with his lips now, a summing up of many thoughts in his brain. The brain went on elaborating the text. "She thinks I'm brave; she thinks it's easy for me to face enlisting, and the rest. She thinks I'm the makeup which can meet horror and suffering light-heartedly. And I'm not. She admires me for that—she said so. I'm not it. I'm fooling her; it's not honest. Yet"—he groaned aloud. "Yet I may lose her if I tell her the truth. I'm afraid. I am. I hate it. I can't bear—I can't bear to leave my job and my future, just when it's opening out. But I could do that. Only I'm—Oh, damnation—I'm afraid. Horror and danger, agony of men and horses, myself wounded maybe, out on No Man's Land—left there—hours. To die like a dog. Oh, my God—must I? If I tell it will break the little hold I have on her. Must I go to this devil's dance that I hate—and give up her love besides? But yet—it isn't honest to fool her. Oh, God, what will I do?" People walking up State Street, meeting a sober-faced young man, glanced at him with no particular interest. A woman waiting on a doorstep regarded him idly.

"Why isn't he in uniform?" she wondered as one does wonder in these days at a strong chap in mufti. Then she rebuked her thought. "Undoubtedly there's a good reason; American boys are not slackers."

His slow steps carried him beyond her vision and casual thought. The people in the street and the woman on the doorstep did not think or care that what they saw was a man fighting his way through the crisis of his life, fighting alone "per aspera ad astra—" through thorns to the stars.

He lunched with a man at a club and after that took his way to the building on Broadway where were the recruiting headquarters. He had told her that he was going to enlist. As he walked he stared at the people in the streets as a man might stare going to his execution. These people went about their affairs, he considered, as if he—who was about to die—did not, in passing their friendly commonplace, salute them. He did salute them. Out of his troubled soul he sent a silent greeting to each ordinary American hurrying along, each standing to him for pleasant and peaceful America, America of all his days up to now. Was he to toss away this comfortable comradeship, his life to be, everything he cared for on earth, to go into hell, and likely never come back? Why? Why must he? There seemed to be plenty who wanted to fight—why not let them? It was the old slacker's argument; the man was ashamed as he caught himself using it; he had the grace to see its selfishness and cowardice. Yet his soul was in revolt as he drove his body to the recruiting office, and the thoughts that filled him were not of the joy of giving but of the pain of giving up. With that he stood on the steps of the building and here was Charlie Thurston hurrying by on the sidewalk.

"Hello, Jim! Going in to enlist? So long till you come back with one leg and an eye out."

It was Thurston's idea of a joke. He would have been startled if he had known into what a trembling balance his sledge-hummer wit cast its unlucky weight. The balance quivered at the blow, shook back and forth an instant and fell heavily. Jim Barlow wheeled, sprang down the stone steps and bolted up the street, panting as one who has escaped a wild beast. Thurston had said it. That was what was due to happen. It was now three o'clock; Barlow fled up State Street to the big hotel and took a room and locked his door and threw himself on the bed. What was he to do? After weeks of hesitation he had come to the decision that he would offer himself to his country. He saw—none plainer—the reasons why it was fit and right so to do. Other men were giving up homes and careers and the whole bright and easy side of life—why not he? It was the greatest cause to fight for in the world's history—should he not fight for it? How, after the war, might he meet friends, his own people, his children to come, if he alone of his sort had no honorable record to show? Such arguments, known to all, he repeated, even aloud he repeated them, tossing miserably about the bed in his hotel room. And his mind at once accepted them, but that was all. His spirit failed to spring to his mind's support with the throb of emotion which is the spark that makes the engine go. The wheels went around over and over but the connection was not made. The human mind is useful machinery, but it is only the machine's master, the soul, which can use it. Over and over he got to his feet and spoke aloud: "Now I will go." Over and over a repulsion seized him so strongly that his knees gave way and he fell back on the bed. If he had a mother, he thought, she might have helped, but there was no one. Mary—but he could not risk Mary's belief in his courage. Only a mother would have understood entirely.

With that, sick at heart, the hideous sea of counter arguments, arguments of a slacker, surged upon him. What would it all matter a hundred years from now? Wasn't he more useful in his place keeping up the industries of the nation? Wasn't he a bigger asset to America as an alive engineer, an expert in his work, than as mere cannon fodder, one of thousands to be shot into junk in a morning's "activity"—just one of them? Because the Germans were devils why should he let them reach over here, away over here, and drag him out of a decent and happy life and throw him like dirt into the horrible mess they had made, and leave him dead or worse—mangled and useless. Then, again—there were plenty of men mad to fight; why not let them?

Through a long afternoon he fought with the beasts, and dinner-time came and he did not notice, and at last he rose and, telephoning first to Mary a terse message that he would not be able to come this evening, he went out, hardly knowing what he did, and wandered up town.

There was a humble church in a quiet street where a service flag hung, thick with dark stars, and the congregation were passing out from a special service for its boys who were going off to camp. The boys were there on the steps, surrounded by people eager to touch their hands, a little group of eight or ten with serious bright faces, and a look in their eyes which stabbed into Barlow. One may see that look any day in any town, meeting the erect stalwart lads in khaki who are about our streets. It is the look of those who have made a vital sacrifice and know the price, and whose minds are at peace. Barlow, lingering on the corner across the way, stared hungrily. How had they got that look, that peace? If only he might talk to one of them! Yet he knew how dumb an animal is a boy, and how helpless these would be to give him the master word.

The master-word, he needed that; he needed it desperately. He must go; he must. Life would be unendurable without self-respect; no amount of explaining could cover the stain on his soul if he failed in the answer to the call of honor. That was it, it was in a nut-shell, the call. Yet he could not hear it as his call. He wandered unhappily away and left the church and its dissolving congregation, and the boys, the pride of the church, the boys who were now, they also, separating and going back each to his home for the last evening perhaps, to be loved and made much of. Barlow vaguely pictured the scenes in those little homes—eyes bright with unshed tears, love and laughter and courage, patriotism as fine as in any great house in America, determination that in giving to America what was dearest it should be given with high spirit—that the boys should have smiling faces to remember, over there. And then again—love and tender words. He was missing all that. He, too, might go back to his father's house an enlisted man, and meet his father's eyes of pride and see his sisters gaze at him with a new respect, feel their new honor of him in the touch of arms about his neck. All these things were for him too, if he would but take them. With that there was the sound of singing, shrill, fresh voices singing down the street. He wheeled about. A company of little girls were marching towards him and he smiled, looking at them, thinking the sight as pretty as a garden of flowers. They were from eight to ten or eleven years old and in the bravery of fresh white dresses; each had a big butterfly of pink or blue or yellow or white ribbon perched on each little fair or dark head, and each carried over her shoulder a flag. Quite evidently they were coming from the celebration at the church, where in some capacity they had figured. Not millionaires children these; the little sisters likely of the boys who were going to be soldiers; just dear things that bloom all over America, the flowering of the land, common to rich and poor. As they sprang along two by two, in unmartial ranks, they sang with all their might "The Long, Long Trail."

> "There's a long, long trail that's leading
>    To No Man's Land in France
> Where the shrapnel shells are bursting
>    And we must advance."

\* \* \* \* \*

And then:

> We're going to show old Kaiser Bill
> What our Yankee boys can do.

Jim Barlow, his hands in his pockets, backed up against a house and listened to the clear, high, little voices. "No Man's Land in France—We must advance—What our Yankee boys can do."

As if his throat were gripped by a quick hand, a storm of emotion swept him. The little girls—little girls who were the joy, each one, of some home! Such little things as the Germans—in Belgium—"Oh, my God!" The words burst aloud from his lips. These were trusting—innocent, ignorant—to "What our Yankee boys can do." Without that, without the Yankee boys, such as these would be in the power of wild beasts. It was his affair. Suddenly he felt that stab through him.

"God," he prayed, whispering it as the little girls passed on singing, "help me to protect them; help me to forget myself." And the miracle that sends an answer sometimes, even in this twentieth century, to true prayer happened to Jim Barlow. Behold he had forgotten himself. With his head up and peace in his breast, and the look in his face already, though he did not know it, that our soldier boys wear, he turned and started at a great pace down the street to the recruiting office.

"Why, you did come."

It was nine o'clock and he stood with lighted face in the middle of the little library. And she came in; it was an event to which he never got used, Mary's coming into a room. The room changed always into such an astonishing place.

"Mary, I've done it. I'm—" his voice choked a bit—"I'm a soldier." He laughed at that. "Well not so you'd notice it, yet. But I've taken the first step."

"I knew, Jim. You said you were going to enlist. Why did you telephone you couldn't come?"

He stared down at her, holding her hands yet. He felt, unphrased, strong, the overwhelming conviction that she was the most desirable thing on earth. And directly on top of that conviction another, that he would be doing her desirableness, her loveliness less than the highest honor if he posed before her in false colors. At whatever cost to himself he must be honest with her. Also—he was something more now than his own man; he was a soldier of America, and inside and out he would be, for America's sake, the best that was in him to be.

"Mary, I've got a thing to tell you."

"Yes?" The sure way in which she smiled up at him made the effort harder.

"I fooled you. You think I'm a hero. And I'm not. I'm a—" for the life of him he could not get out the word "coward." He went on: "I'm a blamed baby." And he told her in a few words, yet plainly enough what he had gone through in the long afternoon. "It was the kiddies who clinched it, with their flags and their hair ribbons—and their Yankee boys. I couldn't stand for—not playing square with them."

Suddenly he gripped her hands so that it hurt. "Mary, God help me, I'll try to fight the devils over there so that kiddies like that, and—you, and all the blessed people, the whole dear shooting-match will be safe over here. I'm glad—I'm so glad I'm going to have a hand in it. Mary, it's queer, but I'm happier than I've been in months. Only"—his brows drew anxiously. "Only I'm scared stiff for fear you think me—a coward."

He had the word out now. Thee taste wasn't so bad after all; it seemed oddly to have nothing to do with himself. "Mary, dear, couldn't you—forget that in time? When I've been over there and behaved decently—and I think I will. Somehow I'm not afraid of being afraid now. It feels like a thing that couldn't be done—by a soldier of Uncle Sam's. I'll just look at the other chaps—all heroes, you know—and be so proud I'm with them and so keen to finish our job that I know—somehow I *know* I'll never think about my blooming self at all. It's queer to say it, Mary, but the way it looks now I'm in it, it's not just country even. It's religion. See, Mary?"

There was no sound, no glance from Mary. But he went on, unaware, so rapt was he in his new illumination.

"And when I come back, Mary, with a decent record—just possibly with a war-cross—oh, my word! Think of me! Then, couldn't you forget this business I've been telling you? Do you think you could marry me then?"

What was the matter? Why did she stand so still with her head bending lower and lower, the color deepening on the bit of cheek that his anxious eyes could see.

"Mary!"

Suddenly she was clutching his collar as if in deadly fear.

"Mary, what's the matter? I'm such a fool, but—oh, Mary, dear!"

With that Mary-dear straightened and, slipping her clutch to the lapel of his old coat, spoke. She looked into his eyes with a smile that was sweeter—oh, much sweeter!—for tears that dimmed it, and she choked most awfully between words. "Jim"—and a choke. "Jim, I'm terrified to think I nearly let you get away. You. And me not worthy to lace your shoes—" ("Oh, gracious, Mary—don't!") "me—the idiot, backing and filling when I had the chance of my life at—at a hero. Oh, Jim!"

"Here! Mary, don't you understand? I've been telling you I was scared blue. I hated to tell you Mary, and it's the devil to tell you twice—"

What was this? Did Heaven then sometimes come down unawares on the head of an every-day citizen with great lapses of character? Jim Barlow, entranced, doubted his senses yet could not doubt the touch of soft hands clasped in his neck. He held his head back a little to be sure that they were real. Yes, they were there, the hands—Barlow's next remark was long, but untranslatable. Minutes later. "Mary, tell me what you mean. Not that I care much if—if this." Language grows elliptical under stress. "But—did you get me? I'm—a coward." A hand flashed across his mouth.

"Don't you dare, Jim, you're the bravest—bravest—"

The words died in a sharp break. "Why, Jim it was a hundred thousand times pluckier to be afraid and then go. Can't you see that, you big stupid?"

"But, Mary, you said you admired it when—when you thought I was a lion of courage."

"Of course. I admired you. Now I adore you."

"Well," summed up, Barlow bewildered, "if women aren't the blamedest!"

And Mary squealed laughter. She put hands each side of his face. "Jim—listen. I'll try to explain because you have a right to understand."

"Well, yes," agreed Jim.

"It's like this. I thought you'd enlist and I never dreamed you were balky. I didn't know you hated it so. Why didn't you tell me?"

"Go on," urged Jim.

"I thought you were mad to be going, like—like these light-headed boys. That you didn't mind leaving me compared to the adventure. That you didn't care for danger. But now—now." She covered his eyes with her fingers, "Now Jim, you need me. A woman can't love a man her best unless she can help him. Against everything—sorrow, mosquitoes, bad food—drink—any old bother. That's the alluring side of tipplers. Women want to help them. So, now I know you need me," the soft, unsteady voice wandered on, and Jim, anchored between, the hands, drank in her look with his eyes and her tones with his ears and prayed that the situation might last a week. "You need me so, to tell you how much finer you are than if you'd gone off without a quiver."

Barlow sighed in contentment. "And me thinking I was the solitary 'fraid-cat of America!"

"Solitary! Why, Jim, there must be at least ten hundred thousand men going through this same battle. All the ones old enough to think, probably. Why Jim—you're only one of them. In that speech the other night the man said this war was giving men their souls. I think it's your kind he meant, the kind that realizes the bad things over there and the good things over here and goes just the same. The kind—you are."

"I'm a hero from Hero-ville," murmured Barlow. "But little Mary, when I come back mangled will you feel the same? Will you marry me then, Mary?"

"I'll marry you any minute," stated Mary, "and when you come back I'll love you one extra for every mangle."

"Any minute," repeated Barlow dramatically. "Tomorrow?"

And summed up again the heaven that he could not understand and did not want to, "Search me," he adjured the skies in good Americanese, "if girls aren't the blamedest."

---

## THE V.C.

I had forgotten that I ordered frogs' legs. When mine were placed before me I laughed. I always laugh at the sight of frogs' legs because of the person and the day of which they remind me. Nobody noticed that I laughed or asked the reason why, though it was an audible chuckle, and though I sat at the head of my own dinner-party at the Cosmic Club.

The man for whom the dinner was given, Colonel Robert Thornton, my cousin, a Canadian, who got his leg shot off at Vimy Ridge, was making oration about the German Crown Prince's tactics at Verdun, and that was the reason that ten men were not paying attention to me and that I was not paying attention to Bobby. When the good chap talks human talk, tells what happened to people and what their psychological processes seemed to be, he is entertaining. He has a genuine gift of sympathy and a power to lead others in the path he treads; in short, he tells a good story. But like most people who do one thing particularly well he is always priding himself on the way he does something else. He likes to look at Colonel Thornton as a student of the war, and he has the time of his life when he can get people to listen to what he knows Joffre and Foch and Haig and Hindenberg ought to have done. So at this moment he was enjoying his evening, for the men I had asked to meet him, all strangers to him, ignorant of his real powers, were hanging on his words, partly because no one can help liking him whatever he talks about, and partly because, with that pathetic empty trouser-leg and the crutch hooked over his chair, he was an undoubted hero. So I heard the sentences ambling, and reflected that Hilaire Belloc with maps and a quiet evening would do my tactical education more good than Bobby Thornton's discursions. And about then I chuckled unnoticed, over the silly frogs' legs.

"Tell me, Colonel Thornton, do you consider that the French made a mistake in concentrating so much of their reserve—" It was the Governor himself who was demanding this earnestly of Bobby. And I saw that the Governor and the rest were hypnotized, and did not need me.

So I sat at the head of the table, and waiters brooded over us, and cucumbers and the usual trash happened, and Bobby held forth while the ten who were bidden listened as to one sent from heaven. And, being superfluous, I withdrew mentally to a canoe in a lonely lake and went frogging.

Vicariously. I do not like frogging in person. The creature smiles. Also he appeals because he is ugly and complacent. But for the grace of God I might have looked so. He sits in supreme hideousness frozen to the end of a wet log, with his desirable hind legs spread in view, and smiles his bronze smile of confidence in his own charm and my friendship. It is more than I can do to betray that smile. So, hating to destroy the beast yet liking to eat the leg, about once in my summer vacation in camp I go frogging, and make the guides do it.

It would not be etiquette to send them out alone, for in our club guides are supposed to do no fishing or shooting—no sport. Therefore, I sit in a canoe and pretend to take a frog in a landing-net and miss two or three and shortly hand over the net to Josef. We have decided on landing-nets as our tackle. I once shot the animals with a .22 Flobert rifle, but almost invariably they dropped, like a larger bullet, off the log and into the mud, and that was the end. We never could retrieve them. Also at one time we fished them with a many-pronged hook and a bit of red flannel. But that seemed too bitter a return for the bronze smile, and I disliked the method, besides being bad at it. We took to the landing-net.

To see Josef, enraptured with the delicate sport, approach a net carefully till within an inch of the smile, and then give the old graven image a smart rap on the legs in question to make him leap headlong into the snare—to see that and Josef's black Indian eyes glitter with joy at the chase is amusing. I make him slaughter the game instantly, which appears supererogatory to Josef who would exactly as soon have a collection of slimy ones leaping around the canoe. But I have them dead and done for promptly, and piled under the stern seat. And on we paddle to the next.

The day to which I had retired from my dinner-party and the tactical lecture of my distinguished cousin was a late August day of two years before. The frogging fleet included two canoes, that of young John Dudley who was doing his vacation with me, and my own. In each canoe, as is Hoyle for canoeing in Canada, were two guides and a "m'sieur." The other boat, John's, was somewhere on the opposite shore of Lac des Passes, the Lake of the Passes, crawling along edges of bays and specializing in old logs and submerged rocks, after frogs with a landing-net, the same as us. But John— to my mind coarser—was doing his own frogging. The other boat was nothing to us except for an occasional yell when geography brought us near enough, of "How many?" and envy and malice and all uncharitableness if the count was more, and hoots of triumph if less.

In my craft sailed, besides Josef and myself, as bow paddler, The Tin Lizzie. We called him that except when he could hear us, and I think it would have done small harm to call him so then, as he had the brain of a jack-rabbit and managed not to know any English, even when soaked in it daily. John Dudley had named him because of the plebeian and reliable way in which he plugged along Canadian trails. He set forth the queerest walk I have ever seen—a human Ford, John said. He was also quite mad about John. There had been a week in which Dudley, much of a doctor, had treated, with cheerful patience and skill, an infected and painful hand of the guide's, and this had won for him the love eternal of our Tin Lizzie. Little John Dudley thought, as he made jokes to distract the boy, and worked over his big throbbing fist, the fist which meant daily bread—little John thought where the plant of love springing from that seed of gratitude would at last blossom. Little he thought as the two sat on the gallery of the camp, and the placid lake broke in silver on pebbles below, through what hell of fire and smoke and danger the kindliness he gave to the stupid young guide would be given back to him. Which is getting ahead of the story.

I suggested that the Lizzie might like a turn at frogging, and Josef, with Indian wordlessness, handed the net to him. Whereupon, with his flabby mouth wide and his large gray eyes gleaming, he proceeded to miss four easy ones in succession. And with that Josef, in a gibberish which is French-Canadian patois of the inner circles, addressed the Tin Lizzie and took away the net from him, asking no orders from me. The Lizzie, pipe in mouth as always, smiled just as pleasantly under this punishment as in the hour of his opportunities. He would have been a very handsome boy, with his huge eyes and brilliant brown and red color and his splendid shoulders and slim waist of an athlete if only he had possessed a ray of sense. Yet he was a good enough guide to fill in, for he was strong and willing and took orders amiably from anybody and did his routine of work, such as chopping wood and filling lamps and bringing water and carrying boats, with entire efficiency. That he had no initiative at all and by no chance did anything he was not told to, even when most obvious, that he was lacking in any characteristic of interest, that he was moreover a supreme coward, afraid to be left alone in the woods—these things were after all immaterial, for, as John pointed out, we didn't really need to love our guides.

John also pointed out that the Lizzie—his name was, incidentally, Aristophe—had one nice quality. Of course, it was a quality which appealed most to the beneficiary, yet it seemed well to me also to have my guests surrounded with mercy and loving kindness. John had but to suggest building a fire or greasing his boots or carrying a canoe over any portage to any lake, and the Lizzie at once leaped with a bright smile as who should say that this was indeed a pleasure. "C'est bien, M'sieur," was his formula. He would gaze at John for sections of an hour, with his flabby mouth open in speechless surprise as if at the unbelievable glory and magnificence of M'sieur. A nice lad, John Dudley was, but no subtle enchanter; a stocky and well-set-up young man with a whole-souled, garrulous and breezy way, and a gift of slang and a brilliant grin. What called forth hero-worship towards him I never understood; but no more had I understood why Mildred Thornton, Colonel Thornton's young sister, my very beautiful cousin, should have selected him, from a large assortment of suitors, to marry. Indeed I did not entirely understand why I liked having John in camp better than anyone else; probably it was essentially the same charm which impelled Mildred to want to live with him, and the Tin Lizzie to fall down and worship. In any case the Lizzie worshipped with a primitive and unashamed and enduring adoration, which stood even the test of fear. That was the supreme test for the Tin Lizzie, who was a coward of cowards. Rather cruelly I bet John on a day that his satellite did not love him enough to go out to the club-house alone for him, and the next day John was in sore need of tobacco, not to be got nearer than the club.

"Aristophe will go out and get it for me," he announced as Aristophe—the Lizzie—trotted about the table at lunch-time purveying us flapjacks.

The Tin Lizzie stood rooted a second, petrified at the revolutionary scheme of his going to the club, companions unmentioned. There one saw as if through glass an idea seeking a road through his smooth gray matter. One had always gone to the club with Josef, or Maxime or Pierre—certainly M'sieur meant that; one would of course be glad to go—with Josef or Maxime or Pierre—to get tobacco for M'sieur John. Of course, the idea slid through the old road in the almost unwrinkled gray matter, and came safely to headquarters.

"C'est bien, M'sieur," answered the Lizzie smiling brightly.

And with that I knocked the silly little smile into a cocked hat. "You may start early tomorrow, Aristophe," I said, "and get back by dark, going light, I can't spare any other men to go with you. But you will certainly not mind going alone—to get tobacco for M'sieur John."

The poor Tin Lizzie turned red and then white, and his weak mouth fell open and his eyebrows lifted till the whites of his eyes showed above the gray irises. And one saw again, through the crystal of his unexercised brain, the operation of a painful and new thought. M'sieur John—a day alone in the woods—love, versus fear—which would win. John and I watched the struggle a bit mercilessly. A grown man gets small sympathy for being a coward. And yet few forms of suffering are keener. We watched; and the Tin Lizzie stood and gasped in the play of his emotions. Nobody had ever given this son of the soil ideals to hold to through sudden danger; no sense of inherited honor to be guarded came to help the Lizzie; he had been taught to work hard and save his skin—little else. The great adoration for John which had swept him off his commonplace feet—was it going to make good against life-long selfish caution? We wondered. It was curious to watch the new big feeling fight the long-established petty one. And it was with a glow of triumph quite out of drawing that we saw the generous instinct win the battle.

"Oui, M'sieur," spoke Aristophe, unconscious of subtleties or watching. "I go tomorrow—alone. *C'est bien, M'sieur*."

It was about the only remark I ever heard him make, that gracious: "*C'est bien, M'sieur!*" But he made it remarkably well. Almost he persuaded me to respect him with that hearty response to the call of duty, that humble and high gift of graciousness. One remembers him as his dolly face lighted at John's order to go and clean trout or carry in logs, and one does not forget the absurd, queer little fast trot at which his powerful young legs would instantaneously swing off to obey the behest. Such was the Tin Lizzie, the guide who paddled bow in my canvas canoe on the day of the celebrated frog hunt.

That the frog hunt was celebrated was owing to the Lizzie. He should have been in John's boat, as one of John's guides, but at the last moment, there was a confusion of tongues and Lizzie was shipped aboard my canoe. In the excitement of the chase Josef, stern man, had faced about to manipulate his landing-net; Aristophe also slewed around and, sitting on the gunwale, became stern paddler. I was in the middle screwed anyhow, watching the frog fishing and enjoying the enjoyment of the men. Poor chaps, it was the only bit of personal play they got out of our month of play. Aristophe, the Tin Lizzie, was quite mad with the excitement even from his very second fiddle standpoint of paddler to Josef's frogging. His enormous gray eyes snapped, his teeth showed white and gold around his pipe—which he nearly bit off— and he even used language.

"*Tiens! Encore un!*" hissed the Lizzie in a blood-curdling whisper as a new pair of pop eyes lifted from the edge of a rotten log.

And Josef, who had always seen the frog first, fired a guttural sentence, full of contempt, full of friendliness, for he sized up the Lizzie, his virtues and his limitations, accurately. And then the boat was pushed and pulled in the shallow water till Josef and the net were within range. With, that came the slow approach of the net to the smile, the swift tap on the eatable legs, and headlong into his finish leaped M. Crapaud. Which is rot his correct name, Josef tells me, in these parts, but M. Guarron. And that, being translated, means Mr. Very-Big-Bull-Frog.

Business had prospered to fourteen or fifteen head of frogs, and we calculated that the other boat might have a dozen when, facing towards Aristophe, I saw his dull, fresh face suddenly change. My pulse missed a beat at that expression. It was adequate to an earthquake or sudden death. How the fatuous doll-like features could have been made to register that stare of a soul in horror I can't guess. But they did. The whites of his eyes showed an eighth of an inch above the irises and his black eyebrows were shot up to the roots of his glossy black hair. In the gleaming white and gold of his teeth the pipe was still gripped. And while I gazed, astonished, his unfitting deep voice issued from that mask of fear:

"*Tiens! Encore un!*" And I screwed about and saw that the Lizzie was running the boat on top of an enormous frog which he had not spied till the last second. With that Josef exploded throaty language and leaning sidewise made a dive at the frog. Aristophe, unbalanced with emotion and Josef's swift movement shot from his poise at the end of the little craft, and landed, in a foot of water, flat on his buck, and the frog seized that second to jump on his stomach.

I never heard an Indian really laugh before that day. The hills resounded with Josef's shouts. We laughed, Josef and I, till we were weak, and for a good minute Aristophe sprawled in the lake, with the frog anchored as if till Kingdom come on his middle, and howled lusty howls while we laughed. Then Josef fished the frog and got him off the Tin Lizzie's lungs. And Aristophe, weeping, scrambled into the boat. And as we went home in the cool forest twilight, up the portage by the rushing, noisy rapids, Josef, walking before us, carrying the landing-net full of frogs' legs, shook with laughter every little while again, as Aristophe, his wet strong young legs, the only section of him showing, toiled ahead up the winding thread of a trail, carrying the inverted canoe on his head.

It was this adventure which came to me and seized me and carried me a thousand miles northward into Canadian forest as I looked at the frogs' legs on my plate at the Cosmic Club, and did not listen to my cousin, the Colonel, talking military tactics.

The mental review took an eighth of the time it has taken me to tell it. But as I shook off my dream of the woods, I realized that, while Thornton still talked, he had got out of his uninteresting rut into his interesting one. Without hearing what he said I knew that from the look of the men's faces. Each man's eyes were bright, through a manner of mistiness, and there was a sudden silence which was perhaps what had recalled me.

"It's a war which is making a new standard of courage," spoke the young Governor in the gentle tone which goes so oddly and so pleasantly with his bull-dog jaw. "It looks as if we were going to be left with a world where heroism is the normal thing," spoke the Governor.

"Heroism—yes," said Bobby, and I knew with satisfaction that he was off on his own line, the line he does not fancy, the line where few can distance him. "Heroism!"

repeated Bobby, "It's all around out there. And it crops out—" he begun to smile—"in unsuspected places, from varied impulses."

He was working his way to an anecdote. The men at the table, their chairs twisted towards him, sat very still.

"What I mean to say is," Bobby began, "that this war, horrible as it is, is making over human, nature for the better. It's burning out selfishness and cowardice and a lot of faults from millions of men, and it's holding up the nobility of what some of them do to the entire world. It takes a character, this débâcle, and smashes out the littleness. Another thing is curious. If a small character has one good point on which to hang heroism, the battle-spirit searches out that point and plants on it the heroism. There was a stupid young private in my command who—but I'm afraid I'm telling too many war stories," Bobby appealed, interrupting himself. "I'm full of it, you see, and when people are so good, and listen—" He stopped, in a confusion which is not his least attractive manner.

From down the table came a quick murmur of voices. I saw more than one glance halt at the crutch on the back of the soldier's chair.

"Thank you. I'd really like to tell about this man. It's interesting, psychologically to me," he went on, smiling contentedly. He is a lovable chap, my cousin Robert Thornton. "The lad whom I speak of, a French-Canadian from Quebec Province, was my servant, my batman, as the Indian army called them and as we refer to them often now. He was so brainless that I just missed firing him the first day I had him. But John Dudley, my brother-in-law and lieutenant, wanted me to give him a chance, and also there was something in his manner when I gave him orders which attracted me. He appeared to have a pleasure in serving, and an ideal of duty. Dudley had used him as a guide, and the man had a dog-like devotion to 'the lieutenant' which counted with me. Also he didn't talk. I think he knew only four words. I flung orders at him and there would be first a shock of excitement, then a second of tense anxiety, then a radiant smile and the four words: '*C'est bien, Mon Capitaine*.' I was captain then."

At that point I dropped my knife and fork and stared at my cousin. He went on.

"'*C'est bien, Mon Capitaine*.' That was the slogan. And when the process was accomplished, off he would trot, eager to do my will. He was powerful and well-built, but he had the oddest manner of locomotion ever I saw, a trot like—like a Ford car. I discovered pretty soon that the poor wretch was a born coward. I've seen him start at the distant sound of guns long before we got near the front, and he was nervous at going out alone at night about the camp. The men ragged him, but he was such a friendly rascal and so willing to take over others' work that he got along with a fraction of the persecution most of his sort would have had. I wondered sometimes what would happen to the poor little devil when actual fighting came. Would it be '*C'est bien, Mon Capitaine*,' at the order to go over the top, or would the terrible force of fear be too much for him and land him at last with his back to a wall and a firing squad in front—a deserter? Meantime he improved and I got dependent on his radiant good will. Being John Dudley's brother-in-law sanctified me with him, and nothing was too much trouble if I'd give him a chance sometimes to clean John's boots. I have a man now who shows no ecstacy at being ordered to do my jobs, and I don't like him.

"We were moved up towards the front, and, though Mr. Winston Churchill has made a row about the O.S.—the officers' servants who are removed from the firing line, I know that a large proportion of them do their share in the trenches. I saw to it that mine did.

"One night there was a digging expedition. An advance trench was to be made in No Man's Land about a hundred and fifty yards from the Germans. I was in command of the covering party of thirty-five men; I was a captain. We, of course, went out ahead. Beauramé was in the party. It was his first fighting. We had rifles, with bayonets, and bombs, and a couple of Lewis guns. We came up to the trenches by a road, then went into the zigzag communication trenches up to the front, the fire-trench. Then, very cautiously, over the top into No Man's Land. It was nervous work, for at any second they might discover us and open fire. It suited us all to be as quiet as human men could be, and when once in a while a star-shell, a Very light, was sent up from the German lines we froze in our tracks till the white glare died out.

"The party had been digging for perhaps an hour when hell broke loose. They'd seen us. All about was a storm of machine-gun and rifle bullets, and we dropped on our faces, the diggers in their trench—pretty shallow it was. As for the covering party, we simply took our medicine. And then the shrapnel joined the music. Word was passed to get back to the trenches, and we started promptly. We stooped low as we ran over No Man's Land, but there were plenty of casualties. I got mine in the foot, but not the wound which rung in this—" Thornton nodded his head at the crutches with a smile. "It was from a bit of shrapnel just as I made the trench, and as I fell in I caught at the sand bags and whirled about facing out over No Man's Land; as I whirled I saw, close by, Beauramé's face in a shaft of light. I don't know why I made conversation at that moment—I did. I said:

"When did you get back?"

And his answer came as if clicked on a typewriter. "Me, I stayed, *Mon Capitaine*. It had an air too dangerous, out there."

I stared in a white rage. You'll imagine—one of my men to dare tell me that! And at that second, simultaneously, came the flare of a shell star and a shout of a man struck down, and I knew the voice—John Dudley. He was out there, the tail end of the party, wounded. I saw him as he fell, on the farther side of the new trench. Of course, one's instinct was to dash back and bring him in, and I started. And I found my foot gone—I couldn't walk. Quicker than I can tell it I turned to Beauramé, the coward, who'd been afraid to go over the top, and I said in French, because, though I hadn't time to think it out, I yet realized that it would get to him faster so—I said:

"Get over there, you deserter. Save the lieutenant—Lieutenant Dudley. Go."

For one instant I thought it was no good and I was due to have him shot, if we both lived through the night. And then—I never in my life saw such a face of abject fear as the one he turned first to me and then across that horror of No Man's Land. The whites of his eyes showed, it seemed, an eighth of an inch above the irises; his black eyebrows were half way up his forehead, and his teeth, luxuriously upholstered with fillings, shone white and gold in the unearthly light. It was such a mad terror as I'd never seen before, and never since. And into it I, mad too with the thought of my sister if I let young John Dudley die before my eyes—I bombed again the order to go out and bring in Dudley. I remember the fading and coming expressions on that Frenchman's face like the changes on a moving picture film. I suppose it was half a minute. And here was the coward face gazing into mine, transfigured into the face of a man who cared about another man more than himself—a common man whose one high quality was love.

"*C'est bien, Mon Capitaine,*" Beauramé spoke, through still clicking teeth, and with his regulation smile of good will he had sprung over the parapet in one lithe movement, and I saw him crouching, trotting that absurd, powerful fast trot through the lane in our barbed wire, like lightning, to the shallow new trench, to Dudley. I saw him—for the Germans had the stretch lighted—I saw the man pick up my brother-in-law and toss him over his shoulders and start trotting back. Then I saw him fall, both of them fall, and I knew that he'd stopped a bullet. And then, as I groaned, somehow Beauramé was on his feet again. I expected, that he'd bolt for cover, but he didn't. He bent over deliberately as if he had been a fearless hero—and maybe he was—and he picked up Dudley again and started on, laboring, this time in walking. He was hit badly. But he made the trench; he brought in Dudley.

Then such a howl of hurrahs greeted him from the men who watched the rescue as poor little Aristophe Beauramé—"

"Ah!" I interjected, and Bobby turned and stared—"as the poor little scared rat had not dreamed, or had any right to dream would ever greet his conduct on earth. He dropped Dudley at my feet and turned with his flabby mouth open and his great stupid eyes like saucers, towards the men who rushed to shake his hand and throw at him words of admiration that choked them to get out. And then he keeled over. So you see. It was an equal chance at one second, whether a man should be shot for a deserter or—win the Victoria Cross."

"What!" I shouted at my guest. "What! Not the Victoria Cross! Not Aristophe!"

Bobby looked at me in surprise. "You're a great claque for me," he said. "You seem to take an interest in my hero. Yes, he got it. He was badly hurt. One hand nearly gone and a wound in his side. I was lucky enough to be in London on a day three months later, and to be present at the ceremony, when the young French-Canadian, spoiled for a soldier, but splendid stuff now for a hero, stood out in the open before the troops in front of Buckingham Palace and King George pinned the V.C. on his breast. They say that he's back in his village, and the whole show. I hear that he tells over and over the story of his heroism and the rescue of '*Mon Lieutenant.*' to never failing audiences. Of course, John is looking after him, for the hand which John saved was the hand that was shot to pieces in saving John, and the Tin Lizzie can never make his living with that hand again. A deserter, a coward—decorated by the King with the Victoria Cross! Queer things happen in war!" There was a stir, a murmur as of voices, of questions beginning, but Bobby was not quite through.

"War takes the best of the best men, and the best of the cheapest, and transfigures both. War doesn't need heroes for heroism. She pins it on anywhere if there's one spot of greatness in a character. War does strange things with humanity," said Bobby.

And I, gasping, broke out crudely in three words: "Our Tin Lizzie!" I said, and nobody knew in the least what I meant, or with what memories I said it.

# HE THAT LOSETH HIS LIFE SHALL FIND IT

The Red Cross women had gone home. Half an hour before, the large library had been filled with white-clad, white-veiled figures. Two long tables full, forty of them today, had been working; three thousand surgical dressings had been cut and folded and put away in large boxes on shelves behind glass doors where the most valuable books had held their stately existence for years. The books were stowed now in trunks in the attic. These were war days; luxuries such as first editions must wait their time. The great living-room itself, the center of home for this family since the two boys were born and ever this family had been, the dear big room with its dark carved oak, and tapestries, and stained glass, and books, and memories was given over now to war relief work.

Sometimes, as the mistress walked into the spacious, low-ceilinged, bright place, presences long past seemed to fill it intolerably. Brock and Hugh, little chaps, roared in untidy and tumultuous from football, or came, decorous and groomed, handsome, smart little lads, to be presented to guests. Her own Hugh, her husband, proud of the beautiful new house, smiled from the hearth to her as he had smiled twenty-six years back, the night they came in, a young Hugh, younger than Brock was now. Her father and mother, long gone over "to the majority," and the exquisite old ivory beauty of a beautiful grandmother—such ghosts rose and faced the woman as she stepped into the room where they had moved in life, the room with its loveliness marred by two long tables covered with green oilcloth, by four rows of cheap chairs, by rows and rows of boxes on shelves where soft and bright and dark colors of books had glowed. She felt often that she should explain matters to the room, should tell the walls which had sheltered peace and hospitality that she had consecrated them to yet higher service. Never for one instant, while her soul ached for the familiar setting, had she regretted its sacrifice. That her soul did ache made it worth while.

And the women gathered for this branch Red Cross organization, her neighbors on the edge of the great city, wives and daughters and mothers of clerks, and delivery-wagon drivers, and icemen, and night-watchmen, women who had not known how to take their part in the war work in the city or had found it too far to go, these came to her house gladly and all found pleasure in her beautiful room. That made it a joy to give it up to them. She stood in the doorway, feeling an emphasis in the quiet of the July afternoon because of the forty voices which had lately gone out of the sunshiny silence, of the forty busy figures in long, white aprons and white, sweeping veils, the tiny red cross gleaming over the forehead of each one, each face lovely in the uniform of service, all oddly equalized and alike under their veils and crosses. She spoke aloud as she tossed out her hands to the room:

"War will be over some day, and you will be our own again, but forever holy because of this. You will be a room of history when you go to Brock—"

Brock! Would Brock ever come home to the room, to this place which he loved? Brock, in France! She turned sharply and went out through the long hall and across the terrace, and sat down where the steps dropped to the garden, on the broad top step, with her head against the pillar of the balustrade. Above her the smell of box in a stone vase on the pillar punctured the mild air with its definite, reminiscent fragrance. Box is a plant of antecedents of sentiment, of memories. The woman inhaling its delicate sharpness, was caught back into days past. She considered, in rapid jumps of thought, events, episodes, epochs. The day Brock was born, on her own twentieth birthday, up-stairs where the rosy chintz curtains blew now out of the window; the first day she had come down to the terrace—it was June—and the baby lay in his bassinet by the balustrade in that spot—she looked at the spot—the baby, her big Brock, a bundle of flannel and fine, white stuff in lacy frills of the bassinet. And she loved him; she remembered how she had loved that baby, how, laughing at herself, she had whispered silly words over the stolid, pink head; how the girl's heart of her had all but burst with the astonishing new tide of a feeling which seemed the greatest of which she was capable. Yet it was a small thing to the way she loved Brock now. A vision came of little Hugh, three years younger, and the two toddling about the terrace together, Hugh always Brock's satellite and adorer, as was fitting; less sturdy, less daring than Brock, yet ready to go anywhere if only the older baby led. She thought of the day when Hugh, four years old, had taken fright at a black log among the bushes under the trees.

"It's a bear!" little Hugh had whispered, shaking, and Brock, brave but not too certain, had looked at her, inquiring.

"No, love, it's not a bear; it's an old log of wood. Go and put your hand on it, Hughie."

Little Hugh had cried out and shrunk back. "I'm afraid!" cried little Hugh.

And Brock, not entirely clear as to the no-bear theory, had yet bluffed manfully. "Come on, Hughie; let's go and bang 'um," said Brock.

Which invitation Hugh accepted reluctantly with a condition, "If you'll hold my hand, B'ocky."

The woman turned her head to see the place where the black log had lain, there in the old high bushes. And behold! Two strong little figures in white marched along— she could all but see them today—and the bigger little figure was dragging the other a bit, holding a hand with masterful grip. She could hear little Hugh's laughter as they arrived at the terrible log and found it truly a log. Even now Hugh's laugh was music.

"Why, it's nuffin but an old log o' wood!" little Hugh had squealed, as brave as a lion.

As she sat seeing visions, old Mavourneen, Brock's Irish wolf-hound, came and laid her muzzle on the woman's shoulder, crying a bit, as was Mavourneen's Irish way, for pleasure at finding the mistress. And with that there was a brown ripple and a patter of many soft feet, and a broken wave of dogs came around the corner, seven little cairn-terriers. Sticky and Sandy and their offspring. The woman let Sticky settle in her lap and drew Sandy under her arm, and the puppies looked up at her from the step below with ten serious, anxious eyes and then fell to chasing quite imaginary game up and down the stone steps. Mavourneen sighed deeply and dropped with a heavy thud, a great paw on the edge of the white dress and her beautiful head resting on her paws, the topaz, watchful eyes gazing over the city. The woman put her free hand back and touched the rough head.

"Dear dog!" she spoke.

Another memory came: how they had bought Mavourneen, she and Hugh and the boys, at the kennels in Ireland, eight years ago; how the huge baby had been sent to them at Liverpool in a hamper; the uproarious drive the four of them—Hugh, the two boys, and herself—and Mavourneen had taken in a taxi across the city. The puppy, astonished and investigating throughout the whole proceeding, had mounted all of them, separately and together, and insisted on lying in big Hugh's lap, crying broken-heartedly at not being allowed. How they had shouted laughter, the four and the boy taxi-driver, all the journey, till they ached! What good times they had always had together, the young father and mother and the two big sons! She reflected how she had not been at all the conventional mother of sons. She had not been satisfied to be gentle and benevolent and look after their clothes and morals. She had lived their lives with them, she had ridden and gone swimming with them, and played tennis and golf, and fished and shot and skated and walked with them, yes, and studied and read with them, all their lives.

"I haven't any respect for my mother," young Hugh told her one day. "I like her like a sister."

She was deeply pleased at this attitude; she did not wish their respect as a visible quality. Vision after vision came of the old times and care-free days while the four, as happy and normal a family as lived in the world, passed their alert, full days together before the war. Memory after memory took form in the brain of the woman, the center of that light-hearted life so lately changed, so entirely now a memory. War had come.

At first, in 1914, there had been excitement, astonishment. Then the horror of Belgium. One refused to believe that at first; it was a lurid slander on the kindly German people; then one believed with the brain; one's spirit could not grasp it. Unspeakable deeds such as the Germans' deeds—it was like a statement made concerning a fourth dimension of space; civilized modern folk were not so organized as to realize the facts of that bestiality.

"Aren't you thankful we're Americans?" the woman had said over and over.

One day her husband, answering usually with a shake of the head, answered in words. "We may be in it yet," he said. "I'm not sure but we ought to be."

Brock, twenty-one then, had flashed at her: "I want to be in it. I may just have to be, mother."

Young Hugh yawned a bit at that, and stretching his long arm, he patted his brother's shoulder. "Good old hero, Brock! I'll beat you a set of tennis. Come on."

That sudden speech of Brock's had startled her, had brought the war, in a jump which was like a stab, close. The war and Lindow—their place—how was it possible that this nightmare in Europe could touch the peace of the garden, the sunlit view of the river, the trees with birds singing in them, the scampering of the dogs down the drive? The distant hint of any connection between the great horror and her own was pain; she put the thought away.

Then the *Lusitania* was sunk. All America shouted shame through sobs of rage. The President wrote a beautiful and entirely satisfactory note.

"It should be war—war. It should be war today," Hugh had said, her husband. "We only waste time. We'll have to fight sooner or later. The sooner we begin, the sooner we'll finish."

"Fight!" young Hugh threw at him. "What with? We can just about make faces at 'em, father."

The boy's father did not laugh. "We had better get ready to do more than make faces; we've got to get ready." He hammered his hand on the stone balustrade. "I'm going to Plattsburg this summer, Evelyn."

"I'm going with you." Brock's voice was low and his mouth set, and the woman, looking at him, saw suddenly that her boy was a man.

"Well, then, as man power is getting low at Lindow, I'll stay and take care of Mummy. Won't I? We'll do awfully well without them, won't we, Mum? You can drive Dad's Rolls-Royce roadster, and if you leave on the handbrake up-hill, I'll never tell."

Father and son had gone off for the month in camp, and, glad as she was to have the younger boy with her, there was yet an uneasy, an almost subconscious feeling about him, which she indignantly denied each time that it raised its head. It never quite phrased itself, this fear, this wonder if Hugh were altogether as American as his father and brother. Question the courage and patriotism of her own boy? She flung the thought from her as again and yet again it came. People of the same blood were widely different. To Brock and his father it had come easily to do the obvious thing, to go to Plattsburg. It had not so come to young Hugh, but that in good time he would see his duty and do it she would not for an instant doubt. She would not break faith with the lad in thought. With a perfect delicacy she avoided any word that would influence him. He knew. All his life he had breathed loyalty. It was she herself, reading to them night after night through years, who had taught the boys hero worship—above all, worship of American heroes, Washington, Paul Jones, Perry, Farragut, Lee; how Dewey had said, "You may fire now, Gridley, if you are ready"; how Clark had brought the *Oregon* around the continent; how Scott had gone alone among angry Indians. She had taught them such names, names which will not die while America lives. It was she who had told the little lads, listening wide-eyed, that as these men had held life lightly for the glory of America, so her sons, if need came, must be ready to offer their lives for their country. She remembered how Brock, his round face suddenly scarlet, had stammered out:

"I *am* ready, Mummy. I'd die this minute for—for America. Wouldn't you, Hughie?"

And young Hugh, a slim, blond angel of a boy, of curly, golden hair and unexpected answers, had ducked beneath the hero, upsetting him into a hedge to his infinite anger. "I wouldn't die right now, Brocky," said Hugh. "There's going to be chocolate cake for lunch."

One could never count on Hugh's ways of doing things, but Brock was a stone wall of reliability. She smiled, thinking of his youth and beauty and entire boyishness, to think yet of the saying from the Bible which always suggested Brock, "Thou shalt keep him in perfect peace whose mind is stayed on Thee." It was so with the lad; through the gay heart and eager interest in life pulsed an atmosphere of deep religiousness. He was always "in perfect peace," and his mother, less balanced, had stayed her mind on that quiet and right young mind from its very babyhood. The lad had seen his responsibilities and lifted them all his life. It came to her how, when her own mother, very dear to Brock, had died, she had not let the lads go with her to the house of death for fear of saddening their youth, and how, when she and their father came home from the hard, terrible business of the funeral, they met little Hugh on the drive, rapturous at seeing them again, rather absorbed in his new dog. But Brock, then fourteen, was in the house alone, quiet, his fresh, dear face red with tears, and a black necktie of his father's, too large for him, tied under his collar. Of all the memories of her boys, that grotesque black tie was the most poignant and most precious. It said much. It said: "I also, O, my mother, am of my people. I have a right to their sorrows as well as to their joys, and if you do not give me my place in trouble, I shall do what I can alone, being but a boy. I shall give up play, and I shall wear mourning as I can, not knowing how very well, but pushed by all my being to be with my own in their mourning."

Quickly affection for the other lad asserted itself. Brock and Hugh were different, but Hugh was a dear boy, too—undeveloped, that was all. He had never taken life seriously, little Hugh, and now that this war-cloud hung over the world, he simply refused to look at it; he turned away his face. That was all, a temperament which loved harmony and shrank from ugliness; these things were young Hugh's limitations, and no ignoble quality.

In a long dream, yet much faster than the words have told it, in comprehensive flashes of memory, her elbows on her knees and her face, in her slender hands, looking out over the garden with its arched way of roses, with its high hedge, looking past the loveliness that was home to the city pulsing in summer heat, to the shining zigzag of river beyond the city, the woman reviewed her boys' lives. Boys were not now merely one phase of humanity; they had suddenly become the nation. They stood in the foreground of a world crisis; back of them America was ranged, orderly, living and moving to feed, clothe, and keep happy these millions of lads holding in their hands the fate of the earth. Her boys were but two, yet necessary. She owed them to the country, as other mothers of men.

There was a whistle under the archway, a flying step, and young Hugh shot from beneath the rosiness of Dorothy Perkins vines and took the stone steps in four bounds. All the dogs fell into a community chorus of barks and whines and patterings about, and Hugh's hands were on this one and that as he bent over the woman.

"A *good* kiss, Mummy; that's cold baked potato," he complained, and she laughed and hugged him.

"Not cold; I was just thinking. Your knee, Hughie? You came up like a bird."

Hugh made a face. "Bad break, that," he grinned, and limped across the terrace and back. "Mummy, it doesn't hurt much now, and I do forget," he explained, and his color deepened. With that: "Tom Arthur is waiting for me in town. We're going to pick up Whitney, the tennis champion, at the Crossroads Club. May I take Dad's roadster?"

"Yes, Hughie. And, Hugh, meet the train, the seven-five. Dad's coming to-night, you know."

The boy took her hand, looked at her uneasily. "Mummy, dear, don't be thinking sinful thoughts about me. And don't let Dad. Hold your fire, Mummy."

She lifted her face, and her eyes were the eyes of faith he had known all his life. "You blessed boy of mine, I will hold my fire." And then Hugh had all but knocked her over with a violent kiss again, and he slammed happily through the screen doors and was leaping up the stairs. Ten minutes later she heard the car purring down the drive.

The dogs settled about her with long dog-sighs again. She looked at her wrist—only five-thirty. She went back with a new unrest to her thoughts. Hugh's knee—it was odd; it had lasted a long time, ever since—she shuddered a bit, so that old Mavourneen lifted her head and objected softly—ever since war was declared. Over a year! To be sure, he had hurt it again badly, slipping on the ice in December, just as it was getting strong. She wished that his father would not be so grim when Hugh's bad knee was mentioned. What did he mean? Did he dare to think her boy—the word was difficult even mentally—a slacker? With that her mind raced back to the days just before Hugh had hurt this knee. It was in February that Germany had proclaimed the oceans closed except along German paths, at German times. "This is war at last," her husband had said, and she knew the inevitable had come.

Night after night she had lain awake facing it, sometimes breaking down utterly and shaking her soul out in sobs, sometimes trying to see ways around the horror, trying to believe that war must end before our troops could get ready, often with higher courage glorying that she might give so much for country and humanity. Then, in the nights, things that she had read far back, unrealizing, rose and confronted her with awful reality. Brutalities, atrocities, wounds, barbarous captivity—nightmares which the Germans had dug out of the grave of savagery and sent stalking over the earth—such rose and stood before the woman lying awake night after night. At first her soul hid its face in terror at the gruesome thoughts; at first her mind turned and fled and refused to believe. Her boys, Brock and Hugh! It was not credible, it was not reasonable, it was out of drawing that her good boys, her precious boys trained to be happy and help the world, to live useful, peaceful lives, should be snatched from home, here in America, and pitched into the ghastly struggle of Europe. Push back the ocean as she might, the ocean surged every day nearer.

Daytimes she was as brave as the best. She could say: "If we had done it the day after the *Lusitania*, that would have been right. It would have been all over now." She could say: "My boys? They will do their duty like other women's boys." But nights, when she crept into bed and the things she had read of Belgium, of Serbia, came and stood about her, she knew that hers were the only boys in the world who could not, *could* not be spared. Brock and Hugh! It seemed as if it would be apparent to the dullest that Brock and Hugh were different from all others. She could suffer; she could have gone over there light-hearted and faced any danger to save *them*. Of course! That was natural! But—Brock and Hugh! The little heads that had lain in the hollow of her arm; the noisy little boys who had muddied their white clothes, and broken furniture, and spilled ink; the tall, beautiful lads who had been her pride and her everlasting joy, her playmates, her lovers—Brock and Hugh! Why, there had never been on earth love and friendship in any family close and unfailing like that of the four.

Night after night, nearer and nearer, the ghosts from Belgium and Serbia and Poland stood about her bed, and she fought with them as one had fought with the beasts at Ephesus. Day after day she cheered Brock and the two Hughs and filled them with fresh patriotism. Of course, she would not have her own fail in a hair's breadth of eager service to their flag. Of course! And as she lifted up, for their sakes, her heart, behold a miracle, for her heart grew high! She began to feel the words she said. It came to her in very truth that to have the world as one wanted it was not now the point; the point was a greater goal which she had never in her happy life even visualized. It began to rise before her, a distant picture glorious through a mist of suffering, something built of the sacrifice, and the honor, and the deathless bravery of millions of soldiers in battle, of millions of mothers at home. The education of a nation to higher ideals was reaching the quiet backwater of this one woman's soul. There were lovelier things than life; there were harder things than death. Service is the measure of living. If the boys were to compress years of good living into a flame of serving humanity for six months, who was she, what was life here, that she should be reluctant? To play the game, for herself and her sons, this was the one thing worth while. More and more entirely, as the stress of the strange, hard vision crowded out selfishness, this woman, as thousands and tens of thousands all over America, lifted up her heart—the dear things that filled and were her heart—unto the Lord.

And with that she was aware of a recurring unrest. She was aware that there was something her husband did not say to her about the boys, about young Hugh. Brock had been hard to hold for nearly two years now, but his father had thought for reasons, that he should not serve until his own flag called him. Now it would soon be calling, and Brock would go instantly. But young Hugh? What did the boy's attitude mean?

"I can't make out Hughie," his father had said to her in March, 1917, when it was certain that war was coming. "What does this devil-may-care pose about the war mean?"

And she answered: "Let Hughie work it out, Hugh. He's in trouble in his mind, but he'll come through. We'll give him time."

"Oh, very well," Hugh the elder had agreed, "but young Americans will have to take their stand shortly. I couldn't bear it if a son of mine were a slacker."

She tossed out her hands. "Slacker! Don't dare say it of my boy!"

The hideous word followed her. That night, when she lay in bed and looked out into the moonlit wood, and saw the pines swaying like giant fans across a pulsing, pale sky, and listened to the summer wind blowing through the tall heads of them, again through the peace of it the word stabbed. A slacker! She set to work to fancy how it would be if Brock and Hugh both went to war and were both killed. She faced the thought. Life—years of it—without Brock and Hugh! She registered that steadily in her mind. Then she painted to herself another picture, Brock and Hugh not going to war, at home ignominiously safe. Other women's sons marching out into the danger—men, heroes! Brock and Hugh explaining, steadily explaining why they had not gone! Brock and Hugh after the war, mature men, meeting returning soldiers, old friends who had borne the burden and heat, themselves with no memories of hideous, infinitely precious days, of hardships, and squalid trench life, and deadly pain—for America! Brock and Hugh going on through life into old age ashamed to hold up their heads and look their comrades in the eye! Or else—it might be—Brock and Hugh lying next year, this year, in unknown, honored graves in France! Which was worse? And the aching heart of the woman did not wait to answer. Better a thousand times brave death than a coward's life. She would choose so if she knew certainly that she sent them both to death. The education of the war, the new glory of patriotism, had already gone far in this one woman.

And then the thought stabbed again—a slacker—Hugh! How did his father dare say it? A poisonous terror, colder than the fear of death, crawled into her soul and hid there. Was it possible that Hugh, brilliant, buoyant, temperamental Hugh was—that? The days went on, and the cold, vile thing stayed coiled in her soul. It was on the very day war was declared that young Hugh injured his knee, a bad injury. When he was carried home, when the doctor cut away his clothes and bent over the swollen leg and said wise things about the "bursa," the boy's eyes were hard to meet. They constantly sought hers with a look questioning and anxious. Words were impossible, but she tried to make her glance and manner say: "I trust you. Not for worlds would I believe you did it on purpose."

And finally the lad caught her hand and with his mouth against it spoke. "*You* know I didn't do it on purpose, Mummy."

And the cold horror fled out of her heart, and a great relief flooded her.

On a day after that Brock came home from camp, and, though he might not tell it in words, she knew that he would sail shortly for France. She kept the house full of brightness and movement for the three days he had at home, yet the four—young Hugh on crutches now—clung to each other, and on the last afternoon she and Brock were alone for an hour. They had sat just here after tennis, in the hazy October weather, and pink-brown leaves had floated down with a thin, pungent fragrance and lay on the stone steps in vague patterns. Scarlet geraniums bloomed back of Brock's head and made a satisfying harmony with the copper of his tanned face. They fell to silence after much talking, and finally she got out something which had been in her mind but which it had been hard to say.

"Brocky," she began, and jabbed the end of her racket into her foot so that it hurt, because physical pain will distract and steady a mind. "Brocky, I want to ask you to do something."

"Yes'm," answered Brock.

"It's this. Of course, I know you're going soon, over there."

Brock looked at her gravely.

"Yes, I know, I want to ask you if—if *it* happens—will you come and tell me yourself? If it's allowed."

Brock did not even touch her hand; he knew well she could not bear it. He answered quietly, with a sweet, commonplace manner as if that other world to which he might be going was a place too familiar in his thoughts for any great strain in speaking of it. "Yes, Mummy," he said. "Of course I will. I'd have wanted to anyway, even if you hadn't said it. It seems to me—" He lifted his young face, square-jawed, fresh-colored, and there was a vision-seeing look in his eyes which his mother had known at times before. He looked across the city lying at their feet, and the river, and the blue hills beyond, and he spoke slowly, as if shaping a thought. "So many fellows have 'gone west' lately that there must he some way. It seems as if all that mass of love and—and desire to reach back and touch—the ones left—as if all that must have built a sort of bridge over the river—so that a fellow might probably come back and—and tell his mother—"

Brock's voice stopped, and suddenly she was in his arms, his face was against hers, and hot tears not her own were on her cheek. Then he was shaking his head as if to shake off the strong emotion.

"It's not likely to happen, dear. The casualties in this war are tremendously lower than in—"

"I know," she interrupted. "Of course, they are. Of course, you're coming home without a scratch, and likely a general, and conceited beyond words. How will we stand you!"

Brock laughed delightedly. "You're a peach," he stated. "That's the sort. Laughing mothers to send us off—it makes a whale of a difference."

That October afternoon had now dropped eight months back, and still the house seemed lost without Brock, especially on this June twentieth, the day that was his and hers, the day when there had always been "doings" second only to Christmas at Lindow. But she gathered up her courage like a woman. Hugh the elder was coming tonight from his dollar-a-year work in Washington, her man who had moved heaven and earth to get into active service, and who, when finally refused because of his forty-nine years and a defective eye, had left his great business as if it were a joke, and had put his whole time, and strength, and experience, and fortune at the service of the Government—as plenty of other American men were doing. Hugh was coming in time for her birthday dinner, and young Hugh was with them—Her heart shrank as if a sharp thing touched it. How would it be when they rose to drink Brock's health? She knew pretty well what her cousin, the judge, would say:

"The soldier in France! God bring him home well and glorious!"

How would it be for her other boy then, the boy who was not in France? Unphrased, a thought flashed, "I hope, I do hope Hughie will be very lame tonight."

The little dog slipped from her and barked in remonstrance as she threw out her hands and stood up. Old Mavourneen pulled herself to her feet, too, a huge, beautiful beast, and the woman stooped and put her arm lovingly about the furry neck. "Mavourneen, you know a lot. You know our Brock's away." At the name the big dog whined and looked up anxious, inquiring. "And you know—do you know, dear dog, that Hughie ought to go? Do you? Mavourneen, it's like the prayer-book says, 'The burden of it is intolerable.' I can't bear to lose him, and I can't, O God! I can't bear to keep him." She straightened. "As you say, Mavourneen, it's time to dress for dinner."

The birthday party went better than one could have hoped. Nobody broke down at Brock's name; everybody exulted in the splendid episode of his heroism, months back, which had won him the war cross. The letter from Jim Colledge and his own birthday letter, garrulous and gay, were read. Brock had known well that the day would be hard to get through and had made that letter out of brutal cheerfulness. Yet every one felt his longing to be at the celebration, missed for the first time in his life, pulsing through the words. Young Hugh read it and made it sweet with a lovely devotion to and pride in his brother. A heart of stone could not have resisted Hugh that night. And then the party was over, and the woman and her man, seeing each other seldom now, talked over things for an hour. After, through her open door, she saw a bar of light under the door of the den, Brock's and Hugh's den.

"Hughie," she spoke, and on the instant the dark panel flashed into light.

"Come in, Mummy, I've been waiting to talk to you."

"Waiting, my lamb?"

Hugh pushed her, as a boy shoves a sister, into the end of the sofa. There was a wood fire on the hearth in front of her, for the June evening was cool, and luxurious Hugh liked a fire. A reading lamp was lighted above Brock's deep chair, and there were papers on the floor by it, and more low lights. There were magazines about, and etchings on the walls, and bits of university plunder, and the glow of rugs and of books. It was as fascinating a place as there was in all the beautiful house. In the midst of the bright peace Hugh stood haggard.

"Hughie! What is it?"

"Mother," he whispered, "help me!"

"With my last drop of blood, Hugh."

"I can't go on—alone—mother." His eyes were wild, and his words labored into utterance. "I—I don't know what to do—mother."

"The war, Hughie?"

"Of course! What else is there?" he flung at her.

"But your knee?"

"Oh, Mummy, you know as well as I that my knee is well enough. Dad knows it, too. The way he looks at me—or dodges looking! Mummy—I've got to tell you— you'll have to know—and maybe you'll stop loving me. I'm—" He threw out his arms with a gesture of despair. "I'm—afraid to go." With that he was on his knees beside her, and his arms gripped her, and his head was hidden in her lap. For a long minute there was only silence, and the woman held the young head tight.

Hugh lifted his face and stared from blurred eyes. "A man might better be dead than a coward—you're thinking that? That's it." A sob stopped his voice, the young, dear voice. His face, drawn into lines of age, hurt her unbearably. She caught him against her and hid the beloved, impossible face.

"Hugh—I—judging you—I? Why, Hughie, I *love* you—I only love you. I don't stand off and think, when it's you and Brock. I'm inside your hearts, feeling it with you. I don't know if it's good or bad. It's—my own. Coward—Hughie! I don't think such things of my darling."

"'There's no—friend like a mother,'" stammered young Hugh, and tears fell unashamed. His mother had not seen the boy cry since he was ten years old. He went on. "Dad didn't say a word, because he wouldn't spoil your birthday, but the way he dodged—my knee—" He laughed miserably and swabbed away tears with the corner of his pajama coat. "I wish I had a hanky," he complained. The woman dried the tear-stained cheeks hastily with her own. "Dad's got it in for me," said Hugh. "I can tell. He'll make me go—now. He—he suspects I went skating that day hoping I'd fall—and—I know it wasn't so darned unlikely. Yes—I did—not the first time—when I smashed it; that was entirely—luck." He laughed again, a laugh that was a sob. "And now—oh, Mummy, have I *got* to go into that nightmare? I hate it so. I am—I *am*—afraid. If—if I should be there and—and sent into some terrible job—shell-fire—dirt—smells—dead men and horses—filth—torture—mother, I might run. I don't feel sure. I can't trust Hugh Langdon—he might run. Anyhow"—the lad sprang to his feet and stood before her—"anyhow—why am *I* bound to get into this? I didn't start it. My Government didn't. And I've everything, *everything* before me here. I didn't tell you, but that editor said—he said I'd be one of the great writers of the time. And I love it, I love that job. I can do it. I can be useful, and successful, and an honor to you—and happy, oh, so happy! If only I may do as Arnold said, be one of America's big writers! I've everything to gain here; I've everything to lose there." He stopped and stood before her like a flame.

And from the woman's mouth came words which she had not thought, as if other than herself spoke them. "'What shall it profit a man,'" she spoke, "'if he gain the whole world and lose his own soul?'"

At that the boy plunged on his knees in collapse and sobbed miserably. "Mother, mother! Don't be merciless."

"Merciless! My own laddie!" There seemed no words possible as she stroked the blond head with shaking hand. "Hughie," she spoke when his sobs quieted. "Hughie, it's not how you feel; it's what you do. I believe thousands and thousands of boys in this unwarlike country have gone—are going—through suffering like yours."

Hugh lifted wet eyes. "Do you think so, Mummy?"

"Indeed I do. Indeed I do. And I pray that the women who love them are—faithful. For I know, I *know* that if a woman lets her men, if a mother let her sons fail their country now, those sons will never forgive her. It's your honor I'm holding to, Hughie, against human instinct. After this war, those to be pitied won't be the sonless mothers or the crippled soldiers—it will be the men of fighting age who have not fought. Even if they could not, even at the best, they will spend the rest of their lives explaining why."

Hugh sat on the sofa now, close to her, and his head dropped on her shoulder. "Mummy, that's some comfort, that dope about other fellows taking it as I do. I felt lonely. I thought I was the only coward in America. Dad's condemning me; he can't speak to me naturally. I felt as if"—his voice faltered—"as if I couldn't stand it if you hated me, too."

The woman laughed a little. "Hughie, you know well that not anything to be imagined could stop my loving you."

He went on, breathing heavily but calmed. "You think that even if I am a blamed fool, if I went anyhow—that I'd rank as a decent white man? In your eyes—Dad's—my own?"

"I know it, Hughie. It's what you do, not how you feel doing it."

"If Brock would hold my hand!" The eyes of the two met with a dim smile and a memory of the childhood so near, so utterly gone. "I'd like Dad to respect me again," the boy spoke in a wistful, uncertain voice. "It's darned wretched to have your father despise you." He looked at her then. "Mummy, you're tired out; your face is gray. I'm a beast to keep you up. Go to bed, dear."

He kissed her, and with his arm around her waist led her through the dark hall to the door of her room, and kissed her again. And again, as she stood and watched there, he turned on the threshold of the den and threw one more kiss across the darkness, and his face shone with a smile that sent her to bed, smiling through her tears. She lay in the darkness, fragrant of honeysuckle outside, and her sore heart was full of the boys—of Hugh struggling in his crisis; still more, perhaps, of Brock whose birthday it was, Brock in France, in the midst of "many and great dangers," yet—she knew—serene and buoyant among them because his mind was "stayed." Not long these thoughts held her; for she was so deadened with the stress of many emotions that nature asserted itself and shortly she feel asleep.

It may have been two or three hours she slept. She knew afterward that it must have been at about three of the summer morning when a dream came which, detailed and vivid as it was, probably filled in time only the last minute or so before awakening. It seemed to her that glory suddenly flooded the troubled world; the infinite, intimate joy, impossible to put into words, was yet a defined and long first chapter of her dream. After that she stood on the bank of a river, a river perhaps miles wide, and with the new light-heartedness filling her she looked and saw a mighty bridge which ran brilliant with many-colored lights, from her to the misty further shore of the river. Over the bridge passed a throng of radiant young men, boys, all in uniform. "How glorious!" she seemed to cry out in delight, and with that she saw Brock.

Very far off, among the crowd of others, she saw him, threading his way through the throng. He came, unhurried yet swift, and on his face was an amused, loving smile which was perhaps the look of him which she remembered best. By his side walked old Mavourneen, the wolf-hound, Brock's hand on the shaggy head. The two swung steadily toward her, Brock smiling into her eyes, holding her eyes with his, and as they were closer, she heard Mavourneen crying in wordless dumb joy, crying as she had not done since the day when Brock came home the last time. Above the sound Brock's voice spoke, every trick of inflection so familiar, so sweet, that the joy of it was sharp, like pain.

"Mother, I'm coming to take Hughie's hand—to take Hughie's hand," he repeated.

And with that Mavourneen's great cry rose above his voice. And suddenly she was awake. Somewhere outside the house, yet near, the dog was loudly, joyfully crying. Out of the deep stillness of the night burst the sound of the joyful crying.

The woman shot from her bed and ran barefooted, her heart beating madly, into the darkness of the hall to the landing on the stairway. Something halted her. There was a broad, uncurtained pane of glass in the front door of the house. From the landing one might look down the stone steps outside and see clearly in the bright moonlight as far as the beginning of the rose archway. As she stood gasping, from beneath the flowers Brock stepped into the moonlight and began, unhurried, buoyant, as she had but now seen him in her dream, to mount the steps. Mavourneen pressed at his side, and his hand was on the dog's head. As he came, he lifted his face to his mother with the accustomed, every-day smile which she knew, as if he were coming home, as he had come home on many a moonlit evening from a dance in town to talk the day over with her. As she stared, standing in the dark on the landing, her pulse racing, yet still with the stillness of infinity, an arm came around her, a hand gripped her shoulder, and young Hugh's voice spoke.

"Mother! It's Brock!" he whispered.

At the words she fled headlong down to the door and caught at the handle. It was fastened, and for a moment she could not think of the bolt. Brock stood close outside; she saw the light on his brown head and the bend in the long, strong fingers that caressed Mavourneen's fur. He smiled at her happily—Brock—three feet away. Just as the bolt loosened, with an inexplicable, swift impulse she was cold with terror. For the half of a second, perhaps, she halted, possessed by some formless fear stronger than herself—humanity dreading something not human, something unknown, overwhelming. She halted not a whole second—for it was Brock. Brock! Wide open she flung the door and sprang out.

There was no one there. Only Mavourneen stood in the cold moonlight, and cried, and looked up, puzzled, at empty air.

"Oh, Brock, Brock! Oh, dear Brock!" the woman called and flung out her arms. "Brock—Brock—don't leave me. Don't go!"

Mavourneen sniffed about the dark hall, investigating to find the master who had come home and gone away so swiftly. With that young Hugh was lifting her in his arms, carrying her up the broad stairs into his room. "You're barefooted," he spoke brokenly.

She caught his hand as he wrapped her in a rug on the sofa. "Hugh—you saw—it was Brock?"

"Yes, dearest, it was our Brock," answered Hugh stumblingly.

"You saw—and I—and Mavourneen."

"Mavonrneen is Irish," young Hugh said. "She has the second sight," and the big old dog laid her nose on the woman's knee and lifted topaz eyes, asking questions, and whimpered broken-heartedly.

"Dear dog," murmured the woman and drew the lovely head to her. "You saw him." And then; "Hughie—he came to tell us. He is—dead."

"I think so," whispered young Hugh with bent head.

Then, fighting for breath, she told what had happened—the dream, the intense happiness of it, how Brock had come smiling. "And Hugh, the only thing he said, two or three times over, was, 'I'm coming to take Hughie's hand.'"

The lad turned upon her a shining look. "I know, mother. I didn't hear, of course, but I knew, when I saw him, it was for me, too. And I'm ready. I see my way now. Mother, get Dad."

Hugh, the elder, still sleeping in his room at the far side of the house, opened heavy eyes. Then he sprang up. "Evelyn! What is it?"

"Oh, Hugh—come! Oh, Hugh! Brock—Brock—" She could not say the words; there was no need. Brock's father caught her hands. In bare words then she told him.

"My dear," urged the man, "you've had a vivid dream. That's all. You were thinking about the boys; you were only half awake; Mavourneen began to cry—the dog means Brock. It was easy—" his voice faltered—"to—to believe the rest."

"Hugh, I *know*, dear. Brock came to tell me. He said he would." Later, that day, when a telegram arrived from the War Office there was no new shock, no added certainty to her assurance. She went on: "Hughie saw him. And Mavourneen. But I can't argue. We still have a boy, Hugh, and he needs us—he's waiting. Oh, my dear, Hughie is going to France!"

"Thank God!" spoke Hugh's father.

Hand tight in hand like young lovers the two came across to the room where their boy waited, tense. "Father—Dad—you'll give me back your respect, won't you?" The strong young hand held out was shaking. "Because I'm going, Dad. But you have to know that I was—a coward."

"*No*, Hugh."

"Yes. And Dad, I'm afraid—now. But I've got the hang of things, and nothing could keep me. Will you, do you despise me—now—that I still hate it—if—if I go just the same?"

The big young chap shook so that his mother, his tall mother, put her arms about him to steady him. He clutched her hand hard and repeated, through quivering lips, "Would you despise me still, Dad?"

For a moment the father could not answer. Then difficult tears of manhood and maturity forced their way from his eyes and unheeded rolled down his cheeks. With a step he put his arms about the boy as if the boy were a child, and the boy threw his about his father's shoulders.

For a long second the two tall men stood so. The woman, standing apart, through the shipwreck of her earthly life was aware only of happiness safe where sorrow and loss could not touch it. What was separation, death itself, when love stronger than death held people together as it held Hugh and her boys and herself? Then the older Hugh stood away, still clutching the lad's hand, smiling through unashamed tears.

"Hugh," he said, "in all America there's not a man prouder of his son than I am of you. There's not a braver soldier in our armies than the soldier who's to take my name into France." He stopped and steadied himself; he went on: "It would have broken my heart, boy, if you had failed—failed America. And your mother—and Brock and me. Failed your own honor. It would have meant for us shame and would have bowed our heads; it would have meant for you disaster. Don't fear for your courage, Hugh; the Lord won't forsake the man who carries the Lord's colors."

Young Hugh turned suddenly to his mother. "I'm at peace now. You and Dad—honor me. I'll deserve respect from—my country. It will be a wall around me—And—" he caught her to him and crushed his mouth to hers—"dearest—Brock will hold my hand."

---

## THE SILVER STIRRUP

In the most unexpected spots vital sparks of history blaze out. Time seems, once in a while, powerless to kill a great memory. Romance blooms sometimes untarnished across centuries of commonplace. In a new world old France lives.

\* \* \* \* \*

It is computed that about one-seventh of the French-Canadian population of Canada enlisted in the great war. The stampede of heroism seems to have left them cold. A Gospel of the Province first congealed the none too fiery blood of the *habitants*, small farmers, very poor, thinking in terms of narrowest economy, of one pig and ten children, of painstaking thrift and a bare margin to subsistence. Such conditions stifle world interests. The earthquake which threatened civilization disturbed the *habitant* merely because it hazarded his critical balance on the edge of want. The cataclysm over the ocean was none of his affair. And his affairs pressed. What about the pig if one went to war? And could Alphonse, who is fourteen, manage the farm so that there would be vegetables for winter? Tell me that.

When in September, 1914, I went to Canada for two weeks of camping I had heard of this point of view. Dick Lindsley and I were met at the Club Station on the casual railway which climbs the mountains through Quebec Province, by four guides, men from twenty to thirty-five, powerfully built chaps, deep-shouldered and slim-waisted, lithe as wild-cats. It was a treat to see their muscles, like machines in the pink of order, adjust to the heavy *pacquetons*, send a canoe whipping through the water. There was one exception to the general physical perfection; one of Dick's men, a youngster of perhaps twenty-two, limped. He covered ground as well as the others, for all of that; he picked the heaviest load and portaged it at an uneven trot, faster than his comrades; he was what the *habitants* call "ambitionné." Dick's canoe was loaded first, owing to the fellow's efficiency, and I waited while it got away and watched the lame boy. He had an interesting face, aquiline and dark, set with vivid light-blue eyes, shooting restless fire. I registered an intention to get at this lad's personality. The chance came two days later. My men were off chopping on a day, and I suddenly needed to go fishing.

"Take Philippe," offered Dick. "He handles a boat better than any of them."

Philippe and I shortly slipped into the Guardian's Pool, at the lower end of the long lake of the Passes. "It is here, M'sieur," Philippe announced, "that it is the custom to take large ones."

By which statement the responsibility of landing record trout was on my shoulders. I thought I would have a return whack. My hands in the snarly flies and my back to Philippe I spoke around my pipe, yet spoke distinctly.

"Why aren't you in France fighting?"

The canoe shivered down its length as if the man at its stern had jumped. There was a silence. Then Philippe's deep, boyish voice answered.

"As M'sieur sees, one is lame."

I felt a hotness emerging from my flannel collar and rushing up my face as I bent over that damned Silver Doctor that wouldn't loose its grip on the Black Hackle. I didn't see the Black Hackle or the Silver Doctor for a moment. "Beg pardon," I growled. "I forgot." I mumbled platitudes.

"M'sieur le Docteur has right," Philippe announced unruffled. "One should fight for France. I have tried to enlist, there are three times, explaining that I am '*capable*' though I walk not evenly. But one will not have me. Therefore I have shame, me. I have, naturally, more shame than another because of Jeanne."

"Because of Jeanne?" I repeated. "Who is Jeanne?"

There was a pause; a queer feeling made me slew around. Philippe's old felt hat was being pulled off as if he were entering a church.

"But—Jeanne, M'sieur," he stated as if I must understand. "Jeanne d'Arc. *Tiens*—the Maid of France."

"The Maid of France!" I was puzzled. "What has she to do with it?"

"But everything, M'sieur." The vivid eyes flamed. "M'sieur does not know, perhaps, that my grandfather fought under Jeanne?"

"Your grandfather!" I flung it at him in scorn. The man was a poor lunatic.

"But yes, M'sieur. My grandfather, lui-même."

"But, Philippe, the Maid of Orleans died in 1431." I remembered that date. The Maid is one of my heroic figures.

Philippe shrugged his shoulders. "Oh—as for a *grandpère*! But not the *grandpère à present*, he who keeps the grocery shop in St. Raymond. Certainly not that grandfather. It is to say the *grandpère* of that *grandpère*. Perhaps another yet, or even two or three more. What does it matter? One goes back a few times of grandfathers and behold one arrives at him who was armorer for the Maid—to whom she gave the silver stirrup."

"The silver stirrup." My Leonard rod bumped along the bow; my flies tangled again in the current. I squirmed about till I faced the guide in the stern. "Philippe, what in hell do you mean by this drool of grandfathers and silver stirrups?"

The boy, perfectly respectful, not forgetting for a second his affair of keeping the canoe away from the fish-hole, looked at me squarely, and his uncommon light eyes gleamed out of his face like the eyes of a prophet. "M'sieur, it is a tale doubtless which seems strange to you, but to us others it is not strange. M'sieur lives in New York, and there are automobiles and trolley-cars and large buildings *en masse*, and to M'sieur the world is made of such things. But there are other things. We who live in quiet places, know. One has not too much of excitement, we others, so that one remembers a great event which has happened to one's family many years. Yes, indeed, M'sieur, centuries. If one has not much one guards as a souvenir the tale of the silver stirrup of Jeanne. Yes, for several generations."

The boy was apparently unconscious that his remarks were peculiar. "Philippe, will you tell me what you mean by a silver stirrup which Jeanne d'Arc gave to your ancestors?"

"But with pleasure, M'sieur," he answered readily, with the gracious French politeness which one meets among the *habitants* side by side with sad lapses of etiquette. "It is all-simple that the old grandfather, the ancient, he who lived in France when the Maid fought her wars, was an armorer. '*Ça fait que*'—*sa fak*, Philippe pronounced it—'so it happened that on a day the stirrup of the Maid broke as her horse plunged, and my grandfather, the ancient, he ran quickly and caught the horse's head. And so it happened—*çe fait que*—that my grandfather was working at that moment on a fine stirrup of gold for her harness, for though they burned her afterwards, they gave her then all that there was of magnificence. And the old follow—*le vieux*—whipped out the golden stirrup from his pocket, quite prepared for use, so it happened—and he put it quickly in the place of the silver one which she had been using. And Jeanne smiled. 'You are ready to serve France, Armorer.'

"She bent then and looked *le vieux* in the face—but he was young at the time.

"'Are you not Baptiste's son, of Doremy?' asked the Maid.

"'Yes, Jeanne,' said my *grandpère*.

"'Then keep the silver stirrup to remember our village, and God's servant Jeanne,' she said, and gave it to him with her hand."

If a square of Gobelin tapestry had emerged from the woods and hung itself across the gunwale of my canvas canoe it would not have been more surprising. I got my breath. "And the stirrup, what became of it?"

The boy shrugged his shoulders. "*Sais pas*," he answered with French nonchalance. "One does not know that. It is a long time, M'sieur le Docteur. It was lost, that stirrup, some years ago. It may be a hundred years. It may be two hundred. My grandfather, he who keeps the grocery shop, has told me that there is a saying that a Martel must go to France to find the silver stirrup. In every case I do not know. It is my wish to fight for France, but as for the stirrup or Jeanne—*sais pas*." Another shrug. With that he was making oration, his light eyes flashing, his dark face working with feeling, about the bitterness of being a cripple, and unable to go into the army.

"It is not *comme il faut*, M'sieur le Docteur, that a man whose very grandfather fought for Jeanne should fail France now in her need. Jeanne, one knows, was the saviour of France. Is it not?" I agreed. "It is my inheritance, therefore, to fight as my ancient grandfather fought." I looked at the lame boy, not knowing the repartee. He began again. "Also I am the only one of the family proper to go, except Adolphe, who is not very proper, having had a tree to fall on the lungs and leave him liable to fits; and also Jacques and Louis are too young, and Jean Baptiste he is blind of one eye, God knows. So it is I who fail! I fail! Jesus Christ! To stay at home like a coward when France needs men!"

"But you are Canadian, Philippe. Your people have been here two hundred years."

"M'sieur, I am of France. I belong there with the fighting men." His look was a flame, and suddenly I know why he was firing off hot shot at me. I am a surgeon.

"What's the matter with your leg?" I asked.

The brilliant eyes flashed. "Ah!" he brought out, "One hoped—If M'sieur le Docteur would but see. I may be cured. To be straight—to march!" He was trembling.

Later, in the shifting sunshine at the camp door, with the odors of hemlocks and balsams about us, the lake rippling below, I had an examination. I found that the lad's lameness was a trouble to be cured easily by an operation. I hesitated. Was it my affair to root this youngster out of safety and send him to death in the *débâcle* over there? Yet what right had I to set limits? He wanted to offer his life; how could I know what I might be blocking if I withheld the cure? My job was to give strength to all I could reach.

"Philippe," I said, "if you'll come to New York next month I'll set you up with a good leg."

In September, 1915, Dick and I came up for our yearly trip, but Philippe was not with us. Philippe, after drilling at Valcartier, was drilling in England. I had lurid post cards off and on; after a while I knew that he was "somewhere in France." A grim gray card came with no post-mark, no writing but the address and Philippe's labored signature; for the rest there were printed sentences: "I am well. I am wounded. I am in hospital. I have had no letter from you lately." All of which was struck out but the welcome words, "I am well." So far then I had not cured the lad to be killed. Then for weeks nothing. It came to be time again to go to Canada for the hunting. I wrote the steward to get us four men, as usual, and Lindsley and I alighted from the rattling train at the club station in September, 1916, with a mild curiosity to see what Fate had provided as guides, philosophers and friends to us for two weeks. Paul Sioui—that was nice—a good fellow Paul; and Josef—I shook hands with Josef; the next face was a new one—ah, Pierre Beauramé—one calls one's self that—*on s'appelle comme ça. Bon jour!* I turned, and got a shock. The fourth face, at which I looked, was the face of Philippe Martel. I looked, speechless. And with that the boy laughed. "It is that M'sieur cannot again cure my leg," answered Philippe, and tapped proudly on a calf which echoed with a wooden sound.

"You young cuss," I addressed him savagely. "Do you mean to say you have gone and got shot in that very leg I fixed up for you?"

Philippe rippled more laughter—of pure joy—of satisfaction. "But, yes, M'sieur le Docteur, that leg *même*. Itself. In a battle, M'sieur le Docteur gave me the good leg for a long enough time to serve France. It was all that there was of necessary. As for now I may not fight again, but I can walk and portage *comme il faut*. I am *capable* as a guide. Is it not, Josef?" He appealed, and the men crowded around to back him up with deep, serious voices.

"Ah, yes, M'sieur."

"*B'en capable!*"

"He can walk like us others—the same!" they assured me impressively.

Philippe was my guide this year. It was the morning after we reached camp. "Would M'sieur le Docteur be too busy to look at something?"

I was not. Philippe stood in the camp doorway in the patch of sunlight where he had sat two years before when I looked over his leg. He sat down again, in the shifting sunshine, the wooden leg sticking out straight and pathetic, and began to take the covers off a package. There were many covers; the package was apparently valuable. As he worked at it the odors of hemlock and balsam, distilled by hot sunlight, rose sweet and strong, and the lake splashed on pebbles, and peace that passes understanding was about us.

"It was in a bad battle in Lorraine," spoke Philippe into the sunshiny peace, "that I lost M'sieur le Docteur's leg. One was in the front trench and there was word passed to have the wire cutters ready, and also bayonets, for we were to charge across the open towards the trenches of the Germans—perhaps one hundred and fifty yards, eight *arpents*—acres—as we say in Canada. Our big guns back did the preparation, making what M'sieur le Docteur well knows is called a *rideau*—a fire curtain. We climbed out of our trench with a shout and followed the fire curtain; so closely we followed that it seemed we should be killed by our own guns. And then it stopped—too soon, M'sieur le Docteur. Very many Boches were left alive in that trench in front, and they fired as we came, so that some of us were hit, and so terrible was the fire that the rest were forced back to our own trench which we had left. It is so sometimes in a fight, M'sieur le Docteur. The big guns make a little mistake, and many men have to die. Yet it is for France. And as I ran with the others for the shelter of the trench, and as the Boches streamed out of their trench to make a counter attack with hand-grenades I tripped on something. It was little Réné Dumont, whom M'sieur le Docteur remembers. He guided for our camp when Josef was ill in the hand two years ago. In any case he lay there, and I could not let him lie to be shot to pieces. So I caught up the child and ran with him across my shoulders and threw him in the trench, and as he went in there was a cry behind me, 'Philippe!'

"I turned, and one waved arms at me—a comrade whom I did not know very well—but he lay in the open and cried for help. So I thought of Jeanne d'Arc, and how she had no fear, and was kind, and with that, back I trotted to get the comrade. But at that second—pouf!—a big noise, and I fell down and could not get up. It was the good new leg of M'sieur le Docteur which those *sacrés* Boches had blown off with a hand-grenade. So that I lay dead enough. And when I came alive it was dark, and also the leg hurt—but yes! I was annoyed to have ruined that leg which you gave me—M'sieur le Docteur."

I grinned, and something ached inside of me.

Philippe went on. "It was then, when I was without much hope and weak and in pain and also thirsty, that a thing happened. It is a business without pleasure, M'sieur le Docteur, that—to lie on a battle-field with a leg shot off, and around one men dead, piled up—yes, and some not dead yet, which is worse. They groan. One feels unable to bear it. It grows cold also, and the searchlights of the Boches play so as to prevent rescue by comrades. They seem quite horrible, those lights. One lives, but one wishes much to die. So it happened that, as I lay there, I heard a step coming, not crawling along as the rescuers crawl and stopping when the lights flare, but a steady step coming freely. And with that I was lifted and carried quickly into a wood. There was a hole in the ground there, torn by a shell deeply, and the friend laid me there and put a flask to my lips, and I was warm and comforted. I looked up and I saw a figure in soldier's clothing of an old time, such as one sees in books—armor of white. And the face smiled down at me. 'You will be saved,' a voice said; and the words sounded homely, almost like the words of my grandfather who keeps the grocery shop. 'You will be saved.' It seemed to me that the voice was young and gentle and like a woman's.

"'Who are you?' I asked, and I had a strange feeling, afraid a little M'sieur, yet glad to a marvel. I got no answer to my question, but I felt something pressed into my hand, and then I spoke, but I suppose I was a little delirious, M'sieur, for I heard myself say a thing I had not been thinking. 'A Martel must return to France to find the silver stirrup'—I said that, M'sieur. Why I do not know. They were the words I had heard my grandfather speak. Perhaps the hard feeling in my hand—but I cannot explain, M'sieur le Docteur. In any case, there was all at once a great thrill through my body, such as I have never known. I sat up quickly and stared at the figure. It stood there. M'sieur will probably not believe me—the figure stood there in white armor, with a sword—and I knew it for Jeanne—the Maid. With that I knew no more. When I woke it was day. I was still lying in the crater of the shell which had torn up the earth of a very old battle-field, but in my hand I held tight—this."

Philippe drew off the last cover with a dramatic flourish and opened the box which had been wrapped so carefully. I bent over him. In the box, before my eyes, lay an ancient worn and battered silver stirrup. There were no words to say. I stared at the boy. And with that suddenly he had slewed around clumsily—because of his poor wooden leg—and was on his knees at my feet. He held out the stirrup.

"M'sieur le Docteur, you gave me a man's chance and honor, and the joy of fighting for France. I can never tell my thanks. I have nothing to give you—but this. Take it, M'sieur le Docteur. It is not much, yet to me the earth holds nothing so valuable. It is the silver stirrup of Jeanne d'Arc. It is yours."

* * * * *

In a glass case on the wall of my library hangs an antique bit of harness which is my most precious piece of property. How its story came about I do not even try to guess. As Philippe said the action of that day took place on a very old battle-field. The shell which made the sheltering crater doubtless dug up earth untouched for hundreds of years. That it should have dug up the very object which was a tradition in the Martel family and should have laid it in the grasp of a Martel fighting for France with that tradition at the bottom of his mind seems incredible. The story of the apparition of the Maid is incredible to laughter, or tears. No farther light is to be got from the boy, because he believes his story. I do not try to explain, I place the episode in my mind alongside other things incredible, things lovely and spiritual, and, to our viewpoint of five years ago, things mad. Many such have risen luminous, undesirable, unexplained, out of these last horrible years, and wait human thought, it may be human development, to be classified. I accept and treasure the silver stirrup as a pledge of beautiful human gratitude. I hold it as a visible sign that French blood keeps a loyalty to France which ages and oceans may not weaken.

---

## THE RUSSIAN

The little dinner-party of grizzled men strayed from the dining-room and across the hall into the vast library, arguing mightily.

"The great war didn't do it. World democracy was on the way. The war held it back."

It was the United States Senator, garrulous and incisive, who issued that statement. The Judge, the host, wasted not a moment in contradicting. "You're mad, Joe," he threw at him with a hand on the shoulder of the man who was still to him that promising youngster, little Joe Burden of The School. "Held back democracy! The war! Quite mad, my son."

The guest of the evening, a Russian General who had just finished five strenuous years in the Cabinet of the Slav Republic, dropped back a step to watch, with amused eyes, strolling through the doorway, the two splendid old boys, the Judge's arm around the Senator's shoulders, fighting, sputtering, arguing with each other as they had fought and argued forty odd years up to date.

Two minutes more and the party of six had settled into deep chairs, into a mammoth davenport, before a blazing fire of spruce and birch. Cigars, liqueurs, coffee, the things men love after dinner, were there; one had the vaguest impression of two vanishing Japanese persons who might or might not have brought trays and touched the fire and placed tiny tables at each right hand; an atmosphere of completeness was present, one did not notice how. One settled with a sigh of satisfaction into comfort, and chose a cigar. One laughed to hear the Judge pound away at the Senator.

"It's all a game." Dr. Rutherford turned to the Russian. "They're devoted old friends, not violent enemies, General. The Senator stirs up the Judge by taking impossible positions and defending them savagely. The Judge invariably falls into the trap. Then a battle. Their battles are the joy of the Century Club. The Senator doesn't believe for an instant that the war held back democracy."

At that the Senator whirled. "I don't? But I do.—Don't *smoke* that cigar, Rutherford, on your life. Peter will have these atrocities. Here—Kaki, bring the doctor the other box.—That's better.—I don't believe what I said? Now listen. How could the fact that the world was turned into a military camp, officers commanding, privates obeying, rank, rank, rank everywhere throughout mankind, how could that fail to hinder democracy, which is in its essence the leveling of ranks? Tell me that!"

The doctor grinned at the Russian. "What about it, General? What do you think?"

The General answered slowly, with a small accent but in the wonderfully good English of an educated Russian. "I do not agree with the Sena-torr," he stated, and five heads turned to listen. There was a quality of large personality in the burr of the voice, in the poise and soldierly bearing, in the very silence of the man, which made his slow words of importance. "I believe indeed that the Sena-torr is partly—shall I say speaking for argument?"

The Senator laughed.

"The great war, in which all of us here had the honor to bear arms—that death grapple of tyranny against freedom—it did not hold back the cause of humanity, of democracy, that war. Else thousands upon thousands of good lives were given in vain."

There was a hushed moment. Each of the men, men now from fifty to sixty years old, had been a young soldier in that Homeric struggle. Each was caught back at the words of the Russian to a vision of terrible places, of thundering of great guns, of young, generous blood flowing like water. The deep, assured tones of the Russian spoke into the solemn pause.

"There is an episode of the war which I remember. It goes to show, so far as one incident may, where every hour was crowded with drama, how forces worked together for democracy. It is the story of a common man of my country who was a private in the army of your country, and who was lifted by an American gentleman to hope and opportunity, and, as God willed it, to honor. My old friend the Judge can tell that episode better than I. My active part in it was small. If you like"—the dark foreign eyes flashed about the group—"if you like I should much enjoy hearing my old friend review that little story of democracy."

There was a murmur of approval. One man spoke, a fighting parson he had been. "It argues democracy in itself, General, that a Russian aristocrat, the brother of a Duke, should remember so well the adventures of a common soldier."

The smouldering eyes of the Slav turned to the speaker and regarded him gravely. "I remember those adventures well," he answered.

The Judge, flung back in a corner of the davenport, his knees crossed and rings from his cigar ascending, stared at the ceiling, "Come along, Peter. You're due to entertain us," the Senator adjured him, and the Judge, staring upwards, began.

"This is the year 1947. It was in 1917 that the United States went into war—thirty years ago. The fifth of June, 1917, was set, as you remember, for the registration of all men in the country over twenty-one and under thirty-one for the draft. I was twenty-three, living in this house with my father and mother, both dead before the war ended. Being outside of the city, the polling place where I was due to register was three miles off, at Hiawatha. I registered in the morning; the polls were open from seven A.M. to nine P.M. My mother drove me over, and the road was being mended, and, as happened in those days in the country, half a mile of it was almost impassable. There were no adjustable lift-roads invented then. We got through the ruts and stonework, but it was hard going, and we came home by a detour through the city rather than pass again that beastly half mile. That night was dark and stormy, with rain at intervals, and as we sat in this room, reading, the three of us—" The Judge paused and gazed a moment at the faces in the lamplight, at the chairs where his guests sat. It was as if he called back to their old environment for a moment the two familiar figures which had belonged here, which had gone out of his life. "We sat in this room, the three of us," he repeated, "and the butler came in.

"'If you please, sir, there's a young man here who wants to register,' he said.

"'Wants to register!' my father threw at him. 'What do you mean?'

"We all went outside, and there we found not one, but five boys, Russians. There was a munitions plant a mile back of us and the lads worked there, and had wakened to the necessity of registering at the last moment, being new in the country and with little English. They had directions to go to the same polling place as mint, Hiawatha, but had gotten lost, and, seeing our lights, brought up here. Hiawatha, as I said, is three miles away. It was eight-thirty and the polls closed at nine. We brought the youngsters inside, and I dashed to the garage for the car and piled the delighted lads into it and drove them across.

"At least I tried to. But when we came to the bad half mile the car rebelled at going the bit twice in a day, and the motor stalled. There we were—eight-forty-five P.M.—polls due to close at nine—a year's imprisonment for five well-meaning boys for neglecting to register. I was in despair. Then suddenly one of the boys saw a small red light ahead, the tail light of an automobile. We ran along and found a big car standing in front of a house. As we got there, out from the car stepped a woman with a lantern, and as the light swung upward I saw that she was tall and fair and young and very lovely. She stopped as the six of us loomed out of the darkness. I knew that a professor from the University in town had taken this house for the summer, but I don't know the people or their name. It was no time to be shy. I gave my name and stated the case.

"The girl looked at me. 'I've seen you,' she said. 'I know you are Mr. McLane. I'll drive you across. One moment, till I tell my mother.'

"She was in the house and out again without wasting a second, and as she flashed into the car I heard a gasp, and I turned and saw in the glare of the headlights as they sprang on one of my Russians, a gigantic youngster of six feet four or so, standing with his cap off and his head bent, as he might have stood before a shrine, staring at the spot where the girl had disappeared into the car. Then the engine purred and my squad tumbled in.

"We made the polls on the tap of nine. Afterwards we drove back to my car and among us, with the lantern, we got the motor running again, the girl helping efficiently. The big fellow, when we told her good-night, astonished me by dropping on his knees and kissing the edge of her skirt. But I put it down to Slavic temperament and took it casually. I've learned since what Russian depth of feeling means—and tenacity of purpose. There was one more incident. When I finally drove the lads up to their village the big chap, who spoke rather good English when he spoke at all, which was seldom, invited me to have some beer. I was tired and wanted to get home, so I didn't. Then the young giant excavated in his pocket and brought out a dollar bill.

"'You get beer tomorrow.' And when I laughed and shoved it back he flushed. 'Excuse—Mr. Sir,' he said. 'I make mistake.' Suddenly he drew himself up—about to the treetops, it looked, for he was a huge, a magnificent lad. He tossed out his arm to me. 'Some day,' he stated dramatically, 'I do two things. Some day I give Mr. Sir somethings more than dollar—and he will take. And—some day I marry—Miss Angel!'

"You may believe I was staggered. But I simply stuck out my fist and shook his and said: 'Good. No reason on earth why a fellow with the right stuff shouldn't get anywhere. It's a free country.' And the giant drew his black brows together and remarked slowly: 'All countries—world—is to be free. War will sweep up kings—and other—rubbish. I—shall be—a man.'

**144**

"Besides his impressive build, the boy had—had—" the Judge glanced at the Russian General, whose eyes glowed at the fire. "The boy had a remarkable face. It was cut like a granite hill, in sweeping masses. All strength. His eyes were coals. I went home thoughtful, and the Russian boy's intense face was in my mind for days, and I told myself many times that he not only would be, but already was, a man.

"Events quickstepped after that. I got to France within the year, and, as you remember, work was ready. It was perhaps eighteen months after that registration day, June fifth, which we keep so rightly now as one of our sacred days, that one morning I was in a fight. Our artillery had demoralized the enemy at a point and sent them running. There was one machine gun left working in the Hun trenches—doing a lot of damage. Suddenly it jammed. I was commanding my company, and I saw the chance, but also I saw a horrid mess of barbed wire. So I just ran forward a bit and up to the wire and started clipping, while that machine gun stayed jammed. Out of the corner of an eye I could see men rushing towards it in the German trench, and I knew I had only a moment before they got it firing again. Then, as I leaped far forward to reach a bit of entanglement, my foot slipped in a puddle and as I sprawled I saw our uniform and a dead American boy's face under me, and I fell headlong in his blood over him and into a bunch of wire. And couldn't get up. The wire held like the devil. I got more tied up at every pull. And my clippers had fallen from my hand and landed out of reach.

"'It's good night for me,' I thought, and was aware of a sharp regret. To be killed because of a nasty bit of wire! I had wanted to do a lot of things yet. With that something leaped, and I saw clippers flashing close by. A big man was cutting me loose, dragging me out, setting me on my feet. Then the roar of an exploding shell; the man fell—fell into the wire from which he had just saved me. There was no time to consider that; somehow I was back and leading my men—and then we had the trenches.

"The rest of that day was confusion, but we won a mile of earthworks, and at night I remembered the incident of the wire and the man who rescued me. By a miracle I found him in the field hospital. His head was bandaged, for the bit of shell had scraped his cheek and jaw, but his eyes were safe, and something in the glance out of them was familiar. Yet I didn't know him till he drew me over and whispered painfully, for it hurt him to talk:

"'Yester—day I did—give Mr. Sir somethings more than dollar. And he did—take it.'

"Then I know the big young Russian of registration day who had tried to tip me. Bless him! I got him transferred to my command and—" the Judge hesitated a bit and glanced at his distinguished guest. One surmised embarrassment in telling the story of the General's humble compatriot.

The General rose to his feet and stood before the fire facing the handful of men. "I can continue this anecdote from the point that is more easily than my friend the Judge," spoke the General. "I was in the confidence of that countryman of mine. I know. It was so that after he had been thus slightly useful to my friend the Judge, who was the Captain McLane at that time—"

The Judge broke in with a shout of deep laughter worthy of a boy of eighteen. "He 'slightly obliged me by saving my life." The American, threw that into the Russian's smooth sentences. "I put that fact before the jury."

The four men listening laughed also, but the Russian held up a hand and went on gravely: "It was quite simple, that episode, and the man's pleasure. I knew him well. But what followed was not ordinary. The Captain McLane saw to it that the soldier had his chance. He became an officer. He went alive through the war, and at the end the Captain McLane made it possible that he should be educated. His career was a gift from the Captain McLane—from my friend the Judge to that man, who is now—" the finished sentence halted a mere second—"who is now a responsible person of Russia.

"And it is the incident of that sort, it is that incident itself which I know, which leads me to combat—" he turned with a deep bow—"the position of the Sena-torr that the great war did not make for democracy. Gentlemen, my compatriot was a peasant, a person of ignorance, yet with a desire of fulfilling his possibilities. He had been born in social chains and tied to most sordid life, beyond hope, in old Russia. To try to shake free he had gone to America. But it was that caldron of fire, the war, which freed him, which fused his life and the life of the Captain McLane, so different in opportunity, and burned from them all trivialities and put them, stark-naked of advantages and of drawbacks artificial, side by side, as two lives merely. It made them—brothers. One gave and the other took as brothers without thought of false pride. They came from the furnace men. Both. Which is democracy—a chance for a tree to grow, for a flame to burn, for a river to flow; a chance for a man to become a man and not rest a vegetable anchored to the earth as—Oh, God!—for many centuries the Russian mujiks have rested. It is that which I understand by democracy. Freedom of development for everything which wants to develop. It was the earthquake of war which broke chains, loosened dams, cleared the land for young forests. It was war which made Russia a republic, which threw down the kingships, which joined common men and princes as comrades. God bless that liberating war! God grant that never in all centuries may this poor planet have another! God save democracy—humanity! Does the Sena-torr yet believe that the great war retarded democracy?" The Russian's brilliant, smouldering eyes swept about, inquiring.

There was a hush in the peaceful, firelit, lamp-lit room. And with that, as of one impulse, led by the Senator, the five men broke into handclapping. Tears stood in eyes, faces were twisted with emotion; each of these men had seen what the thing was—war; each knew what a price humanity had paid for freedom. Out of the stirring of emotion, out of the visions of trenches and charges and blood and agony and heroism and unselfishness and steadfastness, the fighting parson, he who had bent, under fire, many a day over dying men who waited his voice to help them across the border—the parson led the little company from the intense moment to commonplace.

"You haven't quite finished the story, General. The boy promised to do two things. He did the first; he gave the Judge 'something more than a dollar,' and the Judge took it—his life. But he said also he was going to marry—what did he call her?—Miss Angel. How about that?"

The Russian General, standing on the hearthrug, appeared to draw himself up suddenly with an access of dignity, and the Judge's boyish big laugh broke into the silence, "Tell them, Michael," said the Judge. "You've gone so far with the fairy story that they have a right to know the crowning glory of it. Tell them."

And suddenly the men sitting about noticed with one accord what, listening to the General's voice, they had not thought about—that the Russian was uncommonly tall—six feet four perhaps; that his face was carved in sweeping lines like a granite hillside, and that an old, long scar stretched from the vivid eyes to the mouth. The men stared, startled with a sudden simultaneous thought. The Judge, watching, smiled. Slowly the General put his hand into the breast pocket of his evening coat; slowly he drew out a case of dark leather, tooled wonderfully, set with stones. He opened the case and looked down; the strong face changed as if a breeze and sunshine passed over a mountain. He glanced up at the men waiting.

"I am no Duke's brother," he said, smiling, suddenly radiant. "That is a mistake of the likeness of a name, which all the world makes. I am born a mujik of Russia. But you, sir," and he turned to the parson, "you wish an answer of 'Miss Angel,' as the big peasant boy called that lovely spirit, so far above him in that night, so far above him still, and yet, God be thanked, so close today! Yes? Then this is my answer." He held out the miniature set with jewels.

---

## ROBINA'S DOLL

Massive, sprawling, uncertain writing, two sentences to the page; a violent slant in the second line, down right, balanced by a drastic lessening of the letters, up right, in the line underneath; spelling not as advised in the Century Dictionary—a letter from Robina, aged eight. Robina's Aunt Evelyn, sitting in her dress and cap of a Red Cross nurse in the big base hospital in Paris, read the wandering, painstaking, very unsuccessful literary effort, laughing, half-crying, and kissed it enthusiastically.

"The darling baby! She shall have her doll if it takes—" Aunt Evelyn stopped thoughtfully.

It would take something serious to buy and equip the doll that Robina, with eight-year-old definiteness, had specified. The girl in the Red Cross dress read the letter over.

"Dear Aunt Evelyn," began Robina and struck no snags so far. "I liked your postcard so much." (The facilis descensus to an averni of literature began with a swoop down here.) "Mother is wel. Fother is wel. The baby is wel. The dog has sevven kitens." (Robina robbed Peter to pay Paul habitually in her spelling.) "Fother sais they lukk like choklit eclares. I miss you, dere Aunt Evelyn, because I lov you sew. I hope Santa Claus wil bring me a doll. I want a very bigg bride doll with a vale and flours an a trunk of close, and all her under-close to buton and unboton and to have pink ribons run into. I don't want anythig sode on. Come home, Aunt Evelyn, becaus I miss you. But if the poor wundead soljers ned you then don't come. But as soone as you can come to yure loving own girl—ROBINA."

The dear angel! Every affectionate, labored word was from the warm little heart; Evelyn Bruce knew that. She sat, smiling, holding the paper against her, seeing a vision of the faraway, beloved child who wrote it. She saw the dancing, happy brown eyes and the shining, cropped head of pale golden brown, and the straight, strong little figure; she heard the merry, ready giggle and the soft, slow tones that were always full of love to her. Robina, her sister's child, her own god-daughter had been her close friend from babyhood, and between them there was a bond of understanding which made nothing of the difference in years. Darling little Robina! Such a good, unspoiled little girl, for all of the luxury and devotion that surrounded her!

But—there was a difficulty just there. Robina was unspoiled indeed, yet, as the children of the very rich, she was, even at eight, sophisticated in a baby way. She had been given too many grand dolls not to know just the sort she wanted. She did not know that what she wanted cost money, but she knew the points desired—and they did cost money. Aunt Evelyn had not much money.

"This one extravagant thing I will do," said Evelyn Bruce, "and I'll give up my trip to England next week, and I'll do it in style. Robina won't want dolls much longer and this time she's got to have her heart's desire."

Which was doubtless foolish, yet when one is separated by an ocean and a war from one's own, it is perhaps easier to be foolish for a child's face and a child's voice, and love sent across the sea. So Evelyn Bruce wrote a letter to her cousin in England saying that she could not come to her till after Christmas. Then she went out into Paris and ordered the doll, and reveled in the ordering, for a very gorgeous person indeed it was, and worthy to journey from Paris to a little American. It was to be ready in just two weeks, and Miss Bruce was to come in and look over the fine lady and her equipment as often as desired, before she started on her ocean voyage.

"It would simply break my heart if she were torpedoed."

Evelyn confided that, childlike, to the black-browed, stout Frenchwoman who took a personal interest in every "buton," and then she opened her bag and brought out Robina's photograph, standing, in a ruffled bonnet, her solemn West Highland White terrier dog in her arms, on the garden path of "Graystones" between tall foxgloves. And the Frenchwoman tossed up enraptured hands at the beauty of the little girl who was to get the doll, and did not miss the great, splendid house in the background, or the fact that the dog was of a "*chic*" variety.

The two weeks fled, every day full of the breathless life—and death—of a hospital in war-torn France. Every day the girl saw sights and heard sounds which it seemed difficult to see and hear and go on living, but she moved serene through such an environment, because she could help. Every day she gave all that was in her to the suffering boys who were carried, in a never-ending stream of stretchers, into the hospital. And the strength she gave flowed back to her endlessly from, she could not but believe it, the underlying source of all strength, which stretches beneath and about us all, and from which those who give greatly know how to draw.

Two or three times, during the two weeks, Evelyn had gone in to inspect the progress of Robina's doll, and spent a happy and light-hearted quarter of an hour with friendly Madame of the shop, deciding the color of the lady's party coat, and of the ribbons in her minute underclothes, and packing and repacking the trunk with enchanting fairy foolishnesses. Again and again she smiled to herself, in bed at night, going about her work in the long days, as she thought of the little girl's rapture over the many and carefully planned details. For, with all the presents showered on her, Robina's aunt knew that Robina had never had anything as perfect as this exquisite Paris doll and her trousseau.

The day came on which Evelyn was to make her final visit to "La Marquise," as Madame called the doll, and the nurse was needed in the hospital and could not go. But she telephoned Madame and made an appointment for tomorrow.

"'La Marquise' finds herself quite ready for the voyage," Madame spoke over the telephone. "She is all which there is of most lovely; Paris itself has never seen a so ravishing doll. I say it. We wait anxiously to greet Mademoiselle, I and La Marquise,"

Madame assured her. Evelyn, laughing with sheer pleasure, made an engagement for the next day, without fail, and went back to her work.

There was a badly wounded *poilu* in her ward, whom the girl had come to know well. He was young, perhaps twenty-seven, and his warm brown eyes were full of a quality of gentleness which endeared him to everyone who came near him. He was very grateful, very uncomplaining, a simple-minded, honest, common, young peasant, with a charm uncommon. The unending bright courage with which he made light of cruel pain, was almost more than Evelyn, used as she was to brave men's pain, could bear. He could not get well—the doctors said that—and it seemed that he could not die.

"If Corporal Duplessis might die," Evelyn spoke to the surgeon.

He answered, considering: "I don't see what keeps him alive."

"I believe," said Evelyn, "there's something on his mind. He sighs constantly. Broken-heartedly. I believe he can't die until his mind is relieved."

"It may be that," agreed Dr. Norton. "You could help him if you could get him to tell you." And moved on to the next shattered thing that had been, so lately, a strong, buoyant boy.

Evelyn went back to Duplessis and bent over him and spoke cheerful words; he smiled up at her with quick French responsiveness, and then sighed the heavy, anxious sigh which had come to be part of him. With that the girl took his one good hand and stroked it. "If you could tell the American Sister what it is," she spoke softly, "that troubles your mind, perhaps I might help you. We Americans, you know," and she smiled at him, "we are wonderful people. We can do all sorts of magic—and I want to help you to rest, so much. I'd do anything to help you. Won't you tell me what it is that bothers?" Evelyn Bruce's voice was winning, and Duplessis' eyes rested on her affectionately.

"But how the Sister understands one!" he said. "It is true that there is a trouble. It hinders me to die"—and the heavy sigh swept out again. "It would be a luxury for me—dying. The pain is bad, at times. Yet the Sister knows I am glad to have it, for France. Ah, yes! But—if I might be released. Yet the thought of what I said to her keeps me from dying always."

"What you said 'to her,' corporal?" repeated Evelyn. "Can't you tell me what it was? I would try so hard to help you. I might perhaps."

"Who knows?" smiled the corporal, "It is true that Americans work magic. And the Sister is of a goodness! But yes. Yet the Sister may laugh at me, for it is a thing entirely childish, my trouble."

"I will not laugh at you, Corporal," said Evelyn, gravely, and felt something wring her heart.

"If—then—if the Sister will not think it foolish—I will tell." The Sister's answer was to stroke his fingers. "It is my child, my little girl," Duplessis began in his deep, weak tones. "It was to her I made the promise."

"What promise?" prompted Evelyn softly, as he stopped.

"One sees," the deep voice began again, "that when I told them goodbye, the mother and Marie my wife, and the *petite*, who has five years, then I started away, and would not look back, because I could not well bear it, Sister. And suddenly, as I strode to the street from our cottage, down the brick walk, where there are roses and also other flowers, on both sides—suddenly I heard a cry. And it was the voice of little Jeanne, the *petite*. I turned at that sound, for I could not help it, Sister, and between the flowers the little one came running, and as I bent she threw her arms about my neck and held me so tight, tight that I could not loosen the little hands, not without hurting her. 'I will not let you go—I will not let you go.' She cried that again and again. Till my heart was broken. But all the same, one had to go. One was due to join the comrades at the station, and the time was short. So that, immediately, I had a thought. 'My most dear,' I spoke to her. 'If thou wilt let me go, then I promise to send thee a great, beautiful doll, all in white, as a bride, like the cousin Annette at her wedding last week.' And then the clinging little hands loosened, and she said, wondering—for she is but a baby—'Wilt thou promise, my father?' And I said, 'Yes,' and kissed her quickly, and went away. So that now that I am wounded and am to die, that promise which I cannot keep to my *petite*, that promise hinders me to die."

The deep, sad voice stopped and the honest eyes of the peasant boy looked up at Evelyn, burning with the pain of his body and of his soul. And as Evelyn looked back, holding his hand and stroking it, it was as if the furnace of the soldier's pain melted together all the things she had ever cared to do. Yet it was a minute before she spoke.

"Corporal," she said, "your little girl shall have her doll, I will take it to her and tell her that her father sent it. Will you lie very still while I go and get the doll?"

The brown eyes looked up at her astounded, radiant, and the man caught the hem of her white veil and kissed it. "But the Americans—they do magic. You shall see, Sister, if I shall be still. I will not die before the Sister returns. It is a joy unheard of."

The girl ran out of the hospital and away into Paris, and burst upon Madame. Somehow she told the story in a few words, and Madame was crying as she laid "La Marquise" in a box.

"It is Mademoiselle who is an angel of the good God," she whispered, and kissed Evelyn unexpectedly on both cheeks.

Corporal Duplessis lay, waxen, starry-eyed, as the American Sister came back into the ward. His look was on her as she entered the far-away door, and he saw the box in her arms. The girl knelt and drew out the gorgeous plaything and stood it by the side of the still, bandaged figure. An expression as of amazed radiance came into the fast-dimming eyes—into those large, brown, childlike eyes which had seen so little of the gorgeousness of earth. His hand stirred a very little—enough, for Evelyn quickly moved the gleaming satin train of the doll under the groping fingers. The eyes lifted to Evelyn's face and the smile in them was that of a prisoner who suddenly sees the gate of his prison opened and the fields of home beyond. It mattered little, one may believe, to the welcoming hosts of heaven that the angel at the gate of release for the child-soul of Corporal Duplessis, the poilu, was only Robina's doll!

---

## DUNDONALD'S DESTROYER

This is the year 1977. It will be objected that the episode I am going to tell, having happened in 1917, having been witnessed by twenty-odd thousand people, must have been, if true, for sixty years common property and an old tale. But when General Cochrane—who saved England at the end of the great war—told me the Kitchener incident of the story last year, sitting in the rose-garden of the White Hart Inn at Sonning-on-Thames, I had never heard of it.

I wonder why he told me. Probably, as is the case in most things which most people do, from a mixture of impulses. For one thing I am an American girl, with a fresher zest to hear tales of those titanic days than the people or the children of the people who lived through them. Also the great war of 1914 has stirred me since I was old enough to know about it, and I have read everything concerning it which I could lay hands on, and talked to everyone who had knowledge of it. Also, General Cochrane and I made friends from the first minute. I was a quite unimportant person of twenty-four years, he a magnificent hero of eighty, one of the proud figures of England; it made me a bit dizzy when I saw that he liked me. One feels, once in a long time, an unmistakable double pull, and knows that oneself and another are friends, and not age, color, race nor previous condition of servitude makes the slightest difference. To have that happen with a celebrity, a celebrity whom it would have been honor enough simply to meet, is quite dizzying. This was the way of it.

I was staying with my cousin Mildred Ward, an Atlanta girl who married Sir Cecil Ward, an English baronet of Oxfordshire. I reached Martin-Goring on a day in July just in time to dress for dinner. When I came down, a bit early, Milly looked me over and pronounced favorably.

"You're not so hard to look at," she pronounced. "It takes an American really to wear French clothes. I'm glad you're looking well tonight, because one of your heroes—Oh!"

She had floated inconsequently against a bookcase in a voyage along the big room, and a spray of wild roses from a vase on the shelf caught in her pretty gold hair.

"Oh—why does Middleton stick those catchy things up there?" she complained, separating the flowers from her hair, and I followed her eyes above the shelf.

"Why, that's a portrait of Kitchener—the old great Kitchener, isn't it?" I asked. "Did he belong to Cecil's people?"

"No," answered Milly, "only Cecil's grandfather and General Cochrane—or something—" her voice trailed. And then, "I've got somebody you'll be crazy about tonight, General Cochrane."

"General Cochrane?"

"Oh! You pretend to know about the great war and don't know General Cochrane, who saved England when the fleet was wrecked. Don't know him!"

"Oh!" I said again. "Know him? Know him! I know every breath, he drew. Only I couldn't believe my ears. The boy Donald Cochrane? It isn't true is it? How did you ever, ever—?"

"He lives five miles from us," said Milly, unconcernedly. "We see a lot of him. His wife was Cecil's great-aunt. She's dead now. His daughter is my best friend. 'The boy Donald Cochrane'!" She smiled a little. "He's no boy now. He's old. Even heroes do that—get old."

And with that the footman at the door announced "General Cochrane."

I stared away up at a very tall, soldierly old man with a jagged scar across his forehead. His wide-open, black-lashed gray eyes flashed a glance like a menace, like a sword, and then suddenly smiled as if the sun had jumped from a bank of storm-clouds. And I looked into those wonderful eyes and we were friends. As fast as that. Most people would think it nonsense, but it happened so. A few people will understand. He took me out to dinner, and it was as if no one else was at the table. I was aware only of the one heroic personality. At first I dared not speak of his history, and then, without planning or intention, my own voice astonished my own ears. I announced to him:

"You have been my hero since I was ten years old."

It was a marvelous thing he did, the lad of twenty, even considering that the secret was there at his hand, ready for him to use. The histories say that—that no matter if he did not invent the device, it was his ready wit which remembered it, and his persistence which forced the war department to use it. Yes, and his heroism which led the ship and all but gave his life. And when he had fulfilled his mission he stepped back into the place of a subaltern; he was modest, even embarrassed, at the great people who thronged to him. England was saved; that was all his affair; nothing, so the books say, could prod him into prominence—though he rose to be a General later—after that, after being the first man in England for those days. It was this personage with whom I had gone out to dinner, and to whom I dared make that sudden speech: "You have been my hero, General Cochrane, since I was ten years old."

He slued about with the menacing, shrapnel look, and it seemed that there might be an explosion of sharp-pointed small bullets over the dinner-table.

"Don't!" I begged. The sun came out; the artillery attack was over; he looked at me with boyish shyness.

"D'you know, when people say things like that I feel as if I were stealing," he told me confidentially. "Anybody else could have done all I did. In fact, it wasn't I at all," he finished.

"Not you? Who then? Weren't you the boy Donald Cochrane?"

"Yes," he said, and stopped as if he were considering it. "Yes," he said quietly in the clean-cut, terse English manner of speaking, "I suppose I was the boy Donald Cochrane." He gazed across the white lilacs and pink roses on the table as if dreaming a bit. Then he turned with a long breath. "My child," he said, "there is something about you which gives me back my youth, and—the freshness of a great experience. I thank you."

I gazed into those compelling eyes, gasping like a fish with too much oxygen, I felt myself, Virginia Fox, meshed in the fringes of historic days, stirred by the rushing mighty wind of that Great Experience. I was awestruck into silence. Just then Milly got up, and eight women flocked into the library.

I was good for nothing there, simply good for nothing at all. I tried to talk to the nice, sensible English women, and I could not. I knew Milly was displeased with me for not keeping up my end, but I was sodden with thrills. I had sat through a dinner next to General Cochrane, the Donald Cochrane who was the most dramatic figure of the world war of sixty years ago. It has always moved me to meet persons who even existed at that time. I look at them and think what intense living it must have meant to pick up a paper and read—as the news of the day, mind you—that Germany had entered Belgium, that King Albert was fighting in the trenches, that Von Kluck was within seventeen miles of Paris, that Von Kluck was retreating—think of the rapture of that—Paris saved!—that the Germans had taken Antwerp; that the *Lusitania* was sunk; that Kitchener was drowned at sea! I wonder if the people who lived and went about their business in America in those days realized that they were having a stage-box for the greatest drama of history? I wonder. Terror and heroism and cruelty find self-sacrifice on a scale which had never been dreamed, which will never, God grant, need to be dreamed on this poor little racked planet again. Of course, there are plenty of those people alive yet, and I've talked to many and they remember it, all of them remember well, even those who were quite small. And it has stirred me simply to look into the eyes of such an one and consider that those eyes read such things as morning news. The great war has had a hold on me since I first heard of it, and I distinctly remember the day, from my father, at the age of seven.

"Can you remember when it happened, father?" I asked him. And then: "Can you remember when they drove old people out of their houses—and killed them?"

"Yes," said my father. And I burst into tears. And when I was not much older he told me about Donald Cochrane, the boy who saved England.

It was not strange to my own mind that I could not talk commonplaces now, when I had just spent an hour tailing to the man who had been that historic boy—the very Donald Cochrane. I could not talk commonplaces.

Milly's leisurely voice broke my meditation. "I'm sorry that my cousin, Virginia Fox, should have such bad manners, Lady Andover," she was drawling. "She was brought up to speak when spoken to, but I think it's the General who has hypnotized her. Virginia, did you know that Lady Andover asked you—" And I came to life.

"It was Miss Fox who hypnotized the General, I fancy," said Lady Andover most graciously, considering I had overlooked her existence a second before. "He had a word for no one else during dinner." I felt myself go scarlet; it had pleased the Marvelous Person, then, to like me a little, perhaps for the youth and enthusiasm in me.

With that the men straggled into the room and the tall grizzled head of my hero, his lined face conspicuous for the jagged, glorious scar, towered over the rest. I saw the vivid eyes flash about, and they met mine; I was staring at him, as I must, and my heart all but jumped out of me when he came straight to where I stood, my back against the bookcase.

"I was looking for you," he said simply.

Then he glanced over my head and his hand shot up in a manner of salute; I turned to see why. I was in front of the portrait of Lord Kitchener.

"Did you know him, General Cochrane?" I asked.

"Know him?" he demanded, and the gray glance plunged out at me from under the thick lashes.

"Don't do it," I pleaded, putting my hands over my eyes. "When you look at me so it's—bombs and bullets." The look softened, but the lean, wrinkled face did not smile.

"You asked if I knew Kitchener," he stated.

I spoke haltingly. "I didn't know. Ought I to have known?"

General Cochrane gazed down, all at once dreamy, as if he looked through me at something miles and æons away.

"No," he said. "There's no reason why you should. You have an uncommon knowledge of events of that time, an astonishing knowledge for a young thing, so that I forget you can't know—all of it." He stopped, as if considering. "It is because I am old that I have fancies," he went on slowly. "And you have understanding eyes. I have had a fancy this evening that you and I were meant to be friends; that a similarity of interests, a—a likeness—oh, hang it all!" burst out the General like a college boy. "I never could talk except straight and hot. I mean I've a feeling of a bond between us— you'll think me most presuming—"

I interrupted, breathless. "It's so," I whispered. "I felt it, only I'd not have dared—" and I choked.

Old General Cochrane frowned thoughtfully. "Curious," was what he said. "It's psychology of course, but I'm hanged if I know the explanation. However, since it's so, my child, I'm glad. A man as old as I makes few new friends. And a beautiful young woman—with a brain—and charm—and innocent eyes—and French clothes!"

One may guess if I tried to stop this description. I could have listened all night. With that:

"'Did I know Kitchener!' the child asked," reflected the General, and threw back his splendid head and laughed. I stared up, my heart pumping. Then, "Well, rather. Why, little Miss Fox—" and he stopped. "I've a mind to tell the child a fairy-story," he said. "A true fairy-story which is so extraordinary that few have been found to believe it, even of those who saw it happen."

He halted again.

"Tell me!"

General Coehrane looked about the roomful of people and tossed out his hand. "In this mob?" he objected. "It's too long a story in any case. But why shouldn't you and I have a séance, to let a garrulous old fellow talk about his youth?" he demanded in his lordly way. "Why not come out on the river in my boat? They'll let you play about with an octogenarian, won't they?"

"I'll come," I answered the General eagerly.

"Very good. Tomorrow. Oh, by George, no. That confounded Prime Minister comes down to me tomorrow. I detest old men," said General Cochrane. "Well, then, the day after?"

The Thames was a picture-book river that day, gay with row-boats and punts and launches, yet serene for all its gaiety; slipping between grassy banks under immemorial trees with the air of a private stream wandering, protected, through an estate. The English have the gift above other nations of producing an atmosphere of leisure and seclusion, and surely there is no little river on earth so used and so unabused as the Thames. Of all the craft abroad that bright afternoon, General Cochrane's white launch with its gold line above the water and its gleaming brass trimmings was far and away the prettiest, and I was bursting with pride as we passed the rank and file on the stream and they looked at us admiringly. To be alive on such a day in England was something; to be afloat on the silvery Thames was enchantment; to be in that lovely boat with General Cochrane, the boy Donald Cochrane, was a rapture not to be believed without one's head reeling. Yet here it was happening, the thing I should look back upon fifty, sixty years from now, an old gray woman, and tell my grandchildren as the most interesting event of my life. It was happening, and I was enjoying every second, and not in the least awed into misery, as is often the case with great moments. For the old officer was as perfect a playmate as any good-for-nothing young subaltern in England, and that is putting it strongly.

"Wouldn't it be nicer to land at Sonning and have our tea there?" he suggested. We were dropping through the lock just higher than the village; the wet, mossy walls were rising above us on both sides and the tops of the lock-keeper's gorgeous pink snapdragons were rapidly going out of sight. My host went on: "There's rather a nice rose-garden, and it's on the river, and the plum-cake's good. What do you think, that or on board?"

"The rose-garden," I decided.

Sonning is a village cut out of a book and pasted on the earth. It can't be true, it's so pretty. And the little White Hart Inn is adorable.

"Is it really three hundred years old?" I asked. "The standard roses look like an illustration out of 'Alice in Wonderland.' Yes, please—tea in the White Hart garden."

The old General heaved a sigh. "Thank Heaven," he said. "I was most awfully anxious for fear you'd say on the boat, and I didn't order any."

We slipped under an arch of the ancient red bridge and were at the landing. I remember the scene as we stood on shore and looked down the shining way of the river, the tall grasses bending on either side like green fur stroked by the breeze; I remember the trim sea-wall and velvet lawn, and the low, long house with leaded windows of the place next the inn. A house-boat was moored to the shore below, white, with scarlet geraniums flowing the length of the upper deck, and willow chairs and tables; people were having tea up there; muslin curtains blew from the portholes below. Some Americans went past with two enormous Scotch deer-hound puppies on leash. "Be quiet, Jock," one of them said, and the big, gentle-faced beast turned on her with a giant, caressing bound, the last touch of beauty in the beautiful, quiet scene.

It was early, so that we took the table which pleased us, one set a bit aside against a ten-foot hedge, and guarded by a tall bush of tea-roses. A plump maid hurried across the lawn and spread a cloth on our table and waited, smiling, as if seeing us had simply made her day perfect. And the General gave the orders.

"The plum-cake is going to be wonderful," I said then, "and I'm hungry as a bear for tea. But the best thing I've been promised this afternoon is a fairy-story."

The shrapnel look flashed, keen and bright and afire, but I looked back steadily, not afraid. I knew what sunlight was going to break; and it broke.

"D'you know," said he, "I'm really quite mad to talk about myself. Men always are. You've heard the little tale of the man who said, 'Let's have a garden-party. Let's go out on the lawn and talk about me'? One becomes a frightful bore quite easily. So that I've made rules—I don't hector people about—about things I've been concerned with. As to the incident I said I'd tell you, that would be quite impossible to tell to—well, practically anyone."

My circulatory system did a prance; he could tell it practically to no one, yet he was going to tell it to me! I instantly said that. "But you're going to tell it to me?" I was anxious.

"Child, you flatter well," said the Marvelous Person, who had brought me picnicking. "It's the American touch; there's a way with American women quite irresistible."

"Oh—American women!" I remonstrated.

"Yes, indeed. They're delightful—you're witches, every mother's daughter of you. But you—ah—that's different, now. You and I, as we decided long ago, on day before yesterday, have a bond. I can't help the conviction that you're the hundred-thousandth person. You have understanding eyes. If I were a young man—And yet it's not just that; it's something a bit rarer. Moreover, they tell me there's a chap back in America."

"Yes," I owned. "There is a chap." And I persisted: "I'm to have a fairy-story?"

The black-lashed gaze narrowed as it traveled across the velvet turf and the tall roses, down the path of the quiet river. He had a fine head, thick-thatched and grizzled, not white; his nose was of the straight, short English type, slightly chopped up at the end—a good-looking nose; his mouth was wide and not chiseled, yet sensitive as well as strong; the jaw was powerful and the chin square with a marked dimple in it; there was also color, the claret and honey of English tanned complexions. Of course his eyes, with the exaggeratedly thick and long black lashes, were the wonderful part of him, but there is no describing the eyes. It was the look from them, probably, which made General Cochrane's face remarkable. I suppose it was partly that compelling look which had brought about his career. He was six feet four, lean and military, full of presence, altogether a conspicuously beautiful old lion in a land where every third man is beautiful.

"What are you looking munitions-of-war at, General, down the innocent little Thames River? You must be seeing around corners, past Wargrave, as far as Henley."

"I didn't see the Thames River," he shot at me in his masterful way. "I was looking at things past, and people dead and gone. We ancients do that. I saw London streets and crowds; I read the posters which told that Kitchener was drowned at sea, and then I saw, a year later, England in panic; I saw an almighty meeting in Trafalgar Square and I heard speeches which burned my ears—men urging Englishmen to surrender England and make terms with the Huns. Good God!" His fist came down on the rattling little iron table.

"My blood boils now when I remember. Child," he demanded, "I can't see why your alluring ways should have set me talking. Fancy, I've never told this tale but twice, and I'm holding forth to a little alien whom I haven't known two days, a young ne'er-do-well not born till forty years after the tale happened!"

"What difference does that make?" I asked. "Age means nothing to real people. And we've known each other since—since we hunted pterodactyls together, pre-historically. Only—I hate bats," I objected to my own arrangement. I went on: "If you knew how I want to hear! It's the most wonderful thing in my life, this afternoon—you."

"I know you are honest," he said. "Different from the ruck. I knew that the moment I saw you."

"Then," I prodded, "do begin with the posters about Lord Kitchener."

"But that's not the beginning," he protested. "You'll spoil it all," he said.

"Oh, no, then! Begin at the beginning. I didn't know. I wanted to get you started."

The gray eyes dreamed down the placid river water.

"The beginning was before I was born. It began when Kitchener, a young general, picked up a marauding party of black rascals on his way to Khartoum. They had a captive, a white girl, a lady. They had murdered her father and mother and young brother. The father was newly appointed Colonel of a regiment, traveling to his post with his family. The Arabs were saving the girl for their devilish head chieftain. Kitchener had the lot executed, and sent for the girl. She was—"

The old man's hand lifted to his head and he took off his hat and laid it on the ground.

"I cannot speak of that girl without uncovering," he said, quietly. "She was my mother." There was an electrical silence. I knew enough to know that no words fitted here. The old officer went on: "She was one of the wonderful people. What she seemed to think of, after the horrors she had gone through, was not herself or her suffering, but only to show her gratitude. It was a long journey—weeks—through that land of hell, while she was in Kitchener's hands, and not once did she lose courage. The Sirdar told me that it was having an angel in camp—she held that rough soldiery in the hollow of her hand. She told Kitchener her story, and after that she would not talk of herself. You've heard that he never had a love affair? That's wrong. He was in love then, and for the rest of his life, with my mother."

I gasped. The shrapnel eyes menaced me.

"She could not speak of herself, d'you see? It was salvation to think only of others, so that she'd not told him that she was engaged to my father. Love from any other was the last thing she was thinking of. After what had happened she was living from one breath to another and she dared not consider her own affairs. The night before they reached Cairo, Kitchener asked her to marry him. He was over forty then; she was nineteen. She told him of her engagement, of course—told him also that it might be she would never marry at all; a life of her own and happiness seemed impossible now. She might go into a sisterhood. Work for others was what she must have. Then, unexpectedly, my father was at Cairo to meet her, and Kitchener went to him and told him. From that on the two men were close friends. My people were not married till five years later, and when I came to be baptized General Kitchener was godfather. All my young days I was used to seeing him about the house at intervals, as if he belonged to us. I remember his eyes following my mother. Tall and slight she was, with a haunted look, from what she'd seen; she moved softly, spoke softly. It was no secret from the two, my father and mother, that he loved her always. Yet, so loyal, so crystal he was that my father had never one moment of jealousy. On the contrary they were like brothers. Then they died—my father and mother. The two almost together. I came into Kitchener's hands, Lord Kitchener by then. When he met me in London, a long lad of seventeen, he held my fingers a second and looked hard at me.

"'You're very like her, Donald,' he said. And held on. And said it again. 'Your mother's double. I'd know you for her boy if I caught one look of your eyes, anywhere,' he said. 'Her boy.'—Well—what? Do I want more tea? Of course, I do."

For the smiling plump maid had long ago brought the steaming stuff, the bread and butter and jam and plum cake, I had officiated and General Cochrane had been absorbing his tea as an Englishman does, automatically, while he talked.

About us the tables were filling up, all over the rose-garden. The Americans were there with the beautiful long-legged giant deer-hound puppy, Jock, and were having trouble with his table manners. People came in by twos and threes and more, from the river, with the glow of exercise on their faces; an elderly country parson sat near, black-coated, white-collared, with his elderly daughter and their dog, a well-behaved Scottie this one, big-headed, with an age-old, wise, black face. And a group of three pretty girls with their pretty pink-cheeked mother and a young man or so were having a gay time with soft-voiced laughter and jokes, not far away. The breeze lifted the long purple and rose-colored motor veils of mother and daughters. The whole place was full of bright colors and low-toned cheerful talk, yet so English was the atmosphere, that it was as if the General and I were shut into an enchanted forest. No one looked at us, no one seemed to know we were there. The General began to talk again, unconscious as the rest of anything or anybody not his affair.

"I got my commission in 1915 in K-1, Kitchener's first hundred thousand, and I went off to the front in the second year of the war. I had a scratch and was slightly gassed once, but nothing much happened for a long time. And in 1916, in May, came the news that my godfather, the person closest to me on earth, was drowned at sea. I was in London, just out of the hospital and about to go back to France."

The old General stopped and stared down at the graveled path with its trim turf border lying at his feet.

"It was to me as if the world, seething in its troubles, was suddenly empty—with that man gone. I drifted with the crowd about London town, and the crowd appeared to be like myself, dazed. The streets were full and there was continually a profound, sorrowful sound, like the groan of a nation; faces were blank and gray. Those surging, mournful London streets, and the look of the posters with great letters on them—his name—that memory isn't likely to leave me till I die. Of course, I got hold of every detail and tried to picture the manner of it to myself, but I couldn't get it that he was dead. Kitchener, the heart of the nation; I couldn't comprehend that he had stopped breathing. I couldn't get myself satisfied that I wasn't to see him again. It seemed there must be some way out. You'll remember, perhaps, that four boats were seen to put off from the *Hampshire* as she sank? I tried to trace those boats. I traveled up there and interviewed people who had seen them. I got no good from it. But it kept coming to me that it was not a mine that had sunk the ship, that it was a torpedo from a German submarine, and that Kitchener was on one of the boats that put off and that he had been taken prisoner by the enemy. God knows why that thought persisted—there were reasons against it—it was a boy's theory. But it persisted; I couldn't get it out of my head. I was in St. Paul's at the Memorial Service; I heard the 'Last Post' played for him, and I saw the King and Queen in tears; all that didn't settle my mind. I went back to the front, heavy-hearted, and tried to behave myself as I believed he'd have had me—the Sirdar. My people had called him the Sirdar always. Luck was with me in France; I had chances, and did a bit of work, and got advancement."

"I know," I nodded. "I've read history. A few trifles like the rescue of the rifles and holding that trench and—"

The old soldier interrupted, looking thunderous. "It has a bearing on the episode I'm about to tell you. That's why I refer to it."

I didn't mind his haughtiness. It was given me to see the boy's shyness within that grim old hero.

"So that when I landed in London in 1917, having been stupid enough to get my right arm potted, it happened that my name was known. They picked me out to make a doing over. I was most uncommonly conspicuous for nothing more than thousands of other lads had done. They'd given their lives like water, thousands of them—it made me sick with shame, when I thought of those others, to have my name ringing through the land. But so it was, and it served a purpose, right enough, I saw later.

"Then, as I began to crawl about, came the crisis of the war. Ill news piled on ill news; the army in France was down with an epidemic; each day's news was worse than the last; to top all, the Germans found the fleet. It was in letters a foot long about London—newsboys crying awful words:

"'Fleet discovered—German submarines and Zeppelins approaching.'

"A bit later, still worse. 'The *Bellerophon* sunk by German torpedo—ten dreadnoughts sunk—' There were the names of the big ships, the *Queen Elizabeth*, the *Warspite*, the *Thunderer*, the *Agamemnon*, the *King Edward*—a lot more, battle cruisers, too—then ten more dreadnoughts—and more and worse every hour. The German navy was said to be coming into the North Sea and advancing to our coast. And our navy was going—gone—nothing to stand between us and the fate of Belgium.

"Then England went mad! I thank God I'll not live through such days again. The land went mad with fear. You'll remember that there had been a three-year strain which human nerves were not meant to bear. Well, there was a faction who urged that the only sane act now possible was to surrender to Germany quickly and hope for a mercy which we couldn't get if we struggled. The government, under enormous pressure, weakened. It's easy to cry 'Shame!' now, but how could it stand firm with the country stampeding back of it?

"So things were the day of the mass meeting in Trafalgar Square. I was tall, and so thin and gaunt that, with my uniform and my arm in its sling, it was easy to get close to the front, straight under the speakers. And no sooner had I got there than I was seized with a restlessness, an uncontrollable desire to see my godfather—Kitchener. Only to see him, to lay eyes on him. I wish I might express to you the push of that feeling. It was thirst in a desert. With that spell on me I stood down in front of the stone lions and stared up at Nelson on his column, and listened to the speakers. They were mad, quite, those speakers. The crowd was mad, too. It overflowed that great space, and there were few steady heads in the lot. You'll realize it looked a bit of a close shave, with the German navy coming and our fleet being destroyed, no one knew how fast, and the army in France, and struck down by illness. At that moment it looked a matter of three or four days before the Huns would be landing. Never before in a thousand years was England as near the finish. As I stood there fidgeting, with the starvation on me for my godfather, it flashed to me that there's a legend in every nation about some one of its heroes, how in the hour of need he will come back to save the people—Charlemagne in France, don't you know, and Barbarossa and King Arthur and—oh, a number. And I spoke aloud, so that the chap next prodded me in the ribs and said: 'Stop that, will you? I can't hear'—I spoke aloud and said:

"'This is the hour. Come back and save us.'

"The speakers had been ranting along, urging on the people to force the government to give in and make terms with those devils who'd crushed Belgium. Of course there were plenty there ready to die in the last ditch for honor and the country, but the mob was with the speakers. Quite insane with terror the mob was. And I spoke aloud to Kitchener, like a madman of a sort also, begging him to come from another world and save his people.

"'This is the hour; come and save us,' said I, and said it as if my words could get through to Kitchener in eternity.

"With that a taxicab forced through the crowd, close to the platform, and it stopped and somebody got out. I could see an officer's cap and the crowd pressing. My eyes were riveted on that brown cap; my breath came queerly; there was a murmur, a hush and a murmur together, where that tall officer with the cap over his face pushed toward the speakers. I felt I should choke if I didn't see him—and I couldn't see him. Then he made the platform, and before my eyes, before the eyes of twenty thousand people, he stood there—Kitchener!"

General Cochrane stared defiantly at me. "I'm not asking you to believe this," he said. "I'm merely telling you—what happened."

"Go on," I whispered.

He went on: "A silence like death fell on that vast crowd. The voice of the speaker screaming out wild cowardice about mercy from the Germans kept on for a few words, and then the man caught the electrical atmosphere and was aware that something was happening. He halted half-way in a word, and turned and faced the grim, motionless figure—Kitchener. The man stared a half minute and shot his hands up and howled, and ran into the throng. All over the great place, by then, was a whisper swelling into a bass murmur, into a roar, his name.

"'Kitchener—Kitchener!' and 'K. of K.!' and 'Kitchener of Khartoum!'

"Never in my life have I heard a volume of sound like London shouting that day the name of Kitchener. After a time he lifted his hand and stood, deep-eyed and haggard, as the mass quieted. He spoke. I can't tell you what he said. I couldn't have told you the next hour. But he quieted us and lifted us, that crowd, fearstruck, sobbing, into courage. He put his own steady dignity into those cheap, frightened little Johnnies. He gave us strength even if the worst came, and he held up English pluck and doggedness for us to look at and to live by. As his voice stopped, as I stood down in front just under him, I flung up my arms, and I suppose I cried out something; I was but a lad of twenty, and half crazed with the joy of seeing him. And he swung forward a step to me as if he had seen me all the time—and I think he had. 'Do the turn, Donald,' he said, 'The time has come for a Cochrane to save England.'

"And with that he wheeled and without a look to right or left, in his own swift, silent, shy way he was gone.

"Nobody saw where he went. I all but killed myself for an hour trying to find him, but it was of no use. And with that, as I sat at my lunch, too feverish and stirred to eat food, demanding over and over what he meant, what the 'turn' was which I was to do, why a Cochrane should have a chance to save England—with that, suddenly I knew."

General Cochrane halted again, and again he gazed down the little river, the river of England, the river which he, more than any other, had kept for English folk and their peaceful play-times. I knew I must not hurry him; I waited.

"The thing came to me like lightning," he went on, "and I had only to go from one simple step to another; it seemed all thought out for me. It was something, don't you see, which I'd known all my lifetime, but hadn't once thought of since the war began. I went direct to my bankers and got a box out of the safe and fetched it home in a cab. There I opened it and took out papers and went over them.... This part of the tale is mostly in print," General Cochrane interrupted himself. "Have you read it? I don't want to bore you with repetitions."

I answered hurriedly, trembling for fear I might say the wrong thing: "I've read what's in print, but your telling it puts it in another world. Please go on. Please don't shorten anything."

The shadow of a smile played. "I rather like telling you a story, d'you know," he spoke, half absent-mindedly—his real thoughts were with that huge past. He swept back to it. "You know, of course, about Dundonald's Destroyer—the invention of my great-grandfather's kinsman, Thomas Cochrane, tenth Earl of Dundonald? He was a good bit of an old chap in various ways. He did things to the French fleet that put him as a naval officer in the class with Nelson and Drake. But he's remembered in history by his invention. It was a secret, of course, one of the puzzles of the time and of years after, up to 1917. It was known there was something. He offered it to the government in 1811, and the government appointed a committee to examine into it. The chairman was the Duke of York, commander-in-chief of the army, said to be the ablest administrator of military affairs of that time. Also there were Admirals Lord Keith and Exmouth and the Congreve brothers of the ordnance department. A more competent committee of five could not have been gathered in the world. This board would not recommend the adoption of the scheme. Why? They reported that there was no question that the invention would do all which Dundonald claimed, but it was so unspeakably dreadful as to be impossible for civilized men.

"There was not a shadow of doubt, the committee reported, that Dundonald's device would not merely defeat but annihilate and sweep out of existence any hostile force, whole armies and navies. 'No power on earth could stand against it,' said the old fellow, and the five experts backed him up. But they considered that the devastation would be inhuman beyond permissible warfare. Not war, annihilation. In fact, they shelved it because it was too efficient. There was great need of means for fighting Napoleon just then, so they gave it up reluctantly, but it was a bit too shocking.

"The weak point of the business was, as Dundonald himself declared, that it was so simple—as everybody knows now—that its first use would tell the secret and put it in the hands of other nations. Therefore the committee recommended that this incipient destruction should be stowed away and kept secret, so that no power more unscrupulous than England should get it and use it for the annihilation of England and the conquest of the world. Also the committee persuaded the Earl before he went on his South American adventure to swear formally that he would never disclose his device except in the service of England. He kept that oath.

"Well, the formula for this affair was, of course, in pigeonholes or vaults in the British Admiralty ever since the committee in 1811 had examined and refused it. But there was also, unknown to the public, another copy. The Earl was with my great-grandfather, his kinsman and lifelong friend, shortly before his death, and he gave this copy to him with certain conditions. The old chap had an ungovernable temper, quarreled right and left, don't you know, his life long, and at this time and until he died he was not on speaking terms with his son Thomas, who succeeded him as Earl, or indeed with any of the three other sons. Which accounts for his trusting to my great-grandfather the future of his invention. I found a quaint note with the papers. He said in effect that he had come to believe with the committee that it was quite too shocking for decent folk. Yet, he suggested, the time might come when England was in straits and only a sweeping blow could serve her. If that time should come it would be a joy to him in heaven or in hell—he said—to think that a man of his name had used the work of his brains to save England.

"Therefore, the Earl asked my grandfather to guard this gigantic secret and to see to it that one man in each generation of Cochranes should know it and have it at hand for use in an emergency. My grandfather came into the papers when he came of age, and after him my father; I was due to read them when I should be twenty-one. I was only twenty in 1917. But the papers were mine, and from the moment it flashed to me what Kitchener meant I didn't hesitate. It was this enormous power which was placed suddenly in the hands of a lad of twenty. The Sirdar placed it there.

"I went over the business in an hour—it was simple, like most big things. You know what it was, of course; everybody knows now. Wasn't it extraordinary that in five thousand years of fighting no one ever hit on it before? I rushed to the War Office.

"Well, the thing came off. At first they pooh-poohed me as an unbalanced boy, but they looked up the documents in the Admiralty and there was no question. It isn't often a youngster is called into the councils of the government, and I've wondered since how I held my own. I've come to believe that I was merely a body for Kitchener's spirit. I was conscious of no fatigue, no uncertainty. I did things as the Sirdar might have done them, and it appears to me only decent to realize that he did do them, and not I. You probably know the details."

I waited, hoping that he would not stop. Then I said: "I know that the government asked for twenty-five volunteers for a service which would destroy the German fleet, but which would mean almost certain death to the volunteers. I know that you headed the list and that thousands offered." My voice shook and I spoke with difficulty as I realized to whom I was speaking. "I know that you were the only one who came back alive, and that you were barely saved."

General Cochrane seemed not to hear me. He was living over enormous events.

"It was a bright morning in the North Sea," he talked on, but not to me now. "Nobody but ourselves knew just what was to be done, but everybody hoped—they didn't know what. It was a desperate England from which we sailed away. We hadn't long to wait—the second morning. There were their ships, the triumphant long lines of the invader. There were their crowded transports, the soldiers coming to crucify

England as they had crucified Belgium—thousands and tens of thousands of them. Then—we did it. German power was wiped off the face of the earth. German arrogance was ended for all time. And that was the last I knew," said General Cochrane. "I was conscious till it was known that the trick had worked. Of course it couldn't be otherwise, yet it was so beyond anything which mankind had dreamed that I couldn't believe it till I knew. Then, naturally, I didn't much care if I lived or died. I'd done the turn as the Sirdar told me, and one life was a small thing to pay. I dropped into blackness quite happily, and when I woke up to this good earth I was glad. England was right. The Sirdar had saved her."

"And the Sirdar?" I asked him. "Was it—himself?"

"Himself? Most certainly."

"I mean—well—" I stammered. And then I plunged in. "I must know," I said. "Was it Lord Kitchener in flesh and blood? Had he been a prisoner in Germany and escaped? Or was it—his ghost?"

The old lion rubbed his cheek consideringly. "Ah, there you have me," and he smiled. "Didn't I tell you this was a tale which could be told to few people?" he demanded. "'Flesh and blood'—ah, that's what I can't tell you. But—himself? Those people, the immense crowd which saw him and recognized him, they knew. Afterwards they begged the question. The papers were full of a remarkable speech made by an unknown officer who strikingly resembled Kitchener. That's the way they got out of it. But those people knew, that day. There wasn't any doubt in their minds when that roar of his name went up. They knew! But people are ashamed to own to the supernatural. And yet it's all around us," mused General Cochrane.

"Could it have been—did you ever think—" I began, and dared not go on.

"Did I ever think what, child?" repeated the old officer, with his autocratic friendliness. "Out with it. You and I are having a truth-feast."

"Well, then," I said, "if you won't be angry—"

"I won't. Come along."

"Did you ever think that it might have been that—you were only a boy, and wounded and weak and overstrained—and full of longing for your godfather. Did you ever think that you might have mistaken the likeness of the officer for Kitchener himself? That the thought of Dundonald's Destroyer was working in your mind before, and that it materialized at that moment and you—imagined the words he said. Perhaps imagined them afterwards, as you searched for him over London. The two things might have suggested each other in your feverish boy's brain."

I stopped, frightened, fearful that he might think me not appreciative of the honor he had done me in telling this intimate experience. But General Cochrane was in no wise disturbed.

"Yes, I've thought that," he answered dispassionately. "It may be that was the case. And yet—I can't see it. That thing happened to me. I've not been able to explain it away to my own satisfaction. I've not been able to believe otherwise than that the Sirdar, England's hero, came to save England in her peril, and that he did it by breathing his thought into me. His spirit got across somehow from over there—to me. I was the only available person alive. The copy in the archives was buried, dead and buried and forgotten for seventy years. So he did it—that way. And if your explanation is the right one it isn't so much less wonderful, is it?" he demanded. "In these days psychology dares say more than in 1917. One knows that ghost stories, as they called them in those ignorant times, are not all superstition and imagination. One knows that a soul lives beyond the present, that a soul sometimes struggles back from what we call the hereafter to this little earth—makes the difficult connection between an unseen world of spirit, unconditioned by matter, and our present world of spirit, conditioned by matter. When the pull is strong enough. And what pull could be stronger than England's danger? To Kitchener?" The black-lashed, gray eyes flamed at me, unblinking the rift of light through the curtain of eternal silences.

When I spoke again: "It's a story the world ought to own some day," I said. "Love of country, faithfulness that death could not hinder."

"Well," said old General Cochrane, "when I'm gone you may write it for the world if you like, little American. And what I'll do will be to find the Sirdar, the very first instant I'm over the border, and say to him, 'I've known it was your work all along, sir, and however did you get it across?'"

A month ago my cousin sent me some marked newspapers. General Cochrane has gone over the border, and I make no doubt that before now he has found the Sirdar and that the two sons and saviors of a beloved little land on a little planet have talked over that moment, in the leisures and simplicities of eternity, and have wondered perhaps that anyone could wonder how he got it across.

# The Militants, Stories of Some Parsons, Soldiers, and Other Fighters in the World

### THE BISHOP'S SILENCE

The Bishop was walking across the fields to afternoon service. It was a hot July day, and he walked slowly—for there was plenty of time—with his eyes fixed on the far-off, shimmering sea. That minstrel of heat, the locust, hidden somewhere in the shade of burning herbage, pulled a long, clear, vibrating bow across his violin, and the sound fell lazily on the still air—the only sound on earth except a soft crackle under the Bishop's feet. Suddenly the erect, iron-gray head plunged madly forward, and then, with a frantic effort and a parabola or two, recovered itself, while from the tall grass by the side of the path gurgled up a high, soft, ecstatic squeal. The Bishop, his face flushed with the stumble and the heat and a touch of indignation besides, straightened himself with dignity and felt for his hat, while his eyes followed a wriggling cord that lay on the ground, up to a small brown fist. A burnished head, gleaming in the sunshine like the gilded ball on a church steeple, rose suddenly out of the waves of dry grass, and a pink-ginghamed figure, radiant with joy and good-will, confronted him. The Bishop's temper, roughly waked up by the unwilling and unepiscopal war-dance just executed, fell back into its chains.

"Did you tie that string across the path?"

"Yes," The shining head nodded. "Too bad you didn't fell 'way down. I'm sorry. But you kicked awf'ly."

"Oh! I did, did I?" asked the Bishop. "You're an unrepentant young sinner. Suppose I'd broken my leg?"

The head nodded again. "Oh, we'd have patzed you up," she said cheerfully. "Don't worry. Trust in God."

The Bishop jumped. "My child," he said, "who says that to you?"

"Aunt Basha." The innocent eyes faced him without a sign of embarrassment. "Aunt Basha's my old black mammy. Do you know her? All her name's longer'n that. I can say it." Then with careful, slow enunciation, "Bathsheba Salina Mosina Angelica Preston."

"Is that your little bit of name too?" the Bishop asked, "Are you a Preston?"

"Why, of course." The child opened her gray eyes wide. "Don't you know my name? I'm Eleanor. Eleanor Gray Preston."

For a moment again the locust had it all to himself. High and insistent, his steady note sounded across the hot, still world. The Bishop looked down at the gray eyes gazing upward wonderingly, and through a mist of years other eyes smiled at him. Eleanor Gray—the world is small, the life of it persistent; generations repeat themselves, and each is young but once. He put his hand under the child's chin and turned up the baby face.

"Ah!" said he—if that may stand for the sound that stood for the Bishop's reverie. "Ah! Whom were you named for, Eleanor Gray?"

"For my own muvver." Eleanor wriggled her chin from the big hand and looked at him with dignity. She did not like to be touched by strangers. Again the voices stopped and the locust sang two notes and stopped also, as if suddenly awed.

"Your mother," repeated the Bishop, "your mother! I hope you are worthy of the name."

"Yes, I am," said Eleanor heartily. "Bug's on your shoulder, Bishop! For de Lawd's sake!" she squealed excitedly, in delicious high notes that a prima donna might envy; then caught the fat grasshopper from the black clerical coat, and stood holding it, lips compressed and the joy of adventure dancing in her eyes. The Bishop took out his watch and looked at it, as Eleanor, her soul on the grasshopper, opened her fist and flung its squirming contents, with delicious horror, yards away. Half an hour yet to service and only five minutes' walk to the little church of Saint Peter's-by-the-Sea.

"Will you sit down and talk to me, Eleanor Gray?" he asked, gravely.

"Oh, yes, if there's time," assented Eleanor, "but you mustn't be late to church, Bishop. That's naughty."

"I think there's time. How do you know who I am, Eleanor?"

"Dick told me."

The Bishop had walked away from the throbbing sunshine into the green-black shadows of a tree, and seated himself with a boyish lightness in piquant contrast with his gray-haired dignity—a lightness that meant athletic years. Eleanor bent down the branch of a great bush that faced him and sat on it as if a bird had poised there. She smiled as their eyes met, and began to hum an air softly. The startled Bishop slowly made out a likeness to the words of the old hymn that begins

Am I a soldier of the Cross,
A follower of the Lamb?

Sweetly and reverently she sang it, over and over, with a difference.

Am I shoulder of a hoss,
A quarter of a lamb?

sang Eleanor.

The Bishop exploded into a great laugh that drowned the music.

"Aunt Basha taught you that, too, didn't she?" he asked, and off he went into another deep-toned peal.

"I thought you'd like that, 'cause it's a hymn and you're a Bishop," said Eleanor, approvingly. Her effort was evidently meeting with appreciation. "You can talk to me now, I'm here." She settled herself like a Brownie, elbows on knees, her chin in the hollows of small, lean hands, and gazed at him unflinchingly.

"Thank you," said the Bishop, sobering at once, but laughter still in his eyes. "Will you be kind enough to tell me then, Eleanor, who is Dick?"

Eleanor looked astonished, "You don't know anybody much, do you?" and there was gentle pity in her voice. "Why, Dick, he's—why, he's—why, you see, he's my friend. I don't know his uvver names, but Mr. Fielding, he's Dick's favver."

"Oh!" said the Bishop with comprehension. "Dick Fielding. Then Dick is my friend, too. And people that are friends to the same people should be friends to each other—that's geometry, Eleanor, though it's possibly not life."

"Huh?" Eleanor stared, puzzled.

"Will you be friends with me, Eleanor Gray? I knew your mother a long time ago, when she was Eleanor Gray." Eleanor yawned frankly. That might be true, but it did not appear to her remarkable or interesting. The deep voice went on, with a moment's interval. "Where is your mother? Is she here?"

Eleanor laughed. "Oh, no," she said. "Don't you know? What a funny man you are—you know such a few things. My muvver's up in heaven. She went when I was a baby, long, *long* ago. I reckon she must have flewed," she added, reflectively, raising clear eyes to the pale, heat-worn sky that gleamed through the branches.

The Bishop's big hands went up to his face suddenly, and the strong fingers clasped tensely above his forehead. Between his wrists one could see that his mouth was set in a hard line. "Dead!" he said. "And I never knew it."

Eleanor dug a small russet heel unconcernedly into the ground. "Naughty, naughty, naughty little grasshopper," she began to chant, addressing an unconscious insect near the heel. "Don't you go and crawl up on the Bishop. No, just don't you. 'Cause if you do, oh, naughty grasshopper, I'll scrunch you!" with a vicious snap on the "scrunch."

The Bishop lowered his hands and looked at her. "I'm not being very interesting, Eleanor, am I?"

"Not very," Eleanor admitted. "Couldn't you be some more int'rstin'?"

"I'll try," said the Bishop. "But be careful not to hurt the poor grasshopper. Because, you know, some people say that if he is a good grasshopper for a long time, then when he dies his little soul will go into a better body—perhaps a butterfly's body next time."

Eleanor caught the thought instantly. "And if he's a good butterfly, then what'll he be? A hummin'-bird? Let's kill him quick, and see him turn into a butterfly."

"Oh, no, Eleanor, you can't force the situation. He has to live out his little grasshopper life the best that he can, before he's good enough to be a butterfly. If you kill him now you might send him backward. He might turn into what he was before—a poor little blind worm perhaps."

"Oh, my Lawd!" said Eleanor.

The Bishop was still a moment, and then repeated, quietly:

Slay not the meanest creature, lest thou slay
Some humble soul upon its upward way.

"Oughtn't to talk to yourself," Eleanor shook her head disapprovingly. "'Tisn't so very polite. Is that true about the grasshopper, Bishop, or is it a whopper?"

The Bishop thought for a moment. "I don't know, Eleanor," he answered, gently.

"You don't know so very much, do you?" inquired Eleanor, not as despising but as wondering, sympathizing with ignorance.

"Very little," the Bishop agreed. "And I've tried to learn, all my life"—his gaze wandered off reflectively.

"Too bad," said Eleanor. "Maybe you'll learn some time."

"Maybe," said the Bishop and smiled, and suddenly she sprang to her feet, and shook her finger at him.

"I'm afraid," she said, "I'm very much afraid you're a naughty boy."

The Bishop looked up at the small, motherly face, bewildered. "Wh—why?" he stammered.

"Do you know what you're bein'? You're bein' late to church!"

The Bishop sprang up too, at that, and looked at his watch quickly. "Not late yet, but I'll walk along. Where are you going, waif? Aren't you in charge of anybody?"

"Huh?" inquired Eleanor, her head cocked sideways.

"Whom did you come out with?"

"Madge and Dick, but they're off there," nodding toward the wood behind them. "Madge is cryin'. She wouldn't let me pound Dick for makin' her, so I went away."

"Who is Madge?"

Eleanor, drifting beside him through the sunshine like a rose-leaf on the wind, stopped short. "Why, Bishop, don't you know even Madge? Funny Bishop! Madge is my sister—she's grown up. Dick made her cry, but I think he wasn't much naughty, 'cause she would *not* let me pound him. She put her arms right around him."

"Oh!" said the Bishop, and there was silence for a moment. "You mustn't tell me any more about Madge and Dick, I think, Eleanor."

"All right, my lamb!" Eleanor assented, cheerfully, and conversation flagged.

"How old are you, Eleanor Gray?"

"Six, praise de Lawd!"

The Bishop considered deeply for a moment, then his face cleared.

"'Their angels do always behold the face of my Father,'" and he smiled. "I say it too, praise the Lord that she is six."

"Madge is lots more'n that," the soft little voice, with its gay, courageous inflection, went on. "She's twenty. Isn't that old? You aren't much different of that, are you?" and the heavy, cropped, straight gold mass of her hair swung sideways as she turned her face up to scrutinize the tall Bishop.

He smiled down at her. "Only thirty years different. I'm fifty, Eleanor."

"Oh!" said Eleanor, trying to grasp the problem. Then with a sigh she gave it up, and threw herself on the strength of maturity. "Is fifty older'n twenty?" she asked.

More than once as they went side by side on the narrow foot-path across the field the Bishop put out his hand to hold the little brown one near it, but each time the child floated from his touch, and he smiled at the unconscious dignity, the womanly reserve of the frank and friendly little lady. "Thus far and no farther," he thought, with the quick perception of character that was part of his power. But the

Bishop was as unconscious as the child of his own charm, of the magnetism in him that drew hearts his way. Only once had it ever failed, and that was the only time he had cared. But this time it was working fast as they walked and talked together quietly, and when they reached the open door that led from the fields into the little robing-room of Saint Peter's, Eleanor had met her Waterloo. Being six, it was easy to say so, and she did it with directness, yet without at all losing the dignity that was breeding, that had come to her from generations, and that she knew of as little as she knew the names of her bones. Three steps led to the robing-room, and Eleanor flew to the top and turned, the childish figure in its worn pink cotton dress facing the tall powerful one in sober black broadcloth.

"I love you," she said. "I'll kiss you," and the long, strong little arms were around his neck, and it seemed to the Bishop as if a kiss that had never been given came to him now from the lips of the child of the woman he had loved. As he put her down gently, from the belfry above tolled suddenly a sweet, rolling note for service.

When the Bishop came out from church the "peace that passeth understanding" was over him. The beautiful old words that to churchmen are dear as their mothers' faces, haunting as the voices that make home, held him yet in the last echo of their music. Peace seemed, too, to lie across the world, worn with the day's heat, where the shadows were stretching in lengthening, cooling lines. And there at the vestry step, where Eleanor had stood an hour before, was Dick Fielding, waiting for him, with as unhappy a face as an eldest scion, the heir to millions, well loved, and well brought up, and wonderfully unspoiled, ever carried about a country-side. The Bishop was staying at the Fieldings'. He nodded and swung past Dick, with a look from the tail of his eye that said: "Come along." Dick came, and silently the two turned into the path of the fields. The scowl on Dick's dark face deepened as they walked, and that was all there was by way of conversation for some time. Finally:

"You don't know about it, do you, Bishop?" he asked.

"A very little, my boy," the Bishop answered.

Dick was on the defensive in a moment. "My father told you—you agree with him?"

"Your father has told me nothing. I only came last night, remember. I know that you made Madge cry, and that Eleanor wasn't allowed to punish you."

The boyish face cleared a little, and he laughed. "That little rat! Has she been talking? It's all right if it's only to you, but Madge will have to cork her up." Then anxiety and unhappiness seized Dick's buoyant soul again. "Bishop, let me talk to you, will you please? I'm knocked up about this, for there's never been trouble between my father and me before, and I can't give in. I know I'm right—I'd be a cad to give in, and I wouldn't if I could. If you would only see your way to talking to the governor, Bishop! He'll listen to you when he'd throw any other chap out of the house."

"Tell me the whole story if you can, Dick, I don't understand, you see."

"I suppose it will sound rather commonplace to you," said Dick, humbly, "but it means everything to me. I—I'm engaged to Madge Preston. I've known her for a year, and been engaged half of it, and I ought to know my own mind by now. But father has simply set his forefeet and won't hear of it. Won't even let me talk to him about it."

Dick's hands went into his pockets and his head drooped, and his big figure lagged pathetically. The Bishop put his hand on the young man's shoulder, and left it there as they walked slowly on, but he said nothing.

"It's her father, you know," Dick went on. "Such rot, to hold a girl responsible for her ancestors! Isn't it rot, now? Father says they're a bad stock, dissipated and arrogant and spendthrift and shiftless and weak—oh, and a lot more! He's not stingy with his adjectives, bless you! Picture to yourself Madge being dissipated and arrogant and—have you seen Madge?" he interrupted himself.

The Bishop shook his head. "Eleanor made an attempt on my life with a string across the path, to-day. We were friends over that."

"She's a winning little rat," said Dick, smiling absent-mindedly, "but nothing to Madge. You'll understand when you see Madge how I couldn't give her up. And it isn't so much that—my feeling for her—though that's enough in all conscience, but picture to yourself, if you please, a man going to a girl and saying: 'I'm obliged to give you up, because my father threatens to disinherit me and kick me out of the business. He objects because your father's a poor lot.' That's a nice line of conduct to map out for your only son. Yet that's practically what my father wishes me to do. But he's brought me up a gentleman, by George," said Dick straightening himself, "and it's too late to ask me to be a beastly cad. Besides that," and voice and figure drooped to despondency again, "I just can't give her up."

The Bishop's keen eyes were on the troubled face, and in their depths lurked a kindly shade of amusement. He could see stubborn old Dick Fielding in stubborn young Dick Fielding so plainly. Dick the elder had been his friend for forty years. But he said nothing. It was better to let the boy talk himself out a bit. In a moment Dick began again.

"Can't see why the governor's so keen against Colonel Preston, anyway. He's lost his money and made a mess of his life, and I rather fancy he drinks too much. But he's the sort of man you can't help being proud of—bad clothes and vices and all—handsome and charming and thorough-bred—and father must know it. His children love him—he can't be such a brute as the governor says. Anyway, I don't want to marry the Colonel—what's the use of rowing about the Colonel?" inquired Dick, desperately.

The Bishop asked a question now: "How many children are there?"

"Only Madge and Eleanor. They're here with their cousins, the Vails, summers. Two or three died between those two, I believe. Lucky, perhaps, for the family has been awfully hard up. Lived on in their big old place, in Maryland, with no money at all. I've an idea Madge's mother wasn't so sorry to die—had a hard life of it with the fascinating Colonel." The Bishop's hand dropped from the boy's shoulder, and shut tightly. "But that has nothing to do with my marrying Madge," Dick went on.

"No," said the Bishop, shortly.

"And you see," said Dick, slipping to another tangent, "it's not the money I'm keenest about, though of course I want that too, but it's father. You believe I think more of my father than of his money, don't you? We've been good friends all my life, and he's such a crackerjack old fellow. I'd hate to get along without him." Dick

169

sighed, from his boots up—almost six feet. "Couldn't you give him a dressing down, Bishop? Make him see reason?" He looked anxiously up the three inches that the Bishop towered above him.

At ten o'clock the next morning Richard Fielding, owner of the great Fielding Foundries, strolled out on his wide piazza, which, luxurious in deep wicker chairs and Japanese rugs and light, cool furniture, looked under scarlet and white awnings, across long boxes of geraniums and vines, out to the sparkling Atlantic. The Bishop, a friendly light coming into his thoughtful eyes, took his cigar from his lips and glanced up at his friend. Mr. Fielding kicked a hassock aside, moved a table between them, and settled himself in another chair, and with the scratch of a match, but without a word spoken, they entered into the companionship which had been a life-long joy to both.

"Father and the Bishop are having a song and dance without words," Dick was pleased sometimes to say, and felt that he hit it off. The breeze carried the scent of the tobacco in intermittent waves of fragrance, and on the air floated delicately that subtle message of peace, prosperity, and leisure which is part of the mission of a good cigar. The pleasantness of the wide, cool piazza, with its flowers and vines and gay awnings; the charm of the summer morning, not yet dulled by wear and tear of the day; the steady, deliberate dash of the waves on the beach below; the play and shimmer of the big, quiet water, stretching out to the edge of the world; all this filled their minds, rested their souls. There was no need for words. The Bishop sighed comfortably as he pushed his great shoulders back against the cool wicker of the chair and swung one long leg across the other. Fielding, chin up and lips rounded to let out a cloud of smoke, rested his hand, cigar between the fingers, on the table, and gazed at him satisfied. This was the man, after Dick, dearest to him in the world. Into which peaceful Eden stole at this point the serpent, and, as is usual, in the shape of woman. Little Eleanor, long-legged, slim, fresh as a flower in her crisp, faded pink dress, came around the corner. In one hot hand she carried, by their heads, a bunch of lilac and pink and white sweet peas. It cost her no trouble at all, and about half a minute of time, to charge the atmosphere, so full of sweet peace and rest, with a saturated solution of bitterness and disquiet. Her presence alone was a bombshell, and with a sentence or two in her clear, innocent voice, the fell deed was done. Fielding stopped smoking, his cigar in mid-air, and stared with a scowl at the child; but Eleanor, delighted to have found the Bishop, saw only him. A shower of crushed blossoms fell over his knees.

"I ran away from Aunt Basha. I brought you a posy for 'Good-mornin'," she said. The Bishop, collecting the plunder, expressed gratitude. "Dick picked a whole lot for Madge, and then they went walkin' and forgot 'em. Isn't Dick funny?" she went on.

Mr. Fielding looked as if Dick's drollness did not appeal to him, but the Bishop laughed, and put his arm around her.

"Will you give me a kiss, too, for 'Good-morning,'" he said; and then, "That's better than the flowers. You had better run back to Aunt Basha now, Eleanor—she'll be frightened."

Eleanor looked disappointed, "I wanted to ask you 'bout what dead chickens gets to be, if they're good. Pups? Do you reckon it's pups?"

The theory of transmigration of souls had taken strong hold. Mr. Fielding lost his scowl in a look of bewilderment, and the Bishop frankly shouted out a big laugh.

"Listen, Eleanor. This afternoon I'll come for you to walk, and we'll talk that all over. Go home now, my lamb." And Eleanor, like a pale-pink over-sized butterfly, went.

"Do you know that child, Jim?" Mr. Fielding asked, grimly.

"Yes," answered the Bishop, with a serene pull at his cigar.

"Do you know she's the child of that good-for-nothing Fairfax Preston, who married Eleanor Gray against her people's will and took her South to—to—starve, practically?"

The Bishop drew a long breath, and then he turned and looked at his old friend with a clear, wide gaze. "She's Eleanor Gray's child, too, Dick," he said.

Mr. Fielding was silent a moment. "Has the boy talked to you?" he asked. The Bishop nodded. "It's the worst trouble I've ever had. It would kill me to see him marry that man's daughter. I can't and won't resign myself to it. Why should I? Why should Dick choose, out of all the world, the one girl in it who would be insufferable to me. I can't give in about this. Much as Dick is to me I'll let him go sooner. I hope you'll see I'm right, Jim, but right or wrong, I've made up my mind."

The Bishop stretched a large, bony hand across the little table that stood between them. Fielding's fell on it. Both men smoked silently for a minute.

"Have you anything against the girl, Dick?" asked the Bishop, presently.

"That she's her father's daughter—it's enough. The bad blood of generations is in her. I don't like the South—I don't like Southerners. And I detest beyond words Fairfax Preston. But the girl is certainly beautiful, and they say she is a good girl, too," he acknowledged, gloomily.

"Then I think you're wrong," said the Bishop.

"You don't understand, Jim," Fielding took it up passionately. "That man has been the *bête noir* of my life. He has gotten in my way half-a-dozen times deliberately, in business affairs, little as he amounts to himself. Only two years ago—but that isn't the point after all." He stopped gloomily. "You'll wonder at me, but it's an older feud than that. I've never told anyone, but I want you to understand, Jim, how impossible this affair is." He bit off the end of a fresh cigar, lighted it and then threw it across the geraniums into the grass. "I wanted to marry her mother," he said, brusquely. "That man got her. Of course, I could have forgiven that, but it was the way he did it. He lied to her—he threw it in my teeth that I had failed. Can't you see how I shall never forgive him—never, while I live!" The intensity of a life-long, silent hatred trembled in his voice.

"It's the very thing it's your business to do, Dick," said the Bishop, quietly. "'Love your enemies, bless them that curse you'—what do you think that means? It's your very case. It may be the hardest thing in the world, but it's the simplest, most obvious." He drew a long puff at his cigar, and looked over the flowers to the ocean.

"Simple! Obvious!" Fielding's voice was full of bitterness. "That's the way with you churchmen! You live outside passions and temptations, and then preach against them, with no faintest notion of their force. It sounds easy, doesn't it?

Simple and obvious, as you say. You never loved Eleanor Gray, Jim; you never had to give her up to a man you knew beneath her; you never had to shut murder out of your heart when you heard that he'd given her a hard life and a glad death. Eleanor Gray! Do you remember how lovely she was, how high-spirited and full of the joy of life?" The Bishop's great figure was still as if the breath in it had stopped, but Fielding, carried on the flood of his own rushing feeling, did not notice. "Do you remember, Jim?" he repeated.

"I remember," the Bishop said, and his voice sounded very quiet.

"Jove! How calm you are!" exploded the other.

"You're a churchman; you live behind a wall, you hear voices through it, but you can't be in the fight—it's easy for you."

"Life isn't easy for anyone, Dick," said the Bishop, slowly. "You know that. I'm fighting the current as well as you. You are a churchman as well as I. If it's my *métier* to preach against human passion, it's yours to resist it. You're letting this man you hate mould your character; you're letting him burn the kindness out of your soul. He's making you bitter and hard and unjust—and you're letting him. I thought you had more will—more poise. It isn't your affair what he is, even what he does, Dick—it's your affair to keep your own judgment unwarped, your own heart gentle, your own soul untainted by the poison of hatred. We are both churchmen, as you put it—loyalty is for us both. You live your sermon—I say mine. I have said it. Now live yours. Put this wormwood away from you. Forgive Preston, as you need forgiveness at higher hands. Don't break the girl's heart, and spoil your boy's life—it may spoil it—the leaven of bitterness works long. You're at a parting of the ways—take the right turn. Do good and not evil with your strength; all the rest is nothing. After all the years there is just one thing that counts, and that our mothers told us when we were little chaps together—be good, Dick."

The magnetic voice, that had swayed thousands, the indescribable trick of inflection that caught the heart-strings, the pure, high personality that shone through look and tone, had never, in all his brilliant career, been more full of power than for this audience of one. Fielding got up, trembling, and stood before him.

"Jim," he said, "whatever else is so, you are that—you are a good man. The trouble is you want me to be as good as you are; and I can't. If you had had temptations like mine, trials like mine, I might try to follow you—I would try. But you haven't—you're an impossible model for me. You want me to be an angel of light, and I'm only—a man." He turned and went into the house.

The oldest inhabitant had not seen a devotion like the Bishop's and Eleanor's. There was in it no condescension on one side, no strain on the other. The soul that through fulness of life and sorrow and happiness and effort had reached at last a child's peace met as its like the little child's soul, that had known neither life nor sorrow nor conscious happiness, and was without effort as a lily of the field. It may be that the wisdom of babyhood and the wisdom of age will look very alike to us when we have the wisdom of eternity. And as all the colors of the spectrum make sunlight, so all his splendid powers that patient years had made perfect shone through the Bishop's character in the white light of simplicity. No one knew what they talked about, the child and the man, on the long walks that they took together almost every day, except from Eleanor's conversation after. Transmigration, done into the vernacular, and applied with startling directness, was evidently a fascinating subject from the first. She brought back as well a vivid and epigrammatic version of the nebular hypothesis.

"Did you hear 'bout what the world did?" she demanded, casually, at the lunch-table. "We were all hot, nasty steam, just like a tea-kettle, and we cooled off into water, sailin' around so much, and then we got crusts on us, bless de Lawd, and then, sir, we kept on gettin' solid, and circus animals grewed all over us, and then they died, and thank God for that, and Adam and Evenin' camed, and Madge *can't* I have some more gingerbread? I'd just as soon be a little sick if you'll let me have it."

The "fairyland of science and the long results of time," passing from the Bishop's hands into the child's, were turned into such graphic tales, for Eleanor, with all her airy charm, struck straight from the shoulder. Never was there a sense of superiority on the Bishop's side, or of being lectured on Eleanor's.

"Why do you like to walk with the Bishop?" Mrs. Vail asked, curiously.

"Because he hasn't any morals," said the little girl, fresh from a Sunday-school lesson.

Saturday night Mr. Fielding stayed late in the city, and Dick was with his lady-love at the Vails; so the Bishop, after dining alone, went down on the wide beach below the house and walked, as he smoked his cigar. Through the week he had been restless under the constant prick of a duty undone, which he could not make up his mind to do. Over and over he heard his friend's agitated voice. "If you had had temptations like mine, trials like mine, I would try to follow you," it said. He knew that the man would be good as his word. He could perhaps win Dick's happiness for him if he would pick up the gauntlet of that speech. If he could bring himself to tell Fielding the whole story that he had shut so long ago into silence—that he, too, had cared for Eleanor Gray, and had given her up in a harder way than the other, for the Bishop had made it possible that the Southerner should marry her. But it was like tearing his soul to do it. No one but his mother, who was dead, had known this one secret of a life like crystal. The Bishop's reticence was the intense sort, that often goes with a frank exterior, and he had never cared for another woman. Some men's hearts are open pleasure-grounds, where all the world may come and go, and the earth is dusty with many feet; and some are like theatres, shut perhaps to the world in general, but which a passport of beauty or charm may always open; and with many, of finer clay, there are but two or three ways into a guarded temple, and only the touchstone of quality may let pass the lightest foot upon the carefully tended sod. But now and then a heart is Holy of Holies. Long ago the Bishop, lifting a young face from the books that absorbed him, had seen a girl's figure filling the narrow doorway, and dazzled by the radiance of it, had placed that image on the lonely altar, where the flame waited, before unconsecrated. Then the girl had gone, and he had quietly shut the door and lived his life outside. But the sealed place was there, and the fire burned before the old picture. Why should he, for Dick Fielding, for any one, let the light of day upon that stillness? The one thing in life that was his own, and all these years he had kept it sacred—why should he? Fiercely, with the old animal jealousy of ownership, he guarded for himself that memory—what was there on earth that could make him share it? And in answer there rose before him the vision of Madge Preston, with a haunting air of her mother about her; of young Dick Fielding, almost his own child from babyhood, his honest soul torn between two duties; of old Dick Fielding, loyal and kind and obstinate, his stubborn feet, the feet that had walked near his for forty years, needing only a touch to turn them into the right path.

Back and forth the thoughts buffeted each other, and the Bishop sighed, and threw away his cigar, and then stopped and stared out at the darkening, great ocean. The steady rush and pause and low wash of retreat did not calm him to-night.

"I'd like to turn it off for five minutes. It's so eternally right," he said aloud and began to walk restlessly again.

Behind him came light steps, but he did not hear them on the soft sand, in the noise of a breaking wave. A small, firm hand slipped into his was the first that he knew of another presence, and he did not need to look down at the bright head to know it was Eleanor, and the touch thrilled him in his loneliness. Neither spoke, but swung on across the sand, side by side, the child springing easily to keep pace with his great step. Beside the gift of English, Eleanor had its comrade gift of excellent silence. Those who are born to know rightly the charm and the power and the value of words, know as well the value of the rests in the music. Little Eleanor, her nervous fingers clutched around the Bishop's big thumb, was pouring strength and comfort into him, and such an instinct kept her quiet.

So they walked for a long half-hour, the Bishop fighting out his battle, sometimes stopping, sometimes talking aloud to himself, but Eleanor, through it all, not speaking. Once or twice he felt her face laid against his hand, and her hair that brushed his wrist, and the savage selfishness of reserve slowly dissolved in the warmth of that light touch and the steady current of gentleness it diffused through him. Clearly and more clearly he saw his way and, as always happens, as he came near to the mountain, the mountain grew lower. "Over the Alps lies Italy." Why should he count the height when the Italy of Dick's happiness and Fielding's duty done lay beyond? The clean-handed, light-hearted disregard of self that had been his habit of mind always came flooding back like sunshine as he felt his decision made. After all, doing a duty lies almost entirely in deciding to do it. He stooped and picked Eleanor up in his arms.

"Isn't the baby sleepy? We've settled it together—it's all right now, Eleanor. I'll carry you back to Aunt Basha."

"Is it all right now?" asked Eleanor, drowsily. "No, I'll walk," kicking herself downward. "But you come wiv me." And the Bishop escorted his lady-love to her castle, where the warden, Aunt Basha, was for this half hour making night vocal with lamentations for the runaway.

"Po' lil lamb!" said Aunt Basha, with an undisguised scowl at the Bishop. "Seems like some folks dunno nuff to know a baby's bedtime. Seems like de Lawd's anointed wuz in po' business, ti'in' out chillens!"

"I'm sorry, Aunt Basha," said the Bishop, humbly. "I'll bring her back earlier again. I forgot all about the time."

"Huh!" was all the response that Aunt Basha vouchsafed, and the Bishop, feeling himself hopelessly in the wrong, withdrew in discreet silence.

Luncheon was over the next day and the two men were quietly smoking together in the hot, drowsy quiet of the July mid-afternoon before the Bishop found a chance to speak to Fielding alone. There was an hour and a half before service, and this was the time to say his say, and he gathered himself for it, when suddenly the tongue of the ready speaker, the *savoir faire* of the finished man of the world, the mastery of situations which had always come as easily as his breath, all failed him at once.

"Dick," he stammered, "there is something I want to tell you," and he turned on his friend a face which astounded him.

"What on earth is it? You look as if you'd been caught stealing a hat," he responded, encouragingly.

The Bishop felt his heart thumping as that healthy organ had not thumped for years. "I feel a bit that way," he gasped. "You remember what we were talking of the other day?"

"The other day—talking—" Fielding looked bewildered. Then his face darkened. "You mean Dick—the affair with that girl." His voice was at once hard and unresponsive. "What about it?"

"Not at all," said the Bishop, complainingly. "Don't misunderstand like that, Dick—it's so much harder."

"Oh!" and Fielding's look cleared. "Well, what is it then, old man? Out with it—want a check for a mission? Surely you don't hesitate to tell me that! Whatever I have is yours, too—you know it."

The Bishop looked deeply disgusted. "Muddlehead!" was his unexpected answer, and Fielding, serene in the consciousness of generosity and good feeling, looked as if a hose had been turned on him.

"What the devil!" he said. "Excuse me, Jim, but just tell me what you're after. I can't make you out."

"It's most difficult." The Bishop seemed to articulate with trouble. "It was so long ago, and I've never spoken of it." Fielding, mouth and eyes wide, watched him as he stumbled on. "There were three of us, you see—though, of course, you didn't know. Nobody knew. She told my mother, that was all.—Oh, I'd no idea how difficult this would be," and the Bishop pushed back his damp hair and gasped again. Suddenly a wave of color rushed over his face.

"No one could help it, Dick," he said. "She was so lovely, so exquisite, so—"

Fielding rose quickly and put his hand on his friend's forehead, "Jim, my dear boy," he said gravely, "this heat has been too much for you. Sit there quietly, while I get some ice. Here, let me loosen your collar," and he put his fingers on the white clerical tie.

Then the Bishop rose up in his wrath and shook him off, and his deep blue eyes flashed fire.

"Let me alone," he said. "It is inexplicable to me how a man can be so dense. Haven't I explained to you in the plainest way what I have never told another soul? Is this the reward I am to have for making the greatest effort I have made for years?" And after a moment's steady, indignant glare at the speechless Fielding he turned and strode in angry majesty through the wide hall doorway.

When he walked out of the same doorway an hour later, on his way to service, Fielding sat back in a shadowy corner and let him pass without a word. He watched critically the broad shoulders and athletic figure as his friend moved down the narrow walk—a body carefully trained to hold well and easily the trained mind within. But the careless energy that was used to radiate from the great elastic muscles seemed lacking to-day, and the erect head drooped. Fielding shook his own head as the Bishop turned the corner and went out of his view.

"'*Mens sana in corpore sano*,'" he said aloud, and sighed. "He has worked too hard this summer. I never saw him like that. If he should—" and he stopped; then he rose, and looked at his watch and slowly followed the Bishop's steps.

The little church of Saint Peter's-by-the-Sea was filled even on this hot July afternoon, to hear the famous Bishop, and in the half-light that fell through painted windows and lay like a dim violet veil against the gray walls, the congregation with summer gowns and flowery hats, had a billowy effect as of a wave tipped everywhere with foam. Fielding, sitting far back, saw only the white-robed Bishop, and hardly heard the words he said, through listening for the modulations of his voice. He was anxious for the man who was dear to him, and the service and its minister were secondary to-day. But gradually the calm, reverent, well-known tones reassured him, and he yielded to the pleasure of letting his thoughts be led, by the voice that stood to him for goodness, into the spirit of the words that are filled with the beauty of holiness. At last it was time for the sermon, and the Bishop towered in the low stone pulpit and turned half away from them all as he raised one arm high with a quick, sweeping gesture.

"In the name of the Father and of the Son and of the Holy Ghost, Amen!" he said, and was still.

A shaft of yellow light fell through a memorial window and struck a golden bar against the white lawn of his surplice, and Fielding, staring at him with eyes of almost passionate devotion, thought suddenly of Sir Galahad, and of that "long beam" down which had "slid the Holy Grail." Surely the flame of that old vigorous Christianity had never burned higher or steadier. A marvellous life for this day, kept, like the flower of Knighthood, strong and beautiful and "unspotted from the world." Fielding sighed as he thought of his own life, full of good impulses, but crowded with mistakes, with worldliness, with lowered ideals, with yieldings to temptation. Then, with a pang, he thought about Dick, about the crisis for him that the next week must bring, and he heard again the Bishop's steady, uncompromising words as they talked on the piazza. And on a wave of selfish feeling rushed back the old excuses. "It is different. It is easy for him to be good. Dick is not his son. He has never been tempted like other men. He never hated Fairfax Preston—he never loved Eleanor Gray." And back somewhere in the dark places of his consciousness began to work a dim thought of his friend's puzzling words of that day: "No one could help loving her—she was so lovely—so exquisite!"

The congregation rustled softly everywhere as the people settled themselves to listen—they listened always to him. And across the hush that followed came the Bishop's voice again, tranquilly breaking, not jarring, the silence. "Not disobedient to the heavenly vision," were the words he was saying, and Fielding dropped at once the thread of his own thought to listen.

He spoke quickly, clearly, in short Anglo-Saxon words—the words that carry their message straightest to hearts red with Saxon blood—of the complex nature of every man—how the angel and the demon live in each and vary through all the shades of good and bad. How yet in each there is always the possibility of a highest and best that can be true for that personality only—a dream to be realized of the lovely life, blooming into its own flower of beauty, that God means each life to be. In his own rushing words he clothed the simple thought of the charge that each one has to keep his angel strong, the white wings free for higher flights that come with growth.

"The vision," he said, "is born with each of us, and though we lose it again and again, yet again and again it comes back and beckons, calls, and the voice thrills us always. And we must follow, or lose the way. Through ice and flame we must follow. And no one may look across where another soul moves on a quick, straight path and think that the way is easier for the other. No one can see if the rocks are not cutting his friend's feet; no one can know what burning lands he has crossed to follow, to be so close to his angel, his messenger. Believe always that every other life has been more tempted, more tried than your own; believe that the lives higher and better than your own are so not through more ease, but more effort; that the lives lower than yours are so through less opportunity, more trial. Believe that your friend with peace in his heart has won it, not happened on it—that he has fought your very fight. So the mist will melt from your eyes and you will see clearer the vision of your life and the way it leads you; selfishness will fall from your shoulders and you will follow lightly. And at the end, and along the way you will have the glory of effort, the joy of fighting and winning, the beauty of the heights where only an ideal can take you."

What more he said Fielding did not hear—for him one sentence had been the final word. The unlaid ghost of the Bishop's puzzling talk an hour before rose up and from its lips came, as if in full explanation, "He has fought your very fight." He sat in his shadowy, dark corner of the cool, little stone church, and while the congregation rose and knelt and sang and prayed, he was still. Piece by piece he fitted the mosaic of past and present, and each bit slipped faultlessly into place. There was no question in his mind now as to the fact, and his manliness and honor rushed to meet the situation. He had said that where his friend had gone he would go. If it was down the road of renunciation of a life-long enmity, he would not break his word. Complex problems resolve themselves at the point of action into such simple axioms. Dick should have a blessing and his sweetheart; he would do his best for Fairfax Preston; with his might he would keep his word. A great sigh and a wrench at his heart as if a physical growth of years were tearing away, and the decision was made. Then, in a mist of pain and effort, and a surprised new freedom from the accustomed pang of hatred, he heard the rustle and movement of a kneeling congregation, and, as he looked, the Bishop raised his arms. Fielding bent his gray head quickly in his hands, and over it, laden with "peace" and "the blessing of God Almighty," as if a general commended his soldier on the field of battle, swept the solemn words of the benediction.

Peace touched the earth on the blue and white September day when Madge and Dick were married. Pearly piled-up clouds, white "herded elephants," lay still against a sparkling sky, and the air was alive like cool wine, and breathing warm breaths of sunlight. No wedding was ever gayer or prettier, from the moment when the smiling holiday crowd in little Saint Peter's caught their breath at the first notes of "Lohengrin" and turned to see Eleanor, white-clad and solemn, and impressed with responsibility, lead the procession slowly up the aisle, her eyes raised to the Bishop's calm face in the chancel, to the moment when, in showers of rice and laughter and slippers, the Fielding carriage dashed down the driveway, and Dick, leaning out, caught for a last picture of his wedding-day, standing apart from the bright colors grouped on the lawn, the black and white of the Bishop and Eleanor, gazing after them, hand in hand.

Bit by bit the brilliant kaleidoscopic effect fell apart and resolved itself into light groups against the dark foliage or flashing masses of carriages and people and horses, and then even the blurs on the distance were gone, and the place was still and the wedding was over. The long afternoon was before them, with its restless emptiness, as if the bride and groom had taken all the reason for life with them.

There were bridesmaids and ushers staying at the Fieldings'. The graceful girl who poured out the Bishop's tea on the piazza, some hours later, and brought it to him with her own hands, stared a little at his face for a moment.

"You look tired, Bishop. Is it hard work marrying people? But you must be used to it after all these years," and her blue eyes fell gently on his gray hair. "So many love-stories you have finished—so many, many!" she went on, and then quite softly, "and yet never to have a love-story of your own!"

At this instant Eleanor, lolling on the arm of his chair, slipped over on his knee and burrowed against his coat a big pink bow that tied her hair. The Bishop's arm tightened around the warm, alive lump of white muslin, and he lifted his face, where lines showed plainly to-day, with a smile like sunshine.

"You are wrong, my daughter. They never finish—they only begin here. And my love-story"—he hesitated and his big fingers spread over the child's head, "It is all written in Eleanor's eyes."

"I hope when mine comes I shall have the luck to hear anything half as pretty as that. I envy Eleanor," said the graceful bridesmaid as she took the tea-cup again, but the Bishop did not hear her.

He had turned toward the sea and his eyes wandered out across the geraniums where the shadow of a sun-filled cloud lay over uncounted acres of unhurried waves. His face was against the little girl's bright head, and he said something softly to himself, and the child turned her face quickly and smiled at him and repeated the words:

"Many waters shall not wash out love," said Eleanor.

**"Many waters shall not wash out love," said Eleanor.**

---

### *THE WITNESSES*

The old clergyman sighed and closed the volume of "Browne on The Thirty-nine Articles," and pushed it from him on the table. He could not tell what the words meant; he could not keep his mind tense enough to follow an argument of three sentences. It must be that he was very tired. He looked into the fire, which was burning badly, and about the bare, little, dusty study, and realized suddenly that he was tired all the way through, body and soul. And swiftly, by way of the leak which that admission made in the sea-wall of his courage, rushed in an ocean of depression. It had been a hard, bad day. Two people had given up their pews in the little church which needed so urgently every ounce of support that held it. And the junior warden, the one rich man of the parish, had come in before service in the afternoon to complain of the music. If that knife-edged soprano did not go, he said, he was afraid he should have to go himself; it was impossible to have his nerves scraped to the raw every Sunday.

The old clergyman knew very little about music, but he remembered that his ear had been uncomfortably jarred by sounds from the choir, and that he had turned once and looked at them, and wondered if some one had made a mistake, and who it was. It must be, then, that dear Miss Barlow, who had sung so faithfully in St. John's for twenty-five years, was perhaps growing old. But how could he tell her so; how could he deal such a blow to her kind heart, her simple pride and interest in her work? He was growing old, too.

His sensitive mouth carved downward as he stared into the smoldering fire, and let himself, for this one time out of many times he had resisted, face the facts. It was not Miss Barlow and the poor music; it was not that the church was badly heated, as one of the ex-pewholders had said, nor that it was badly situated, as another had claimed; it was something of deeper, wider significance, a broken foundation, that made the ugly, widening crack all through the height of the tower. It was his own inefficiency. The church was going steadily down, and he was powerless to lift it. His old enthusiasm, devotion, confidence—what had become of them? They seemed to have slipped by slow degrees, through the unsuccessful years, out of his soul, and in their place was a dull distrust of himself; almost—God forgive him—distrust in God's kindness. He had worked with his might all the years of his life, and what he had to show for it was a poor, lukewarm parish, a diminished congregation, debt—to put it in one dreadful word, failure!

**He stared into the smoldering fire.**

By the pitiless searchlight of hopelessness, he saw himself for the first time as he was—surely devoted and sincere, but narrow, limited, a man lacking outward expression of inward and spiritual grace. He had never had the gift to win hearts. That had not troubled him much, earlier, but lately he had longed for a little appreciation, a little human love, some sign that he had not worked always in vain. He remembered the few times that people had stopped after service to praise his sermons, and to-night he remembered not so much the glow at his heart that the kind words had brought, as the fact that those times had been very few. He did not preach good sermons; he faced that now, unflinchingly. He was not broad minded; new thoughts were unattractive, hard for him to assimilate; he had championed always theories that were going out of fashion, and the half-consciousness of it put him ever on the defensive; when most he wished to be gentle, there was something in his manner which antagonized. As he looked back over his colorless, conscientious past, it seemed to him that his life was a failure. The souls he had reached, the work he had done with such infinite effort—it might all have been done better and easily by another man. He would not begrudge his strength and his years burned freely in the sacred fire, if he might know that the flame had shone even faintly in dark places, that the heat had warmed but a little the hearts of men. But—he smiled grimly at the logs in front of him, in the small, cheap, black marble fireplace—his influence was much like that, he thought, cold, dull, ugly with uncertain smoke. He, who was not worthy, had dared to consecrate himself to a high service, and it was his reasonable punishment that his life had been useless.

Like a stab came back the thought of the junior warden, of the two more empty pews, and then the thought, in irresistible self-pity, of how hard he had tried, how well he had meant, how much he had given up, and he felt his eyes filling with a man's painful, bitter tears. There had been so little beauty, reward, in his whole past. Once, thirty years before, he had gone abroad for six weeks, and he remembered the trip with a thrill of wonder that anything so lovely could have come into his sombre life—the voyage, the bit of travel, the new countries, the old cities, the expansion, broadening of mind he had felt for a time as its result. More than all, the delight of the people whom he had met, the unused experience of being understood at once, of light touch and easy flexibility, possible, as he had not known before, with good and serious qualities. One man, above all, he had never forgotten. It had been a pleasant memory always to have known him, to have been friends with him even, for he had felt to his own surprise and joy that something in him attracted this man of men. He had followed the other's career, a career full of success unabused, of power grandly used, of responsibility lifted with a will. He stood over thousands and ruled rightly—a true prince among men. Somewhat too broad, too free in his thinking—the old clergyman deplored that fault—yet a man might not be perfect. It was pleasant to know that this strong and good soul was in the world and was happy; he had seen him once with his son, and the boy's fine, sensitive face, his honest eyes, and pretty deference of manner, his pride, too, in his distinguished father, were surely a guaranty of happiness. The old man felt a sudden generous gladness that if some lives must be wasted, yet some might be, like this man's whom he had once known, full of beauty and service. It would be good if he might add a drop to the cup of happiness which meant happiness to so many—and then he smiled at his foolish thought. That he should think of helping that other—a man of so little importance to help a man of so much! And suddenly again he felt tears that welled up hotly.

He put his gray head, with its scanty, carefully brushed hair, back against the support of the worn armchair, and shut his eyes to keep them back. He would try not to be cowardly. Then, with the closing of the soul-windows, mental and physical fatigue brought their own gentle healing, and in the cold, little study, bare, even, of many books, with the fire smoldering cheerlessly before him, he fell asleep.

---

A few miles away, in a suburb of the same great city, in a large library peopled with books, luxurious with pictures and soft-toned rugs and carved dark furniture, a man sat staring into the fire. The six-foot logs crackled and roared up the chimney, and the blaze lighted the wide, dignified room. From the high chimney-piece, that had been the feature of a great hall in Florence two centuries before, grotesque heads of black oak looked down with a gaze which seemed weighted with age-old wisdom and cynicism, at the man's sad face. The glow of the lamp, shining like a huge gray-green jewel, lighted unobtrusively the generous sweep of table at his right hand, and on it were books whose presence meant the thought of a scholar and the broad interests of a man of affairs. Each detail of the great room, if there had been an observer of its quiet perfection, had an importance of its own, yet each exquisite belonging fell swiftly into the dimness of the background of a picture when one saw the man who was the master. Among a thousand picked men, his face and figure would have been distinguished. People did not call him old, for the alertness and force of youth radiated from him, and his gray eyes were clear and his color fresh, yet the face was lined heavily, and the thick thatch of hair shone in the firelight silvery white. Face and figure were full of character and breeding, of life lived to its utmost, of will, responsibility, success. Yet to-night the spring of the mechanism seemed broken, and the noble head lay back against the brown leather of his deep chair as listlessly as a tired girl's. He watched the dry wood of the fire as it blazed and fell apart and blazed up brightly again, yet his eyes did not seem to see it—their absorbed gaze was inward.

The distant door of the room swung open, but the man did not hear, and, his head and face clear cut like a cameo against the dark leather, hands stretched nervelessly along the arms of the chair, eyes gazing gloomily into the heart of the flame, he was still. A young man, brilliant with strength, yet with a worn air about him, and deep circles under his eyes, stood inside the room and looked at him a long minute—those two in the silence. The fire crackled cheerfully and the old man sighed.

"Father!" said the young man by the door.

In a second the whole pose changed, and he sat intense, staring, while the son came toward him and stood across the rug, against the dark wood of the Florentine fireplace, a picture of young manhood which any father would be proud to own.

"Of course, I don't know if you want me, father," he said, "but I've come to tell you that I'll be a good boy, if you do."

The gentle, half-joking manner was very winning, and the play of his words was trembling with earnest. The older man's face shone as if lamps were lighted behind his eyes.

"If I want you, Ted!" he said, and held out his hand.

With a quick step forward the lad caught it, and then, with quick impulsiveness, as if his childhood came back to him on the flood of feeling unashamed, bent down and kissed him. As he stood erect again he laughed a little, but the muscles of his face were working, and there were tears in his eyes. With a swift movement he had drawn a chair, and the two sat quiet a moment, looking at each other in deep and silent content to be there so, together.

"Yesterday I thought I'd never see you again this way," said the boy; and his father only smiled at him, satisfied as yet without words. The son went on, his eager, stirred feelings crowding to his lips. "There isn't any question great enough, there isn't any quarrel big enough, to keep us apart, I think, father. I found that out this afternoon. When a chap has a father like you, who has given him a childhood and a youth like mine—" The young voice stopped, trembling. In a moment he had mastered himself. "I'll probably never be able to talk to you like this again, so I want to say it all now. I want to say that I know, beyond doubt, that you would never decide anything, as I would, on impulse, or prejudice, or from any motives but the highest. I know how well-balanced you are, and how firmly your reason holds your feelings. So it's a question between your judgment and mine—and I'm going to trust yours. You may know me better than I know myself, and anyway you're more to me than any career, though I did think—but we won't discuss it again. It would have been a tremendous risk, of course, and it shall be as you say. I found out this afternoon how much of my life you were," he repeated.

The older man kept his eyes fixed on the dark, sensitive, glowing young face, as if they were thirsty for the sight. "What do you mean by finding it out this afternoon, Ted? Did anything happen to you?"

The young fellow turned his eyes, that were still a bit wet with the tears, to his father's face, and they shone like brown stars. "It was a queer thing," he said, earnestly, "It was the sort of thing you read in stories—almost like," he hesitated, "like Providence, you know. I'll tell you about it; see if you don't think so. Two days ago, when I—when I left you, father—I caught a train to the city and went straight to the club, from habit, I suppose, and because I was too dazed and wretched to think. Of course, I found a grist of men there, and they wouldn't let me go. I told them I was ill, but they laughed at me. I don't remember just what I did, for I was in a bad dream, but I was about with them, and more men I knew kept turning up—I couldn't seem to escape my friends. Even if I stayed in my room, they hunted me up. So this morning I shifted to the Oriental, and shut myself up in my room there, and tried to think and plan. But I felt pretty rotten, and I couldn't see daylight, so I went down to lunch, and who should be at the next table but the Dangerfields, the whole outfit, just back from England and bursting with cheerfulness! They made me lunch with them, and it was ghastly to rattle along feeling as I did, but I got away as soon us I decently could—rather sooner, I think—and went for a walk, hoping the air would clear my head. I tramped miles—oh, a long time, but it seemed not to do any good; I felt deadlier and more hopeless than ever—I haven't been very comfortable fighting you," he stopped a minute, and his tired face turned to his father's with a smile of very winning gentleness.

The father tried to speak, but, his voice caught harshly. Then, "We'll make it up, Ted," he said, and laid his hand on the boy's shoulder.

The young fellow, as if that touch had silenced him, gazed into the fire thoughtfully, and the big room was very still for a long minute. Then he looked up brightly.

"I want to tell you the rest. I came back from my tramp by the river drive, and suddenly I saw Griswold on his horse trotting up the bridle-path toward me. I drew the line at seeing any more men, and Griswold is the worst of the lot for wanting to do things, so I turned into a side-street and ran. I had an idea he had seen me, so when I came to a little church with the doors open, in the first half-block, I shot in. Being Lent, you know, there was service going on, and I dropped quietly into a seat at the back, and it came to me in a minute, that I was in fit shape to say my prayers, so—I said 'em. It quieted me a bit, the old words of the service. They're fine English, of course, and I think words get a hold on you when they're associated with every turn of your life. So I felt a little less like a wild beast, by the time the clergyman began his sermon. He was a pathetic old fellow, thin and ascetic and sad, with a narrow forehead and a little white hair, and an underfed look about him. The whole place seemed poor and badly kept. As he walked across the chancel, he stumbled on a hole in the carpet. I stared at him, and suddenly it struck me that he must be about your age, and it was like a knife in me, father, to see him trip. No two men were ever more of a contrast, but through that very fact he seemed to be standing there as a living message from you. So when he opened his mouth to give out his text I fell back as if he had struck me, for the words he said were, 'I will arise and go to my father.'"

The boy's tones, in the press and rush of his little story, were dramatic, swift, and when he brought out its climax, the older man, though his tense muscles were still, drew a sudden breath, as if he, too, had felt a blow. But he said nothing, and the eager young voice went on.

"The skies might have opened and the Lord's finger pointed at me, and I couldn't have felt more shocked. The sermon was mostly tommy-rot, you know—platitudes. You could see that the man wasn't clever—had no grasp—old-fashioned ideas—didn't seem to have read at all. There was really nothing in it, and after a few sentences I didn't listen particularly. But there were two things about it I shall never forget, never, if I live to a hundred. First, all through, at every tone of his voice, there was the thought that the brokenhearted look in the eyes of this man, such a contrast to you in every way possible, might be the very look in your eyes after a while, if I left you. I think I'm not vain to know I make a lot of difference to you, father—considering we two are all alone." There was a questioning inflection, but he smiled, as if he knew.

"You make all the difference. You are the foundation of my life. All the rest counts for nothing beside you." The father's voice was slow and very quiet.

"That thought haunted me," went on the young man, a bit unsteadily, "and the contrast of the old clergyman and you made it seem as if you were there beside me. It sounds unreasonable, but it was so. I looked at him, old, poor, unsuccessful, narrow-minded, with hardly even the dignity of age, and I couldn't help seeing a vision of you, every year of your life a glory to you, with your splendid mind, and splendid body, and all the power and honor and luxury that seem a natural background to you. Proud as I am of you, it seemed cruel, and then it came to my mind like a stab that perhaps without me, your only son, all of that would—well, what you said just now. Would count for nothing—that you would be practically, some day, just a lonely and pathetic old man like that other."

The hand on the boy's shoulder stirred a little. "You thought right, Ted."

"That was one impression the clergyman's sermon made, and the other was simply his beautiful goodness. It shone from him at every syllable, uninspired and uninteresting as they were. You couldn't help knowing that his soul was white as an angel's. Such sincerity, devotion, purity as his couldn't be mistaken. As I realized it, it transfigured the whole place. It made me feel that if that quality—just goodness—could so glorify all the defects of his look and mind and manner, it must be worth while, and I would like to have it. So I knew what was right in my heart—I think you can always know what's right if you want to know—and I just chucked my pride and my stubbornness into the street, and—and I caught the 7:35 train."

The light of renunciation, the exhaustion of wrenching effort, the trembling triumph of hard-won victory, were in the boy's face, and the thought, as he looked at it, dear and familiar in every shadow, that he had never seen spirit shine through clay more transparently. Never in their lives had the two been as close, never had the son so unveiled his soul before. And, as he had said, in all probability never would it be again. To the depth where they stood words could not reach, and again for minutes, only the friendly undertone of the crackling fire stirred the silence of the great room. The sound brought steadiness to the two who sat there, the old hand on the young shoulder yet. After a time, the older man's low and strong tones, a little uneven, a little hard with the effort to be commonplace, which is the first readjustment from deep feeling, seemed to catch the music of the homely accompaniment of the fire.

"It is a queer thing, Ted," he said, "but once, when I was not much older than you, just such an unexpected chance influence made a crisis in my life. I was crossing to England with the deliberate intention of doing something which I knew was wrong. I thought it meant happiness, but I know now it would have meant misery. On the boat was a young clergyman of about my own age making his first, very likely his only, trip abroad. I was thrown with him—we sat next each other at table, and our cabins faced—and something in the man attracted me, a quality such as you speak of in this other, of pure and uncommon goodness. He was much the same sort as your old man, I fancy, not particularly winning, rather narrow, rather limited in brains and in advantages, with a natural distrust of progress and breadth. We talked together often, and one day, I saw, by accident, into the depths of his soul, and knew what he had sacrificed to become a clergyman—it was what meant to him happiness and advancement in life. It had been a desperate effort, that was plain, but it was plain, too, that from the moment he saw what he thought was the right, there had been no hesitation in his mind. And I, with all my wider mental training, my greater breadth—as I looked at it—was going, with my eyes open, to do a wrong because I wished to do it. You and I must be built something alike, Ted, for a touch in the right spot seems to penetrate to the core of us—the one and the other. This man's simple and intense flame of right living, right doing, all unconsciously to himself, burned into me, and all that I had planned to do seemed scorched in that fire—turned to ashes and bitterness. Of course it was not so simple as it sounds. I went through a great deal. But the steady influence for good was beside me through that long passage—we were two weeks—the stronger because it was unconscious, the stronger, I think, too, that it rested on no intellectual basis, but was wholly and purely spiritual—as the confidence of a child might hold a man to his duty where the arguments of a sophist would have no effect. As I say, I went through a great deal. My mind was a battle-field for the powers of good and evil during those two weeks, but the man who was leading the forces of the right never knew it. The outcome was that as soon as I landed I took my passage back on the next boat, which sailed at once. Within a year, within a month almost, I knew that the decision I made then was a turning-point, that to have done otherwise would have meant ruin in more than one way. I tremble now to think how close I was to shipwreck. All that I am, all that I have, I owe more or less directly to that man's unknown influence. The measure of a life is its service. Much opportunity for that, much power has been in my hands, and I have tried to hold it humbly and reverently, remembering that time. I have thought of myself many times us merely the instrument, fitted to its special use, of that consecrated soul."

The voice stopped, and the boy, his wide, shining eyes fixed on his father's face, drew a long breath. In a moment he spoke, and the father knew, as well as if he had said it, how little of his feeling he could put into words.

"It makes you shiver, doesn't it," he said, "to think what effect you may be having on people, and never know it? Both you and I, father—our lives changed, saved—by the influence of two strangers, who hadn't the least idea what they were doing. It frightens you."

"I think it makes you know," said the older man, slowly, "that not your least thought is unimportant; that the radiance of your character shines for good or evil where you go. Our thoughts, our influences, are like birds that fly from us as we walk along the road; one by one, we open our hands and loose them, and they are gone and forgotten, but surely there will be a day when they will come back on white wings or dark like a cloud of witnesses—"

The man stopped, his voice died away softly, and he stared into the blaze with solemn eyes, as if he saw a vision. The boy, suddenly aware again of the strong hand on his shoulder, leaned against it lovingly, and the fire, talking unconcernedly on, was for a long time the only sound in the warmth and stillness and luxury of the great room which held two souls at peace.

---

At that hour, with the volume of Browne under his outstretched hand, his thin gray hair resting against the worn cloth of the chair, in the bare little study, the old clergyman slept. And as he slept, a wonderful dream came to him. He thought that he had gone from this familiar, hard world, and stood, in his old clothes, with his old discouraged soul, in the light of the infinitely glorious Presence, where he must surely stand at last. And the question was asked him, wordlessly, solemnly:

"Child of mine, what have you made of the life given you?" And he looked down humbly at his shabby self, and answered:

"Lord, nothing. My life is a failure. I worked all day in God's garden, and my plants were twisted and my roses never bloomed. For all my fighting, the weeds grew thicker. I could not learn to make the good things grow, I tried to work rightly, Lord, my Master, but I must have done it all wrong."

And as he stood sorrowful, with no harvest sheaves to offer as witnesses for his toiling, suddenly back of him he heard a marvellous, many-toned, soft whirring, as of innumerable light wings, and over his head flew a countless crowd of silver-white birds, and floated in the air beyond. And as he gazed, surprised, at their loveliness, without speech again it was said to him:

"My child, these are your witnesses. These are the thoughts and the influences which have gone from your mind to other minds through the years of your life." And they were all pure white.

And it was borne in upon him, as if a bandage had been lifted from his eyes, that character was what mattered in the great end; that success, riches, environment, intellect, even, were but the tools the master gave into his servants' hands, and that the honesty of the work was all they must answer for. And again he lifted his eyes to the hovering white birds, and with a great thrill of joy it came to him that he had his offering, too, he had this lovely multitude for a gift to the Master; and, as if the thought had clothed him with glory, he saw his poor black clothes suddenly transfigured to shining garments, and, with a shock, he felt the rush of a long-forgotten feeling, the feeling of youth and strength, beating in a warm glow through his veins. With a sigh of deep happiness, the old man awoke.

A log had fallen, and turning as it fell, the new surface had caught life from the half-dead ashes, and had blazed up brightly, and the warmth was penetrating gratefully through him. The old clergyman smiled, and held his thin hands to the flame as he gazed into the fire, but the wonder and awe of his dream were in his eyes.

"My beautiful white birds!" he said, aloud, but softly. "Mine! They were out of sight, but they were there all the time. Surely the dream was sent from Heaven—surely the Lord means me to believe that my life has been of service after all." And as he still gazed, with rapt face, into his study fire, he whispered: "Angels came and ministered unto him."

---

### THE DIAMOND BROOCHES

The room was filled with signs of breeding and cultivation; it was bare of the things which mean money. Books were everywhere; family portraits, gone brown with time, hung on the walls; a tall silver candlestick gleamed from a corner; there was the tarnished gold of carved Florentine frames, such as people bring still from Italy. But the furniture-covering was faded, the carpet had been turned, the place itself was the small parlor of a cheap apartment, and the wall-paper was atrocious. The least thoughtful, listening for a moment to that language which a room speaks of those who live in it, would have known this at once as the home of well-bred people who were very poor.

So quiet it was that it seemed empty. If an observer had stood in the doorway, it might have been a minute before he saw that a man sat in front of the fireless hearth with his arms stretched before him on the table and his head fallen into them. For many minutes there was no sound, no stir of the man's nerveless pose; it might have been that he was asleep. Suddenly the characterless silence of the place was flooded with tragedy, for the man groaned, and a child would have known that the sound came from a torn soul. He lifted his face—a handsome, high-bred face, clever, a bit weak,—and tears were wet on his cheeks. He glanced about as if fearing to be seen as he wiped them away, and at the moment there was a light bustle, low voices down the hall. The young man sprang to his feet and stood alert as a step came toward him. He caught a sharp breath as another man, iron-gray, professional, stood in the doorway.

"Doctor! You have made the examination—you think—" he flung at the newcomer, and the other answered with the cool incisive manner of one whose words weigh.

"Mr. Newbold," he said, "when you came to my office this morning I told you my conjectures and my fear. I need not, therefore, go into details again. I am very sorry to have to say to you—" he stopped, and looked at the younger man kindly. "I wish I might make it easier, but it is better that I should tell you that your mother's condition is as I expected."

Newbold gave way a step as if under a blow, and his color went gray. The doctor had seen souls laid bare before, yet he turned his eyes to the floor as the muscles pulled and strained in this young face. It seemed minutes that the two faced each other in the loaded silence, the doctor gazing gravely at the worn carpet, the other struggling for self-control. At last Newbold spoke, in the harsh tone which often comes first after great emotion.

"You mean that there is—no hope?"

And the doctor, relieved at the loosening of the tension, answered readily, glad to merge his humanity in his professional capacity: "No, Mr. Newbold; I do not mean just that. It is this bleak climate, the raw winds from the lake, which make it impossible for your mother to take the first step which might lead to recovery. There is, in fact—" he hesitated. "I may say that there is no hope for her cure while here. But if she is taken to a warm climate at once—at once—within two weeks— and kept there until summer, then, although I have not the gift of prophecy, yet I believe she would be in time a well woman. No medicine, can do it, but out-of-doors and warmth would do it—probably."

He put out his hand with a smile. "I am indeed glad that I may temper judgment with mercy," he said. "Try the south, Mr. Newbold,—try Bermuda, for instance. The sea air and the warmth there might set your mother up marvellously." And as the young man stared at him unresponsively he gave a grasp to the hand he held, and turning, found his way out alone. He stumbled down the dark steps of the third-rate apartment-house and into his brougham, and as the rubber tires bowled him over the asphalt he communed with himself:

"Queer about those Newbolds. Badly off, of course, to live in that place, yet they know what it means to call me in. There must be some money. I wonder if they have enough for a trip, poor souls. Bah! they must have—everybody has when it comes to life and death. They'll get it somehow—rich relations and all that. Burr Claflin is their cousin, I know. David Newbold himself was rich enough five years ago, when he made that unlucky gamble in stocks—which killed him, they say. Well—life is certainly hard." And the doctor turned his mind to a new pair of horses he had been looking at in the afternoon, with a comfortable sense of a wind-guard or so, at the least, between himself and the gales of adversity.

In the little drawing-room, with its cheap paper and its old portraits, Randolph Newbold faced his sister with the news. He knew her courage, yet, even in the stress of his feeling, he wondered at it now; he felt almost a pang of jealousy when he saw her take the blow as he had not been able to take it.

"It is a death-sentence," he said, brokenly. "We have not the money to send her south, and we cannot get it."

Katherine Newbold's hands clenched. "We will get it," she said. "I don't know how just now, but we'll get it, Randolph. Mother's life shall not go for lack of a few hundred dollars. Oh, think—just think—six years ago it would have meant nothing. We went south every winter, and we were all well. It is too cruel! But we'll get the money—you'll see."

"How?" the young man asked, bitterly. "The last jewel went so that we could have Dr. Renfrew. There's nothing here to sell—nobody would buy our ancestors," and he looked up mournfully at the painted figures on the wall. The very thought seemed an indignity to those stately personalities—the English judge in his wig, the colonial general in his buff-faced uniform, harbored for a century proudly among their own, now speculated upon as possible revenue. The girl put up a hand toward them as if deprecating her brother's words, and his voice went on: "You know the doctor practically told me this morning. I have had no hope all day, and all day I have lived in hell. I don't know how I did my work. To-night, coming home, I walked past Litterny's. The windows were lighted and filled with a gorgeous lot of stones—there were a dozen big diamond brooches. I stopped and looked at them, and thought how she used to wear such things, and how now her life was going for the value of one of them, and—you may be horrified, Katherine, but this is true: If I could have broken into that window and snatched some of that stuff, I'd have done it. Honesty and all I've been brought up to would have meant nothing—nothing. I'd do it now, in a second, if I could, to get the money to save my mother. God! The town is swimming in money, and I can't get a little to keep her alive!"

The young man's eyes were wild with a passion of helplessness, but his sister gazed at him calmly, as if considering a question. From a room beyond came a painful cough, and the girl was on her feet.

"She is awake; I must go to her. But I shall think—don't be hopeless, boy—I shall think of a way." And she was gone.

Worn out with emotion, Randolph Newbold was sleeping a deep sleep that night. With a start he awoke, staring at a white figure with long, fair braids.

"Randolph, it's I—Katherine. Don't be startled."

"What's the matter? Is she worse?" He lifted himself anxiously, blinking sleep from his eyes.

"No—oh no! She's sleeping well. It's just that I have to talk to you, Randolph. Now. I can't wait till morning—you'll understand when I tell you. I haven't been asleep at all; I've been thinking. I know now how we can get the money."

"Katherine, are you raving?" the brother demanded; but the girl was not to be turned aside.

"Listen to me," she said, and in her tone was the authority of the stronger personality, and the young man listened. She sat on the edge of his bed and held his hand as she talked, and through their lives neither might ever forget that midnight council.

---

The room had an air of having come in perfect and luxurious condition, fur-lined and jewel-clasped, as it were, from the hands of a good decorator, and of having stopped at that. The great triple lamp glowed green as if set with gigantic emeralds; and its soft light shone on a scheme of color full of charm for the eye. The stuffs, the woodwork, were of a delightful harmony, but it seemed that the books and the pictures were chosen to match them. The man talking, in the great carved armchair by the fire, fitted the place. His vigorous, pleasant face looked prosperous, and so kindly was his air that one might not cavil at a lack of subtler qualities. He drew a long breath as he brought out the last words of the story he was telling.

"And that, Mr. North," he concluded, "is the way the firm of Litterny Brothers, the leading jewellers of this city, were done yesterday by a person or persons unknown, to the tune of five thousand dollars." His eyes turned from the blazing logs to his guest.

The young man in his clerical dress stood as he listened, with eyes wide like a child's, fixed on the speaker. He stooped and picked up a poker and pushed the logs together as he answered. The deliberateness of the action would not have prepared one for the intensity of his words. "I never wanted to be a detective before," he said, "but I'd give a good deal to catch the man who did that. It was such planned rascality, such keen-witted scoundrelism, that it gives me a fierce desire to show him up. I'd like to teach the beggar that honesty can be as intelligent as knavery; that in spite of his strength of cunning, law and right are stronger. I wish I could catch him," and the brass poker gleamed in a savage flourish. "I'd have no mercy. The hungry wretch who steals meat, the ignorant sinner taught to sin from babyhood—I have infinite patience for such. But this thief spoke like a gentleman, and the maid said he was 'a pretty young man'—there's no excuse for him. He simply wanted money that wasn't his,—there's no excuse. It makes my blood boil to think of a clever rascal like that succeeding in his rascality." With that the intense manner had dropped from him as a garment, and he was smiling the gentlest, most whimsical smile at the older man. "You'll think, Mr. Litterny, that it's the loss of my new parish-house that's making me so ferocious, but, honestly, I'd forgotten all about it." And no one who heard him could doubt his sincerity. "I was thinking of the case from your point of view. As to the parish-house, it's a disappointment, but of course I know that a large loss like this must make a difference in a man's expenditures. You have been very good to St. John's already,—a great many times you have been good to us."

"It's a disappointment to me as well," Litterny said. "Old St. John's of Newburyport has been dear to me many years. I was confirmed and married there—but *you* know. Everything I could do for it has been a satisfaction. And I looked forward to giving this parish-house. In ordinary years a theft of five thousand dollars would not have prevented me, but there have been complications and large expenses of late, to which this loss is the last straw. I shall have to postpone the parish-house,—but it shall be only postponed, Mr. North, only postponed."

The young rector answered quietly: "As I said before, Mr. Litterny, you have been most generous. We are grateful more than I know how to say." His manner was very winning, and the older man's kind face brightened.

"The greatest luxury which money brings is to give it away. St. John's owes its thanks not to me, but to you, Mr. North. I have meant for some time to put into words my appreciation of your work there. In two years you have infused more life and earnestness into that sleepy parish than I thought possible. You've waked them up, put energy into them, and got it out of them. You've done wonders. It's right you should know that people think this of you, and that your work is valued."

"I am glad," Norman North said, and the restraint of the words carried more than a speech.

Mr. Litterny went on: "But there's such a thing as overdoing, young man, and you're shaving the edge of it. You're looking ill—poor color—thin as a rail. You need a rest."

"I think I'll go to Bermuda. My senior warden was there last year, and he says it's a wonderful little place—full of flowers and tennis and sailing, and blue sea and nice people." He stood up suddenly and broadened his broad shoulders. "I love the south," he said. "And I love out-of-doors and using my muscles. It's good to think of whole days with no responsibility, and with exercise till my arms and legs ache. I get little exercise, and I miss it. I was on the track team at Yale, you see, and rather strong at tennis."

Mr. Litterny smiled, and his smile was full of sympathy. "We try to make a stained-glass saint out of you," he said, "and all the time you're a human youngster with a human desire for a good time. A mere lad," he added, reflectively, and went on: "Go down to Bermuda with a light heart, my boy, and enjoy yourself,—it will do your church as much good as you. Play tennis and sail—fall in love if you find the right girl,—nothing makes a man over like that." North was putting out his hand. "And remember," Litterny added, "to keep an eye out for my thief. You're retained as assistant detective in the case."

---

On a bright, windy morning a steamship wound its careful way through the twisted water-road of Hamilton Harbor, Bermuda. Up from cabins mid corners poured figures unknown to the decks during the passage, and haggard faces brightened under the balmy breeze, and tired eyes smiled at the dark hills and snowy sands of the sliding shore. In a sheltered corner of the deck a woman lay back in a chair and drew in breaths of soft air, and a tall girl watched her.

"You feel better already, don't you?" she demanded, and Mrs. Newbold put her hand into her daughter's.

"It is Paradise," she said. "I am going to get well."

In an hour the landing had been made, the custom-house passed; the gay, exhilarating little drive had been taken to the hotel, through white streets, past white-roofed houses buried in trees and flowers and vines; the sick woman lay quiet and happy on her bed, drawn to the open window, where the healing of the breeze touched her gently, and where her eyes dreamed over a fairy stretch of sea and islands. Katherine, moving about the room, unpacking, came to sit in a chair by her mother and talk to her for a moment.

"To-morrow, if you're a good child, you shall go for a drive. Think—a drive in an enchanted island. It's Shakespeare's *Tempest* island,—did I tell you I heard that on the boat? We might run across Caliban any minute, and I think at least we'll find 'M' and 'F', for Miranda and Ferdinand, cut into the bark of a tree somewhere. We'll go for a drive every day, every single day, till we find it. You'll see."

Mrs. Newbold's eyes moved from the sea and rested, perplexed, on her daughter. "Katherine, how can we afford to drive every day? How can we be here at all? I don't understand it. I'm sure there was nothing left to sell except the land out west, and Mr. Seaton told us last spring that it was worthless. How did you and Randolph conjure up the money for this beautiful journey that is going to save my life?"

The girl bent impulsively and kissed her with tender roughness. "It is going to do that—it is!" she cried, and her voice broke. Then: "Never mind how the money came, dear,—invalids mustn't be curious. It strains their nerves. Wait till you're well and perhaps you'll hear a tale about that land out west."

Day after day slipped past in the lotus-eating land whose unreality makes it almost a change of planets from every-day America. Each day brought health with great rapidity, and soon each day brought new friends. Mrs. Newbold was full of charm, and the devotion between the ill mother and the blooming daughter was an attractive sight. Yet the girl was not light-hearted. Often the mother, waking in the night, heard a shivering sigh through the open door between their rooms; often she surprised a harassed look in the young eyes which, with all that the family had gone through, was new to them. But Katherine laughed at questions, and threw herself so gayly into the pleasures which came to her that Mrs. Newbold, too happy to be analytical, let the straws pass and the wind blow where it would.

There came a balmy morning when the two were to take, with half a dozen others, the long drive to St. George's. The three carriage-loads set off in a pleasant hubbub from the white-paved courtyard of the hotel, and as Katherine settled her mother with much care and many rugs, her camera dropped under the wheels. Everybody was busy, nobody was looking, and she stooped and reached for it in vain. Then out of a blue sky a voice said:

"I'll get it for you," She was pushed firmly aside and a figure in a blue coat was grovelling adventurously beneath the trap. It came out, straightened; she had her camera; she was staring up into a face which contemplated her, which startled her, so radiant, so everything desirable it seemed to her to be. The man's eyes considered her a moment as she thanked him, and then he had lifted his hat and was gone, running, like a boy in a hurry for a holiday, toward the white stone landing. An empty sail flopped big at the landing, and the girl stood and looked as he sprang in under it and took the rudder. Joe, the head porter, the familiar friend of every one, was stowing in a rug.

"That gen'l'man's the Reverend Norman North,—he come by the *Trinidad* last Wednesday; he's sailin' to St. George's," Joe volunteered. "Don't look much like a reverend, do he?" And with that the carriage had started.

Seeing the sights at St. George's, they came to the small old church, on its western side a huge flight of steps, capped with a meek doorway; on its eastern end a stone tower guarding statelily a flowery graveyard. The moment the girl stepped inside, the spell of the bright peace which filled the place caught her. The Sunday decorations were still there, and hundreds of lilies bloomed from the pillars; sunshine slanted through the simple stained glass and lay in colored patches on the floor; there were square pews of a bygone day; there was a pulpit with a winding stair; there were tablets on the walls to shipwrecked sailors, to governors and officers dead here in harness. The clumsy woodwork, the cheap carpets, the modest brasses, were in perfect order; there were marks everywhere of reverent care.

"Let me stay," the girl begged. "I don't want to drive about. I want to stay in this place. I'll meet you at the hotel for lunch, if you'll leave me." And they left her.

The verger had gone, and she was quite alone. Deep in the shadow of a gallery she slid to her knees and hid her face. "O God!" she whispered,—"O God, forgive me!" And again the words seemed torn from her—"O God, forgive me!"

There were voices in the vestibule, but the girl in the stress of her prayer did not hear.

"Deal not with us according to our sins, neither reward us according to our iniquities," she prayed, the accustomed words rushing to her want, and she was suddenly aware that two people stood in the church. One of them spoke.

"Don't bother to stay with me," he said, and in the voice, it seemed, were the qualities that a man's speech should have—strength, certainty, the unteachable tone of gentle blood, and beyond these the note of personality, always indescribable, in this case carrying an appeal and an authority oddly combined. "Don't stay with me. I like to be alone here. I'm a clergyman, and I enjoy an old church like this. I'd like to be alone in it," and a bit of silver flashed.

If the tip did it or the compelling voice, the verger murmured a word about luncheon, was gone, and the girl in her dim corner saw, as the other turned, that he was the rescuer of her camera, whose name was, Joe had said and she remembered, Norman North. She was about to move, to let herself be seen, when the young man knelt suddenly in the old-fashioned front pew, as a good child might kneel who had been taught the ways of his mother church, and bent his dark head. She waited quietly while this servant spoke to his Master. There was no sound in the silent, sun-lanced church, but outside one heard as from far away the noises of the village. Katherine's eyes rested on the bowed head, and she wondered uncertainly if she should let him know of her presence, or if it might not be better to slip out unnoticed, when in a moment he had risen and was swinging with a vigorous step up the little corkscrew stairway of the pulpit. There he stood, facing the silence, facing the flower-starred shadows, the empty spaces; facing her, but not seeing her.

And the girl forgot herself and the question of her going as she saw the look in his face, the light which comes at times to those who give their lives to holiness, since the day when the people, gazing at Stephen, the martyr, "saw his face as it had been the face of an angel." When his voice floated out on the dim, sunny atmosphere it rested as lightly on the silence as if the notes of an organ rolled through its own place. He spoke a prayer of a service which, to those whose babyhood has been consecrated by it, whose childhood and youth have listened to its simple and stately words, whose manhood and womanhood have been carried over many a hard place by the lift of its familiar sentences,—he spoke a prayer of that service which is less dear only, to those bred in it, than the voices of their dearest. As a priest begins to speak to his congregation he began, and the hearer in the shadow of the gallery listened, awed:

"The Lord is in His holy temple: let all the earth keep silence before Him."

And in the little church was silence as if all the earth obeyed. The collect for the day came next, and a bit of jubilant Easter service, and then his mind seemed to drift back to the sentences with which the prayer-book opens.

"This is the day which the Lord hath made," the ringing voice announced. "Let us rejoice and be glad in it." And then, stabbing into the girl's fevered conscience, "I acknowledge my transgressions, and my sin is ever before me." It was as if an inflexible judge spoke the words for her. "When the wicked man turneth away from his wickedness, and doeth that which is lawful and right, he shall save his soul alive," the pure, stern tones went on.

She was not turning away from wickedness; she did not mean to turn away; she would not do that which was lawful. The girl shivered. She could not hear this dreadful accusal from the very pulpit. She must leave this place. And with that the man, as if in a sudden passion of feeling, had tossed his right hand high above him; his head was thrown back; his eyes shone up into the shadows of the roof as if they would pierce material things and see Him who reigned; he was pleading as if for his life, pleading for his brothers, for human beings who sin and suffer.

"O Lord," he prayed, "spare all those who confess their sins unto Thee, that they whose consciences by sin are accused, by Thy merciful pardon may be absolved; through Christ our Lord." And suddenly he was using the very words which had come to her of themselves a few minutes before. "Deal not with us according to our sins—deal not with us," he repeated, as if wresting forgiveness for his fellows from the Almighty. "Deal not with us according to our sins, neither reward us according to our iniquities." And while the echo of the words yet held the girl motionless he was gone.

---

Down by the road which runs past the hotel, sunken ten feet below its level, are the tennis-courts, and soldiers in scarlet and khaki, and blue-jackets with floating ribbons, and negro bell-boys returning from errands, and white-gowned American women with flowery hats, and men in summer flannels stop as they pass, and sit on the low wall and watch the games. There is always a gallery for the tennis-players. But on a Tuesday morning about eleven o'clock the audience began to melt away in disgust. Without doubt they were having plenty of amusement among themselves, these tennis-players grouped at one side of the court and filling the air with explosions of laughter. But the amusement of the public was being neglected. Why in the world, being rubber-shod as to the foot and racqueted as to the hand, did they not play tennis? A girl in a short white dress, wearing white tennis-shoes and carrying a racquet, came tripping down the flight of stone steps, and stopped as she stood on the last landing and seemed to ask the same question. She came slowly across the empty court, looking with curiosity at the bunch of absorbed people, and presently she caught her breath. The man who was the centre of the group, who was making, apparently, the amusement, was the young clergyman, Norman North.

There was an outburst, a chorus of: "You can't have that one, Mr. North!" "That's been used!" "That's Mr. Dennison's!"

A tall English officer—a fine, manly mixture of big muscles and fresh color and khaki—looked up, saw the girl, and swung toward her. "Good morning, Miss Newbold. Come and join the fun. Devil of a fellow, that North,—they say he's a parson."

"What is it? What are they laughing at?" Katherine demanded.

"They're doing a Limerick tournament, which is what North calls the game. Mr. Gale is timekeeper. They're to see which recites most rhymes inside five minutes. The winner picks his court and plays with Miss Lee."

Captain Comerford imparted this in jerky whispers, listening with one ear all the time to a sound which stirred Katherine, the voice which she had heard yesterday in the church at St. George's. The Englishman's spasmodic growl stopped, and she drifted a step nearer, listening. As she caught the words, her brows drew together with displeasure, with shocked surprise. The inspired saint of yesterday was reciting with earnestness, with every delicate inflection of his beautiful voice, these words:

"There was a young curate of Kidderminster,
Who kindly, but firmly, chid a spinster,
Because on the ice
She said something not nice
When he quite inadvertently slid ag'inst her."

As the roar which followed this subsided, Katherine's face cleared. What right had she to make a pattern of solemn righteousness for this stranger and be insulted if he did not fit? Certainly he was saintly—she had seen his soul bared to her vision; but certainly he was human also, as this moment was demonstrating. It flashed over her vaguely to wonder which was the dominant quality—which would rule in a stress of temptation—the saintly side or the human? But at least he was human with a winning humanity. His mirth and his enjoyment of it were as spontaneous as a mischievous, bright child's, and it was easy to see that the charm of his remarkable voice attracted others as it had attracted her.

"There was a young fellow from Clyde,

Who was often at funerals espied—"

he had begun, and with that, between her first shock and her swift recovery, with the contrast between the man of yesterday and the man of to-day, Katherine suddenly laughed aloud. North stopped short, and turned and looked at her, and for a second and their eyes met, and each read recognition and friendliness. The Limerick went on:

"When asked who was dead,
He nodded and said,
'*I* don't know—*I* just came for the ride.'"

"Eleven for Mr. North—one-half minute more," called Mr. Gale, and instantly North was in the breach:

"A sore-hipped hippopotamus quite flustered
Objected to a poultice made of custard;
'Can't you doctor up my hip
With anything but flip?'
So they put upon the hip a pot o' mustard.'"

And the half-minute was done and North had won, and there was clapping of hands for the victor, and at once, before the little uproar was over, Katherine saw him speak a word to Mr. Gale, and saw the latter, turning, stare about as if searching for some one, and, meeting her glance, smile.

"I want to present Mr. North, Miss Newbold," Gale said.

"Why did you laugh in the middle of my Limerick? Had you heard it?" North demanded, as if they had known each other a year instead of a minute.

"No, I had not heard it." Katherine shook her head.

"Then why did you laugh?"

She looked at him reflectively. "I don't know you well enough to tell you that."

"How soon will you know me well enough—if I do my best?"

She considered. "About three weeks from yesterday."

---

Many things grow fast in southern climates—fruits, flowers, even friendship and love. Three weeks later, on a hot, bright morning of April, North and Katherine Newbold were walking down a road of Bermuda to the sea, and between them was what had ripened in the twenty-one days from a germ to a full-grown bud, ready to open at the lightest touch into flower. As they walked down such a road of a dream, the man talked to the girl as he had never talked to any one before. He spoke of his work and its hopes and disappointments, of the pathos, the tragedy, the comedy often of a way of life which leads by a deeper cut through men's hearts than any other, and he told her also, modestly indeed, and because he loved to tell her what meant much to him, of the joy of knowing himself successful in his parish. He went into details, absorbingly interesting to him, and this new luxury of speaking freely carried him away.

"I hope I'm not boring you." His frank gaze turned on her anxiously. "I don't know what right I have to assume that the increase in the Sunday-school, or even the new brass pulpit, is a fascinating subject to you. I never did this before," he said, and there was something in his voice which hindered the girl from answering his glance. But there was no air of being bored about her, and he went on. "However, life isn't all good luck. I had a serious blow just before I came down here—a queer thing happened. I told you just now that all the large gifts to St. John's had come from one man—a former parishioner. The man was James Litterny, of the great firm of—Why, what's the matter—what is it?" For Katherine had stopped short, in her fast, swinging walk, and without a sound had swayed and caught at the wall as if to keep herself from falling. Before he could reach her she had straightened herself and was smiling.

"I felt ill for a second—it's nothing,—let's go along."

North made eager suggestions for her comfort, but the girl was firm in her assertion, that she was now quite well, so that, having no sisters and being ignorant that a healthy young woman does not, any more than a healthy young man, go white and stagger without reason, he yielded, and they walked briskly on.

"You were telling me something that happened to you—something connected with Mr.—with the rich parishioner." Her tone was steady and casual, but looking at her, he saw that she was still pale.

"Do you really want to hear my yarns? You're sure it isn't that which made you feel faint—because I talked so much?"

"It's always an effort not to talk myself," she laughed up at him, yet with a strange look in her eyes. "All the same, talk a little more. Tell me what you began to tell about Mr. Litterny." The name came out full and strong.

"Oh, that! Well, it's a story extraordinary enough for a book. I think it will interest you."

"I think it will," Katherine agreed.

"You see," he went on, "Mr. Litterny promised us a new parish-house, the best and largest practicable. It was to cost, with the lot, ten thousand dollars. It was to be begun this spring. Not long before I came to Bermuda, I had a note one morning from him, asking me to come to his house the next evening. I went, and he told me that the parish-house would have to be given up for the present, because the firm of Litterny Brothers had just met with a loss, through a most skilful and original robbery, of five thousand dollars."

"A robbery?" the girl repeated. "Burglars, you mean?"

"Something much more artistic than burglars. I told you this story was good enough for a book. It's been kept quiet because the detectives thought the chance better that way of hunting the thief to earth." (Why should she catch her breath?) "But I'm under no promise—I'm sure I may tell you. You're not likely to have any connection with the rascal."

Katherine's step hung a little as if she shrank from the words, but she caught at a part of the sentence and repeated it, "'Hunting the thief to earth'—you say that as if you'd like to see it done."

"I would like to see it done," said North, with slow emphasis. "Nothing has ever more roused my resentment. I suppose it's partly the loss of the parish-house, but, aside from that, it makes me rage to think of splendid old James Litterny, the biggest-hearted man I know, being done in that way. Why, he'd have helped the scoundrel in a minute if he'd gone to him instead of stealing from him. Usually my sympathies are with the sinner, but I believe if I caught this one I'd be merciless."

"Would you mind sitting down here?" Katherine asked, in a voice which sounded hard. "I'm not ill, but I feel—tired. I want to sit here and listen to the story of that unprincipled thief and his wicked robbery."

North was all solicitude in a moment, but the girl put him aside impatiently.

"I'm quite right. Don't bother. I just want to be still while you talk. See what a good seat this is."

Over the russet sand of the dunes the sea flashed a burning blue; storm-twisted cedars led a rutted road down to it; in the salt air the piny odor was sharp with sunlight. Katherine had dropped beneath one of the dwarfed trees, and leaning back, smiled dimly up at him with a stricken face which North did not understand.

"You are ill," he said, anxiously. "You look ill. Please let me take care of you. There is a house back there—let me—" but she interrupted:

"I'm not ill, and I won't be fussed over. I'm not exactly right, but I will be in a few minutes. The best thing for me is just to rest here and have you talk to me. Tell me that story you are so slow about."

He took her at her word. Lying at full length at her feet—his head propped on a hillock so that he might look into her face, one of his hands against the hem of her white dress,—the shadows of the cedars swept back and forth across him, the south sea glittered beyond the sand-dunes, and he told the story.

"Mr. Litterny was in his office in the early afternoon of February 18," he began, "when a man called him up on the telephone. Mr. Litterny did not recognize the voice, but the man stated at once that he was Burr Claflin, whose name you may know. He is a rich broker, and a personal friend of both the Litternys. Voice is so uncertain a quantity over a telephone that it did not occur to Mr. Litterny to be suspicious on that point, and the conversation was absolutely in character otherwise. The talker used expressions and a manner of saying things which the jeweller knew to be characteristic of Claflin.

"He told Mr. Litterny that he had just made a lucky hit in stocks, and 'turned over a bunch of money,' as he put it, and that he wanted to make his wife a present. 'Now—this afternoon—this minute,' he said, which was just like Burr Claflin, who is an impetuous old chap. 'I want to give her a diamond brooch, and I want her to wear it out to dinner to-night,' he said. 'Can't you send two or three corkers up to the house for me?' That surprised Mr. Litterny and he hesitated, but finally said that he would do it. It was against the rules of the house, but as it was for Mr. Claflin he would do it. They had a little talk about the details, and Claflin arranged to call up his wife and tell her that the jewels would be there at four-thirty, so that she could look out for them personally. All that was the Litterny end of the affair. Simple enough, wasn't it?"

Katherine's eyes were so intent, so brilliant, that Norman North went on with a pleased sense that he told the tale well:

"Now begins the Claflin experience. At half past four a clerk from Litterny's left a package at the Claflin house in Cleveland Avenue, which was at once taken, as the man desired, to Mrs. Claflin. She opened it and found three very handsome diamond brooches, which astonished her extremely, as she knew nothing about them. However, it was not unusual for Claflin to give her jewelry, and he is, as I said, an impulsive man, so that unexpected presents had come once or twice before; and altogether, being much taken with the stones, she concluded simply that she would understand when her husband came home to dinner.

"However, her hopes were dashed, for twenty minutes later, barely long enough for the clerk to have got back to the shop, she was called to the telephone by a message, said to be from Litterny's, and a most polite and apologetic person explained over the line that a mistake had been made; that the diamonds had been addressed and sent to her by an error of the shipping-clerk; that they were not intended for Mrs. Burr Claflin, but for Mrs. Bird Catlin, and that the change in name had been discovered on the messenger's return. Would Mrs. Claflin pardon the trouble caused, and would she be good enough to see that the package was given to their man, who would call for it in fifteen minutes? Now the Catlins, as you must know, are richer people even than the Claflins, so that the thing was absolutely plausible. Mrs. Claflin tied up the jewels herself, and entrusted them to her own maid, who has been with her for years, and this woman answered the door and gave the parcel into the hands of a man who said that he was sent from Litterny's for it. All that the maid could say of him was that he was 'a pretty young man, with a speech like a gentleman.' And that was the last that has been seen of the diamond brooches. Wasn't it simple? Didn't I tell you that this affair was an artistic one?" North demanded.

Katherine Newbold drew a deep breath, and the story-teller, watching her face, saw that she was stirred with an emotion which he put down, with a slight surprise, to interest in his narrative.

"Is there no clew to the—thief? Have they no idea at all? Haven't those wonderful detectives yet got on—his track?"

North shook his head. "I had a letter by yesterday's boat from Mr. Litterny about another matter, and he spoke of this. He said the police were baffled—that he believed now that it could never be traced."

"Thank God!" Katherine said, slowly and distinctly, and North stared in astonishment.

"What?" His tone was incredulous.

"Oh; don't take me so seriously," said the girl, impatiently. "It's only that I can't sympathize with your multimillionaire, who loses a little of his heaps of money, against some poor soul to whom that little may mean life or death—life or death, maybe, for his nearest and dearest. Mr. Litterny has had a small loss, which he won't feel in a year from now. The thief, the rascal, the scoundrel, as you call him so fluently, has escaped for now, perhaps, with his ill-gotten gains, but he is a hunted thing, living with a black terror of being found out—a terror which clutches him when he prays and when he dances. It's the thief I'm sorry for—I'm sorry for him—I'm sorry for him." Her voice was agitated and uneven beyond what seemed reasonable.

"'The way of the transgressor is hard,'" Norman North said, slowly, and looked across the shifting sand-stretch to the inevitable sea, and spoke the words pitilessly, as if an inevitable law spoke through him.

They cut into the girl's soul. A quick gasp of pain broke from her, and the man turned and saw her face and sprang to his feet.

"Come," he said,—"come home," and held out his hands.

She let him take hers, and he lifted her lightly, and did not let her hands go. For a second they stood, and into the silence a deep boom of the water against the beach thundered and died away. He drew the hands slowly toward him till he held them against him. There seemed not to be any need for words.

Half an hour later, as they walked back through the sweet loneliness of Springfield Avenue, North said: "You've forgotten something. You've forgotten that this is the day you were to tell me why you had the bad manners to laugh at me before you knew me. Now that we are engaged it's your duty to tell me if I'm ridiculous."

There was none of the responsive, soft laughter he expected. "We're not engaged—we can't be engaged," she threw back, impetuously, and as he looked at her there was suffering in her face.

"What do you mean? You told me you loved me." His voice was full of its curious mixture of gentleness and sternness, and she shrank visibly from the sternness.

"Don't be hard on me," she begged, like a frightened child, and he caught her hand with a quick exclamation. "I'll tell you—everything. Not only that little thing about my laughing, but—but more—everything. Why I cannot be engaged to you. I must tell you—I know it—but, oh! not to-day—not for a little while! Let me have this little time to be happy. You sail a week from to-day. I'll write it all for you, and you can read it on the way to New York. That will do—won't that do?" she pleaded.

North took both her hands in a hard grasp and searched her face and her eyes—eyes clear and sweet, though filled with misery. "Yes, that will do," he said. "It's all nonsense that you can't be engaged to me. You are engaged to me, and you are going to marry me. If you love me—and you say you do,—there's nothing I'll let interfere. Nothing—absolutely nothing." There was little of the saint in his look now; it was filled with human love and masterful determination, and in his eyes smouldered a recklessness, a will to have his way, that was no angel, but all man.

A week later Norman North sailed to New York, and in his pocket was a letter which was not to be read till Bermuda was out of sight. When the coral reef was passed, when the fairy blue of the island waters had changed to the dark swell of the Atlantic, he slipped the bolt in the door of his cabin and took out the letter.

"I laughed because you were so wonderfully two men in one," it began, "I was in the church at St. George's the day when you sent the verger away and went into the pulpit and said parts of the service. I could not tell you this before because it came so close to the other thing which I must tell you now; because I sat trembling before you that day, hidden in the shadow of a gallery, knowing myself a criminal, while you stood above me like a pitiless judge and rolled out sentences that were bolts of fire emptied on my soul. The next morning I heard you reciting Limericks.

Are you surprised that I laughed when the contrast struck me? Even then I wondered which was the real of you, the saint or the man,—which would win if it came to a desperate fight. The fight is coming, Norman.

"That's all a preamble. Here is what you must know: I am the thief who stole Mr. Litterny's diamonds."

The letter fell, and the man caught at it as it fell. His hand shook, but he laughed aloud.

"It is a joke," he said, in a queer, dry voice. "A wretched joke. How can she?" And he read on:

"You won't believe this at first; you will think I am making a poor joke; but you will have to believe it in the end. I will try to put the case before you as an outside person would put it, without softening or condoning. My mother was very ill; the specialist, to pay whom we had sold her last jewel, said that she would die if she were not taken south; we had no money to take her south. That night my brother lost his self-control and raved about breaking into a shop and stealing diamonds, to get money to save her life. That put the thought into my mind, and I made a plan. Randolph, my brother, is a clever amateur actor, and the rich Burr Claflin is our distant cousin. We both know him fairly well, and it was easy enough for Randolph to copy his mannerisms. We knew also, of course, more or less, his way of living, and that it would not be out of drawing that he should send up diamonds to his wife unexpectedly. I planned it all, and I made Randolph do it. I have always been able to influence him to what I pleased. The sin is all mine, not his. We had been selling my mother's jewels little by little for several years, so we had no difficulty in getting rid of the stones, which Randolph took from their settings and sold to different dealers. My mother knows nothing of where the money came from. We are living in Bermuda now, in comfort and luxury, I as well as she, on the profits of my thievery. I am not sorry. It has wrecked life, perhaps eternity, for me, but I would do it again to save my mother.

"I put this confession into your hands to do with, as far as I am concerned, what you like. If the saint in you believes that I ought to be sent to jail, take this to Mr. Litterny and have him send me to jail. But you shan't touch Randolph—you are not free there. It was I who did it—he was my tool,—any one will tell you I have the stronger will. You shall not hurt Randolph—that is barred.

"You see now why I couldn't be engaged to you—you wouldn't want to marry a thief, would you, Norman? I can never make restitution, you know, for the money will be mostly gone before we get home, and there is no more to come. You could not, either, for you said that you had little beyond your salary. We could never make it good to Mr. Litterny, even if you wanted to marry me after this. Mr. Litterny is your best friend; you are bound to him by a thousand ties of gratitude and affection. You can't marry a thief who has robbed him of five thousand dollars, and never tell him, and go on taking his gifts. That is the way the saint will look at it—the saint who thundered awful warnings at me in the little church at St. George's. But even that day there was something gentler than the dreadful holiness of you. Do you remember how you pleaded, begged as if of your father, for your brothers and sisters? 'Deal not with us according to our sins, neither reward us according to our iniquities,' you said. Do you remember? As you said that to God, I say it to you, I love you. I leave my fate at your mercy. But don't forget that you yourself begged that, with your hands stretched out to heaven, as I stretch my hands to you, Norman, Norman—'Deal not with me according to my sins, neither reward me according to my iniquities.'"

The noises of a ship moving across a quiet ocean went on steadily. Many feet tramped back and forth on the deck, and cheerful voices and laughter floated through the skylight, and down below a man knelt in a narrow cabin with his head buried in his arms, motionless.

---

### *CROWNED WITH GLORY AND HONOR*

Mists blew about the mountains across the river, and over West Point hung a raw fog. Some of the officers who stood with bared heads by the heap of earth and the hole in the ground shivered a little. The young Chaplain read, solemnly, the solemn and grand words of the service, and the evenness of his voice was unnatural enough to show deep feeling. He remembered how, a year before, he had seen the hero of this scene playing football on just such a day, tumbling about and shouting, his hair wild and matted and his face filled with fresh color. Such a mere boy he was, concerned over the question as to where he could hide his contraband dress boots, excited by an invitation to dine out Saturday night. The dear young chap! There were tears in the Chaplain's eyes as he thought of little courtesies to himself, of little generosities to other cadets, of a manly and honest heart shown everywhere that character may show in the guarded life of the nation's schoolboys.

The sympathetic, ringing voice stopped, and he watched the quick, dreadful, necessary work of the men at the grave, and then his sad eyes wandered pitifully over the rows of boyish faces where the cadets stood. Just such a child as those, thought the Chaplain—himself but a few years older—no history; no life, as we know life; no love, and what was life without—you may see that the Chaplain was young; the poor boy was taken from these quiet ways and sent direct on the fire-lit stage of history, and in the turn, behold! he was a hero. The white-robed Chaplain thrilled and his dark eyes flashed. He seemed to see that day; he would give half his life to have seen it—this boy had given all of his. The boy was wounded early, and as the bullets poured death down the hill he crept up it, on hands and knees, leading his men. The strong life in him lasted till he reached the top, and then the last of it pulled him to his feet and he stood and waved and cheered—and fell. But he went up San Juan Hill. After all, he lived. He missed fifty years, perhaps, but he had Santiago. The flag wrapped him, he was the honored dead of the nation. God keep him! The Chaplain turned with a swing and raised his prayer-book to read the committal. The long black box—the boy was very tall—was being lowered gently, tenderly. Suddenly the heroic vision of Santiago vanished and he seemed to see again the rumpled head and the alert, eager, rosy face of the boy playing football—the head that lay there! An iron grip caught his throat, and if a sound had come it would have been a sob. Poor little boy! Poor little hero! To exchange all life's sweetness for that fiery glory! Not to have known the meaning of living—of loving—of being loved!

The beautiful, tender voice rang out again so that each one heard it to the farthest limit of the great crowd—"We therefore commit his body to the ground; earth to earth, ashes to ashes, dust to dust; looking for the general resurrection in the last day, and the life of the world to come."

---

An hour later the boy's mother sat in her room at the hotel and opened a tin box of letters, found with his traps, and given her with the rest. She had planned it for this time and had left the box unopened. To-morrow she must take up life and try to carry it, with the boy gone, but to-day she must and would be what is called morbid. She looked over the bend in the river to the white-dotted cemetery—she could tell where lay the new mound, flower-covered, above his yellow head. She looked away quickly and bent over the box in her lap and turned the key. Her own handwriting met her eyes first; all her letters for six months back were there, scattered loosely about the box. She gathered them up, slipping them through her fingers to be sure of the writing. Letter after letter, all hers.

"They were his love-letters," she said to herself. "He never had any others, dear little boy—my dear little boy!"

Underneath were more letters, a package first; quite a lot of them, thirty, fifty—it was hard to guess—held together by a rubber strap. The strap broke as she drew out the first envelope and they fell all about her, some on the floor, but she did not notice it, for the address was in a feminine writing that had a vague familiarity. She stopped a moment, with the envelope in one hand and the fingers of the other hand on the folded paper inside. It felt like a dishonorable thing to do—like prying into the boy's secrets, forcing his confidence; and she had never done that. Yet some one must know whether these papers of his should be burned or kept, and who was there but herself? She drew out the letter. It began "My dearest." The boy's mother stopped short and drew a trembling breath, with a sharp, jealous pain. She had not known. Then she lifted her head and saw the dots of white on the green earth across the bay and her heart grew soft for that other woman to whom he had been "dearest" too, who must suffer this sorrow of losing him too. But she could not read her letters, she must send them, take them to her, and tell her that his mother had held them sacred. She turned to the signature.

"And so you must believe, darling, that I am and always will be—always, always, with love and kisses, your own dear, little 'Good Queen Bess.'"

It was not the sort of an ending to a letter she would have expected from the girl he loved, for the boy, though most undemonstrative, had been intense and taken his affections seriously always. But one can never tell, and the girl was probably quite young. But who was she? The signature gave no clew; the date was two years before, and from New York—sufficiently vague! She would have to read until she found the thread, and as she read the wonder grew that so flimsy a personality could have held her boy. One letter, two, three, six, and yet no sign to identify the writer. She wrote first from New York on the point of starting for a long stay abroad, and the other letters were all from different places on the other side. Once in awhile a familiar name cropped up, but never to give any clew. There were plenty of people whom she called by their Christian names, but that helped nothing. And often she referred to their engagement—to their marriage to come. It was hard for the boy's mother, who believed she had had his confidence. But there was one letter from Vienna that made her lighter-hearted as to that.

"My dear sweet darling," it began, "I haven't written you very often from here, but then I don't believe you know the difference, for you never scold at all, even if I'm ever so long in writing. And as for you, you rascal, you write less and less, and shorter and shorter. If I didn't know for certain—but then, of course, you love me? Don't you, you dearest boy? Of course you do, and who wouldn't? Now don't think I'm really so conceited as that, for I only mean it in joke, but in earnest, I might think it if I let myself, for they make such a fuss over me here—you never saw anything like it! The Prince von H—— told Mamma yesterday I was the prettiest girl who had been here in ten years—what do you think of that, sir? The officers are as thick as bees wherever I go, and I ride with them and dance with them and am having just the loveliest time! You don't mind that, do you, darling, even if we are engaged? Oh, about telling your mother—no, sir, you just cannot! You've begged me all along to do that, but you might as well stop, for I won't. You write more about that than anything else, it seems to me, and I'll believe soon you are more in love with your mother than with me. So take care! Remember, you promised that night at the hop at West Point—what centuries ago it seems, and it was a year and a half!—that you would not tell a living soul, not even your mother, until I said so. You see, it might get out and—oh, what's the use of fussing? It might spoil all my good time, and though I'm just as devoted as ever, and as much in love, you big, handsome thing—yes, just exactly!—still, I want to have a good time. Why shouldn't I? As the Prince would say, I'm pretty enough—but that's nonsense, of course."

The letter was signed like all the others "Good Queen Bess," a foolish enough name for a girl to call herself, the boy's mother thought, a touch contemptuously. She sat several minutes with that letter in her hand.

"I'll believe soon that you are more in love with your mother than you are with me"—that soothed the sore spot in her heart wonderfully. Wasn't it so, perhaps. It seemed to her that the boy had fallen into this affair suddenly, impulsively, without realizing its meaning, and that his loyalty had held him fast, after the glamour was gone. And perhaps the girl, too. For the boy had much besides himself, and there were girls who might think of that.

The next letter went far to confirm this theory.

"Of course I don't want to break our engagement," the girl wrote. "What makes you ask such a question? I fully expect to marry you some day, of course, when I have had my little 'fling,' and I should just go crazy if I thought you didn't love me as much as always. You would if you saw me, for they all say I'm prettier than ever. You don't want to break the engagement, do you? Please, please, don't say so, for I couldn't bear it."

And in the next few lines she mentioned herself by name. It was a well-known name to the boy's mother, that of the daughter of a cousin with whom she had never been over-intimate. She had had notes from the girl a few times, once or twice from abroad, which accounted for the familiarity of the writing. So she gathered the letters together, the last one dated only a month before, and put them one side to send back.

"She will soon get over it," she said, and sighed as she turned to the papers still left in the bottom of the box. There were only a few, a thin packet of six or eight, and one lying separate. She slipped the rubber band from the packet and looked hard at the irregular, strong writing, woman's or man's, it was hard to say which. Then she spread out the envelopes and took them in order by the postmarks. The first was a little note, thanking him for a book, a few lines of clever nothing signed by a woman's name which she had never heard.

---

"My dear Mr. ———," it ran. "Indeed you did get ahead of 'all the others' in sending me 'The Gentleman from Indiana,' So far ahead that the next man in the procession is not even in sight yet. I hate to tell you that, but honesty demands it. I have taken just one sidewise peep at 'The Gentleman'—and like his looks immensely—but to-morrow night I am going to pretend I have a headache and stay home from the concert where the family are going, and turn cannibal and devour him. I hope nothing will interrupt me. Unless—I wonder if you are conceited enough to imagine what is one of the very few things I would like to have interrupt me? After that bit of boldness I think I must stop writing to you. I mean it just the same. And thanking you a thousand times again, I am,

"Sincerely yours."

There were four or five more of this sort, sometimes only a day or two, sometimes a month apart; always with some definite reason for the writing, flowers or books to thank him for, a walk to arrange, an invitation to dinner. Charming, bright, friendly notes, with the happy atmosphere of a perfect understanding between them, of mutual interests and common enthusiasms.

"She was very different from the other," the boy's mother sighed, as she took up an unread letter—there were but two more. There was no harm in reading such letters as these, she thought with relief, and noticed as she drew the paper from the envelope that the postmark was two months later.

"You want me to write once that I love you"—that is the way it began.

The woman who read dropped it suddenly as if it had burned her. Was it possible? Her light-hearted boy, whose short life she had been so sure had held nothing but a boy's, almost a child's, joys and sorrows! The other affair was surprise enough, and a sad surprise, yet after all it had not touched him deeply, she felt certain of that; but this was another question. She knew instinctively that if love had grown from such a solid foundation as this sweet and happy and reasonable friendship with this girl, whose warm heart and deep soul shone through her clear and simple words, it would be a different love from anything that other poor, flimsy child could inspire. "L'amitié, c'est l'amour sans ailes." But sometimes when men and women have let the quiet, safe god Friendship fold his arms gently around them, he spreads suddenly a pair of sinning wings and carries them off—to heaven—wherever he wills it, and only then they see that he is not Friendship, but Love.

She picked up the letter again and read on:

"You want me to write once that I love you, so that you may read it with your eyes, if you may not hear it with your ears. Is that it—is that what you want, dear? Which question is a foolish sort of way for me to waste several drops of ink, considering that your letter is open before me. And your picture just back of it, your brown eyes looking over the edge so eagerly, so actually alive that it seems very foolish to be making signs to you on paper at all. How much simpler just to say half a word and then—then! Only we two can fill up that dash, but we can fill it full, can't we? However, I'm not doing what you want, and—will you not tell yourself, if I tell you something? To do what you want is just the one thing on earth I like most to do. I think you have magnetized me into a jelly-fish, for at times I seem to have no will at all. I believe if you asked me to do the Chinese kotow, and bend to the earth before you, I'd secretly be dying to do it. But I wouldn't, you know, I promise you that. I give you credit for liking a live woman, with a will of her own, better than a jelly-fish. And anyway I wouldn't—if you liked me for it or not—so you see it's no use urging me. And still I haven't done what you want—what was it now? Oh, to tell you that—but the words frighten me, they are so big. That I—I—I—love you. Is it that? I haven't said it yet, remember. I'm only asking a question. Do you know I have an objection to sitting here in cold blood and writing that down in cold ink? If it were only a little dark now, and your shoulder—and I could hide my head—you can't get off for a minute? Ah, I am scribbling along light-heartedly, when all the time the sword of Damocles is hanging over us both, when my next letter may have to be good-by for always. If that fate comes you will find me steady to stand by you, to help you. I will say those three little words, so little and so big, to you once again, and then I will live them by giving up what is dearest to me—that's you, dear—that your 'conduct' may not be 'unbecoming an officer and a gentleman.' You must keep your word. If the worst comes, will you always remember that as an American woman's patriotism. There could be none truer. I could send you marching off to Cuba—and how about that, is it war surely?—with a light heart, knowing that you were giving yourself for a holy cause and going to honor and fame, though perhaps, dear, to a soldier's death. And I would pray for you and remember your splendid strength, and think always of seeing you march home again, and then only your mother could be more proud than I. That would be easy, in comparison. Write me about the war—but, of course, you would not be sent.

"Now here is the very end of my letter, and I haven't yet said it—what you wanted. But here it Is, bend your head, from away up there, and listen. Now—do you hear—I love you. Good-by, good-by, I love you."

The papers rustled softly in the silent room, and the boy's mother, as she put the letter back, kissed it, and it was as if ghostly lips touched hers, for the boy had kissed those words, she knew.

The next was only a note, written just before his sailing to Cuba.

"A fair voyage and a short one, a good fight and a quick one," the note said. "It is my country as well as yours you are going to fight for, and I give you with all my heart. All of it will be with you and all my thoughts, too, every minute of every day, so you need never wonder if I'm thinking of you. And soon the Spaniards will be beaten and you'll be coming home again 'crowned with glory and honor,' and the bands will play fighting music, and the flag will be flying over you, for you, and in all proud America there will be no prouder soul than I—unless it is your mother. Good-by, good-by—God be with you, my very dearest."

He had come home "crowned with glory and honor." And the bands had played martial music for him. But his horse stood riderless by his grave, and the empty cavalry boots hung, top down, from the saddle.

Loose in the bottom of the box lay a folded sheet of paper, and, hidden under it, an envelope, the face side down. When the boy's mother opened the paper, it was his own crabbed, uneven writing that met her eye.

"They say there will be a fight to-morrow," he wrote, "and we're likely to be in it. If I come out right, you will not see this, and I hope I shall, for the world is sweet with you in it. But if I'm hit, then this will go to you. I'm leaving a line for my mother and will enclose this and ask her to send it to you. You must find her and be good to her, if that happens. I want you to know that if I die, my last thought will have been of you, and if I have the chance to do anything worth while, it will be for your sake. I could die happy if I might do even a small thing that would make you proud of me."

The sorrowful woman drew a long, shivering breath as she thought of the magnificent courage of that painful passing up San Juan Hill, wounded, crawling on, with a pluck that the shades of death could not dim. Would she be proud of him?

The line for herself he had never written. There was only the empty envelope lying alone in the box. She turned it in her hand and saw it was addressed to the girl to whom he had been engaged. Slowly it dawned on her that to every appearance this envelope belonged to the letter she had just read, his letter of the night before the battle. She recoiled at the thought—those last sacred words of his, to go to that empty-souled girl! All that she would find in them would be a little fuel for her vanity, while the other—she put her fingers on the irregular, back writing, and felt as if a strong young hand held hers again. She would understand, that other; she had thought of his mother in the stress of her own strongest feeling; she had loved him for himself, not for vanity. This letter was hers, the mother knew it. And yet the envelope, with the other address, had lain just under it, and she had been his promised wife. She could not face her boy in heaven if this last earthly wish of his should go wrong through her. How could she read the boy's mind now? What was right to do?

The twilight fell over Crow Nest, and over the river and the heaped-up mountains that lie about West Point, and in the quiet room the boy's mother sat perplexed, uncertain, his letter in her hands; yet with a vague sense of coming comfort in her heart as she thought of the girl who would surely "find her and be good to her," But across the water, on the hillside, the boy lay quiet.

---

### A MESSENGER

How oft do they their silver bowers leave,
To come to succour us that succour want!
How oft do they with golden pineons cleave
The flitting skyes, like flying Pursuivant,
Against fowle feendes to ayd us militant!
They for us fight, they watch and dewly ward,
And their bright Squadrons round about us plant;
And all for love, and nothing for reward.
O! Why should heavenly God to men have such regard?
—*Spenser's "Faerie Queene."*

That the other world of our hope rests on no distant, shining star, but lies about us as an atmosphere, unseen yet near, is the belief of many. The veil of material life shades earthly eyes, they say, from the glories in which we ever are. But sometimes when the veil wears thin in mortal stress, or is caught away by a rushing, mighty wind of inspiration, the trembling human soul, so bared, so purified, may look down unimagined heavenly vistas, and messengers may steal across the shifting boundary, breathing hope and the air of a brighter world. And of him who speaks his vision, men say "He is mad," or "He has dreamed."

---

The group of officers in the tent was silent for a long half minute after Colonel Wilson's voice had stopped. Then the General spoke.

"There is but one thing to do," he said. "We must get word to Captain Thornton at once."

The Colonel thought deeply a moment, and glanced at the orderly outside the tent. "Flannigan!" The man, wheeling swiftly, saluted. "Present my compliments to Lieutenant Morgan and say that I should like to see him here at once," and the soldier went off, with the quick military precision in which there is no haste and no delay.

"You have some fine, powerful young officers, Colonel," said the General casually. "I suppose we shall see in Lieutenant Morgan one of the best. It will take strength and brains both, perhaps, for this message."

A shadow of a smile touched the Colonel's lips. "I think I have chosen a capable man, General," was all he said.

Against the doorway of the tent the breeze blew the flap lazily back and forth. A light rain fell with muffled gentle insistence on the canvas over their heads, and out through the opening the landscape was blurred—the wide stretch of monotonous, billowy prairie, the sluggish, shining river, bending in the distance about the base of Black Wind Mountain—Black Wind Mountain, whose high top lifted, though it was almost June, a white point of snow above dark pine ridges of the hills below. The five officers talked a little as they waited, but spasmodically, absent-mindedly. A shadow blocked the light of the entrance, and in the doorway stood a young man, undersized, slight, blond. He looked inquiringly at the Colonel.

"You sent for me, sir?" and the General and his aide, and the grizzled old Captain, and the big, fresh-faced young one, all watched him.

In direct, quiet words—words whose bareness made them dramatic for the weight of possibility they carried—the Colonel explained. Black Wolf and his band were out on the war-path. A soldier coming in wounded, escaped from the massacre of the post at Devil's Hoof Gap, had reported it. With the large command known to be here camped on Sweetstream Fork, they would not come this way; they would swerve up the Gunpowder River twenty miles away, destroying the settlement and Little Fort Slade, and would sweep on, probably for a general massacre, up the Great Horn as far as Fort Doncaster. He himself, with the regiment, would try to save Fort Slade, but in the meantime, Captain Thornton's troop, coming to join him, ignorant that Black Wolf had taken the war-path, would be directly in their track. Some one must be sent to warn them, and of course the fewer the quicker. Lieutenant Morgan would take a sergeant, the Colonel ordered quietly, and start at once.

In the misty light inside the tent, the young officer looked hardly more than seventeen years old as he stood listening. His small figure was light, fragile; his hair was blond to an extreme, a thick thatch of pale gold; and there was about him, among these tanned, stalwart men in uniform, a presence, an effect of something unusual, a simplicity out of place yet harmonious, which might have come with a little child into a scene like this. His large blue eyes were fixed on the Colonel as he talked, and in them was just such a look of innocent, pleased wonder, as might be in a child's eyes, who had been told to leave studying and go pick violets. But as the Colonel ended he spoke, and the few words he said, the few questions he asked, were full of poise, of crisp directness. As the General volunteered a word or two, he turned to him and answered with a very charming deference, a respect that was yet full of gracious ease, the unconscious air of a man to whom generals are first as men, and then as generals. The slight figure in its dark uniform was already beyond the tent doorway when the Colonel spoke again, with a shade of hesitation in his manner.

"Mr. Morgan!" and the young officer turned quickly. "I think it may be right to warn you that there is likely to be more than usual danger in your ride."

"Yes, sir." The fresh, young voice had a note of inquiry.

"You will—you will"—what was it the Colonel wanted to say? He finished abruptly. "Choose the man carefully who goes with you."

"Thank you, Colonel," Morgan responded heartily, but with a hint of bewilderment. "I shall take Sergeant O'Hara," and he was gone.

There was a touch of color in the Colonel's face, and he sighed as if glad to have it over. The General watched him, and slowly, after a pause, he demanded:

"May I ask, Colonel, why you chose that blond baby to send on a mission of uncommon danger and importance?"

The Colonel answered quietly: "There were several reasons, General—good ones. The blond baby"—that ghost of a smile touched the Colonel's lips again—"the blond baby has some remarkable qualities. He never loses his head; he has uncommon invention and facility of getting out of bad holes; he rides light and so can make a horse last longer than most, and"—the Colonel considered a moment—"I may say he has no fear of death. Even among my officers he is known for the quality of his courage. There is one more reason: he is the most popular man I have, both with officers and men; if anything happened to Morgan the whole command would race into hell after the devils that did it, before they would miss their revenge."

The General reflected, pulling at his mustache. "It seems a bit like taking advantage of his popularity," he said.

"It is," the Colonel threw back quickly. "It's just that. But that's what one must do—a commanding officer—isn't it so, General? In this war music we play on human instruments, and if a big chord comes out stronger for the silence of a note, the note must be silenced—that's all. It's cruel, but it's fighting; it's the game."

The General, as if impressed with the tense words, did not respond, and the other officers stared at the Colonel's face, as carved, as stern as if done in marble—a face from which the warm, strong heart seldom shone, held back always by the stronger will.

The big, fresh-colored young Captain broke the silence. "Has the General ever heard of the trick Morgan played on Sun Boy, sir?" he asked.

"Tell the General, Captain Booth," the Colonel said briefly, and the Captain turned toward the higher officer.

"It was apropos of what the Colonel said of his inventive faculties, General," he began. "A year ago the youngster with a squad of ten men walked into Sun Boy's camp of seventy-five warriors. Morgan had made quite a pet of a young Sioux, who was our prisoner for five months, and the boy had taught him a lot of the language, and assured him that he would have the friendship of the band in return for his kindness to Blue Arrow—that was the chap's name. So he thought he was safe; but it turned out that Blue Arrow's father, a chief, had got into a row with Sun Boy, and the latter would not think of ratifying the boy's promise. So there was Morgan with his dozen men, in a nasty enough fix. He knew plenty of Indian talk to understand that they were discussing what they would do with him, and it wasn't pleasant.

"All of a sudden he had an inspiration. He tells the story himself, sir, and I assure you he'd make you laugh—Morgan is a wonderful mimic. Well, he remembered suddenly, as I said, that he was a mighty good ventriloquist, and he saw his chance. He gave a great jump like a startled fawn, and threw up his arms and stared like one demented into the tree over their heads. There was a mangy-looking crow sitting up there on a branch, and Morgan pointed at him as if at something marvellous, supernatural, and all those fool Indians stopped pow-wowing and stared up after him, as curious as monkeys. Then to all appearances, the crow began to talk. Morgan said they must have thought that spirits didn't speak very choice Sioux, but he did his best. The bird cawed out:

"'Oh, Sun Boy, great chief, beware what you do!'

"And then the real bird flapped its wings and Morgan thought it was going to fly, and he was lost. But it settled back again on the branch, and Morgan proceeded to caw on:

"'Hurt not the white man, or the curses of the gods will come upon Sun Boy and his people.'

"And he proceeded to give a list of what would happen if the Indians touched a hair of their heads. By this time the red devils were all down on their stomachs, moaning softly whenever Morgan stopped cawing. He said he quite got into the spirit of it and would have liked to go on some time, but he was beginning to get hoarse, and besides he was in deadly terror for fear the crow would fly before he got to the point. So he had the spirit order them to give the white men their horses and turn them loose instanter; and just as he got all through, off went the thing with a big flap and a parting caw on its own account. I wish I could tell it as Morgan does—you'd think he was a bird and an Indian rolled together. He's a great actor spoiled, that lad."

"You leave out a fine point, to my mind, Captain Booth," the Colonel said quickly. "About his going back."

"Oh! certainly that ought to be told," said the Captain, and the General's eyes turned to him again. "Morgan forgot to see young Blue Arrow, his friend, before he got away, and nothing would do but that he should go back and speak to him. He said the boy would be disappointed. The men were visibly uneasy at his going, but that didn't affect him. He ordered them to wait, and back he went, pell-mell, all alone into that horde of fiends. They hadn't got over their funk, luckily, and he saw Blue Arrow and made his party call and got out again all right. He didn't tell that himself, but Sergeant O'Hara made the camp ring with it. He adores Morgan, and claims that he doesn't know what fear is. I believe it's about so. I've seen him in a fight three times now. His cap always goes off—he loses a cap every blessed scrimmage—and with that yellow mop of hair, and a sort of rapt expression he gets, he looks like a child saying its prayers all the time he is slashing and shooting like a berserker." Captain Booth faced abruptly toward the Colonel. "I beg your pardon for talking so long, sir," he said. "You know we're all rather keen about little Miles Morgan."

The General lifted his head suddenly. "Miles Morgan?" he demanded. "Is his name Miles Morgan."

The Colonel nodded. "Yes. The grandson of the old Bishop—named for him."

"Lord!" ejaculated the General. "Miles Morgan was my earliest friend, my friend until he died! This must be Jim's son—Miles's only child. And Jim is dead these ten years," he went on rapidly. "I've lost track of him since the Bishop died, but I knew Jim left children. Why, he married"—he searched rapidly in his memory—"he married a daughter of General Fitzbrian's. This boy's got the church and the army both in him. I knew his mother," he went on, talking to the Colonel, garrulous with interest. "Irish and fascinating she was—believed in fairies and ghosts and all that, as her father did before her. A clever woman, but with the superstitious, wild Irish blood strong in her. Good Lord! I wish I'd known that was Miles Morgan's grandson."

The Colonel's voice sounded quiet and rather cold after the General's impulsive enthusiasm. "You have summed him up by his antecedents, General," he said. "The church and the army—both strains are strong. He is deeply religious."

The General looked thoughtful. "Religious, eh? And popular? They don't always go together."

Captain Booth spoke quickly. "It's not that kind, General," he said. "There's no cant in the boy. He's more popular for it—that's often so with the genuine thing, isn't it? I sometimes think"—the young Captain hesitated and smiled a trifle deprecatingly—"that Morgan is much of the same stuff as Gordon—Chinese Gordon; the martyr stuff, you know. But it seems a bit rash to compare an every-day American youngster to an inspired hero."

"There's nothing in Americanism to prevent either inspiration or heroism that I know of," the General affirmed stoutly, his fine old head up, his eyes gleaming with pride of his profession.

Out through the open doorway, beyond the slapping tent-flap, the keen, gray eyes of the Colonel were fixed musingly on two black points which crawled along the edge of the dulled silver of the distant river—Miles Morgan and Sergeant O'Hara had started.

---

"Sergeant!" They were eight miles out now, and the camp had disappeared behind the elbow of Black Wind Mountain. "There's something wrong with your horse. Listen! He's not loping evenly." The soft cadence of eight hoofs on earth had somewhere a lighter and then a heavier note; the ear of a good horseman tells in a minute, as a musician's ear at a false note, when an animal saves one foot ever so slightly, to come down harder on another.

"Yessirr. The Lieutenant'll remimber 'tis the horrse that had a bit of a spavin, Sure I thot 'twas cured, and 'tis the kindest baste in the rigiment f'r a pleasure ride, sorr—that willin' 'tis. So I tuk it. I think 'tis only the stiffness at furrst aff. 'Twill wurruk aff later. Plaze God, I'll wallop him." And the Sergeant walloped with a will.

But the kindest beast in the regiment failed to respond except with a plunge and increased lameness. Soon there was no more question of his incapacity.

Lieutenant Morgan halted his mount, and, looking at the woe-begone O'Hara, laughed. "A nice trick this is, Sergeant," he said, "to start out on a trip to dodge Indians with a spavined horse. Why didn't you get a broomstick? Now go back to camp as fast as you can go; and that horse ought to be blistered when you get there. See if you can't really cure him. He's too good to be shot." He patted the gray's nervous head, and the beast rubbed it gently against his sleeve, quiet under his hand.

"Yessirr. The Lieutenant'll ride slow, sorr, f'r me to catch up on ye, sorr?"

Miles Morgan smiled and shook his head. "Sorry, Sergeant, but there'll be no slow riding in this. I'll have to press right on without you; I must be at Massacre Mountain to-night to catch Captain Thornton to-morrow."

Sergeant O'Hara's chin dropped. "Sure the Lieutenant'll niver be thinkin' to g'wan alone—widout *me*?" and with all the sergeant's respect of his superiors, it took the Lieutenant ten valuable minutes to get the man started back, shaking his head and muttering forebodings, to the camp.

It was quiet riding on alone. There were a few miles to go before there was any chance of Indians, and no particular lookout to be kept, so he put the horse ahead rapidly while he might, and suddenly he found himself singing softly as he galloped. How the words had come to him he did not know, for no conscious train of thought had brought them; but they surely fitted to the situation, and a pleasant sense of companionship, of safety, warmed him as the swing of an old hymn carried his voice along with it.

> God shall charge His angel legions
> Watch and ward o'er thee to keep;
> Though thou walk through hostile regions,
> Though in desert wilds thou sleep.

Surely a man riding toward—perhaps through—skulking Indian hordes, as he must, could have no better message reach him than that. The bent of his mind was toward mysticism, and while he did not think the train of reasoning out, could not have said that he believed it so, yet the familiar lines flashing suddenly, clearly, on the curtain of his mind, seemed to him, very simply, to be sent from a larger thought than his own. As a child might take a strong hand held out as it walked over rough country, so he accepted this quite readily and happily, as from that Power who was never far from him, and in whose service, beyond most people, he lived and moved. Low but clear and deep his voice went on, following one stanza with its mate:

> Since with pure and firm affection
> Thou on God hast set thy love,
> With the wings of His protection
> He will shield thee from above.

The simplicity of his being sheltered itself in the broad promise of the words.

Light-heartedly he rode on and on, though now more carefully; lying flat and peering over the crests of hills a long time before he crossed their tops; going miles perhaps through ravines; taking advantage of every bit of cover where a man and a horse might be hidden; travelling as he had learned to travel in three years of experience in this dangerous Indian country, where a shrub taken for granted might mean a warrior, and that warrior a hundred others within signal. It was his plan to ride until about twelve—to reach Massacre Mountain, and there rest his horse and himself till gray daylight. There was grass there and a spring—two good and innocent things that had been the cause of the bad, dark thing which had given the place its name. A troop under Captain James camping at this point, because of the water and grass, had been surprised and wiped out by five hundred Indian braves of the wicked and famous Red Crow. There were ghastly signs about the place yet; Morgan had seen them, but soldiers may not have nerves, and it was good camping ground.

On through the valleys and half-way up the slopes, which rolled here far away into a still wilder world, the young man rode. Behind the distant hills in the east a glow like fire flushed the horizon. A rim of pale gold lifted sharply over the ridge; a huge round ball of light pushed faster, higher, and lay, a bright world on the edge of the world, great against the sky—the moon had risen. The twilight trembled as the yellow rays struck into its depths, and deepened, dying into purple shadows. Across the plain zigzagged pools of a level stream, as if a giant had spilled handfuls of quicksilver here and there.

Miles Morgan, riding, drank in all the mysterious, wild beauty, as a man at ease; as open to each fair impression as if he were not riding each moment into deeper danger, as if his every sense were not on guard. On through the shining moonlight and in the shadow of the hills he rode, and, where he might, through the trees, and stopped to listen often, to stare at the hill-tops, to question a heap of stones or a bush.

At last, when his leg-weary horse was beginning to stumble a bit, he saw, as he came around a turn, Massacre Mountain's dark head rising in front of him, only half a mile away. The spring trickled its low song, as musical, as limpidly pure as if it had never run scarlet. The picketed horse fell to browsing and Miles sighed restfully as he laid his head on his saddle and fell instantly to sleep with the light of the moon on his damp, fair hair. But he did not sleep long. Suddenly with a start he awoke, and sat up sharply, and listened. He heard the horse still munching grass near him, and made out the shadow of its bulk against the sky; he heard the stream, softly falling and calling to the waters where it was going. That was all. Strain his hearing as he might he could hear nothing else in the still night. Yet there was something. It might not be sound or sight, but there was a presence, a something— he could not explain. He was alert in every nerve. Suddenly the words of the hymn he had been singing in the afternoon flashed again into his mind, and, with his cocked revolver in his hand, alone, on guard, in the midnight of the savage wilderness, the words came that were not even a whisper:

God shall charge His angel legions
Watch and ward o'er thee to keep;
Though thou walk through hostile regions,
Though in desert wilds thou sleep.

He gave a contented sigh and lay down. What was there to worry about? It was just his case for which the hymn was written. "Desert wilds"—that surely meant Massacre Mountain, and why should he not sleep here quietly, and let the angels keep their watch and ward? He closed his eyes with a smile. But sleep did not come, and soon his eyes were open again, staring into blackness, thinking, thinking.

It was Sunday when he started out on this mission, and he fell to remembering the Sunday nights at home—long, long ago they seemed now. The family sang hymns after supper always; his mother played, and the children stood around her—five of them, Miles and his brothers and sisters. There was a little sister with brown hair about her shoulders, who always stood by Miles, leaned against him, held his hand, looked up at him with adoring eyes—he could see those uplifted eyes now, shining through the darkness of this lonely place. He remembered the big, home-like room; the crackling fire; the peaceful atmosphere of books and pictures; the dumb things about its walls that were yet eloquent to him of home and family; the sword that his great-grandfather had worn under Washington; the old ivories that another great-grandfather, the Admiral, had brought from China; the portraits of Morgans of half a dozen generations which hung there; the magazine table, the books and books and books. A pang of desperate homesickness suddenly shook him. He wanted them—his own. Why should he, their best-beloved, throw away his life—a life filled to the brim with hope and energy and high ideals—on this futile quest? He knew quite as well as the General or the Colonel that his ride was but a forlorn hope. As he lay there, longing so, in the dangerous dark, he went about the library at home in his thought and placed each familiar belonging where he had known it all his life. And as he finished, his mother's head shone darkly golden by the piano; her fingers swept over the keys; he heard all their voices, the dear never-forgotten voices. Hark! They were singing his hymn—little Alice's reedy note lifted above the others—"God shall charge His angel legions—"

Now! He was on his feet with a spring, and his revolver pointed steadily. This time there was no mistaking—something had rustled in the bushes. There was but one thing for it to be—Indians. Without realizing what he did, he spoke sharply.

"Who goes there?" he demanded, and out of the darkness a voice answered quietly:

"A friend."

"A friend?" With a shock of relief the pistol dropped by his side, and he stood tense, waiting. How might a friend be here, at midnight in this desert? As the thought framed itself swiftly the leaves parted, and his straining eyes saw the figure of a young man standing before him.

"How came you here?" demanded Miles sternly. "Who are you?"

Even in the dimness he could see the radiant smile that answered him. The calm voice spoke again: "You will understand that later. I am here to help you."

As if a door had suddenly opened into that lighted room of which he dreamed, Miles felt a sense of tranquillity, of happiness stirring through him. Never in his life had he known such a sudden utter confidence in anyone, such a glow of eager friendliness as this half-seen, mysterious stranger inspired. "It is because I was lonelier than I knew," he said mentally. "It is because human companionship gives courage to the most self-reliant of us"; and somewhere in the words he was aware of a false note, but he did not stop to place it.

The low, even voice of the stranger spoke again. "There are Indians on your trail," he said. "A small band of Black Wolf's scouts. But don't be troubled. They will not hurt you."

"You escaped from them?" demanded Miles eagerly, and again the light of a swift smile shone into the night. "You came to save me—how was it? Tell me, so that we can plan. It is very dark yet, but hadn't we better ride? Where is your horse?"

He threw the earnest questions rapidly across the black night, and the unhurried voice answered him. "No," it said, and the verdict was not to be disputed. "You must stay here."

Who this man might be or how he came Miles could not tell, but this much he knew, without reason for knowing it; it was someone stronger than he, in whom he could trust. As the newcomer had said, it would be time enough later to understand the rest. Wondering a little at his own swift acceptance of an unknown authority, wondering more at the peace which wrapped him as an atmosphere at the sound of the stranger's voice, Miles made a place for him by his side, and the two talked softly to the plashing undertone of the stream.

Easily, naturally, Miles found himself telling how he had been homesick, longing for his people. He told him of the big familiar room, and of the old things that were in it, that he loved; of his mother; of little Alice, and her baby adoration for the big brother; of how they had always sung hymns together Sunday night; he never for a moment doubted the stranger's interest and sympathy—he knew that he cared to hear.

"There is a hymn," Miles said, "that we used to sing a lot—it was my favorite; 'Miles's hymn,' the family called it. Before you came to-night, while I lay there getting lonelier every minute, I almost thought I heard them singing it. You may not have heard it, but it has a grand swing. I always think"—he hesitated—"it always seems to me as if the God of battles and the beauty of holiness must both have filled the man's mind who wrote it." He stopped, surprised at his own lack of reserve, at the freedom with which, to this friend of an hour, he spoke his inmost heart.

"I know," the stranger said gently. There was silence for a moment, and then the wonderful low tones, beautiful, clear, beyond any voice Miles had ever heard, began again, and it was as if the great sweet notes of an organ whispered the words:

God shall charge His angel legions
Watch and ward o'er thee to keep;
Though thou walk through hostile regions,
Though in desert wilds thou sleep.

"Great Heavens!" gasped Miles. "How could you know I meant that? Why, this is marvellous—why, this"—he stared, speechless, at the dim outlines of the face which he had never seen before to-night, but which seemed to him already familiar and dear beyond all reason. As he gazed the tall figure rose, lightly towering above him. "Look!" he said, and Miles was on his feet. In the east, beyond the long sweep of the prairie, was a faint blush against the blackness; already threads of broken light, of pale darkness, stirred through the pall of the air; the dawn was at hand.

"We must saddle," Miles said, "and be off. Where is your horse picketed?" he demanded again.

But the strange young man stood still; and now his arm was stretched pointing. "Look," he said again, and Miles followed the direction with his eyes.

From the way he had come, in that fast-growing glow at the edge of the sky, sharp against the mist of the little river, crept slowly half a dozen pin points, and Miles, watching their tiny movement, knew that they were ponies bearing Indian braves. He turned hotly to his companion.

"It's your fault," he said. "If I'd had my way we'd have ridden from here an hour ago. Now here we are caught like rats in a trap; and who's to do my work and save Thornton's troop—who's to save them—God!" The name was a prayer, not an oath.

"Yes," said the quiet voice at his side, "God,"—and for a second there was a silence that was like an Amen.

Quickly, without a word, Miles turned and began to saddle. Then suddenly as he pulled at the girth, he stopped. "It's no use," he said. "We can't get away except over the rise, and they'll see us there"; he nodded at the hill which rose beyond the camping ground three hundred yards away, and stretched in a long, level sweep into other hills and the west. "Our chance is that they're not on my trail after all—it's quite possible." There was a tranquil unconcern about the figure near him; his own bright courage caught the meaning of its relaxed lines with a hound of pleasure. "As you say, it's best to stay here," he said, and as if thinking aloud—"I believe you must always be right." Then he added, as if his very soul would speak itself to this wonderful new friend: "We can't be killed, unless the Lord wills it, and if he does it's right. Death is only the step into life; I suppose when we know that life, we will wonder how we could have cared for this one."

Through the gray light the stranger turned his face swiftly, bent toward Miles, and smiled once again, and the boy thought suddenly of the martyrdom of St. Stephen, and how those who were looking "saw his face as it had been the face of an angel."

Across the plain, out of the mist-wreaths, came rushing, scurrying, the handful of Indian braves. Pale light streamed now from the east, filtering over a hushed world. Miles faced across the plain, stood close to the tall stranger whose shape, as the dawn touched it, seemed to rise beyond the boy's slight figure wonderfully large and high. There was a sense of unending power, of alertness, of great, easy movement about him; one might have looked at him, and looking away again, have said that wings were folded about him. But Miles did not see him. His eyes were on the fast-nearing, galloping ponies, each with its load of filthy, cruel savagery. This was his death coming; there was disgust, but not dread in the thought for the boy. In a few minutes he should be fighting hopelessly, fiercely against this froth of a lower world; in a few minutes after that he should be lying here still—for he meant to be killed; he had that planned. They should not take him—a wave of sick repulsion at that thought shook him. Nearer, nearer, right on his track came the riders pell-mell. He could hear their weird, horrible cries; now he could see gleaming through the dimness the huge headdress of the foremost, the white coronet of feathers, almost the stripes of paint on the fierce face.

Suddenly a feeling that he knew well caught him, and he laughed. It was the possession that had held in him in every action which he had so far been in. It lifted his high-strung spirit into an atmosphere where there was no dread and no disgust, only a keen rapture in throwing every atom of soul and body into physical intensity; it was as if he himself were a bright blade, dashing, cutting, killing, a living sword rejoicing to destroy. With the coolness that may go with such a frenzy he felt that his pistols were loose; saw with satisfaction that he and his new ally were placed on the slope to the best advantage, then turned swiftly, eager now for the fight to come, toward the Indian band. As he looked, suddenly in mid-career, pulling in their plunging ponies with a jerk that threw them, snorting, on their haunches, the warriors halted. Miles watched in amazement. The bunch of Indians, not more than a hundred yards away, were staring, arrested, startled, back of him to his right, where the lower ridge of Massacre Mountain stretched far and level over the valley that wound westward beneath it on the road to Fort Rain-and-Thunder. As he gazed, the ponies had swept about and were galloping back as they had come, across the plain.

Before he knew if it might be true, if he were not dreaming this curious thing, the clear voice of his companion spoke in one word again, like the single note of a deep bell. "Look!" he said, and Miles swung about toward the ridge behind, following the pointing finger.

**"Look!" he said, and Miles swung about toward the ridge behind.**

In the gray dawn the hill-top was clad with the still strength of an army. Regiment after regiment, silent, motionless, it stretched back into silver mist, and the mist rolled beyond, above, about it; and through it he saw, as through rifts in broken gauze, lines interminable of soldiers, glitter of steel. Miles, looking, knew.

He never remembered how long he stood gazing, earth and time and self forgotten, at a sight not meant for mortal eyes; but suddenly, with a stab it came to him, that if the hosts of heaven fought his battle it was that he might do his duty, might save Captain Thornton and his men; he turned to speak to the young man who had been with him. There was no one there. Over the bushes the mountain breeze blew damp and cold; they rustled softly under its touch; his horse stared at him mildly; away off at the foot-hills he could see the diminishing dots of the fleeing Indian ponies; as he wheeled again and looked, the hills that had been covered with the glory of heavenly armies, lay hushed and empty. And his friend was gone.

Clatter of steel, jingle of harness, an order ringing out far but clear—Miles threw up his head sharply and listened. In a second he was pulling at his horse's girth, slipping the bit swiftly into its mouth—in a moment more he was off and away to meet them, as a body of cavalry swung out of the valley where the ridge had hidden them.

"Captain Thornton's troop?" the officer repeated carelessly. "Why, yes; they are here with us. We picked them up yesterday, headed straight for Black Wolf's war-path. Mighty lucky we found them. How about you—seen any Indians, have you?"

Miles answered slowly: "A party of eight were on my trail; they were riding for Massacre Mountain, where I camped, about an hour—about half an hour—awhile ago." He spoke vaguely, rather oddly, the officer thought, "Something—stopped them about a hundred yards from the mountain. They turned, and rode away."

"Ah," said the officer. "They saw us down the valley."

"I couldn't see you," said Miles.

The officer smiled. "You're not an Indian, Lieutenant. Besides, they were out on the plain and had a farther view behind the ridge." And Miles answered not a word.

General Miles Morgan, full of years and of honors, has never but twice told the story of that night of forty years ago. But he believes that when his time comes, and he goes to join the majority, he will know again the presence which guarded him through the blackness of it, and among the angel legions he looks to find an angel, a messenger, who was his friend.

---

### THE AIDE-DE-CAMP

Age has a point or two in common with greatness; few willingly achieve it, indeed, but most have it thrust upon them, and some are born old. But there are people who, beginning young, are young forever. One might fancy that the careless fates who shape souls—from cotton-batting, from stone, from wood and dynamite and cheese—once in an æon catch, by chance, a drop of the fountain of youth, and use it in their business, and the soul so made goes on bubbling and sparkling eternally, and gray dust of years cannot dim it. It might be imagined, in another flight of fancy, that a spark of divine fire from the brazier of the immortals snaps loose once in a century and lodges in somebody, and is a heart—with such a clean and happy flame burns sometimes a heart one knows.

On a January evening, in a room where were books and a blazing hearth, a man with a famous name and a long record told me a story, and through his blunt speech flashed in and out all the time the sparkle of the fire and the ripple of the fountain. Unsuspecting, he betrayed every minute the queer thing that had happened to him—how he had never grown up and his blood had never grown cold. So that the story, as it fell in easy sequence, had a charm which was his and is hard to trap, yet it is too good a story to leave unwritten. A picture goes with it, what I looked at as I listened: a massive head on tremendous shoulders; bright white hair and a black bar of eyebrows, striking and dramatic; underneath, eyes dark and alive, a face deep red-and-brown with out of doors. His voice had a rough command in it, because, I suppose, he had given many orders to men. I tell the tale with this memory for a setting; the firelight, the soldierly presence, the gayety of youth echoing through it.

The fire had been forgotten as we talked, and I turned to see it dull and lifeless. "It hasn't gone out, however," I said, and coughed as I swallowed smoke. "There's no smoke without some fire," I poked the logs together. "That's an old saw; but it's true all the same."

"Old saws always are true," said the General. "If there isn't something in them that people know is so they don't get old—they die young. I believe in the ridden-to-death proverbs—little pitchers with big ears—cats with nine lives—still waters running deep—love at first sight, and the rest. They're true, too." His straight look challenged me to dispute him.

The pine knots caught and blazed up, and I went back comfortably into my chair and laughed at him.

"O General! Come! You don't believe in love at first sight."

I liked to make him talk sentiment. He was no more afraid of it than of anything else, and the warmest sort came out of his handling natural and unashamed.

"I don't? Yes, I do, too," he fired at me. "I know it happens, sometimes."

With that the lines of his face broke into the sunshiniest smile. He threw back his head with sudden boyishness, and chuckled, "I ought to know; I've had experience," he said. His look settled again thoughtfully. "Did I ever tell you that story—the story about the day I rode seventy-five miles? Well, I did that several times—I rode it once to see my wife. But this was the first time, and a good deal happened. It was a history-making day for me all right. That was when I was aide-de-camp to General Stoneman. Have I told you that?"

"No," I said; and "oh, do tell me." I knew already that a fire and a deep chair and one of the General's stories made a good combination.

His manner had a quality uncommon to storytellers; he spoke as if what he told had occurred not in times gone by, but perhaps last week; it was more gossip than history. Probably the sharp, full years had been so short to him that the interval between twenty and seventy was no great matter; things looked as clear and his interest was as lively as a half-century ago. This trick of mind made a narrative of his vivid. With eyes on the fire, with his dominant voice absorbing the crisp sound of the crackling wood, he began to talk.

"It was down in Virginia in—let me see—why, certainly, it was in '63—right away after the battle of Chancellorsville, you know." I kept still and hoped the

General thought I knew the date of the battle of Chancellorsville. "I was part of a cavalry command that was sent from the Army of the Potomac under General Stoneman—I was his aide. Well, we did a lot of things—knocked out bridges and railroads, and all that; our object was, you see, to destroy communication between Lee's army and Richmond. We even got into Richmond—we thought every Confederate soldier was with Lee at the front, and we had a scheme to free the prisoners in Libby, and perhaps capture Jefferson Davis—but we counted wrong. The defence was too strong, and our force too small; we had to skedaddle, or we'd have seen Libby in a way we didn't like. We found a negro who could pilot us, and we slipped out through fields and swamps beyond the reach of the enemy. Then the return march began. Let me put that log on."

"No. Talk," I protested; but the General had the wood in his vigorous left hand—where a big scar cut across the back.

"You needn't be so independent," he threw at me. "Now you've got a splinter in your finger—serves you right." I laughed at the savage tone, and his eyes flashed fiercely—and he laughed back.

"What was I talking about—you interrupted. Oh, that march. Well, we'd had a pretty rough time when the march back began. For nine days we hadn't had a real meal—just eaten standing up, whatever we could get cooked—or uncooked. We hadn't changed our clothes, and we'd slept on the ground every night."

"Goodness!" I interjected with amateur vagueness. "What about the horses?"

"Oh, they got it, too," the General said carelessly. "We seldom unsaddled them at all, and when we did it was just to give them a rub-down and saddle again. We'd made one march toward home and halted, late at night, when General Stoneman called for his aide-de-camp. I went to him, rather sleepy, and he told me he'd decided to communicate with his chief and report his success, and that I was to start at daylight and find the Army of the Potomac. I had my pick of ten of the best men and horses from the brigade, and I got off at gray dawn with them, and with the written report in my boot to the commanding general, and verbal orders to find him wherever he might be. Nothing else, except the tools—swords and pistols, and that sort of thing. Oh, yes, there was one thing more. General Ladd, who was a Virginian, had given my chief a letter for his people, thinking we'd get into their country. His family were all on the Confederate side of the fence, while he was a Union officer. That was not uncommon in our civil war. But we didn't get near the Ladd estate, and so Stoneman commissioned me to return the letter to the general with the explanation. Does this bore you?" he stopped suddenly to ask, and his alert eye shot the glance at me like a bullet.

"Stop once more and I'll be likely to cry," I predicted.

"For Heaven's sake don't do that." He reached across and took the poker. "Here's the Rapidan River," he sketched down the rug. "Runs east and west. And this blue diagonal north of it is the Rappahannock. I started south of the Rapidan, to cross it and go north, hoping to find our army victorious and south of the Rappahannock. Which I didn't—but that's farther along. Well, we were off at daylight, ten men and the officer—me. It was a fine spring morning, and the bunch of horsemen made a pretty sight as the sun came up, moving through the greenness—the foliage is well out down there in May. The bits jingled and the saddles creaked under our legs—I remember how it sounded as we started off. We'd had a strenuous week, but we were a strong lot and ready for anything. We were going to get it, too." The General chuckled suddenly, as if something had hit his funny-bone. "I skirted along the south bank of the Rapidan, keeping off the roads most of the time, and out of sight, which was better for our health—we were in Confederate country—and we got to Germania Ford without seeing anybody, or being seen. Said I, 'Here's the place we'll cross.' We'd had breakfast before starting, but we'd been in the saddle three hours since that, and I was thirsty. I could see a house back in the trees as we came to the ford—a beautiful old house—the kind you see a lot of in the South—high white pillars—dignified and aristocratic. It seemed to be quiet and safe, so we trotted up the drive, the eleven of us. The front door was open, and I jumped off my horse and ran up the steps and stood in the doorway. There were four or five people in the hall, and they'd seen us coming and were scared. A nice old lady was lying back in a chair, as pale as ashes, with her hand to her heart, gasping ninety to the second, and two or three negroes stood around her with their eyes rolling. And right in the middle of the place a red-headed girl in a white dress was bending over a grizzled old negro man who was locking a large travelling-bag. As cool as a cucumber that girl was."

The General stopped and considered.

"I wish I could describe the scene the way I saw it—I remember exactly. It was a big, square hall running through from front to back, and the back door was open, and you saw a garden with box hedges, and woods behind it. Stairs went up each side the hall and a balcony ran around the second story, with bedrooms opening off it. There was a high, oval window at the back over the balcony, and the sun poured through.

"The girl finished locking her bag as if she hadn't noticed scum of the earth like us, and then she deliberately picked up a bunch of long white flowers that lay by the bag—lilies, I think you call them—and stood up, and looked right past me, as if she was struck with the landscape, and didn't see me. She was a tall girl, and when she stood straight the light from the back window just hit her hair and shone through the loose part of it—there was a lot, and it was curly. I give you my word that, as she stood there and looked calmly beyond me, in her white dress, with the stalk of flowers over her shoulder, and the sun turning that wonderful red-gold hair into a halo—I give you my word she was a perfect picture of a saint out of a stained-glass window in a church. But she didn't act like one."

The General was seized with sudden, irresistible laughter. He sobered quickly.

"I took one look at the vision, and I knew it was all up with me. Talk about love at first sight—before she ever spoke a word I—well." He pulled up the sentence as if it were a horse. "I snatched off my cap and I said, said I, 'I'm very sorry to disturb you,' just as politely as I knew how, but all the answer she gave me was to glance across at the old lady. Then she went find put her arm around her as she lay back gasping in a great curved chair.

"'Don't be afraid, Aunt Virginia,' she said. 'Nothing shall hurt you. I can manage this man.'

"The way she said 'this man' was about as contemptuous as they make 'em. I guess she was right, too—I guess she could. She turned her head toward me, but did not look at me.

"'Do you want anything here?' she asked.

"Her voice was the prettiest, softest sound you ever heard—she was mad as a hornet, too." The General's swift chuckle caught him. "'Hyer,' she said it," he repeated. "'Hyer.'" He liked to say it, evidently. "I stood holding my cap in my hand, so tame by this time you could have put me on a perch in a cage, for the pluck of the girl was as fascinating as her looks. I spoke up like a man all the same.

"'I wanted to ask,' said I, 'if I might send my men around to your well for a drink of water. They're thirsty.'

"The way she answered, looking all around me and never once at me, made me uncomfortable. 'I suppose you can if you wish,' she said. 'You're stronger than we are. You can take what you choose. But I won't give you anything—not if you were dying—not a glass of water.'

"Well, in spite of her having played football with my heart, that made me angry.

"'I didn't know before that to be Southern made a woman unwomanly,' I said. 'Where I came from I don't believe there's a girl would say a cruel thing like that or refuse a drink of cold water to soldiers doing their duty, friends or enemies. We've slept on the ground nine nights and ridden nine days, and had very little to eat—my men are tired and thirsty. I shan't make them go without any refreshment they can get, even if it is grudged.'

"I gave an order over my shoulder, and my party went off to the back of the house. Then I made a low bow to the old lady and to Miss High-and-Mighty, and I swung about and walked down the steps and mounted my horse. I was parched for water, but I wouldn't have had it if I'd choked, after that. Between taking an almighty shine to the girl and getting stirred up that way, and then being all frozen over with icicles by her cool insultingness, I was pretty savage, and I stared away from the place and thought the men would never come. All of a sudden I felt something touch my arm, and I looked around quick, and there was the girl. She stood by the horse, her red hair close to my elbow as I sat in the saddle, and she held up a glass of water. I never was so astonished in my life.

"'You're thirsty and tired, too,' she said, speaking as low as if she was afraid the horse might hear. 'For my self-respect—for Southern women'—she brought it out in that soft, sliding way, but the words were all mixed up with embarrassment— and red—my, but she blushed! Then she went on. 'You were right,' said she. 'I was cruel; you're my enemy and I hate you, but I ought not to grudge you water. Take it.'

"I put my hand right on top of hers as she held the glass, and bent down and drank so, making her hold it to my lips, and my hand over hers—bless her heart!"

The General came to a full stop. He was smiling into the fire, and his face was as if a flame burned back of it. I waited very quietly, fearing to change the current by a word, and in a moment the strong voice, with its vibrating note, not to be described, began again.

"I drained every drop," he said, "I'd have drunk a hogshead. When I finished I raised my head and looked down at her without a word said—but I didn't let go of the glass with her hand holding it inside mine—and she lifted her eyes very slowly, and for the first time looked at me. Well—" he shut his lips a moment—"these things don't tell well, but something happened. I held her eyes into mine, us if I gripped them with my muscles, and there came over her face an extraordinary expression—first as if she was surprised that it was me, then as if she was glad, and then—well, you may believe it or not, but I knew that second that the girl—loved me. She hated me all right five minutes before—I was her people's enemy—the chances were she'd never see me again—all that's true, but it simply didn't count. She cared for me, and I for her, and we both knew it—that's all there was about it. People live faster in war-time, I think—anyhow, that's the way it was.

"The men and horses came pouring around the house, and I let her hand loose—it was hard to do it, too—and then she was gone, and we rode on to the ford. We stopped when we got to the stream to let the horses have their turn at drinking, and as I sat loafing in the saddle, with my mind pretty full of what had just passed, my eyes were all over. Every cavalry officer, and especially an aide-de-camp, gets to be a sort of hawk in active service—nothing can move within range that he doesn't see. So as I looked about me I took in among other things the house we'd just left, and suddenly I spied a handkerchief waving from behind one of the big white pillars. Of course you've got to be wary in an enemy's country, and these people were rabid Confederates, as I'd occasion to know. All the same it would have been bad judgment to neglect such a signal, and what's more, I'd have staked my life on that girl's honesty. If the handkerchief had been a cannon I'd have gone back. So back I went, taking a couple of men with me. As I jumped off my horse I saw her standing inside the front door, back in the shadow, and I ran up the steps to her.

"'Well?' said I.

"She looked up at me and laughed, showing a row of white teeth. That was the first time I ever saw her laugh. 'I knew you'd come back,' said she, as mischievous as a child, and her eyes danced.

"I didn't mean to be made a fool of, for I had my duty to think about, so I spoke rather shortly. 'Well, and now I'm here—what?'

"With that she drew an excited little gasp. 'I couldn't let you be killed,' she brought out in a sort of breathless whisper, so low I had to bend over close to hear her. 'You mustn't go on—in that direction—you'll be taken. The Union army's been defeated—at Chancellorsville. They're driven north of the Rappahannock—to Falmouth. Our troops are in their old camps. There's an outpost across the ford—just over the hill.'

"It was the first I'd heard of the defeat at Chancellorsville, and it stunned me for a second. 'Are you telling me the truth?' I asked her pretty sharply.

"'You know I am,' she said, as haughty as you please all of a sudden, and drew herself up with her head in the air.

"And I did know it. Something else struck me just about then. The old lady and the servants were gone from the hall. There wasn't anybody in it but herself and me; my men were out of sight on the driveway. I forgot our army and the war and everything else, and I caught her bands in between mine, and said I, 'Why couldn't you let me be killed?'"

At his words I drew a quick breath, too. For a moment I was the Southern girl with the red-gold hair. I could feel the clasp of the young officer's hands; I could hear his voice asking the rough, tender question, "Why couldn't you let me be killed?"

"It was mighty still for a minute. Then she lifted up her eyes as I held her fingers in a vise, and gave me a steady look. That was all—but it was plenty.

"I don't know how I got on my horse or what order I gave, but my head was clear enough for business purposes, and I had to use it—quickly, too. There were thick woods near by, and I hurried my party into them and gave men and horses a short rest till I could decide what to do. The Confederates were east of us, around Chancellorsville and in the triangle between the Rapidan and the Rappahannock, so that It was unsafe travelling in that direction. It's the business of an aide-de-camp carrying despatches to steal as quietly as possible through an enemy's country, and the one fatal thing is to be captured. So I concluded I wouldn't get into the thick of it till I had to, but would turn west and make a *détour*, crossing by Morton's Ford, farther up the Rapidan. Germania Ford lies in a deep loop of the river, and that made our ride longer, but we found a road and crossed all right as I planned it, and then we doubled back, as we had to, eastward.

"It was a pretty ride in the May weather, through that beautiful Virginia country. We kept in the woods and the lonely roads as much as we could and hardly saw a soul for hours, and though I knew we were getting into dangerous parts again, I hoped we might work through all right. Of course I thought first about my errand, and my mind was on every turn of the road and every speck in the landscape, but all the same there was one corner of it—or of something—that didn't forget that red-headed girl—not an instant. I kept wondering if I'd ever see her again, and I was mighty clear that I would, if there was enough left of me by the time I could get off duty to go and look her up. The touch of her hands stayed with me all day.

"About two o'clock or so we passed a house, just a cabin, but a neat sort of place, and I looked at it as I did at everything, and saw an old negro with grizzled hair standing some distance in front of it. Now everything reminded me of that girl because she was on my mind, and instantly I was struck with the idea, that the old fellow looked like the servant who had been locking the bag in the house by Germania Ford. I wasn't sure it was the same darky, but I thought I'd see. There was a patch of woods back of the house, and I ordered the party to wait there till I joined them, and I threw my bridle to a soldier and turned in at the gate. The man loped out for the house, but I halted him. Then I went along past the negro to the cabin, and opened the door, which had been shut tight.

"There was a table littered with papers in the middle of the room, and behind it, in a gray riding-habit, with a gray soldier-cap on her red hair, writing for dear life, sat the girl. She lifted her head quick, as the door swung open, and then made a jump to get between me and the table. I took off my cap, and said I:

"'I'm very glad to see you. I was just wondering if we'd ever meet again.' She only stared at me. Then I said: 'I'm sorry, but I'll have to ask you for those papers.' I knew by the look of them that they were some sort of despatches.

"At that she laughed in a kind of a friendly, cocksure way. She wasn't afraid of anything, that girl. 'No,' she threw at me—just like that—'No.'" The General tossed back his big head and did a poor imitation of a girl's light tone—a poor imitation, but the way he did it was winning. "'No,' said she, shaking her head sidewise. 'You can't have those papers—not ever,' and with that she swept them together and popped them into a drawer of the table and then hopped up on the table and sat there laughing at me, with her little riding-hoots swinging. 'At least, unless you knock me down, and I don't believe you'll do that,' said she.

"Well, I had to have those papers. I didn't know how important they might be, but if this girl was sending information to the Southern commanders I was inclined to think it would be accurate and worth while. It wouldn't do not to capture it. At the same time I wouldn't have laid a finger on her, to compel her, for a million dollars. I stood and stared like a blockhead for a minute, at my wit's end, and she sat there and smiled. All of a sudden I had an idea. I caught the end of the table and tipped it up, and off slid the young lady, and I snatched at the knob of the drawer, and had the papers in a second.

"It was simple, but it worked. Then it was her turn to look foolish. Of course she had a temper, with that colored hair, and she was raging. She looked at me as if she'd like to tear me to pieces. There wasn't anything she could say, however, and not lose her dignity, and I guess she pretty nearly exploded for a minute, and then, in a flash, the joke of it struck her. Her eyes began to dance, and she laughed because she couldn't help it, and I with her. For a whole minute we forgot what a big business we were both after, and acted like two children.

"'That's right,' said I finally. 'I had to get them, but I did it in the kindest spirit. I see you understand that.'

"'Oh, I don't care,' she answered with her chin up—a little way she had. 'They're not much, anyway. I hadn't got to the important part.'

"'Won't you finish?' said I politely, and pretended to offer her the papers—and then I got serious. 'What are you doing here?' I asked her. 'Where are you going?'

"She looked up at me, and—I knew she liked me. She caught her breath before she answered. 'What right have you got to ask me questions?' said she, making a bluff at righteous indignation.

"But I just gripped her fingers into mine—it was getting to be a habit, holding her hand.

"'And what are *you* doing here?' she went on saucily, but her voice was a whisper, and she let her hand lie.

"'I'll tell you what I'm doing,' said I. 'I'm obeying the Bible. My Bible tells me to love my enemies, and I'm going to. I do,' said I. 'What does your Bible tell you?'

"'My Bible tells me to resist the devil and he will flee from me,' she answered back like a flash, standing up straight and looking at me squarely, as solemn as a church.

"'Well, I guess I'm not that kind of a devil,' said I. 'I don't want to flee worth a cent.'

"And at that she broke into a laugh and showed all her little teeth at me. That was one of the prettiest things about her, the row of small white teeth she showed every time she laughed.

"'Just at that second the old negro stuck his head in at the door. 'We're busy, uncle,' said I. 'I'll give you five dollars for five minutes.'

"But the girl put her hand on my arm to stop me, 'What is it, Uncle Ebenezer?' she asked him anxiously.

"'It's young Marse, Miss Lindy,' the man said, 'Him'n Marse Philip Breck'nridge 'n' Marse Tom's ridin' down de branch right now. Close to hyer—dey'll be hyer in fo'-five minutes.'

"She nodded at him coolly. 'All right. Shut the door, Uncle Ebenezer,' said she, and he went out and shut it.

"And before I could say Jack Robinson she was dragging me into the next room, and pushing me out of a door at the back.

"'Go—hurry up—oh, go!' she begged. 'I won't let them take you.'

"Well, I didn't like to leave her suddenly like that, so I said, said I: 'What's the hurry? I want to tell you something.'

"'*No*,' she shot at me. 'You can't. Go—won't you, please go?' Then I picked up a little hand and hold it against my coat. I knew by now just how she would catch her breath when I did it."

At about this point the General forgot me. Such good comrades we were that my presence did not trouble him, but as for telling the story to me, that was past—he was living it over, to himself alone, with every nerve in action.

"'Look here,' said I, 'I don't believe a thing like this ever happened on the globe before, but this has. It's so—I love you, and I believe you love me, and I'm not going till you tell me so.'

"By that time she was in a fit. 'They'll be here in two minutes; they're Confederate officers. Oh, and you mustn't cross at Kelly's Ford—take the ford above it'—and she thumped me excitedly with the hand I held. I laughed, and she burst out again: 'They'll take you—oh, please go!'

"'Tell me, then,' said I, and she stopped half a second, and gasped again, and looked up in my eyes and said it. 'I love you,' said she. And she meant it.

"'Give me a kiss,' said I, and I leaned close to her, but she pulled away.

"'Oh, no—oh, please go now,' she begged.

"'All right,' said I, 'but you don't know what you're missing,' and I slid out of the back door at the second the Southerners came in at the front.

"There were bushes back there, and I crawled behind them and looked through into the window, and what do you suppose I saw? I saw the biggest and best-looking man of the three walk up to the girl who'd just told me she loved me, and I saw her put up her face and give him the kiss she wouldn't give me. Well, I went smashing down to the woods, making such a rumpus that if those officers had been half awake they'd have been after me twice over. I was so maddened at the sight of that kiss that I didn't realize what I was doing or that I was endangering the lives of my men. 'Of course,' said I to myself, 'it's her brother or her cousin,' but I knew it was a hundred to one that it wasn't, and I was in a mighty bad temper.

"I got my men away from the neighborhood quietly, and we rode pretty cautiously all that afternoon, I knew the road leading to Kelly's Ford, and I bore to the north, away from there, for I trusted the girl and believed I'd be safe if I followed her orders. She'd saved my life twice that day, so I had reason to trust her. But all the time as I jogged along I was wondering about that man, and wondering what the dickens she was up to, anyway, and why she was travelling in the same direction that I was, and where she was going—and over and over I wondered if I'd ever see her again. I felt sure I would, though—I couldn't imagine not seeing her, after what she'd said. I didn't even know her name, except that the old negro had called her 'Miss Lindy.' I said that a lot of times to myself as I rode, with the men's bits jingling at my buck and their horses' hoofs thud-thudding. 'Lindy—Miss Lindy—Linda—my Linda—I said it half aloud. It kept first-rate time to the hoof-beats—'Lindy—Miss Lindy.'

"I wondered, too, why she wouldn't let me cross the Rappahannock by Kelly's Ford, for I had reason to think there'd be a Union post on the east side of the river there, but there was a sense of brains and capability about the girl, as well as charm—in fact, that's likely to be a large part of any real charm—and so I trusted to her.

**"I got behind a turn and fired as a man came on alone."**

"Well, late in the afternoon we were trotting along, feeling pretty secure. I'd left the Kelly's Ford road at the last turn, and was beginning to think that we ought to be within a few miles of the river, when all of a sudden, coming out of some woods into a small clearing with a farmhouse about the centre of it, we rode on a strong outpost of the enemy, infantry and cavalry both. We were in the open before I saw them, so there was nothing to do but make a dash for it and rush past the cabin before they could reach their arms, and we drew our revolvers and put the spurs in deep and flew past with a fire that settled some of them. But a surprise of this sort doesn't last long, and it was only a few minutes before they were after us—and with fresh mounts. Then it was a horse-race for the river, and I wasn't certain of the roads. However, I knew a trick or two about this business, and I was sure some of the pursuers would forge ahead; so three times I got behind a turn and fired as a man came on alone. I dismounted several that way. This relieved the strain enough so that I got within sight of the river with all my men. It was a quarter of a mile away when I saw it, and at that point the road split, and which branch led to the ford for the life of me I didn't know. There wasn't time for meditation, however, so I shot down the turn to the left, on the gamble, and sure enough there was the ford—only it wasn't any ford. The Rappahannock was full to the banks and perhaps two hundred yards across. The Confederates were within rifle-shot, so there were exactly two things to do—surrender or swim. I gave my men the choice—to follow me or be captured—and I plunged in, without any of them."

"What!" I demanded here, puzzled. "Didn't the men know how to swim?"

"Oh, yes, they knew how," the General answered, and looked embarrassed.

"Well, then, why didn't they?" It began to dawn on me, "Were they afraid—was it dangerous—was the river swift?"

"Yes," he acknowledged. "The river was swift—it was a foaming torrent."

"They were afraid—all ten of them—and you weren't—you alone?" The General looked annoyed. "I didn't want to be captured," he explained crossly. "I had the despatches besides." He went on: "I slipped off my horse, keeping hold of the bridle to guide him, and swam low beside him, because they were firing from the bank. But all at once the shots stopped, and I heard shouting, and shortly after I got a glimpse, over my horse's back, of a rider in the water near me, and there was a flash of a gray cap. One of the Southerners was swimming after me, and I was due for a tussle when we landed. I made it first. I scrambled to shore and snatched out my sword—the pistols were wet—and rushed for the other man as he jumped to the bank, and just as I got to him—just in time—I saw him. It wasn't him—it was her—the girl. Heavens!" gasped the General; "she gave me a start that time. I dropped my sword on the ground, I was so surprised, and stared at her with my mouth open.

"'Oo-ee!' said that girl, shaking her skirt, as calm as a May morning. 'Oo-ee!' like a baby crowing. 'My, but that's a cold river!' And her teeth chattered.

"Well, that time I didn't ask permission. I took her in my arms and held her—I had to, to keep her warm. Couldn't let her stand there and click her teeth—could I? And she didn't fight me. 'What did you do such a crazy thing for?' asked I.

"'Well, you're mighty par-particular,' said she as saucy as you please, but still shivering so she couldn't talk straight. 'They were popping g-guns at you—that's what for. Roger's a right bad shot, but he might have hit you.'

"'And he might, have hit you,' said I. 'Did you happen to think of that?'

"She just laughed. 'Oh, no—they wouldn't risk hitting me. I'm too valuable—that's why I jumped in—to protect you.'

"'Oh!' said I. 'I'm a delicate flower, it seems. You've been protecting me all day. Who's Roger?'

"'My brother,' said she, smiling up at me.

"'Was that the man you kissed in the cabin back yonder?'

"'Shame!' said she. 'You peeped.'

"'Was it?' I insisted, for I wanted to know. And she told me.

"'Yes,' she told me, in that low voice of hers that was hard to hear, only it paid to listen.

"'Did you ever kiss any other man?' said I.

"'It's none of your business,' said the girl. 'But I didn't—the way you mean.'

"'Well, it wouldn't make any difference, anyway—nothing would,' I said. 'Except this—are you ever going to?'

"All this time that bright-colored head of hers was on my shoulder, Confederate cap and all, and I was afraid of my life to stir, for fear she'd take it away. But when I said that I put my face down against hers and repeated the question, 'Are you ever going to?'

"It seemed like ages before she answered and I was scared—yet she didn't pull away,—and finally the words came—low, but I heard. 'One,' said she. 'If he wants it.'

"Then—" the General stopped suddenly, and the splendid claret and honey color of his cheeks went a dark shade more to claret. He had come to from his trance, and remembered me. "I don't know why I'm telling you all these details," he declared abruptly. "I suppose you're tired to death listening." His alert eyes questioned me.

"General," I begged, "don't stop like that again. Don't leave out a syllable. 'Then—'"

But he threw back his head boyishly and laughed with a touch of self-consciousness. "No, madam, I won't tell you about 'then.' I'll leave so much to your imagination. I guess you're equal to it. It wasn't a second anyway before she gave a jump that took her six feet from me, and there she was tugging at the girth of her saddle.

"'Quick—change the saddles!' she ordered me. 'I must be out of my mind to throw away time when your life's in danger. They're coming around by the bridge,' she explained, 'two miles down. And you have to have a fresh mount. They'd catch you on that.' She threw a contemptuous glance at my tired brute, and began unbuckling the wet straps with her little wet fingers.

"'Don't do that,' said I. 'Let me.' But she pushed me away. 'Mustn't waste time.' She gave her orders as business-like as an officer. 'Do your own saddle while I attend to this. Zero can run right away from anything they're riding—from anything at all. Can't you, Zero?' and she gave the horse a quick pat in between unbuckling. He was a powerful, rangy bay, and not winded by his run and his swim. 'He's my father's,' she went on. 'He'll carry you through to General Hooker's camp at Falmouth—he knows that camp. It's twenty-five miles yet, and you've ridden fifty to-day, poor boy.'

"I wish I could tell you how pretty her voice was when she said things like that, as if she cared that I'd had a strenuous day and was a little tired.

"'How do you know I'm going to Falmouth? How do you know how far I've ridden?' I asked her, astonished again.

"'I'm a witch,' she said. 'I find out everything about you-all by magic, and then I tell our officers. They know it's so if I tell them. Ask Stonewall Jackson how he discovered the road to take his cavalry around for the attack on Howard. I reckon I helped a lot at Chancellorsville.'

"'Do you reckon you're helping now?' I asked, throwing my saddle over Zero's back. 'Strikes me you're giving aid and comfort to the enemy hand over fist.'

"That girl surprised me whatever she did, and the reason was—I figured it out afterward—that she let herself be what few people let themselves be—absolutely straightforward. She had the gentlest ways, but she always hit straight from the shoulder, and that's likely to surprise people. This time she took three steps to where I stood by Zero and caught my finger in the middle of pulling up the cinch and held to it.

"'I'm not a traitor,' she threw at me. 'I'm loyal to my people, and you're my enemy—and I'm saving you from them. But it's you—it's you,' she whispered, looking up at me. It was getting dark by now, but I could see her eyes. 'When you put your hand over mine this morning it was like somebody'd telegraphed that the one man was coming; and then I looked at you, and I knew he'd got there. I've never bothered about men—mostly they're not worth while, when there are horses—but ever since I've been grown I've known that you'd come some time, and that I'd know you when you came. Do you think I'm going to let you be taken—shot, maybe? Not much—I'll guard your life with every breath of mine—and I'll keep it safe, too.'

"Now, wasn't that a strange way for a girl to talk? Did you ever hear of another woman who could talk that way, and live up to it?" he demanded of me unexpectedly.

I was afraid to say the wrong thing and I spoke timidly. "What did you do then?"

He gave me a glance smouldering with mischief. "I didn't do it. I tried to, but she wouldn't let me.

"'Hurry, hurry,' said she, in a panic all of a sudden. 'They'll be coming. Zero's fast, but you ought to get a good start.'

"And she hustled me on the horse. And just as I was off, as I bent from the saddle to catch her hand for the last time, she gave me two more shocks together." Silent reminiscent laughter shook him.

"'When am I going to see you again?' asked I hopelessly, for I felt as if everything was mighty uncertain, and I couldn't bear to leave her.

"'To-morrow,' said she, prompt as taxes. 'To-morrow. Good-by, Captain Carruthers.'

"And she gave the horse a slap that scared him into a leap, and off I went galloping into darkness, with my brain in a whirl as to where I could see her to-morrow, and how under creation she knew my name. The cold bath had refreshed me—I hadn't had the like of it for nine days—and I galloped on for a while feeling fine, and thinking mighty hard about the girl I'd left behind me. Twenty-four hours before I'd never seen her, yet I felt, as if I had known her all my life. I was sure of this, that in all my days I'd never seen anybody like her, and never would. And that's true to this minute. I'd had sweethearts a-plenty—in a way—but the affair of that day was the only time I was ever in love in my life."

To tell the truth I had been a little scandalized all through this story, for I knew well enough that there was a Mrs. Carruthers. I had not met her—she had been South through the months which her husband had spent in New York—but the General's strong language concerning the red-haired girl made me sympathize with his wife, and this last sentiment was staggering. Poor Mrs. Carruthers! thought I—poor, staid lady, with this gay lad of a husband declaring his heart forever buried with the adventure of a day of long ago. Yet, a soldier boy of twenty-three—the romance of war-time—the glamour of lost love—there were certainly alleviating circumstances. At all events, it was not my affair—I could enjoy the story as it came with a clear conscience. So I smiled at the wicked General—who looked as innocent as a baby—and he went on.

"I knew every road on that side the river, and I knew the Confederates wouldn't dare chase me but a few miles, as it wasn't their country any longer, so pretty soon I began to take things easy. I thought over everything that had happened through the day, everything she'd said and done, every look—I could remember it all. I can now. I wondered who under heaven she was, and I kicked myself that I hadn't asked her name. 'Lindy'—that's all I knew, and I guess I said that over a hundred times. I wondered why she'd told me not to go to Kelly's Ford, but I worked that out the right way—as I found later—that her party expected to cross there, and she didn't want me to encounter them; and then the river was too full and they tried a higher ford. And I'd run into them. Yet I couldn't understand why she planned to cross at Kelly's, anyway, because there was pretty sure to be a Union outpost on the east bank there, and she'd have landed right among them. That puzzled me. Who was the girl, and why on earth was she travelling in that direction, and where could she be going? I went over that problem again and again, and couldn't find an answer.

"Meanwhile it was getting late, and the bracing effect of the cold water of the Rappahannock was wearing off, and I began to feel the fatigue of an exciting day and a seventy-five-mile ride—on top of nine other days with little to eat and not much rest. My wet clothes chilled me, and the last few miles I have never been able to remember distinctly—I think I was misty in my mind. At any rate, when I got to headquarters camp I was just about clear enough to guide Zero through the maze of tents, and not any more, and when the horse stopped with his nose against the front pole of the general's fly I was unconscious."

I exclaimed, horrified: "It was too much for human nature! You must have been nearly dead. Did you fall off? Were you hurt?"

"Oh, no—I was all right," he said cheerfully. "I just sat there. But an equestrian statue in front of the general's tent at 11 P.M. wasn't usual, and there was a small sensation. It brought out the adjutant-general and he recognized me, and they carried me into a tent, and got a surgeon, and he had me stripped and rubbed and rolled in blankets. They found the despatches in my boots, and those gave all the information necessary. They found the letter, too, which Stoneman had given me to hand back to General Ladd, and they didn't understand that, as it was addressed simply to 'Miss Ladd, Ford Hall,' so they left it till I waked up. That wasn't till noon the next day."

The General began chuckling contagiously, and I was alive with curiosity to know the coming joke.

"I believe every officer in the camp, from the commanding general down, had sent me clothes. When I unclosed my eyes that tent was alive with them. It was a spring opening, I can tell you—all sorts. Well, when I got the meaning of the array, I lay there and laughed out loud, and an orderly appeared at that, and then the adjutant-general, and I reported to him. Then I got into an assortment of the clothes, and did my duty by a pile of food and drink, and I was ready to start back to join my chief. Except for the letter of General Ladd—I had to deliver that in person to give the explanation. General Ladd had been wounded, I found, at

Chancellorsville, but would see me. So off I went to his tent, and the orderly showed me in at once. He was in bed with his arm and shoulder bandaged, and by his side, looking as fresh as a rose and as mischievous as a monkey, sat a girl with red hair—Linda Ladd—Miss Ladd, of Ford Hall—the old house where I first saw her. Her father presented me in due form and told me to give her the letter and—that's all."

The General stopped short and regarded me quietly.

"Oh, but—" I stammered. "But that isn't all—why, I don't understand—it's criminal not to tell the rest—there's a lot."

"What do you want to hear?" he demanded, "I don't know any more—that's all that happened."

"Don't be brutal," I pleaded. "I want to know, for one thing, how she knew your name."

"Oh—that." He laughed like an amused child. "That was rather odd. You remember I told you that when they were chasing us I took shelter and shot the horses from under some of the Southerners."

"I remember."

"Well, the first man dismounted was Tom Ladd, the girl's cousin, who'd been my classmate at the Point, and he recognized me. He ran back and told them to make every effort to capture the party, as its leader was Captain Carruthers, of Stoneman's staff, and undoubtedly carried despatches."

"Oh!" I said. "I see. And where was Miss Ladd going, travelling your way all day?"

"To see her wounded father at Falmouth, don't you understand? She'd had word from him the day before. She was escorted by a strong party of Confederates, including her brother and cousin. She started out with just the old negro, and it was arranged that she should meet the party at the cabin where I found her writing. They were to go with her to Kelly's Ford, where she was to pass over to the Union post on the other bank—she had a safe-conduct."

"Oh!" I assimilated this. "And she and her brother were Confederates, and the father was a Northern general—how extraordinary!"

"Not in the least," the General corrected me. "It happened so in a number of cases. She was a power in that campaign. She did more work than either father or brother. A Southern officer told me afterward that the men half believed what she said—that she was a witch, and got news of our movements by magic. Nothing escaped her—she had a wonderful mind, and did not know what fear was. A wonderful woman!"

He was smiling to himself again as he sat, with his great shoulders bent forward and his scarred hand on his knee, looking into the fire.

"General," I said tentatively, "aren't you going to tell me what she said when she saw you come into her father's tent?"

"Said?" asked the General, looking up and frowning. "What could she say? Good-morning, I guess."

I wasn't afraid of his frown or of his hammer-and-tongs manner. I'd got behind both before now. I persisted.

"But I mean—what did you say to each other, like the day before—how did it all come out?"

"Oh, we couldn't do any love-making, if that's what you mean," he explained in a business-like way, "because the old man was on deck. And I had to leave in about ten minutes to ride back to join my command. That was all there was to it."

I sighed with disappointment. Of course I knew it was just an idyll of youth, a day long, and that the book was closed forty years before. But I could not bear to have it closed with a bang. Somewhere in the narrative had come to me the impression that the heroine of it had died young in those exciting war-times of long ago. I had a picture in my mind of the dancing eyes closed meekly in a last sleep; of the young officer's hand laid sorrowing on the bright halo of hair.

"Did you ever see the girl again?" I asked softly.

The General turned on me a quick, queer look. Fun was in it, and memory gave it gentleness; yet there was impatience, too, at my slowness, in the boyish brown eyes.

"Mrs. Carruthers has red hair," he said briefly.

---

### *THROUGH THE IVORY GATE*

Breeze-filtered through shifting leafage, the June morning sunlight came in at the open window by the boy's bed, under the green shades, across the shadowy, white room, and danced a noiseless dance of youth and freshness and springtime against the wall opposite. The boy's head stirred on his pillow. He spoke a quick word from out of his dream. "The key?" he said inquiringly, and the sound of his own voice awoke him. Dark, drowsy eyes opened, and he stared half seeing, at the picture that hung facing him. Was it the play of mischievous sunlight, was it the dream that still held his brain? He knew the picture line by line, and there was no such figure in it. It was a large photograph of Fairfield, the Southern home of his mother's people, and the boy remembered it always hanging there, opposite his bed, the first sight to meet his eyes every morning since his babyhood. So he was certain there was no figure in it, more than all one so remarkable as this strapping little chap in his queer clothes; his dress of conspicuous plaid with large black velvet squares sewed on it, who stood now in front of the old manor-house. Could it be only a dream? Could it be that a little ghost, wandering childlike in dim, heavenly fields, had joined the gay troop of his boyish visions and shipped in with them through the ivory gate of pleasant dreams? The boy put his fists to his eyes and rubbed them and looked again. The little fellow was still there, standing with sturdy legs wide apart as if owning the scene; he laughed as he held toward the boy a key—a small key tied with a scarlet ribbon. There was no doubt in the boy's mind that the key was for him, and out of the dim world of sleep he stretched his young arm for it; to reach it he sat up in bed. Then he was awake and knew himself alone in the peace of his own little room, and laughed shamefacedly at the reality of the vision which had followed him from dreamland into the very boundaries of consciousness, which held him even now with gentle tenacity, which drew him back through the day, from his studies, from his play, into the strong current of its fascination.

The first time Philip Beckwith had this dream he was only twelve years old, and, withheld by the deep reserve of childhood, he told not even his mother about it, though he lived in its atmosphere all day and remembered it vividly days longer. A year after it came again; and again it was a June morning, and as his eyes opened the little boy came once more out of the picture toward him, laughing and holding out the key on its scarlet string. The dream was a pleasant one, and Philip welcomed it eagerly from his sleep as a friend. There seemed something sweet and familiar in the child's presence beyond the one memory of him, as again the boy, with eyes half open to every-day life, saw him standing, small but masterful, in the garden of that old house where the Fairfields had lived for more than a century. Half consciously he tried to prolong the vision, tried not to wake entirely for fear of losing it; but the picture faded surely from the curtain of his mind as the tangible world painted there its heavier outlines. It was as if a happy little spirit had tried to follow him, for love of him, from a country lying close, yet separated; it was as if the common childhood of the two made it almost possible for them to meet; as if a message that might not be spoken, were yet almost delivered.

The third time the dream came it was a December morning of the year when Philip was fifteen, and falling snow made wavering light and shadow on the wall where hung the picture. This time, with eyes wide open, yet with the possession of the dream strongly on him, he lay sub-consciously alert and gazed, as in the odd, unmistakable dress that Philip knew now in detail, the bright-faced child swung toward him, always from the garden of that old place, always trying with loving, merry efforts to reach Philip from out of it—always holding to him the red-ribboned key. Like a wary hunter the big boy lay—knowing it unreal, yet living it keenly—and watched his chance. As the little figure glided close to him he put out his hand suddenly, swiftly for the key—he was awake. As always, the dream was gone; the little ghost was baffled again; the two worlds might not meet.

That day Mrs. Beckwith, putting in order an old mahogany secretary, showed him a drawer full of photographs, daguerrotypes. The boy and his gay young mother were the best of friends, for, only nineteen when he was born, she had never let the distance widen between them; had held the freshness of her youth sacred against the time when he should share it. Year by year, living in his enthusiasms, drawing him to hers, she had grown young in his childhood, which year by year came closer to her maturity. Until now there was between the tall, athletic lad and the still young and attractive woman, an equal friendship, a common youth, which gave charm and elasticity to the natural tie between them. Yet even to this comrade-mother the boy had not told his dream, for the difficulty of putting into words the atmosphere, the compelling power of it. So that when she opened one of the old-fashioned black cases which held the early sun-pictures, and showed him the portrait within, he startled her by a sudden exclamation. From the frame of red velvet and tarnished gilt there laughed up at him the little boy of his dream. There was no mistaking him, and if there were doubt about the face, there was the peculiar dress—the black and white plaid with large squares of black velvet sewed here and there as decoration. Philip stared in astonishment at the sturdy figure, the childish face with its wide forehead and level, strong brows; its dark eyes straight-gazing and smiling.

"Mother—who is he? Who is he?" he demanded.

"Why, my lamb, don't you know? It's your little uncle Philip—my brother, for whom you were named—Philip Fairfield the sixth. There was always a Philip Fairfield at Fairfield since 1790. This one was the last, poor baby! and he died when he was five. Unless you go back there some day—that's my hope, but it's not likely to come true. You are a Yankee, except for the big half of you that's me. That's Southern, every inch." She laughed and kissed his fresh cheek impulsively. "But what made you so excited over this picture, Phil?"

Philip gazed down, serious, a little embarrassed, at the open case in his hand. "Mother," he said after a moment, "you'll laugh at me, but I've seen this chap in a dream three times now."

"Oh!" She did laugh at him. "Oh, Philip! What have you been eating for dinner, I'd like to know? I can't have you seeing visions of your ancestors at fifteen—it's unhealthy."

The boy, reddening, insisted. "But, mother, really, don't you think it was queer? I saw him as plainly as I do now—and I've never seen this picture before."

"Oh, yes, you have—you must have seen it," his mother threw back lightly. "You've forgotten, but the image of it was tucked away in some dark corner of your mind, and when you were asleep it stole out and played tricks on you. That's the way forgotten ideas do: they get even with you in dreams for having forgotten them."

"Mother, only listen—" But Mrs. Beckwith, her eyes lighting with a swift turn of thought, interrupted him—laid her finger on his lips.

"No—you listen, boy dear—quick, before I forget it! I've never told you about this, and it's very interesting."

And the youngster, used to these wilful ways of his sister-mother, laughed and put his fair head against her shoulder and listened.

"It's quite a romance," she began, "only there isn't any end to it; it's all unfinished and disappointing. It's about this little Philip here, whose name you have—my brother. He died when he was five, as I said, but even then he had a bit of dramatic history in his life. He was born just before war-time in 1859, and he was a beautiful and wonderful baby; I can remember all about it, for I was six years older. He was incarnate sunshine, the happiest child that ever lived, but far too quick and clever for his years. The servants used to ask him, 'Who is you, Marse Philip, sah?' to hear him answer, before he could speak it plainly, 'I'm Philip Fairfield of Fairfield'; he seemed to realize that, and his responsibility to them and to the place, as soon as he could breathe. He wouldn't have a darky scolded in his presence, and every morning my father put him in front of him in the saddle, and they rode together about the plantation. My father adored him, and little Philip's sunshiny way of taking possession of the slaves and the property pleased him more deeply, I think, than anything in his life. But the war came before this time, when the child was about a year old, and my father went off, of course, as every Southern man went who could walk, and for a year we did not see him. Then he was badly wounded at the battle of Malvern Hill; and came home to get well. However, it was more serious than he knew, and he did not get well. Twice he went off again to join our army, and each time he was sent back within a month, too ill to be of any use. He chafed constantly, of course, because he must stay at home and farm, when his whole soul ached to be fighting for his flag; but finally in December, 1863, he thought he was well enough at last for service. He was to join General John Morgan, who had just made his wonderful escape from prison at Columbus, and it was planned that my mother should take little Philip and me to England to live there till the war was over and we could all be together at Fairfield again. With that in view my father drew all of his ready money—it was ten thousand dollars in gold—from the banks in Lexington, for my mother's use in the years they might be separated. When suddenly, the day before he was to have gone, the old wound broke out again, and he was helplessly ill in bed at the hour when he should have been on his horse riding toward Tennessee. We were fifteen miles out from Lexington, yet it might be rumored that father had drawn a large sum of money, and, of course, he was well known as a Southern officer. Because of the Northern soldiers, who held the city, he feared very much to have the money in the house, yet he hoped still to join Morgan a little later, and then it would be needed as he had planned. Christmas morning my father was so much better that my mother went to church, taking me, and leaving little Philip, then four years old, to amuse him. What happened that morning was the point of all this rambling; so now listen hard, my precious thing."

The boy, sitting erect now, caught his mother's hand silently, and his eyes stared into hers as he drunk in every word:

"Mammy, who was, of course, little Philip's nurse, told my mother afterward that she was sent away before my father and the boy went into the garden, but she saw them go and saw that my father had a tin box—a box about twelve inches long, which seemed very heavy—in his arms, and on his finger swung a long red ribbon with a little key strung on it. Mother knew it as the key of the box, and she had tied the ribbon on it herself.

"It was a bright, crisp Christmas day, pleasant in the garden—the box hedges were green and fragrant, aromatic in the sunshine. You don't even know the smell of box in sunshine, you poor child! But I remember that day, for I was ten years old, a right big girl, and it was a beautiful morning for an invalid to take the air. Mammy said she was proud to see how her 'handsome boy' kept step with his father, and she watched the two until they got away down by the rose-garden, and then she couldn't see little Philip behind the three-foot hedge, so she turned away. But somewhere in that big garden, or under the trees beside it, my father buried the box that held the money—ten thousand dollars. It shows how he trusted that baby, that he took him with him, and you'll see how his trust was only too well justified. For that evening, Christmas night, very suddenly my father died—before he had time to tell my mother where he had hidden the box. He tried; when consciousness came a few minutes before the end he gasped out, 'I buried the money'—and then he choked. Once again he whispered just two words: 'Philip knows.' And my mother said, 'Yes, dearest—Philip and I will find it—don't worry, dearest,' and that quieted him. She told me about it so many times.

"After the funeral she took little Philip and explained to him as well as she could that he must tell mother where he and father had put the box, and—this is the point of it all, Philip—he wouldn't tell. She went over and over it all, again and again, but it was no use. He had given his word to my father never to tell, and he was too much of a baby to understand how death had dissolved that promise. My mother tried every way, of course, explanations and reasoning first, then pleading, and finally severity; she even punished the poor little martyr, for it was awfully important to us all. But the four-year-old baby was absolutely incorruptible, he cried bitterly and sobbed out:

"'Farver said I mustn't never tell anybody—never! Farver said Philip Fairfield of Fairfield mustn't *never* bweak his words,' and that was all.

"Nothing could induce him to give the least hint. Of course there was great search for it, but it was well hidden and it was never found. Finally, mother took her obdurate son and me and came to New York with us, and we lived on the little income which she had of her own. Her hope was that as soon as Philip was old enough she could make him understand, and go back with him and get that large sum lying underground—lying there yet, perhaps. But in less than a year the little boy was dead and the secret was gone with him."

Philip Beckwith's eyes were intense and wide. The Fairfield eyes, brown and brilliant, their young fire was concentrated on his mother's face.

"Do you mean that money is buried down there, yet, mother?" he asked solemnly.

Mrs. Beckwith caught at the big fellow's sleeve with slim fingers. "Don't go to-day, Phil—wait till after lunch, anyway!"

"Please don't make fun, mother—I want to know about it. Think of it lying there in the ground!"

"Greedy boy! We don't need money now, Phil. And the old place will be yours when I am dead—" The lad's arm went about his mother's shoulders. "Oh, but I'm not going to die for ages! Not till I'm a toothless old person with side curls, hobbling along on a stick. Like this!"—she sprang to her feet and the boy laughed a great peal at the hag-like effect as his young mother threw herself into the part. She dropped on the divan again at his side.

"What I meant to tell you was that your father thinks it very unlikely that the money is there yet, and almost impossible that we could find it in any case. But some day when the place is yours you can have it put through a sieve if you choose. I wish I could think you would ever live there, Phil; but I can't imagine any chance by which you should. I should hate to have you sell it—it has belonged to a Philip Fairfield so many years."

A week later the boy left his childhood by the side of his mother's grave. His history for the next seven years may go in a few lines. School days, vacations, the four years at college, outwardly the commonplace of an even and prosperous development, inwardly the infinite variety of experience by which each soul is a person; the result of the two so wholesome a product of young manhood that no one realized under the frank and open manner a deep reticence, an intensity, a sensitiveness to impressions, a tendency toward mysticism which made the fibre of his being as delicate as it was strong.

Suddenly, in a turn of the wheel, all the externals of his life changed. His rich father died penniless and he found himself on his own hands, and within a month the boy who had owned five polo ponies was a hard-working reporter on a great daily. The same quick-wittedness and energy which had made him a good polo player made him a good reporter. Promotion came fast and, as those who are busiest have most time to spare, he fell to writing stories. When the editor of a large magazine took one, Philip first lost respect for that dignified person, then felt ashamed to have imposed on him, then rejoiced utterly over the check. After that editors fell into the habit; the people he ran against knew about his books; the checks grew better reading all the time; a point came where it was more profitable to stay at home and imagine events than to go out and report them. He had been too busy as the days marched, to generalize, but suddenly he knew that he was a successful writer; that if he kept his head and worked, a future was before him. So he soberly put his own English by the side of that of a master or two from his bookshelves, to keep his perspective clear, and then he worked harder. And it came to be five years after his father's death.

At the end of those years three things happened at once. The young man suddenly was very tired and knew that he needed the vacation he had gone without; a check came in large enough to make a vacation easy—and he had his old dream. His fagged brain had found it but another worry to decide where he should go to rest, but the dream settled the vexed question off-hand—he would go to Kentucky. The very thought of it brought rest to him, for like a memory of childhood, like a bit of his own soul, he knew the country—the "God's Country" of its people—which he had never seen. He caught his breath as he thought of warm, sweet air that held no hurry or nerve strain; of lingering sunny days whose hours are longer than in other places; of the soft speech, the serene and kindly ways of the people; of the royal welcome waiting for him as for every one, heartfelt and heartwarming; he knew it all from a daughter of Kentucky—his mother. It was May now, and he remembered she had told him that the land was filled with roses at the end of May—he would go then. He owned the old place, Fairfield, and he had never seen it. Perhaps it had fallen to pieces; perhaps his mother had painted it in colors too bright; but it was his, the bit of the earth that belonged to him. The Anglo-Saxon joy of land-owning stirred for the first time within him—he would go to his own place. Buoyant with the new thought he sat down and wrote a letter. A cousin of the family, of a younger branch, a certain John Fairfield, lived yet upon the land. Not in the great house, for that had been closed many years, but in a small house almost as old, called Westerly. Philip had corresponded with him once or twice about affairs of the estate, and each letter of the older man's had brought a simple and urgent invitation to come South and visit him. So, pleased as a child with the plan, he wrote that he was coming on a certain Thursday, late in May. The letter sent, he went about in a dream of the South, and when its answer, delighted and hospitable, came simultaneously with one of those bleak and windy turns of weather which make New York, even in May, a marvellously fitting place to leave, he could not wait. Almost a week ahead of his time he packed his bag and took the

Southwestern Limited, and on a bright Sunday morning he awoke in the old Phoenix Hotel in Lexington. He had arrived too late the night before to make the fifteen miles to Fairfield, but he had looked over the horses in the livery-stable and chosen the one he wanted, for he meant to go on horseback, as a Southern gentleman should, to his domain. That he meant to go alone, that no one, not even John Fairfield, knew of his coming, was not the least of his satisfactions, for the sight of the place of his forefathers, so long neglected, was becoming suddenly a sacred thing to him. The old house and its young owner should meet each other like sweethearts, with no eyes to watch their greeting, their slow and sweet acquainting; with no living voices to drown the sound of the ghostly voices that must greet his home-coming from those walls—voices of his people who had lived there, voices gone long since into eternal silence.

A little crowd of loungers stared with frank admiration at the young fellow who came out smiling from the door of the Phoenix Hotel, big and handsome in his riding clothes, his eyes taking in the details of girths and bits and straps with the keenness of a horseman.

Philip laughed as he swung into the saddle and looked down at the friendly faces, most of them black faces, below, "Good-by," he said. "Wish me good luck, won't you?" and a willing chorus of "Good luck, boss," came flying after him as the horse's hoofs clattered down the street.

Through the bright drowsiness of the little city he rode in the early Sunday morning, and his heart sang for joy to feel himself again across a horse, and for the love of the place that warmed him already. The sun shone hotly, but he liked it; he felt his whole being slipping into place, fitting to its environment; surely, in spite of birth and breeding, he was Southern born and bred, for this felt like home more than any home he had known!

As he drew away from the city, every little while, through stately woodlands, a dignified sturdy mansion peeped down its long vista of trees at the passing cavalier, and, enchanted with its beautiful setting, with its air of proud unconsciousness, he hoped each time that Fairfield would look like that. If he might live here—and go to New York, to be sure, two or three times a year to keep the edge of his brain sharpened—but if he might live his life as these people lived, in this unhurried atmosphere, in this perfect climate, with the best things in his reach for every-day use; with horses and dogs, with out-of-doors and a great, lovely country to breathe in; with—he smiled vaguely—with sometime perhaps a wife who loved it as he did—he would ask from earth no better life than that. He could write, he felt certain, better and larger things in such surroundings.

But he pulled himself up sharply as he thought how idle a day-dream it was. As a fact, he was a struggling young author, he had come South for two weeks' vacation, and on the first morning he was planning to live here—he must be light-headed. With a touch of his heel and a word and a quick pull on the curb, his good horse broke into a canter, and then, under the loosened rein, into a rousing gallop, and Philip went dashing down the country road, past the soft, rolling landscape, and under cool caves of foliage, vivid with emerald greens of May, thoughts and dreams all dissolved in exhilaration of the glorious movement, the nearest thing to flying that the wingless animal, man, may achieve.

He opened his coat as the blood rushed faster through him, and a paper fluttered from his pocket. He caught it, and as he pulled the horse to a trot, he saw that it was his cousin's letter. So, walking now along the brown shadows and golden sunlight of the long white pike, he fell to wondering about the family he was going to visit. He opened the folded letter and read:

"My dear Cousin," it said—the kinship was the first thought in John Fairfield's mind—"I received your welcome letter on the 14th. I am delighted that you are coming at last to Kentucky, and I consider that it is high time you paid Fairfield, which has been the cradle of your stock for many generations, the compliment of looking at it. We closed our house in Lexington three weeks ago, and are settled out here now for the summer, and find it lovelier than ever. My family consists only of myself and Shelby, my one child, who is now twenty-two years of age. We are both ready to give you an old-time Kentucky welcome, and Westerly is ready to receive you at any moment you wish to come."

The rest was merely arrangement for meeting the traveller, all of which was done away with by his earlier arrival.

"A prim old party, with an exalted idea of the family," commented Philip mentally. "Well-to-do, apparently, or he wouldn't be having a winter house in the city. I wonder what the boy Shelby is like. At twenty-two he should be doing something more profitable than spending an entire summer out here, I should say."

The questions faded into the general content of his mind at the glimpse of another stately old pillared homestead, white and deep down its avenue of locusts. At length he stopped his horse to wait for a ragged negro trudging cheerfully down the road.

"Do you know a place around here called Fairfield?" he asked.

"Yessah. I does that, sah. It's that ar' place right hyeh, sah, by yo' hoss. That ar's Fahfiel'. Shall I open the gate fo' you, boss?" and Philip turned to see a hingeless ruin of boards held together by the persuasion of rusty wire.

"The home of my fathers looks down in the mouth," he reflected aloud.

The old negro's eyes, gleaming from under shaggy sheds of eyebrows, watched him, and he caught the words.

"Is you a Fahfiel', boss?" he asked eagerly. "Is you my young Marse?" He jumped at the conclusion promptly. "You favors de fam'ly mightily, sah. I heard you was comin'"; the rag of a hat went off and he bowed low. "Hit's cert'nly good news fo' Fahfiel', Marse Philip, hit's mighty good news fo' us niggers, sah. I'se b'longed to the Fahfiel' fam'ly a hund'ed years, Marse—me and my folks, and I wishes yo' a welcome home, sah—welcome home, Marse Philip."

Philip bent with a quick movement from his horse, and gripped the twisted old black hand, speechless. This humble welcome on the highway caught at his heart deep down, and the appeal of the colored people to Southerners, who know them, the thrilling appeal of a gentle, loyal race, doomed to live forever behind a veil and hopeless without bitterness, stirred for the first time his manhood. It touched him to be taken for granted as the child of his people; it pleased him that he should be "Marse Philip" as a matter of course, because there had always been a Marse Philip at the place. It was bred deeper in the bone of him than he knew, to understand the soul of the black man; the stuff he was made of had been Southern two hundred years.

The old man went off down the white limestone road singing to himself, and Philip rode slowly under the locusts and beeches up the long drive, grass-grown and lost in places, that wound through the woodland three-quarters of a mile to his house. And as he moved through the park, through sunlight and shadow of these great trees that were his, he felt like a knight of King Arthur, like some young knight long exiled, at last coming to his own. He longed with an unreasonable seizure of desire to come here to live, to take care of it, beautify it, fill it with life and prosperity as it had once been filled, surround it with cheerful faces of colored people whom he might make happy and comfortable. If only he had money to pay off the mortgage, to put the place once in order, it would be the ideal setting for the life that seemed marked out for him—the life of a writer.

The horse turned a corner and broke into a canter up the slope, and as the shoulder of the hill fell away there stood before him the picture of his childhood come to life, smiling drowsily in the morning sunlight with shuttered windows that were its sleeping eyes—the great white house of Fairfield. Its high pillars reached to the roof; its big wings stretched away at either side; the flicker of the shadow of the leaves played over it tenderly and hid broken bits of woodwork, patches of paint cracked away, window-panes gone here and there. It stood as if too proud to apologize or to look sad for such small matters, as serene, as stately as in its prime. And its master, looking at it for the first time, loved it.

He rode around to the side and tied his mount to an old horse-rack, and then walked up the wide front steps as if each lift were an event. He turned the handle of the big door without much hope that it would yield, but it opened willingly, and he stood inside. A broom lay in a corner, windows were open—his cousin had been making ready for him. There was the huge mahogany sofa, horse-hair-covered, in the window under the stairs, where his mother had read "Ivanhoe" and "The Talisman." Philip stepped softly across the wide hall and laid his head where must have rested the brown hair of the little girl who had come to be, first all of his life, and then its dearest memory. Half an hour he spent in the old house, and its walls echoed to his footsteps as if in ready homage, and each empty room whose door he opened met him with a sweet half familiarity. The whole place was filled with the presence of the child who had loved it and left it, and for whom this tall man, her child, longed now as if for a little sister who should be here, and whom he missed. With her memory came the thought of the five-year-old uncle who had made history for the family so disastrously. He must see the garden where that other Philip had gone with his father to hide the money on the fated Christmas morning. He closed the house door behind him carefully, as if he would not disturb a little girl reading in the window, a little boy sleeping perhaps in the nursery above. Then he walked down the broad sweep of the driveway, the gravel crunching under the grass, and across what had been a bit of velvet lawn, and stood for a moment with his hand on a broken vase, weed-filled, which capped the stone post of a gateway.

All the garden was misty with memories. Where a tall golden flower nodded alone, from out of the tangled thicket of an old flower-bed, a bright-haired child might have laughed with just that air of startled, gay naughtiness, from the forbidden centre of the blossoms. In the moulded tan-bark of the path was a vague print, like the ghost of a footprint that had passed down the way a lifetime ago. The box, half dead, half sprouted into high unkept growth, still stood stiffly against the riotous overflow of weeds as if it yet held loyally to its business of guarding the borders, Philip shifted his gaze slowly, lingering over the dim contours, the shadowy shape of what the garden had been. Suddenly his eyes opened wide. How was this? There was a hedge as neat, as clipped, as any of Southampton in mid-season, and over it a glory of roses, red and white and pink and yellow, waved gay banners to him in trim luxuriance. He swung toward them, and the breeze brought him for the first time in his life the fragrance of box in sunshine.

Four feet tall, shaven and thick and shining, the old hedge stood, and the garnered sweetness of a hundred years' slow growth breathed delicately from it toward the great-great-grandson of the man who planted it. A box hedge takes as long in the making as a gentleman, and when they are done the two are much of a sort. No plant in all the garden has so subtle an air of breeding, so gentle a reserve, yet so gracious a message of sweetness for all of the world who will stop to learn it. It keeps a firm dignity under the stress of tempest when lighter growths are tossed and torn; it shines bright through the snow; it has a well-bred willingness to be background, with the well-bred gift of presence, whether as background or foreground. The soul of the box-tree is an aristocrat, and the sap that runs through it is the blue blood of vegetation.

Saluting him bravely in the hot sunshine with its myriad shining sword-points, the old hedge sent out to Philip on the May breeze its ancient welcome of aromatic fragrance, and the tall roses crowded gayly to look over its edge at the new master. Slowly, a little dazed at this oasis of shining order in the neglected garden, he walked to the opening and stepped inside the hedge. The rose garden! The famous rose garden of Fairfield, and as his mother had described it, in full splendor of cared-for, orderly bloom. Across the paths he stepped swiftly till he stood amid the roses, giant bushes of Jacqueminot and Maréchal Niel; of pink and white and red and yellow blooms in thick array. The glory of them intoxicated him. That he should own all of this beauty seemed too good to be true, and instantly he wanted to taste his ownership. The thought came to him that he would enter into his heritage with strong hands here in the rose garden; he caught a deep-red Jacqueminot almost roughly by its gorgeous head and broke off the stem. He would gather a bunch, a huge, unreasonable bunch of his own flowers. Hungrily he broke one after another; his shoulders bent over them, he was deep in the bushes.

"I reckon I shall have to ask you not to pick any more of those roses," a voice said.

**"I reckon I shall have to ask you not pick any more of those roses," a voice said.**

Philip threw up his head as if he had been shot; he turned sharply with a great thrill, for he thought his mother spoke to him. Perhaps it was only the Southern inflection so long unheard, perhaps the sunlight that shone in his eyes dazzled him, but, as he stared, the white figure before him seemed to him to look exactly as his mother had looked long ago. Stumbling over his words, he caught at the first that came.

"I—I think it's all right," he said.

The girl smiled frankly, yet with a dignity in her puzzled air. "I'm afraid I shall have to be right decided," she said. "These roses are private property and I mustn't let you have them."

"Oh!" Philip dropped the great bunch of gorgeous color guiltily by his side, but still held tightly the prickly mass of stems, knowing his right, yet half wondering if he could have made a mistake. He stammered:

"I thought—to whom do they belong?"

"They belong to my cousin, Mr. Philip Fairfield Beckwith"—the sound of his own name was pleasant as the falling voice strayed through it. "He is coming home in a few days, so I want them to look their prettiest for him—for his first sight of them. I take care of this rose garden," she said, and laid a motherly hand on the nearest flower. Then she smiled. "It doesn't seem right hospitable to stop you, but if you will come over to Westerly, to our house, father will be glad to see you, and I will certainly give you all the flowers you want." The sweet and masterful apparition looked with a gracious certainty of obedience straight into Philip's bewildered eyes.

"The boy Shelby!" Many a time in the months after Philip Beckwith smiled to himself reminiscently, tenderly, as he thought of "the boy Shelby" whom he had read into John Fairfield's letter; "the boy Shelby" who was twenty-two years old and the only child; "the boy Shelby" whom he had blamed with such easy severity for idling at Fairfield; "the boy Shelby" who was no boy at all, but this white flower of girlhood, called—after the quaint and reasonable Southern way—as a boy is called, by the surname of her mother's people.

Toward Westerly, out of the garden of the old time, out of the dimness of a forgotten past, the two took their radiant youth and the brightness of to-day. But a breeze blew across the tangle of weeds and flowers as they wandered away, and whispered a hope, perhaps a promise; for as it touched them each tall stalk nodded gayly and the box hedges rustled delicately an answering undertone. And just at the edge of the woodland, before they were out of sight, the girl turned and threw a kiss back to the roses and the box.

"I always do that," she said. "I love them so!"

Two weeks later a great train rolled into the Grand Central Station of New York at half-past six at night, and from it stepped a monstrosity—a young man without a heart. He had left all of it, more than he had thought he owned, in Kentucky. But he had brought back with him memories which gave him more joy than ever the heart had done, to his best knowledge, in all the years. They were memories of long and sunshiny days; of afternoons spent in the saddle, rushing through grassy lanes where trumpet-flowers flamed over gray farm fences, or trotting slowly down white roads; of whole mornings only an hour long, passed in the enchanted stillness of an old garden; of gay, desultory searches through its length and breadth, and in the park that held it, for buried treasure: of moonlit nights; of roses and June and Kentucky—and always, through all the memories, the presence that made them what they were, that of a girl he loved.

No word of love had been spoken, but the two weeks had made over his life; and he went back to his work with a definite object, a hope stronger than ambition, and, set to it as music to words, came insistently another hope, a dream that he did not let himself dwell on—a longing to make enough money to pay off the mortgage and put Fairfield in order, and live and work there all his life—with Shelby. That was where the thrill of the thought came in, but the place was very dear to him in itself.

The months went, and the point of living now were the mails from the South, and the feast days were the days that brought letters from Fairfield. He had promised to go back for a week at Christmas, and he worked and hoarded all the months between with a thought which he did not formulate, but which ruled his down-sitting and his up-rising, the thought that if he did well and his bank account grew enough to justify it he might, when he saw her at Christmas, tell her what he hoped; ask her—he finished the thought with a jump of his heart. He never worked harder or better, and each check that came in meant a step toward the promised land; and each seemed for the joy that was in it to quicken his pace, to lengthen his stride, to strengthen his touch. Early in November he found one night when he came to his rooms two letters waiting for him with the welcome Kentucky postmark. They were in John Fairfield's handwriting and in his daughter's, and "*place aux dames*" ruled rather than respect to age, for he opened Shelby's first. His eyes smiling, he read it.

"I am knitting you a diamond necklace for Christmas," she wrote. "Will you like that? Or be sure to write me if you'd rather have me hunt in the garden and dig you up a box of money. I'll tell you—there ought to be luck in the day, for it was hidden on Christmas and it should be found on Christmas; so on Christmas morning we'll have another look, and if you find it I'll catch you 'Christmas gif'' as the darkies do, and you'll have to give it to me, and if I find it I'll give it to you; so that's fair, isn't it? Anyway—" and Philip's eyes jumped from line to line, devouring the clear, running writing. "So bring a little present with you, please— just a tiny something for me," she ended, "for I'm certainly going to catch you 'Christmas gif.'"

Philip folded the letter back into its envelope and put it in his pocket, and his heart felt warmer for the scrap of paper over it. Then he cut John Fairfield's open dreamily, his mind still on the words he had read, on the threat—"I'm going to catch you 'Christmas gif.'" What was there good enough to give her? Himself, he thought humbly, very far from it. With a sigh that was not sad he dismissed the question and began to read the other letter. He stood reading it by the fading light from the window, his hat thrown by him on a chair, his overcoat still on, and, as he read, the smile died from his face. With drawn brows he read on to the end, and then the letter dropped from his fingers to the floor and he did not notice; his eyes stared widely at the high building across the street, the endless rows of windows, the lights flashing into them here and there. But he saw none of it. He saw a stretch of quiet woodland, an old house with great white pillars, a silent, neglected garden, with box hedges sweet and ragged, all waiting for him to come and take care of them—the home of his fathers, the home he had meant, had expected—he knew it now—would be some day his own, the home he had lost! John Fairfield's letter was to tell him that the mortgage on the place, running now so many years, was suddenly to be foreclosed; that, property not being worth much in the neighborhood, no one would take it up; that on January 2nd, Fairfield, the house and land, were to be sold at auction. It was a hard blow to Philip Beckwith. With his hands in his overcoat pockets he began to walk up and down the room, trying to plan, to see if by any chance he might save this place he loved. It would mean eight thousand dollars to pay the mortgage. One or two thousand more would put the estate in order, but that might wait if he could only tide over this danger, save the house and land. An hour he walked so, forgetting dinner, forgetting the heavy coat which he still wore, and then he gave it up. With all he had saved—and it was a fair and promising beginning—he could not much more than half pay the mortgage, and there was no way, which he would consider, by which he could get the money. Fairfield would have to go, and he set his teeth and clinched his fists as he thought how he wanted to keep it. A year ago it had meant nothing to him, a year from now if things went his way he could have paid the mortgage. That it should happen just this year—just now! He could not go down at Christmas; it would break his heart to see the place again as his own when it was just slipping from his grasp. He would wait until it was all over, and go, perhaps, in the spring. The great hope of his life was still his own, but Fairfield had been the setting of that hope; he must readjust his world before he saw Shelby again. So he wrote them that he would not come at present, and then tried to dull the ache of his loss with hard work.

But three days before Christmas, out of the unknown forces beyond his reasoning swept a wave of desire to go South, which took him off his feet. Trained to trust his brain and deny his impulse as he was, yet there was a vein of sentiment, almost of superstition, in him which the thought of the old place pricked sharply to life. This longing was something beyond him—he must go—and he had thrown his decisions to the winds and was feverish until he could get away.

As before, he rode out from the Phoenix Hotel, and at ten o'clock in the morning he turned into Fairfield. It was a still, bright Christmas morning, crisp and cool, and the air like wine. The house stood bravely in the sunlight, but the branches above it were bare and no softening leafage hid the marks of time; it looked old and sad and deserted to-day, and its master gazed at it with a pang in his heart. It was his, and he could not save it. He turned away and walked slowly to the garden, and stood a moment as he had stood last May, with his hand on the stone gateway. It was very silent and lonely here, in the hush of winter; nothing stirred; even the shadows of the interlaced branches above lay almost motionless across the walks.

Something moved to his left, down the pathway—he turned to look. Had his heart stopped, that he felt this strange, cold feeling in his breast? Were his eyes—could he be seeing? Was this insanity? Fifty feet down the path, half in the weaving shadows, half in clear sunlight, stood the little boy of his life-long vision, in the dress with the black velvet squares, his little uncle, dead forty years ago. As he gazed, his breath stopping, the child smiled and held up to him, as of old, a key on a scarlet string, and turned and flitted as if a flower had taken wing, away between the box hedges. Philip, his feet moving as if without his will, followed him. Again the baby face turned its smiling dark eyes toward him, and Philip knew that the child was calling him, though there was no sound; and again without volition of his own his feet took him where it led. He felt his breath coming difficultly, and suddenly a gasp shook him—there was no footprint on the unfrozen earth where the vision had passed. Yet there before him, moving through the deep sunlit silence of the garden, was the familiar, sturdy little form in its old-world dress. Philip's eyes were open; he was awake, walking; he saw it. Across the neglected tangle it glided, and into the trim order of Shelby's rose garden; in the opening between the box walls it wheeled again, and the sun shone clear on the bronze hair and fresh face, and the scarlet string flashed and the key glinted at the end of it. Philip's fascinated eyes saw all of that. Then the apparition slipped into the shadow of the beech trees and Philip quickened his step breathlessly, for it seemed that life and death hung on the sight. In and out through the trees it moved; once more the face turned toward him; he caught the quick brightness of a smile. The little chap had disappeared behind the broad tree-trunk, and Philip, catching his breath, hurried to see him appear again. He was gone. The little spirit that had strayed from over the border of a world—who can say how far, how near?—unafraid in this earth-corner once its home, had slipped away into eternity through the white gate of ghosts and dreams.

Philip's heart was pumping painfully as he came, dazed and staring, to the place where the apparition had vanished. It was a giant beech tree, all of two hundred and fifty years old, and around its base ran a broken wooden bench, where pretty girls of Fairfield had listened to their sweethearts, where children destined to be generals and judges had played with their black mammies, where gray-haired judges and generals had come back to think over the fights that were fought out. There were letters carved into the strong bark, the branches swung down whisperingly, the green tent of the forest seemed filled with the memory of those who had camped there and gone on. Philip's feet stumbled over the roots as he circled the veteran; he peered this way and that, but the woodland was hushed and empty; the birds whistled above, the grasses rustled below, unconscious, casual, as if they knew nothing of a child-soul that had wandered back on Christmas day with a Christmas message, perhaps, of good-will to its own.

As he stood on the farther side of the tree where the little ghost had faded from him, at his feet lay, open and conspicuous, a fresh, deep hole. He looked down absent-mindedly. Some animal—a dog, a rabbit—had scratched far into the earth. A bar of sunlight struck a golden arm through the branches above, and as he gazed at the upturned, brown dirt the rays that were its fingers reached into the hollow and touched a square corner, a rusty edge of tin. In a second the young fellow was down on his knees digging as if for his life, and in less than five minutes he had loosened the earth which had guarded it so many years, and staggering with it to his feet had lifted to the bench a heavy tin box. In its lock was the key, and dangling from it a long bit of no-colored silk, that yet, as he untwisted it, showed a scarlet thread in the crease. He opened the box with the little key; it turned scrapingly, and the ribbon crumbled in his fingers, its long duty done. Then, as he tilted the heavy weight, the double eagles, packed closely, slipped against each other with a soft clink of sliding metal. The young man stared at the mass of gold pieces as if he could not trust his eyesight; he half thought even then that he dreamed it. With a quick memory of the mortgage he began to count. It was all there—ten thousand dollars in gold! He lifted his head and gazed at the quiet woodland, the open shadow-work of the bare branches, the fields beyond lying in the calm sunlit rest of a Southern winter. Then he put his hand deep into the gold pieces, and drew a long breath. It was impossible to believe, but it was true. The lost treasure was found. It meant to him Shelby and home; as he realized what it meant his heart felt as if it would break with the joy of it. He would give her this for his Christmas gift, this legacy of his people and hers, and then he would give her himself. It was all easy now—life seemed not to hold a difficulty. And the two would keep tenderly, always, the thought of a child who had loved his home and his people and who had tried so hard, so long, to bring them together. He knew the dream-child would not visit him again—the little ghost was laid that had followed him all his life. From over the border whence it had come with so many loving efforts it would never come again. Slowly, with the heavy weight in his arms, he walked back to the garden sleeping in the sunshine, and the box hedges met him with a wave of fragrance, the sweetness of a century ago; and as he passed through their shining door, looking beyond, he saw Shelby. The girl's figure stood by the stone column of the garden entrance, the light shone on her bare head, and she had stopped, surprised, as she saw him. Philip's pace quickened with his heart-throb as he looked at her and thought of the little ghostly hands that had brought theirs together; and as he looked the smile that meant his welcome and his happiness broke over her face, and with the sound of her voice all the shades of this world and the next dissolved in light.

"'Christmas gif',' Marse Philip!" called Shelby.

## *THE WIFE OF THE GOVERNOR*

The Governor sat at the head of the big black-oak table in his big stately library. The large lamps on either end of the table stood in old cloisonné vases of dull rich reds and bronzes, and their shades were of thick yellow silk. The light they cast on the six anxious faces grouped about them was like the light in Rembrandt's picture of The Clinic.

It was a very important meeting indeed. A city official, who had for months been rather too playfully skating on the thin ice of bare respect for the law, had just now, in the opinion of many, broken through. He had followed a general order of the Governor's by a special order of his own, contradicting the first in words not at all, but in spirit from beginning to end. And the Governor wished to make an example of him—now, instantly, so promptly and so thoroughly that those who ran might read, in large type, that the attempt was not a success. He was young for a Governor—thirty-six years old—and it may be that care for the dignity of his office was not his only feeling on the subject.

"I won't be badgered, you know," he said to the senior Senator of the State. "If the man wishes to see what I do when I'm ugly, I propose to show him. Show me reason, if you can, why this chap shouldn't be indicted."

To which they answered various things; for while they sympathized, and agreed in the main, yet several were for temporizing, and most of them for going a bit slowly. But the Governor was impetuous and indignant. And here the case stood when there came a knock at the library door.

The Governor looked up in surprise, for it was against all orders that he should be disturbed at a meeting. But he spoke a "Come in," and Jackson, the stately colored butler, appeared, looking distressed and alarmed.

"Oh, Lord! Gov'ner, suh!" was all he got out for a moment, fear at his own rashness seizing him in its grip at the sight of the six distinguished faces turned toward him.

"Jackson! What do you want?" asked the Governor, not so very gently.

Jackson advanced, with conspicuous lack of his usual style and sang-froid, a tray in his hand, and a quite second-class-looking envelope upon it. "Beg pardon, suh. Shouldn't 'a' interrupted, Gov'nor; please scuse me, suh; but they boys was so pussistent, and it comed fum the deepo, and I was mos' feared the railways was done gone on a strike, and I thought maybe you'd oughter know, suh—Gov'ner."

And in the meantime, while the scared Jackson rambled on thus in an undertone, the Governor had the cheap, bluish-white envelope in his hand, and with a muttered "Excuse me" to his guests, had cut it across and was reading, with a face of astonishment, the paper that was enclosed. He crumpled it in his hand and threw it on the table.

"Absurd!" he said, half aloud; and then, "No answer, Jackson," and the man retired.

"Now, then, gentlemen, as we were saying before this interruption"—and in clear, eager sentences he returned to the charge. But a change had come over him. The Attorney-General, elucidating a point of importance, caught his chief's eye wandering, and followed it, surprised, to that ball of paper on the table. The Secretary of State could not understand why the Governor agreed in so half-hearted a way when he urged with eloquence the victim's speedy sacrifice. Finally, the august master of the house growing more and more distrait, he suddenly rose, and picking up the crumpled paper—

"Gentlemen, will you have the goodness to excuse me for five minutes?" he said. "It is most annoying, but I cannot give my mind to business until I attend to the matter on which Jackson interrupted us. I beg a thousand pardons—I shall only keep you a moment."

The dignitaries left cooling their heels looked at each other blankly, but the Lieutenant-Governor smiled cheerfully.

"One of the reasons he is Governor at thirty-six is that he always does attend to the matters that interrupt him."

Meanwhile the Governor, rushing out with his usual impulsive energy, had sent two or three servants flying over the house. "Where's Mrs. Mooney? Send Mrs. Mooney to me here instantly—and be quick;" and he waited, impatient, although it was for only three minutes, in a little room across the hall, where appeared to him in that time a square-shaped, gray-haired woman with a fresh face and blue eyes full of intelligence and kindliness.

"Mary, look here;" and the big Governor put his hand on the stout little woman's arm and drew her to the light. Mary and his Excellency were friends of very old standing indeed, their intimacy having begun thirty-five years before, when the future great man was a rampant baby, and Mary his nurse and his adorer, which last she was still. "I want to read you this, and then I want you to telephone to Bristol at once." He smoothed out the wrinkled single sheet of paper.

"My dear Governor Rudd," he read,—"My friends the McNaughtons of Bristol are friends of yours too, I think, and that is my reason for troubling you with this note. I am on my way to visit them now, and expected to take the train for Bristol at twenty minutes after eight to-night, but when I reached here at eight o'clock I found the time-table had been changed, and the train had gone out twenty minutes before. And there is no other till to-morrow. I don't know what to do or where to go, and you are the only person in the city whose name I know. Would it trouble you to advise me where to go for the night—what hotel, if it is right for me to go to a hotel? With regret that I should have to ask this of you when you must be busy with great affairs all the time, I am,

"Very sincerely,

"LINDSAY LEE."

Mary listened, attentive but dazed, and was about to burst out at once with voluble exclamations and questions when the Governor stopped her.

"Now, Mary, don't do a lot of talking. Just listen to me. I thought at first this note was from a man, because it is signed by a man's name. But it looks and sounds like a woman, and I think it should be attended to. I want you to telephone to Mr. George McNaughton, at Bristol, and ask if Mr. or Miss Lindsay Lee is a friend of theirs, and say that, if so, he—or she—is all right, and is spending the night here. Then, in that case, send Harper to the station with the brougham, and say that I beg to have the honor of looking after Mrs. McNaughton's friend for the night. And you'll see that whoever it is is made very comfortable."

"Indeed I will, the poor young thing," said Mary, jumping at a picturesque view of the case. "But, Mr. Jack, do you want me to telephone to Mr. McNaughton's and ask if a friend of theirs—"

The Governor cut her short. "Exactly. You know just what I said, Mary Mooney; you only want to talk it over. I'm much too busy. Tell Jackson not to come to the library again unless the State freezes over. Good-night.—I don't think the McNaughtons can complain that I haven't done their friend brown," said the Governor to himself as he went back across the hall.

---

Down at the station, beneath the spirited illumination of one whistling gas-jet, the station-master and Lindsay Lee waited wearily for an answer from the Governor. It was long in coming, for the station-master's boys, the Messrs. O'Milligan, seizing the occasion for foreign travel offered by a sight of the Executive grounds, had made a détour by the Executive stables, and held deep converse with the grooms. Just as the thought of duty undone began to prick the leathery conscience of the older one, the order came for Harper and the brougham. Half an hour later, at the station, Harper drew up with a sonorous clatter of hoofs. The station-master hurried forward to interview the coachman. In a moment he turned with a beaming face.

"It's good news for ye, miss. The Governor's sent his own kerridge for ye, then. Blessed Mary, but it's him that's condescendin'. Get right in, miss."

Such a sudden safe harbor seemed almost too good to be true. Lindsay was nearly asleep as the rubber-tired wheels rolled softly along through the city. The carriage turned at length from the lights and swung up a long avenue between trees, and then stopped. The door flew open, and Lindsay looked up steps and into a wide, lighted doorway, where stood a stout woman, who hastened to seize her bag and umbrella and take voluble possession of her. The sleepy, dazed girl was vaguely conscious of large halls and a wide stair and a kind voice by her side that flowed ever on in a gentle river of words. Then she found herself in a big, pleasant bed-room, and beyond was the open door of a tiled bath-room.

"Oh—oh!" she said, and dropped down sideways on the whiteness of the brass bed, and put her arms around the pillow and her head, hat and all, on it.

"Poor child!" said pink-cheeked, motherly Mrs. Mooney. "You're more than tired, that I can see without trying, and no wonder, too! I shan't say another word to you, but just leave you to get to bed and to sleep, and I'm sure it's the best medicine ever made, is a good comfortable bed and a night's rest. So I shan't stop to speak another word. But is there anything at all you'd like, Miss Lee? And there, now, what am I thinking about? I haven't asked if you wouldn't have a bit of supper! I'll bring it up myself—just a bit of cold bird and a glass of wine? It will do you good. But it will," as Lindsay shook her head, smiling. "There's nothing so bad as going to sleep on an empty stomach when you're tired."

"But I had dinner on the train, and I'm not hungry; sure enough, I'm not; thank you a thousand times."

Mrs. Mooney reluctantly took two steps toward the door, the room shaking under her soft-footed, heavy tread.

"You're sure you wouldn't like—" She stopped, embarrassed, and the blue eyes shone like kindly sapphires above the always-blushing cheeks. "I'm mortified to ask you for fear you'd laugh at me, but you seem like such a child, and—would you let me bring you—just a slice of bread and butter with some brown sugar on it?"

Lindsay had a gracious way of knowing when people really wished to do something for her. She flapped her hands, like the child she looked. "Oh, how did you think of it? I used to have that for a treat at home. Yes, I'd *love* it!" And Mrs. Mooney beamed.

"There! I thought you would! You see, Miss Lee, that's what I used sometimes to give my boy—that's the Governor—when he was little and got hungry at bedtime."

Lindsay, left alone, took off her hat, and with a pull and screw at her necktie and collar-button, dropped into a chair that seemed to hold its fat arms up for her. She smiled sleepily and comfortably. "I'm having a right good time," she said to herself, "but it's funny. I feel as if I lived here, and I love that old housekeeper-nurse of the Governor's. I wonder what the Governor is like? I wonder—" And at this point she became aware, with only slight surprise, of a little boy with a crown on his head who offered her a slice of bread and butter and sugar a yard square, and told her he had kept it for her twenty-five years. She was about to reason with him that it could not possibly be good to eat in that case, when something jarred the brain that was slipping so easily down into oblivion, and as her eyes opened again she saw Mrs. Mooney's solid shape bending over the tub in the bath-room, and a noise of running water sounded pleasant and refreshing.

"Oh, did I go to sleep?" she asked, sitting up straight and blinking wide-open eyes.

"There! I knew it would wake you, and I couldn't a-bear to do it, my dear, but it would never do for you to sleep like that in your clothes, and I drew your bath warm, thinking it would rest you better, but I can just change it hot or cold as it suits you. And here's the little lunch for you, and I feel as if it was my own little boy I was taking care of again; the year he was ten it was he ate so much at night. I saw him just now, and he's that tired from his meeting—it's a shame how hard he has to work for this State, time and time again. He said 'Good-night, Mary,' he said, just the way he did years ago—such a little gentleman he always was. The dearest and the handsomest thing he was; they used to call him 'the young prince,' he was that handsome and full of spirit. He told me to say he hoped for the pleasure of seeing Miss Lee at breakfast to-morrow at nine; but if you should be tired, Miss Lee, or prefer your breakfast up here, which you can have it just as well as not, you know. And here I'm talking you to death again, and you ought to stop me, for when I begin about the Governor I never know when to stop myself. Just put up your foot, please, and I'll take your shoes off," And while she unlaced Lindsay's small boots with capable fingers she apologized profusely for talking—talking as much again.

"There's nothing to excuse. It's mighty interesting to hear about him," said Lindsay. "I shall enjoy meeting him that much more. Is there a picture of him anywhere around?" looking about the room.

That was a lucky stroke. Mary Mooney parted the black ribbon that was tied beneath her neat white collar and turned her face up, all pleased smiles, to the girl, who leaned down to examine an ivory miniature set as a brooch. It was a sunny-faced little boy, with thick straight golden hair and fearless brown eyes—a sweet childish face very easy to admire, and Lindsay admired it enough to satisfy even Mrs. Mooney.

"I had it for a Christmas gift the year he was nine," she said. Mary's calendar ran from The Year of the Governor, 1. "He had whooping-cough just after that, and was ill seven weeks. Dear me, what teeny little feet you have!" as she put on them the dressing-slippers from the bag, and struggled up to her own, heavily but cheerfully.

Lindsay looked at her thoughtfully. "You haven't mentioned the Governor's wife," she said. "Isn't she at home?" and she leaned over to pull up the furry heel of the little slipper. So that she missed seeing Mary Mooney's face. Expression chased expression over that smiling landscape—astonishment, perplexity, anxiety, the gleam of a new-born idea, hesitation, and at last a glow of unselfish kindliness which often before had transfigured it.

"No, Miss Lee," said Mary. "She's away from home just now." And then, unblushingly, "But she's a lovely lady, and she'll be very disappointed not to see you."

Almost the next thing Lindsay knew she was watching dreamily spots of sunlight that danced on a pale pink wall. Then a bird began to sing at the edge of the window; there was a delicate rustle of skirts, and she turned her head and saw a maid—not Mary Mooney this time—moving softly about, opening part way the outside shutters, drawing lip the shades a bit, letting the light and shadow from tossing trees outside and the air and the morning in with gentle slowness. She dressed with deliberation, and, lo! it was a quarter after nine o'clock.

So that the Governor waited for his breakfast. For ten minutes, while the paper lasted, waiting was unimportant; and then, being impatient by nature, and not used to it, he suddenly was cross.

"Confound the girl!" soliloquized the Governor. "I'll have her indicted too! First she breaks up a meeting, then she gets the horses out at all hours, and now, to cap it, she makes me wait for breakfast. Why should I wait for my breakfast? Why the devil can't she—Now, Mary, what is it? I warn you I'm cross, and I shan't listen well till I've had breakfast. I'm waiting for that young lady you're coddling. Where's that young lady? Why doesn't she—What?"

For the flood-gates were open, and the soft verbal oceans of Mary were upon him. He listened two minutes, mute with astonishment, and then he rose up in his wrath and was verbal also.

"What! You told her I was *married*? What the dev—And you're actually asking *me* to tell her so *too*? Mary, are you insane? Embarrassed? What if she is embarrassed? And what do I care if—What? Sweet and pretty? Mary, don't be an idiot. Am I to improvise a wife, in my own house, because a stray girl may object to visiting a bachelor? Not if I know it. Not much." The Governor bristled with indignation. "Confound the girl, I'll—" At this point Mary, though portly, vanished like a vision of the night, and there stood in the doorway a smiling embodiment of the morning, crisp in a clean shirt-waist, and free from consciousness of crime.

"Is it Governor Rudd?" asked Lindsay; and the Governor was, somehow, shaking hands like a kind and cordial host, and the bitterness was gone from his soul. "I certainly don't know how to thank you," she said. "You-all have been very good to me, and I've been awfully comfortable. I was so lost and unhappy last night; I felt like a wandering Jewess. I hope I haven't kept you waiting for breakfast?"

"Not a moment," said the Governor, heartily, placing her chair, and it was five minutes before he suddenly remembered that he was cross. Then he made an effort to live up to his convictions. "This is a mistake," he said to himself. "I had no intention of being particularly friendly with this young person. Rudd, I can't allow you to be impulsive in this way. You're irritated by the delay and by last night: you're bored to be obliged to entertain a girl when you wish to read the paper; you're anxious to get down to the Capitol to see those men; all you feel is a perfunctory politeness for the McNaughtons' friend. Kindly remember these facts, Rudd, and don't make a fool of yourself gambolling on the green, instead of sustaining the high dignity of your office." So reasoned the Governor secretly, and made futile attempts at high dignity, while his heart became as wax, and he questioned of his soul at intervals to see if it knew what was going on.

So the Governor sat before Lindsay Lee at his own table, momentarily more surprised and helpless. And Lindsay, eating her grape-fruit with satisfaction, thought him delightful, and wondered what his wife was like, and how many children he had, and where they all were. It was at least safe to speak of the wife, for the old house-keeper-nurse had given her an unqualified recommendation. So she spoke.

"I'm sorry to hear that Mrs. Rudd is not at home," she began. "It must be rather lonely in this big house without her."

The Governor looked at her and laughed. "Not that I've noticed," he said, and was suddenly seized with a sickness of pity that was the inevitable effect of Lindsay Lee. She needed no pity, being healthy, happy, and well-to-do, but she had, for the punishment of men's sins, sad gray eyes and a mouth whose full lips curved sorrowfully down. Her complexion was the colorless, magnolia-leaf sort that is typically Southern; her dark hair lay in thick locks on her forehead as if always damp with emotion; her swaying, slender figure seemed to appeal to masculine strength; and the voice that drawled a syllable to twice its length here, to slide over mouthfuls of words there, had an upward inflection at the end of sentences that brought tears to one's eyes. There was no pose about her, but the whole effect of her was pathetic—illogically, for she caught the glint of humor from every side light of life, which means pleasure that other people miss. The old warning against vice says that we "first endure, then pity, then embrace"; but Lindsay differed from vice so far that people never had to endure her, but began with pity, finding it often a very short step to the wish, at least, to embrace her. The Governor after fifteen minutes' acquaintance had arrived at pitying her, intensely and with his whole soul, as he did most things. He held another interview with himself. "Lord! what an innocent face it is!" he said. "Mary said she would be embarrassed—the brute that would embarrass her! Hanged if I'll do it! If she would rather have me married, married I'll be." He raised candid eyes to Lindsay's face.

"I'm afraid I've shocked you. You mustn't think I shall not be glad when—Mrs. Rudd—is here. But, you see, I've been very busy lately. I've hardly had time to breathe—haven't had time to miss—her—at all, really. All the same—" Now what was the queer feeling in his throat and lungs—yes, it must be the lungs—as the Governor framed this sentence? He went on: "All the same, I shall be a happy man when—my wife—comes home."

Lindsay's face cleared. This was satisfactory and proper; there was no more to be said about it. She looked up with a smile to where the old butler beamed upon her for her youth and beauty and her accent and her name.

A handful of busy men left the Capitol in some annoyance that morning because the Governor had telephoned that he could not be there before half past eleven. They would have been more annoyed, perhaps, if they had seen him dashing about the station light-heartedly just before the eleven-o'clock train for Bristol left. They said to each other: "It must be a matter of importance that keeps him. Governor Rudd almost never throws over an appointment. He has been working like the devil over that street-railway franchise case; probably it's that."

And the Governor stood by a chair in a parlor-car, his world cleared of street railways and indictments and their class as if they had never been, and in his hand was a small white oblong box tied with a tinsel cord.

"Good-by," he said, "but remember I'm to be asked down for the garden party next week, and I'm coming."

"I certainly won't forget. And I reckon I'd better not try to thank you for—Oh, thank you! I thought that looked like candy. And bring Mrs. Rudd with you next week. I want to see her. And—Oh, get off, please; it's moving. Good-by, good-by."

And to the mighty music of a slow-clanging bell and the treble of escaping steam and the deep-rolling accompaniment of powerful wheels the Governor escaped to the platform, and the capital city of that sovereign State was empty—practically empty. He noticed it the moment he turned his eyes from the disappearing train and moved toward Harper and the brougham. He also noticed that he had never noticed it before.

A solid citizen, catching a glimpse of the well-known, thoughtful face through the window of the Executive carriage as it bowled across toward the Capitol, shook his head. "He works too hard," he said to himself. "A fine fellow, and young and strong, but the pace is telling. He looks anxious to-day. I wonder what scheme is revolving in his brain at this moment."

And at that moment the Governor growled softly to himself. "I've overdone it," he said. "She's sure to be offended. No one likes to be taken in. I ought not to have showed her Mrs. Rudd's conservatory; that was a mistake. She won't let them ask me down; I shan't see her. Hanged if I won't telephone Mrs. McNaughton to keep the secret till I've been down." And he did, before Lindsay could get there, amid much laughter at both ends of the wire, and no small embarrassment at his own.

And he was asked down, and having enjoyed himself, was asked again. And again. So that during the three weeks of Lindsay's visit Bristol saw more of the Chief Executive officer of the State than Bristol had seen before, and everybody but Lindsay had an inkling of the reason. But the time never came to tell her of the shadowy personality of Mrs. Rudd, and between the McNaughton girls and the Governor, whom they forced into unexpected statements, to their great though secret glee, Lindsay was informed of many details in regard to the missing first lady of the commonwealth. Such a dialogue as the following would occur at the lunch table:

*Alice McNaughton* (speaking with ceremonious politeness from one end of the table to the Governor at the other end). "When is Mrs. Rudd coming, Governor?"

*The Governor* (with a certain restraint). "Before very long, I hope, Miss Alice. Mrs. McNaughton, may I have more lobster? I've never in my life had as much lobster as I wanted."

*Alice* (refusing to be side-tracked). "And when did you last hear from her, Governor?"

*Chuck McNaughton* (ornament of the Sophomore class at Harvard. In love with Lindsay, but more so with the joke. Gifted with a sledgehammer style of wit). "I've been hoping for a letter from her myself, Governor, but it doesn't come."

*The Governor* (with slight hauteur). "Ah, indeed!"

*Lindsay* (at whose first small peep the Governor's eyes turn to hers and rest there shamelessly). "Why haven't you any pictures of Mrs. Rudd in the house, Mrs. McNaughton? The Governor's is everywhere and you all tell me how fascinating she is, and yet don't have her about. It looks like you don't love her as much as the Governor." (At the mention of being loved, in that voice, cold shivers seize the Executive nerves.)

*Mrs. McNaughton* (entranced with the airy persiflage, but knowing her own to be no light hand at repartee). "Ask the others, my dear."

*Alice* (jumping at the chance). "Oh, the reason of that is very interesting! Mrs. Rudd has never given even the Governor her picture. She—she has principles against it. She belongs, you see, to an ancient Hebrew family—in fact, she is a Jewess" ("A wandering Jewess," the Governor interjected, *sotto voce*, his glance veering again to Lindsay's face), "and you know that Jewish families have religious scruples about portraits of any sort" (pauses, exhausted).

*Chuck* (with heavy artillery). "Alice, *taisez-vous*. You're doing poorly. You can't converse. Your best parlor trick is your red hair. Miss Lee, I'll show you a picture of Mrs. Rudd some day, and I'll tell you now what she looks like. She has exquisite melancholy gray eyes, a mouth like a ripe tomato" (shouts from the table *en masse*, but Chuck ploughs along cheerily), "hair like the braided midnight" (cries of "What's that?" and "Hear! Hear!"), "a figure slim and willowy as a vaulting-pole" (a protest of "No track athletics at meals; that's forbidden!"), "and a voice—well, if you ever tasted New Orleans molasses on maple sugar, with 'that tired feeling' thrown in, perhaps you'll have a glimpse, a mile off, of what that voice is like." (Eager exclamations of "That's near enough," "Don't do it any more, Chuck," and "For Heaven's sake, Charlie, stop." Lindsay looks hard with the gray eyes at the Governor.)

*Lindsay*, "Why don't you pull your bowie-knife out of your boot, Governor? It looks like he's making fun of your wife, to me. Isn't anybody going to fight anybody?"

And then Mr. McNaughton would reprove her as a bloodthirsty Kentuckian, and the whole laughing tableful would empty out on the broad porch. At such a time the Governor, laughing too, amused, yet uncomfortable, and feeling himself in a false and undignified position, would vow solemnly that a stop must be put to all this. It would get about, into the papers even, by horrid possibility; even now a few intimates of the McNaughton family had been warned "not to kill the Governor's wife." He would surely tell the girl the next time he could find her alone, and then the absurdity would collapse. But the words would not come, or if he carefully framed them beforehand, this bold, aggressive leader of men, whose nickname was "Jack the Giant-killer," made a giant of Lindsay's displeasure, and was afraid of it. He had never been afraid of anything before. He would screw his courage up to the notch, and then, one look at the childlike face, and down it would go, and he would ask her to go rowing with him. They were such good friends; it was so dangerous to change at a blow existing relations, to tell her that he had been deceiving her all these weeks. These exquisite June weeks that had flown past to music such as no June had made before; days snowed under with roses, nights that seemed, as he remembered them, moonlit for a solid month. The Governor sighed a lingering sigh, and quoted,

"Oh what a tangled web we weave
When first we practise to deceive!"

Yes, he must really wait—say two days longer. Then he might be sure enough of her—regard—to tell her the truth. And then, a little later, if he could control himself so long, another truth. Beyond that he did not allow himself to think.

"Governor Rudd," asked Lindsay suddenly as they walked their horses the last mile home from a ride on which they had gotten separated—the Governor knew how—from the rest of the party, "why do they bother you so about your wife, and why do you let them?"

"Can't help it, Miss Lindsay. They have no respect for me. I'm that sort of man. Hard luck, isn't it?"

Lindsay turned her sad, infantile gray eyes on him searchingly. "I reckon you're not," she said. "I reckon you're the sort of man people don't say things to unless they're right sure you will stand it. They don't trifle with you." She nodded her head with conviction. "Oh, I've heard them talk about you! I like that; that's like our men down South. You're right Southern, anyhow, in some ways. You see, I can pay you compliments because you're a safe old married man," and her eyes smiled up at him: she rarely laughed or smiled except with those lovely eyes. "There's some joke about your wife," she went on, "that you-all won't tell me. There certainly is. I *know* it, sure enough I do, Governor Rudd."

There is a common belief that the Southern accent can be faithfully rendered in writing if only one spells badly enough. No amount of bad spelling could tell how softly Lindsay Lee said those last two words.

"I love to hear you say that—'Guv'na Rudd.' I do, 'sho 'nuff,'" mused the Governor out loud and irrelevantly. "Would you say it again?"

"I wouldn't," said Lindsay, with asperity. "Ridiculous! If you are a Governor! But I was talking about your wife. Isn't she coming home before I go? Sometimes I don't believe you have a wife."

That was his chance, and he saw it. He must tell her now or never, and he drew a long breath. "Suppose I told you that I had not," he said, "that she was a myth, what would you say?"

"Oh, I'd just never speak to you again," said Lindsay, carelessly. "I wouldn't like to be fooled like that. Look, there are the others!" and off she flew at a canter.

It is easy to see that the Governor was not hurried headlong into confession by that speech. But the crash came. It was the night before Lindsay was to go back home to far-off Kentucky, and with infinite expenditure of highly trained intellect, for which the State was paying a generous salary, the Governor had managed to find himself floating on a moonlit flood through the Forest of Arden with the Blessed Damozel. That, at least, is the rendering of a walk in the McNaughtons' wood with Lindsay Lee as it appeared that night to the intellect mentioned. But the language of such thoughts is idiomatic and incapable of exact translation. A flame of eagerness to speak, quenched every moment by a shower-bath of fear, burned in his soul, when suddenly Lindsay tripped on a root and fell, with an exclamation. Then fear dried beneath the flames. It is unnecessary to tell what the Governor did, or what he said. The language, as language, was unoriginal and of striking monotony, and as to what happened, most people have had experience which will obviate the necessity of going into brutal facts. But when, trembling and shaken, he realized a material world again, Lindsay was fighting him, pushing him away, her eyes blazing fiercely.

"What do you mean? What *do* you mean?" she was saying.

"Mean—mean? That I love you—that I want you to love me, to be my wife!" She stood up like a white ghost in the silver light and shadow of the wood.

"Governor Rudd, are you crazy?" she cried. "You have a wife already."

The tall Governor threw back his head and laughed a laugh like a child. The people away off on the porch heard him and smiled. "They are having a good time, those two," Mrs. McNaughton said.

"Lindsay—Lindsay," and he bent over and caught her hands and kissed them. "There isn't any wife—there never will be any but you. It was all a joke. It happened because—Oh, never mind! I can't tell you now; it's a long story. But you must forgive that; that's all in the past now. The question is, will you love me—will you love me, Lindsay? Tell me, Lindsay!" He could not say her name often enough. But there came no answering light in Lindsay's face. She looked at him as if he were a striped convict.

"I'll never forgive you," she said, slowly. "You've treated me like a child; you've made a fool of me, all of you. It was insulting. All a joke, you call it? And I was the joke; you've been laughing at me all these weeks. Why was it funny, I'd like to know?"

"Great heavens, Lindsay—you're not going to take it that way? I insult you—laugh at you! I'd give my life; I'd shoot down any one—Lindsay!" he broke out appealingly, and made a step toward her.

"Don't touch me!" she cried. "Don't touch me! I hate you!" And as he still came closer she turned and ran up the path, into the moonlight of the driveway, and so, a dim white blotch on the fragrant night, disappeared.

When the Governor, walking with dignity, came up the steps of the porch, three minutes later, he was greeted with questions.

"What have you done to Lindsay Lee, I'd like to know?" asked Alice McNaughton. "She said she had fallen and hurt her foot, but she wouldn't let me go up with her, and she was dignified, which is awfully trying. Why did you quarrel with her, this last night?"

"Governor," said Chuck, with more discernment than delicacy, "if you will accept the sympathies of one not unacquainted with grief—" But at this point his voice faded away as he looked at the Governor.

The Governor never remembered just how he got away from the friendly hatefulness of that porchful. An early train the next morning was inevitable, for there was a meeting of real importance this time, and at all events everything looked about the same shade of gray to him; it mattered very little what he did. Only he must be doing something every moment. He devoured work as if it were bread and meat and he were famished. People said all that autumn and winter that anything like the Governor's energy had never been seen. He evidently wanted a second term, and really he ought to have it. He was working hard enough to get it. About New-Year's he went down to Bristol for the first time since June, for a dinner at the McNaughtons'. Alice McNaughton's friendly face, under its red-gold hair, beamed at him from far away down the table, but after dinner, when the men came in from the dining-room, she took possession of him boldly.

"Governor, I want to tell you about Lindsay Lee. I know you'll be interested, though you did have some mysterious fight before she left. She's been awfully ill with pleurisy, a painful attack, and she's getting well very slowly. They have just taken her to Paul Smith's. I'm writing her to-morrow, and I want you to send a good message; it would please her."

It was hard to stand with eighteen people grouped about him, all more or less with an eye on his motions, and be the Governor, calm and dignified, while hot irons were being applied to his heart by this smiling girl.

"But, Miss Alice," he said, slowly, "I'm afraid you are wrong. I was unfortunate enough to make Miss Lee very angry. I am afraid she would think a message from me only an impertinence."

"Sir," said Alice, with decision, "I'm right sometimes, if I'm not Governor; and it's better to be right than to be Governor, I've heard—or something. You trust me. Just try the effect of a message, and see if it isn't a success. What shall I say?"

The Governor was impetuous, and in spite of all the work he had done so fiercely, the longing the work had been meant to quiet surged up as strong as ever. "Miss Alice," he said, eagerly, "if you are right, would it do—do you think I might deliver the message myself?"

"Do I think? Well, if *I* were a man! Faint heart, you know!"

And the Governor, at that choppy eloquence, openly seized the friendly young hand and wrung it till Alice begged, laughing but bruised, for mercy. When he came up, later, to bid her good-night, his face was bright, and,

"Good-night, Angel of Peace," he said.

---

Mary Mooney, who through the dark days had watched with anxious though uncomprehending eyes her boy's dejection and hard effort to live it down, and had applied partridges and sweetbreads and other forms of devotion steadily but unsuccessfully, saw at once and with, rapture the change when the Governor greeted her the next morning. Light-heartedly she packed his traps two days later—she had done it jealously for thirty-five years, though almost over the dead body of the Governor's man sometimes in these later days. And when he told her good-by she had her reward. The man's boyish heart went out in a burst of gratitude to the tireless love that had sought only his happiness all his life. He put his arm around the stout little woman's neck.

"Mary," he said, "I'm going to see Miss Lee."

Mary's pink cheeks were scarlet as she patted with a work-worn palm the strong hand on her shoulder. "Then I know what will happen," she said, "and I'm glad. And if you don't bring her back with you, Mr. Jack, I won't let you in."

So the stately Governor went off like a schoolboy with his nurse's blessing. And later like an arrow from a bow he swung around the corner of the snowy piazza at Paul Smith's, where Mrs. Lee had told him he would find her daughter. There was a bundle of fur in a big chair in the sunlight, dark against the white hills beyond, with their black lines of pine-trees. As the impetuous steps came nearer, it turned, and—the Governor's methods were again such that words do them no justice. But this time with happier result. Half an hour later, when some coherency was established, he said:

"You waited for me! You've been *waiting* for me!" as if it were the most astonishing fact in history. "And since when have you been waiting for me, you—"

Lindsay laughed, not only with her eyes, but with her soft voice. "Ever since the morning after, your Excellency. Alice told me all about it before I left, and made me see reason. And I—and I was right sorry I'd been so cross. I thought you'd come some time—but you came right slow," she said, and her eyes travelled over his face as if she were making sure he was really there.

"And I never dared to think you would see me!" he said. "But now!"

And again there were circumstances that are best described by a hiatus.

The day after, when Mary Mooney, discreetly letting her soul's idol get into his library before greeting him, trotted into that stately chamber with soft, heavy footsteps, she was met with a kiss and a bear's hug that, as she told Mrs. Rudd later, "was like the year he was nine."

"I didn't bring her, Mary," the Governor said, "but you'd better let me stay, for she's coming."

---

## THE LITTLE REVENGE

Suddenly a gust of fresh wind caught Sally's hat, and off it flew, a wide-winged pink bird, over the old, old sea-wall of Clovelly, down among the rocks of the rough beach, tumbling and jumping from one gray stone to another, and getting so far away that, in the soft violet twilight, it seemed as lost as any ship of the Spanish Armada wrecked long ago on this wild Devonshire coast.

"Oh!" cried Sally distractedly, and clapped her hands to her head with the human instinct to shut the stable door after the horse is gone. "Oh!" she cried again; "my pretty hat! And *oh*! it's in the water!"

But suddenly, out of somewhere in the twilight, there was a man chasing it. Sally leaned over the rugged, yellowish, grayish stone wall and excitedly called to him.

"Oh, thank you!" she cried, and "That's so good of you!"

The hat had tacked and was sailing inshore now, one stiff pink taffeta sail set to the breeze. And in a minute, with a reckless splash into the dashing waves, the man had it, and an easy, athletic figure swung up the causeway, holding it away from him, as if it might nip at him. He wore a dark blue jersey, and loose, flapping trousers of a seaman.

"He's only a sailor," Sally said under her breath; "I'd better tip him." Her hand slipped into her pocket and I heard the click of her purse.

He looked from one to the other of us in the dim light inquiringly, as he came up, and then off went his cap, and his face broke into the gentlest, most charming smile as he delivered the hat into Sally's outstretched hands.

"I'm afraid it's a bit damp," he said.

All dark-eyed, stalwart young fellows are attractive to me for the sake of one like that who died forty years ago, but this sailor had a charm of manner that is a gift of the gods, let it fall to prince or peasant; the pretty deference of his few words, and the quick, radiant smile, were enough to win friendliness from me. More than that, something in the set of his head, in the straight gaze of his eyes, held a likeness that made my memory ache. I smiled back at him instantly. But Sally's heart was on her hat; hats from good shops did not grow on trees for Sally Meade.

"I hope it isn't hurt," she said, anxiously, and shook it carefully, and hardly glanced at the rescuer, who was watching with something that looked like amusement in his face. Then her good manners came back.

"Thank you a thousand times," she said, and turned to him brightly. "You were so quick—but, oh! I'm afraid you're wet." She looked at him, and I saw a little shock of surprise in her face. Beauty so striking will be admired, even in a common sailor.

"It's nothing," he said, looking down at his sopping, wide trousers; "I'm used to it," and as Sally's hand went forward I caught the flash of silver, and at the same moment another flash, from the man's eyes.

It was enough to startle me for the fraction of a second, but, as I looked again, his expression held only a serious respect, and I was sure I had been mistaken. He took the money and touched his cap and said, "Thank you, miss," with perfect dignity. Yet my imagination must have been lively, for as he slipped it in his pocket, his look turned toward me, and for another breath of time a gleam of mischief—certainly mischief—flashed from his dark eyes to mine.

Then Sally, quite unconscious of this, perhaps imaginary, by-play, had an idea. "Are you a sailor?" she asked.

The man looked at her. "Yes—miss," he answered, a little slowly.

"We want to engage a boat and a man to take us out. Do you know of one? Have you a boat?"

The young fellow glanced down across the wall where a hull and mast gleamed indistinctly through the falling night, swinging at the side of the quay. "That's mine, yonder," he said, nodding toward it. And then, with the graceful, engaging frankness that I already knew as his, "I shall be very glad to take you out"—including us both in his glance.

"Sally," I said, five minutes later, as we trudged up the one steep, rocky street of Clovelly,—the picturesque old street that once led English smugglers to their caves, and that is more of a staircase than a street, with rows of stone steps across its narrow width—"Sally, you are a very unexpected girl. You took my breath away, engaging that man so suddenly to take us sailing to-morrow. How do you know he is reliable? It would have been safer to try one of the men they recommended from the Inn. And certainly it would have been more dignified to let me make the arrangements. You seem to forget that I am older than you."

"You aren't," said Sully, giving a squeeze to my arm that she held in the angle of hers, pushing me with her young strength up the hill. "You're not as old, cousin Mary. I'm twenty-two, and you're only eighteen, and I believe you will never be any older."

I think perhaps I like flattery. I am a foolish old woman, and I have noticed that it is not the young girls who treat me with great deference and rise as soon as I come who seem to me the most charming, but the ones who, with proper manners, of course, yet have a touch of comradeship, as if they recognized in me something more than a fossil exhibit. I like to have them go on talking about their beaux and their work and play, and let me talk about it, too. Sally Meade makes me feel always that there is in me an undying young girl who has outlived all of my years and is her friend and equal.

"I'm sorry if I was forward, cousin Mary, but the sailing is to be my party, you know, and then I thought you liked him. He had a pretty manner for a common sailor, didn't he? And his voice—these low-class English people have wonderfully well-bred, soft voices. I suppose it's particularly so here in the South. Cousin Mary, did you see the look he gave you with those delicious dark eyes? It's always the way—gentleman or hod-carrier—no one has a chance with men when you are about."

It is pleasant to me, old woman as I am, to be told that people like me—more pleasant, I think, every year. I never take it for truth, of course, but I believe it means good feeling, and it makes an atmosphere easy to breathe. I purred like a contented cat under Sally's talking, yet, to save my dignity, kept up a protest.

"Sally, my dear! Delicious dark eyes! I'm ashamed of you—a common sailor!"

"I didn't smile at him," said Sally, reflectively.

So, struggling up the steep street of Clovelly, we went home to the "New Inn," to cold broiled lobster, to strawberries and clotted Devonshire cream, and dreamless sleep in the white beds of the quiet rooms whose windows looked toward the woods and cliffs of Hobby Drive on one side, and on the other toward the dark, sparkling jewel of the moon-lighted ocean, and the shadowy line of Lundy Island far in the distance.

That I, an inland woman, an old maid of sixty, should tell a story of sailing and of love seems a little ridiculous. My nephews at college beguile me to talk about boats, and then laugh to hear me, for I think I get the names of things twisted. And as for what I know of the other—the only love-making to which I ever listened was ended forty years ago by one of the northern balls that fell in fiery rain on Pickett's charge at Gettysburg. Yet, if I but tell the tale as it came to me, others may feel as I did the thrill of the rushing of the keel through dashing salt water, the swing of the great white sail above, the flapping of the fresh wind in the slack of it, the exhilaration of moving with power like the angels, with the great forces of nature for muscles, the joy of it all expanding, pulsing through you, till it seems as if the sky might crack if once you let your delight go free. And some may catch, too, that other thrill, of the hidden feeling that glorified those days. Few lives are so poor that the like of it has not brightened them, and no one quite forgets.

It is partly Sally Meade's Southern accent that has made me love her above nearer cousins, from her babyhood. The modulations of her voice seem always to bring me close to the sound of the voice that went into silence when Geoffrey Meade, her father's young kinsman, was killed long ago.

The Meades, old-time planters in Virginia, have been very poor since the distant war of the sixties, and it has been one of my luxuries to give Sally a lift over hard places. Always with instant reward, for the smallest bit of sunlight, going into her prismatic spirit, comes out a magnificent rainbow of happiness. So when the idea came that they might let me have the girl to take abroad that summer, her friend, the girl spirit in me, jumped for joy. There was no difficulty made; it was one of the rare good things too good to be true, that yet are true. She did more for me than I for her, for I simply spent some superfluous idle money, while she filled every day with a new enjoyment, the reflection of her own fresh pleasure in every day as it came.

So here we were prowling about the south of England with "Westward Ho!" for a guide-book; coaching through deep, tawny Devonshire lanes from Bideford to Clovelly; searching for the old tombstone of Will Cary's grave in the churchyard on top of the hill; gathering tales of Salvation Yeo and of Amyas Leigh; listening to echoes of the three-hundred-year-old time when the great sea-battle was fought in the channel and many ships of the Armada wrecked along this Devonshire coast. And always coming back to sleep in the fascinating little "New Inn," as old as the hills, built on both sides of the one rocky ladder street of Clovelly, the street so steep that no horses can go in it, and at the bottom of whose breezy tunnel one sees the rolling floor of the sea. In so careless a way does the Inn ramble about the cliff that when I first went to my room, two flights up from the front, I caught my breath at a blaze of scarlet and yellow nasturtiums that faced me through a white-painted doorway opening on the hillside and on a tiny garden at the back.

The irresponsible pleasure of our first sail the next afternoon was never quite repeated. The boat shot from the landing like a high-strung horse given his head, out across the unbordered road of silver water, and in a moment, as we raced toward the low white clouds, we turned and saw the cliffs of the coast and the tiny village, a gay little pile of white, green-latticed houses steeped in foliage lying up a crack in the precipice. Above was the long stretch of the woods of Hobby Drive. Clovelly is so old that its name is in Domesday Book; so old, some say, that it was a Roman station, and its name was Clausa Vaillis. But it is a nearer ancientness that haunts it now. Every wave that dashes on the rocky shore carries a legend of the ships of the Invincible Armada. As we asked question after question of our sailor, handsomer than ever to-day with a red silk handkerchief knotted sailor-fashion about his strong neck, story after story flashed out, clear and dramatic, from his answers. The bunch of houses there on the shore? Yes, that had a history. The people living there were a dark-featured, reticent lot, different from other people hereabouts. It was said that one of the Spanish galleons went ashore there, and the men had been saved and had settled on the spot and married Devonshire women, but their descendants had never lost the tradition of their blood. Certainly their speech and their customs were peculiar, unlike those of the villages near. He had been there and had seen them, had heard them talk. Yes, they were distinct. He laughed a little to acknowledge it, with an Englishman's distrust of anything theatrical. A steep cliff started out into the waves, towering three hundred feet in almost perpendicular lines. Had that a name? Yes, that was called "Gallantry Bower." No; it was not a sentimental story—it was the old sea-fight again. It was said that an English sailor threw a rope from the height and saved life after life of the crew of a Spaniard wrecked under the point.

"You know the history of your place very well," said Sally. The young man kept his eyes on his steering apparatus and a slow half-smile troubled his face and was gone.

"I've had a bit of an education for a seaman—Miss," he said. And then, after apparently reflecting a moment, "My people live near the Leighs of Burrough Court, and I was playmate to the young gentlemen and was given a chance to learn with them, with their tutors, more than a common man is likely to get always."

At that Sally's enthusiasm broke through her reserve, and I was only a little less eager.

"The Leighs! The real, old Leighs of Burrough? Amyas Leigh's descendants? Was that story true? Oh!—" And here manners and curiosity met and the first had the second by the throat. She stopped. But our sailor looked up with a boyish laugh that illumined his dark face.

"Is it so picturesque? I have been brought up so close that it seems commonplace to me. Every one must be descended from somebody, you know."

"Yes, but Amyas Leigh!" went on Sally, flushed and excited, forgetting the man in his story. "Why, he's my hero of all fiction! Think of it, Cousin Mary—there are men near here who are his great—half-a-dozen greats—grandchildren! Cousin Mary," she stopped and looked at me impressively, oblivious of the man so near her, "if I could lay my hands on one of those young Leighs of Burrough I'd marry him in spite of his struggles, just to be called by that name. I believe I would."

"Sally!" I exclaimed, and glanced at the man; Sally's cheeks colored as she followed my look. His mouth was twitching, and his eyes smouldered with fun. But he behaved well. On some excuse of steering he turned his back instantly and squarely toward us. But Sally's interest was irrepressible.

"Would you mind telling me their names, Cary?" she asked. He had told us to call him Cary. "The names of the Mr. Leighs of Burrough."

"No, Cary," I said. "I think Miss Meade doesn't notice that she is asking you personal questions about your friends."

Cary turned on me a look full of gentleness and chivalry. "Miss Meade doesn't ask anything that I cannot answer perfectly well," he said. "There are two sons of the Leighs, Richard Grenville, the older, and Amyas Francis, the younger. They keep the old names you see. Richard—Sir Richard, I should say—is the head of the family, his father being dead."

"Sir Richard Grenville Leigh!" said Sally, quite carried away by that historic combination. "That's better than Amyas," she went on, reflectively. "Is he decent? But never mind. I'll marry *him*, Cousin Mary."

At that our sailor-man shook with laughter, and as I met his eyes appealing for permission, I laughed as hard as he. Only Sally was apparently quite serious.

"He would be very lucky—Miss," he said, restraining his mirth with a respect that I thought remarkable, and turned again to his rudder.

Sally, for the first time having felt the fascination of breathing historic air, was no longer to be held. The sweeping, free motion, the rush of water under the bow as we cut across the waves, the wide sky and the air that has made sailors and soldiers and heroes of Devonshire men for centuries on end, the exhilaration of it all had gone to the girl's head. She was as unconscious of Cary as if he had been part of his boat. I had seen her act so when she was six, and wild with the joy of an autumn morning, intoxicated with oxygen. We had been put for safety into the hollow part of the boat where the seats are—I forget what they call it—the scupper, I think. But I am apt to be wrong on the nomenclature. At all events, there we were, standing up half the time to look at the water, the shore, the distant sails, and because life was too intense to sit down. But when Sally, for all her gentle ways, took the bit in her teeth, it was too restricted for her there.

"Is there any law against my going up and holding on to the mast?" she asked Cary.

"Not if you won't fall overboard, Miss," he answered.

The girl, with a strong, self-reliant jump, a jump that had an echo of tennis and golf and horseback, scrambled up and forward, Cary taking his alert eyes a moment from his sailing, to watch her to safety, I thought her pretty as a picture as she stood swaying with one arm around the mast, in her white shirt-waist and dark dress, her head bare, and brown, untidy hair blowing across the fresh color of her face, and into her clear hazel eyes.

"What is the name of this boat?" she demanded, and Cary's deep, gentle voice lifted the two words of his answer across the twenty feet between them.

"The Revenge" he said.

Then there was indeed joy. "The Revenge! The Revenge! I am sailing on the Revenge, with a man who knows Sir Richard Grenville and Amyas Leigh! Cousin Mary, listen to that—this is the Revenge we're on—this!" She hugged the mast, "And there are Spanish galleons, great three-deckers, with yawning tiers of guns, all around us! You may not see them, but they are here! They are ghosts, but they are here! There is the great San Philip, hanging over us like a cloud, and we are—we are—Oh, I don't know who we are, but we're in the fight, the most beautiful fight in history!" She began to quote:

And half of their fleet to the right, and half to the left were seen,
And the little Revenge ran on through the long sea-lane between.

And then:

Thousands of their sailors looked down from the decks and laughed;
Thousands of their soldiers made mock at the mad little craft
Running on and on till delayed
By the mountain-like San Philip that, of fifteen hundred tons,
And towering high above us with her yawning tiers of guns,
Took the breath from our sails, and we stayed.

The soft, lingering voice threw the words at us with a thrill and a leap forward, just us the Revenge was carrying us with long bounds, over the shining sea. We were spinning easily now, under a steady light wind, and Cary, his hand on the rudder, was opposite me. He turned with a start as the girl began Tennyson's lines, and his shining dark eyes stared up at her.

"Do you know that?" he said, forgetting the civil "Miss" in his earnestness.

"Do I know it? Indeed I do!" cried Sally from her swinging rostrum. "Do you know it, too? I love it—I love every word of it—listen," And I, who knew her good memory, and the spell that the music of a noble poem cast over her, settled myself with resignation. I was quite sure that, short of throwing her overboard, she would recite that poem from beginning to end. And she did. Her skirts and her hair blowing, her eyes full of the glory of that old "forlorn hope," gazing out past us to the seas that had borne the hero, she said it.

At Flores in the Azores, Sir Richard Grenville lay,
And a pinnace, like a frightened bird, came flying from far away;
Spanish ships of war at sea, we have sighted fifty-three!
Then up spake Sir Thomas Howard
"'Fore God, I am no coward"—

She went on and on with the brave, beautiful story. How Sir Thomas would not throw away his six ships of the line in a hopeless fight against fifty-three; how yet Sir Richard, in the Revenge, would not leave behind his "ninety men and more, who were lying sick ashore"; how at last Sir Thomas

sailed away
With five ships of war that day
Till they melted like a cloud in the silent summer heaven,
But Sir Richard bore in hand
All his sick men from the land,
Very carefully and slow,
Men of Bideford in Devon—
And he laid them on the ballast down below;
And they blessed him in their pain
That they were not left to Spain,
To the thumbscrew and the stake, for the glory of the Lord.

The boat sailed softly, steadily now, as if it would not jar the rhythm of the voice telling, with soft inflections, with long, rushing meter, the story of that other Revenge, of the men who had gone from these shores, under the great Sir Richard, to that glorious death.

And the sun went down, and the stars came out far over the summer sea,
And not one moment ceased the fight of the one and the fifty-three.
Ship after ship, the whole night long, their high-built galleons came;
Ship after ship, the whole night long, with their battle thunder and flame;
Ship after ship, the whole night long, drew back with her dead and her shame;
For some they sunk, and many they shattered so they could fight no more.
God of battles! Was ever a battle like this in the world before?

As I listened, though I knew the words almost, by heart too, my eyes filled with tears and my soul with the desire to have been there, to have fought as they did, on the little Revenge one after another of the great Spanish ships, till at last the Revenge was riddled and helpless, and Sir Richard called to the master-gunner to sink the ship for him, but the men rebelled, and the Spaniards took what was left of ship and fighters. And Sir Richard, mortally wounded, was carried on board the flagship of his enemies, and died there, in his glory, while the captains

—praised him to his face.
With their courtly Spanish grace.

So died, never man more greatly, Sir Richard Grenville, of Stow in Devon.

The crimson and gold of sunset were streaming across the water as she ended, and we sat silent. The sailor's face was grim, as men's faces are when they are deeply stirred, but in his dark eyes burned an intensity that reserve could not bold back, and as he still stared at the girl a look shot from them that startled me like speech. She did not notice. She was shaken with the passion of the words she had repeated, and suddenly, through the sunlit, rippling silence, she spoke again.

"It's a great thing to be a Devonshire sailor," she said, solemnly. "A wonderful inheritance—it ought never to be forgotten. And as for that man—that Sir Richard Grenville Leigh—he ought to carry his name so high that nothing low or small could ever touch it. He ought never to think a thought that is not brave and fine and generous."

There was a moment's stillness and then I said, "Sally, my child, it seems to me you are laying down the law a little freely for Devonshire. You have only been here four days." And in a second she was on her usual gay terms with the world again.

"A great preacher was wasted in me," she said. "How I could have thundered at everybody else about their sins! Cousin Mary, I'm coming down—I'm all battered, knocking against the must, and the little trimmings hurt my hands."

Cary did not smile. His face was repressed and expressionless and in it was a look that I did not understand. He turned soberly to his rudder and across the broken gold and silver of the water the boat drew in to shadowy Clovelly.

It was a shock, after we had landed and I had walked down the quay a few yards to inspect the old Red Lion Inn, the house of Salvation Yeo, to come back and find Sally dickering with Cary. I had agreed that this sail should be her "party," because it pleased the girl's proud spirit to open her small purse sometimes for my amusement. But I did not mean to let her pay for all our sailing, and I was horrified to find her trying to get Cary cheaper by the quantity. When I arrived, Sally, a little flustered and very dignified and quite evidently at the end of a discussion as to terms, was concluding an engagement, and there was a gleam in the man's wonderful eyes, which did much of his talking for him.

"You see the boat is very new and clean, Miss," he was saying, "and I hope you were satisfied with me?"

## "You see, the boat is very new and clean, Miss," he was saying.

I upset Sally's business affairs at once, engaged Cary, and told him he must take out no one else without knowing our plans. My handkerchief fell as I talked to him and he picked it up and presented it with as much ease and grace as if he had done such things all his life. It was a remarkable sailor we had happened on. A smile came like sunshine over his face—the smile that made him look as Geoffrey Meade looked, half a century ago.

"I'll promise not to take any one else, ma'am," he said. And then, with the pretty, engaging frankness that won my heart over again each time, "And I hope you'll want to go often—not so much for the money, but because it is a pleasure to me to take you—both."

There was mail for us waiting at the Inn. "Listen, Sally," I said, as I read mine in my room after dinner. "This is from Anne Ford. She wants to join us here the 6th of next month, to fill in a week between visits at country-houses."

Sally, sitting on the floor before the fire, her dark hair loose and her letters lying about her, looked up attentively, and discreetly answered nothing. Anne Ford was my cousin, but not hers, and I knew without discussing it, that Sally cared for her no more than I. She was made of showy fibre, woven in a brilliant pattern, but the fibre was a little coarse, and the pattern had no shading. She was rich and a beauty and so used to being the centre of things, and largely the circumference too, that I, who am a spoiled old woman, and like a little place and a little consideration, find it difficult to be comfortable as spoke upon her wheel.

"It's too bad," I went on regretfully. "Anne will not appreciate Clovelly, and she will spoil it for us. She is not a girl I care for. I don't see why I should he made a convenience for Anne Ford," I argued in my selfish way. "I think I shall write her not to come."

Sally laughed cheerfully. "She won't bother us, Cousin Mary. It would be too bad to refuse her, wouldn't it? She can't spoil Clovelly—it's been here too long. Anne is rather overpowering," Sally went on, a bit wistfully. "She's such a beauty, and she has such stunning clothes."

The firelight played on the girl's flushed, always-changing face, full of warm light and shadow; it touched daintily the white muslin and pink ribbons of the pretty negligee she wore, Sally was one of the poor girls whose simple things are always fresh and right. I leaned over and patted her rough hair affectionately.

"Your clothes are just as pretty," I said, "and Anne doesn't compare with you in my eyes." I lifted the unfinished letter and glanced over it. "All about her visit to Lady Fisher," I said aloud, giving a résumé as I read. "What gowns she wore to what functions; what men were devoted to her—their names—titles—incomes too." I smiled. "And—what is this?" I stopped talking, for a name had caught my eye. I glanced over the page. "Isn't this curious! Listen, my dear," I said. "This will interest you!" I read aloud from Anne's letter.

"'But the man who can have me if he wants me is Sir Richard Leigh. He is the very best that ever happened, and moreover, quite the catch of the season. His title is old, and he has a yacht and an ancestral place or two, and is very rich, they say—

but that isn't it. My heart is his without his decorations—well, perhaps not quite that, but it's certainly his with the decorations. He is such a beauty, Cousin Mary! Even you would admire him. It gives you quite a shock when he comes into a room, yet he is so unconscious and modest, and has the most graceful, fascinatingly quiet manners and wonderful brown eyes that seem to talk for him. He does everything well, and everything hard, is a dare-devil on horseback, a reckless sailor, and a lot besides. If you could see the way those eyes look at me, and the smile that breaks over his face as if the sun had come out suddenly! But alas! the sun has gone under now, for he went this morning, and it's not clear if he's coming back or not. They say his yacht is near Bideford, where his home is, and Clovelly is not far from that, is it?'"

I stopped and looked at Sally, listening, on the floor. She was staring into the fire.

"What do you think of that?" I asked. Sally was slow at answering; she stared on at the burning logs that seemed whispering answers to the blaze.

"Some girls have everything," she said at length. "Look at Anne. She's beautiful and rich and everybody admires her, and she goes about to big country-houses and meets famous and interesting people. And now this Sir Richard Leigh comes like the prince into the story, and I dare say he will fall in love with her and if she finds no one that suits her better she will marry him and have that grand old historic name."

"Sally, dear," I said, "you're not envying Anne, are you?"

A quick blush rushed to her face. "Cousin Mary! What foolishness I've been talking! How could I! What must you think of me! I didn't mean it—please believe I didn't. I'm the luckiest girl on earth, and I'm having the most perfect time, and you are a fairy godmother to me, except that you're more like a younger sister. I was thinking aloud. Anne is such a brilliant being compared to me, that the thought of her discourages me sometimes. It was just Cinderella admiring the princess, you know."

"Cinderella got the prince," I said, smiling.

"I don't want the prince," said Sally, "even if I could get him. I wouldn't marry an Englishman. I don't care about a title. To be a Virginian is enough title for me. It was just his name, magnificent Sir Richard Grenville's name and the Revenge-Armada atmosphere that took my fancy. I don't know if Anne would care for that part," she added, doubtfully.

"I'm sure Anne would know nothing about it," I answered decidedly, and Sally went on cheerfully.

"She's very welcome to the modern Sir Richard, yacht and title and all. I don't believe he's as attractive as your sailor, Cousin Mary. Something the same style, I should say from the description. If you hadn't owned him from the start, I'd rather like that man to be my sailor, Cousin Mary—he's so everything that a gentleman is supposed to be. How did he learn that manner—why, it would flatter you if he let the boom whack you on the head. Too bad he's only a common sailor—such a prince gone wrong!"

I looked at her talking along softly, leaning back on one hand and gazing at the fire, a small white Turkish slipper—Southern girls always have little feet—stuck out to the blaze, and something in the leisurely attitude and low, unhurried voice, something, too, in the reminiscent crackle of the burning wood, invited me to confidence. I went to my dressing-table, and when I came back, dropped, as if I were another girl, on the rug beside her. "I want to show you this," I said, and opened a case that travels always with me. From the narrow gold rim of frame inside, my lover smiled gayly up at her brown hair and my gray, bending over it together.

None of the triumphs of modern photographers seem to my eyes so delicately charming as the daguerrotypes of the sixties. As we tipped the old picture this way and that, to catch the right light on the image under the glass, the very uncertainty of effect seemed to give it an elusive fascination. To my mind the birds in the bush have always brighter plumage than any in the hand, and one of these early photographs leaves ever, no matter from what angle you look upon it, much to the imagination. So Geoff in his gray Southern uniform, young and soldierly, laughed up at Sally and me from the shadowy lines beneath the glass, more like a vision of youth than like actual flesh and blood that had once been close and real. His brown hair, parted far to one side, swept across his forehead in a smooth wave, as was the old-fashioned way; his collar was of a big, queer sort unknown to-day; the cut of his soldier's coat was antique; but the beauty of the boyish face, the straight glance of his eyes, and ease of the broad shoulders that military drill could not stiffen, these were untouched, were idealized even by the old-time atmosphere that floated up from the picture like fragrance of rose-leaves. As I gazed down at the boy, it came to me with a pang that he was very young and I growing very old, and I wondered would he care for me still. Then I remembered that where he lived it was the unworn soul and not the worn-out body that counted, and I knew that the spirit within me would meet his when the day came, with as fresh a joy as forty years ago. And as I still looked, happy in the thought, I felt all at once as if I had seen his face, heard his voice, felt the touch of his young hand that day—could almost feel it yet. Perhaps my eyes were a little dim, perhaps the uncertainty of the old daguerrotype helped the illusion, but the smile of the master of the Revenge seemed to shine up at me from my Geoff's likeness, and then Sally's slow voice broke the pause.

"It's Cousin Geoffrey, isn't it?" she asked. Her father was Geoffrey Meade's cousin—a little boy when Geoff died, "Was he as beautiful as that?" she said, gently, putting her hand over mine that held the velvet case. And then, after another pause, she went on, hesitatingly; "Cousin Mary, I wonder if you would mind if I told you whom he looks like to me?"

"No, my dear," I answered easily, and like an echo to my thought her words came.

"It is your sailor. Do you see it? He is only a common seaman, of course, but I think he must have a wonderful face, for with all his dare-devil ways I always think of 'Blessed are the pure in spirit' when I see him. And the eyes in the picture have the same expression—do you mind my saying it, Cousin Mary?"

"I saw it myself the first time I looked at him," I said. And then, as people do when they are on the verge of crying, I laughed. "Anne Ford would think me ridiculous, wouldn't she?" and I held Geoff's picture in both my hands. "He is much better suited to her or to you. A splendid young fellow of twenty-four to belong to an old woman like me—it is absurd, isn't it?"

"He is suited to no one but you, dear, and you are just his age and always will be," and as Sally's arms caught me tight I felt tears that were not my own on my cheek.

It was ten days yet before Anne was due to arrive, and almost every day of the ten we sailed. The picturesque coast of North Devon, its deep bays, its stretches of high, tree-topped cliffs, grew to be home-like to us. We said nothing of Cary and his boat at the Inn, for we soon saw that both were far-and-away better than common, and we were selfish. Nor did the man himself seem to care for more patronage. He was always ready when we wished to go, and jumped from his spick-and-span deck to meet us with a smile that started us off in sunshine, no matter what the weather. And with my affection for the lovely, uneven coast and the seas that held it in their flashing fingers, grew my interest in the winning personality that seemed to combine something of the strength of the hills and the charm of the seas of Devonshire.

One day after another he loosed the ropes with practised touch, and the wind taught the sail with a gay rattle and the little Revenge flung off the steep street and the old sea-wall and the green cliffs of Clovelly, and first yards and then miles of rippling ocean lay between us and land, and we sailed away, we did not need to know or care where, with our fate for the afternoon in his reliable hands. Little by little we forgot artificial distinctions in the out-of-doors, natural atmosphere, or that the man was anything but himself—a self always simple, always right. Looking back, I see how deeply I was to blame, to have been so blind, at my age, but the figure by the rudder, swinging to the boat's motion, grew to be so familiar and pleasant a sight, that I did not think of being on guard against him. Little as he talked, his moods were varied, grave or gay or with a gleam of daring in his eyes that made him, I think, a little more attractive than any other way. Yet when a wind of seriousness lifted the still or impetuous surface, I caught a glimpse, sometimes, of a character of self-reliance, of decision as solid as the depths under the shifting water of his ocean. There was never a false note in his gentle manner, and I grew to trust serenely to his tact and self-respect, and talked to him freely as I chose. Which of course I should not have done. But there was a temptation to which I yielded in watching for the likeness in his face, and in listening for a tone or two of his voice that caught my heart with the echo of a voice long silent.

One morning to our astonishment Cary sent up to break our engagement for the afternoon. Something had happened so that he could not possibly get away. But it was moonlight and warm—would we not go out in the evening? The idea seemed to me a little improper, yet very attractive, and Sally's eyes danced.

"Let's be bold and bad and go, Cousin Mary," she pleaded, and we went.

A shower of moonlight fell across the sea and on the dark masses of the shore; it lay in sharp patches against the black shadows of the sail; it turned Sally's bare, dark head golden, and tipped each splashing wave with a quick-vanishing electric light. It was not earth or ocean, but fairyland. We were sailing over the forgotten, sea-buried land of Lyonesse; forests where Tristram and Iseult had ridden, lay under our rushing keel; castles and towers and churches were there—hark! could I not hear the faint bells in the steeples ringing up through the waves? The old legend, half true, half fable, was all real to me as I sat in the shadow of the sail and stared, only half seeing them, at Sally standing with her hands on the rudder and Cary leaning over her, teaching her to sail the Revenge. Their voices came to me clear and musical, yet carrying no impression of what they were saying. Then I saw Sally's little fingers slip suddenly, and Cary's firm hand close over them, pushing the rudder strongly to one side. His face was toward me, and I saw the look that went over it as his hand held hers. It startled me to life again, and I sat up straight, but he spoke at once with quiet self-possession.

"I beg your pardon, Miss Meade. She was heading off a bit dangerously."

And he went on with directions, laughing at her a little, scolding her a little, yet all with a manner that could not be criticised. I still wonder how he could have poised so delicately and so long on that slender line of possible behavior.

As the boat slipped over the shimmering ocean, back into the harbor again, most of the houses up the sharp ascent of Clovelly street were dark, but out on the water lay a mass of brilliant lights, rocking slowly on the tide. Sally was first to notice it.

"There is a ship lying out there. Is it a ship or is it an enchantment? She is lighted all over. What is it—do you know?"

Cary was working at the sail and he did not look at us or at it as he answered.

"Yes, Miss—I know her. She is Sir Richard Leigh's yacht the Rose. She was there as we went out, but she was dark and you did not notice her."

I exclaimed, full of interest, at this, but Sally, standing ghost-like in her white dress against the sinking sail, said nothing, but stared at the lights that outlined the yacht against the deep distance of the sky, and that seemed, as the shadowy hull swung dark on the water, to start out from nowhere in pin-pricks of diamonds set in opal moonlight.

Lundy Island lies away from Clovelly to the northwest seventeen miles off on the edge of the world. Each morning as I opened my window at the Inn, and looked out for the new day's version of the ocean, it lifted a vague line of invitation and of challenge. Since we had been in Devonshire the atmosphere of adventure that hung over Lundy had haunted me with the wish to go there. It was the "Shutter," the tall pinnacle of rock at its southern end, that Amyas Leigh saw for his last sight of earth, when the lightning blinded him, in the historic storm that strewed ships of the Armada along the shore. I am not a rash person, yet I was so saturated with the story of "Westward Ho!" that I could not go away satisfied unless I had set foot on Lundy. But it had the worst of reputations, and landing was said to be hazardous.

"It isn't that I can't get you there," said Cary when I talked to him, "but I might not be able to get you away."

Then he explained in a wise way that I did not entirely follow, how the passage through the rocks was intricate, and could only be done with a right wind, and how, if the wind changed suddenly, it was impossible to work out until the right wind came again. And that might not be for days, if one was unlucky. It had been known to happen so. Yet I lingered over the thought, and the more I realized that it was unreasonable, the more I wanted to go. The spirit of the Devonshire seas seemed, to my fancy, to live on the guarded, dangerous rocks, and I must pay tribute before I left his kingdom. Cary laughed a little at my one bit of adventurous spirit so out of keeping with my gray hairs, but it was easy to see that he too wanted to go, and that only fear for our safety and comfort made him hesitate. The day before Anne Ford was due we went. It was the day, too, after our sail in the moonlight that I half believed, remembering its lovely unreality, had been a dream. But as we sailed out, there lay Sir Richard Leigh's yacht to prove it, smart and impressive, shining and solid in the sunlight as it had been ethereal the night before. I gazed at her with some curiosity.

"Have you been on board?" I asked our sailor. "Is Sir Richard there?"

Cary glanced at Sally, who had turned a cold shoulder to the yacht and was looking back at Clovelly village, crawling up its deep crack in the cliff. "Yes," he said; "I've been on her twice. Sir Richard is living on her."

"I suppose he's some queer little rat of a man," Sally brought out in her soft voice, to nobody in particular.

I was surprised at the girl's incivility, but Cary answered promptly, "Yes, Miss!" with such cheerful alacrity that I turned to look at him, more astonished. I met eyes gleaming with a hardly suppressed amusement which, if I had stopped to reason about it, was much out of place. But yet, as I looked at him with calm dignity and seriousness, I felt myself sorely tempted to laugh back. I am a bad old woman sometimes.

The Revenge careered along over the water as if mad to get to Lundy, under a strong west wind. In about two hours the pile of fantastic rocks lay stretched in plain view before us. We were a mile or more away—I am a very uncertain judge of distance—but we could see distinctly the clouds of birds, glittering white sea-gulls, blowing hither and thither above the wild little continent where were their nests. There are thousands and thousands of gulls on Lundy. We had sailed out from Clovelly at two in bright afternoon sunshine, but now, at nearly four, the blue was covering with gray, and I saw Cary look earnestly at the quick-moving sky.

"Is it going to rain?" I asked.

He stood at the rudder, feet apart and shoulders full of muscle and full of grace, the handkerchief around his neck a line of flame between blue clothes and olive face. A lock of bronze hair blew boyishly across his forehead.

"Worse than that," he said, and his eyes were keen as he stared at the uneven water in front of us. A basin of smoother water and the yellow tongue of a sand-beach lay beyond it at the foot of a line of high rocks. "The passage is there"—he nodded. "If I can make it before the squall catches us"—he glanced up again and then turned to Sally. "Could you sail her a moment while I see to the sheet? Keep her just so." His hand placed Sally's with a sort of roughness on the rudder. "Are you afraid?" He paused a second to ask it.

"Not a bit," said the girl, smiling up at him cheerfully, and then he was working away, and the little Revenge was flying, ripping the waves, every breath nearer by yards to that tumbling patch of wolf-gray water.

As I said, I know less about a boat than a boy of five. I can never remember what the parts of it are called and it is a wonder to me how they can make it go more than one way. So I cannot tell in any intelligent manner what happened. But, as it seemed, suddenly, while I watched Sally standing steadily with both her little hands holding the rudder, there was a crack as if the earth had split, then, with a confused rushing and tearing, a mass of something fell with a long-drawn crash, and as I stared, paralyzed, I saw the mast strike against the girl as she stood, her hands still firmly on the rudder, and saw her go down without a sound. There were two or three minutes of which I remember nothing but the roaring of water. I think I must have been caught under the sail, for the next I knew I was struggling from beneath its stiff whiteness, and as I looked about, dazed, behold! we had passed the reefs and lay rocking quietly. I saw that first, and then I saw Cary's head as it bent over something he held in his arms—and it was Sally! I tried to call, I tried to reach them, but the breath must have been battered out of me, for I could not, and Cary did not notice me. I think he forgot I was on earth. As I gazed at them speechless, breathless, Sally's eyes opened and smiled up at him, and she turned her face against his shoulder like a child. Cary's dark cheek went down against hers, and through the sudden quiet I heard him whisper.

"Sweetheart! sweetheart!" he said.

Both heads, close against each other, were still for a long moment, and then my gasping, rasping voice came back to me.

"Cary!" I cried, "for mercy's sake, come and take me out of this jib!"

I have the most confused recollection of the rest of that afternoon. Cary hammered and sawed and worked like a beaver with the help of two men who lived on Lundy, fishermen by the curious name of Heaven. Sally and I helped, too, whenever we could, but all in a heavy silence. Sally was wrapped in dignity as in a mantle, and her words were few and practical. Cary, quite as practical, had no thought apparently for anything but his boat. As for me, I was like a naughty old cat. I fussed and complained till I must have been unendurable, for the emotions within me were all at cross-purposes. I was frightened to death when I thought of General Meade; I was horrified at the picture stamped on my memory of his daughter, trusted to my care, smiling up with that unmistakable expression into the eyes of a common sailor. Horrified! My blood froze at the thought. Yet—it was unpardonable of me—yet I felt a thrill as I saw again those two young heads together, and heard the whispered words that were not meant for me to hear.

Somehow or other, after much difficulty, and under much mental strain, we got home. Sally hardly spoke as we toiled up the stony hill in the dark beneath a pouring rain, and I, too, felt my tongue tied in an embarrassed silence. At some time, soon, we must talk, but we both felt strongly that it was well to wait till we could change our clothes.

At last we reached the friendly brightness of the New Inn windows; we trudged past them to the steps, we mounted them, and as the front door opened, the radiant vision burst upon us of Anne Ford, come a day before her time, fresh and charming and voluble—voluble! It seemed the last straw to our tired and over-taxed nerves, yet no one could have been more concerned and sympathetic, and that we were inclined not to be explicit as to details suited her exactly. All the sooner could she get to her own affairs. Sir Richard Leigh's yacht was the burden of her lay, and that it was here and we had seen it added lustre to our adventures. That we had not been on board and did not know him, was satisfactory too, and neither of us had the heart to speak of Cary. We listened wearily, feeling colorless and invertebrate beside this brilliant creature, while Anne planned to send her card to him to-morrow, and conjectured gayeties for all of us, beyond. Sir Richard Leigh and his yacht did not fill a very large arc on our horizon to-night. Sally came into my room to tell me good-night, when we went up-stairs, and she looked so wistful and tired that I gave her two kisses instead of one.

"Thank you," she said, smiling mistily. "We won't talk to-night, will we, Cousin Mary?" So without words, we separated.

Next morning as I opened my tired eyes on a world well started for the day, there came a tap at the door and in floated Anne Ford, a fine bird in fine feathers, wide-awake and brisk.

"Never saw such lazy people!" she exclaimed. "I've just been in to see Sally and she refuses to notice me. I suppose it's exhaustion from shipwreck. But I wasn't shipwrecked, and I've had my breakfast, and it's too glorious a morning to stay indoors, so I'm going to walk down to the water and look at Sir Richard's boat, and send off my card to him by a sailor or something. Then, if he's a good boy, he will turn up to-day, and then—!" The end of Anne's sentence was wordless ecstasy.

But the mention of the sailor had opened the flood-gates for me, and in rushed all my responsibilities. What should I do with this situation into which I had so easily slipped, and let Sally slip? Should I instantly drag her off to France like a proper chaperone? Then how could I explain to Anne—Anne would be heavy dragging with that lodestone of a yacht in the harbor. Or could we stay here as we had planned and not see Cary again? The unformed shapes of different questions and answers came dancing at me like a legion of imps as I lay with my head on the pillow and looked at Anne's confident, handsome face, and admired the freshness and cut of her pale blue linen gown.

"Well, Cousin Mary," she said at last, "you and Sally seem both to be struck dumb from your troubles. I'm going off to leave you till you can be a little nicer to me. I may come back with Sir Richard—who knows! Wish me good luck, please!" and she swept off on a wave of good-humor and good looks.

I lay and thought. Then, with a pleasant leisure that soothed my nerves a little, I dressed, and went down to breakfast in the quaint dining-room hung from floor to ceiling with china brought years ago from the far East by a Clovelly sailor. As I sat over my egg and toast Sally came in, pale, but sweet and crisp in the white that Southern girls wear most. There was a constraint over us for the reckoning that we knew was coming. Each felt guilty toward the other and the result was a formal politeness. So it was a relief when, just at the last bit of toast, Anne burst in, all staccato notes of suppressed excitement.

"Cousin Mary! Sally! Sir Richard Leigh is here! He's there!" nodding over her shoulder. "He walked up with me—he wants to see you both. But"—her voice dropped to an intense whisper—"he has asked to see Miss Walton first—wants to speak to her alone! What does he mean?" Anne was in a tremendous flutter, and it was plain that wild ideas were coursing through her. "You are my chaperone, of course, but what can he want to see you for alone—Cousin Mary?"

I could not imagine, either, yet it seemed quite possible that this beautiful creature had taken a susceptible man by storm, even so suddenly. I laid my napkin on the table and stood up.

"The chaperone is ready to meet the fairy prince," I said, and we went across together to the little drawing-room.

It was a bit dark as Anne opened the door and I saw first only a man's figure against the window opposite, but as he turned quickly and came toward us, I caught my breath, and stared, and gasped and stared again. Then the words came tumbling over each other before Anne could speak.

"Cary!" I cried. "What are you doing here—in those clothes?"

Poor Anne! She thought I had made some horrid mistake, and had disgraced her. But I forgot Anne entirely for the familiar brown eyes that were smiling, pleading into mine, and in a second he had taken my hand and bending over, with a pretty touch of stateliness, had kissed it, and the charm that no one could resist had me fast in its net.

"Miss Walton! You will forgive me? You were always good to me—you won't lay it up against me that I'm Richard Leigh and not a picturesque Devonshire sailor! You won't be angry because I deceived you! The devil tempted me suddenly and I yielded, and I'm glad. Dear devil! I never should have known either of you if I had not."

There were more of the impetuous sentences that I cannot remember, and somewhere among them Anne gathered that she was not the point of them, and left the room like a slighted but still reigning princess. It was too bad that any one should feel slighted, but if it had to be, it was best that it should be Anne.

Then my sailor told me his side of the story; how Sally's tip for the rescue of her hat had showed him what we took him to be; how her question about a boat had suggested playing the part; how he had begun it half for the fun of it and half, even then, for the interest the girl had roused in him—and he put in a pretty speech for the chaperone just there, the clever young man! He told me how his yacht had come sooner than he had expected, and that he had to give up one afternoon with her was so severe a trial that he knew then how much Sally meant to him.

"That moonlight sail was very close sailing indeed," he said, his face full of a feeling that he did not try to hide. "There was nearly a shipwreck, when—when she steered wrong." And I remembered.

Then, with no great confidence in her mood, I went in search of my girl. She is always unexpected, and a dead silence, when I had anxiously told my tale, was what I had not planned for. After a minute,

"Well?" I asked.

And "Well?" answered Sally, with scarlet cheeks, but calmly.

"He is waiting for you down-stairs," I said.

Then she acted in the foolish way that seemed natural. She dropped on her knees and put her face against my shoulder.

"Cousin Mary! I can't! It's a strange man—it isn't our sailor any more. I hate it. I don't like Englishmen."

"He's very much the same as yesterday," I said. "You needn't like him if you don't want to, but you must go and tell him so yourself." I think that was rather clever of me.

So, holding my hand and trembling, she went down. When I saw Richard Leigh's look as he stood waiting, I tried to loosen that clutching hand and leave them, but Sally, always different from any one else, held me tight.

"Cousin Mary, I won't stay unless you stay," she said, firmly.

I looked at the young man and he laughed.

"I don't care. I don't care if all the world hears me," he said, and he took a step forward and caught her hands.

Sally looked up at him. "You're a horrid lord or something," she said.

He laughed softly. "Do you mind? I can't help it. It's hard, but I want you to help me try to forget it. I'd gladly he a sailor again if you'd like me better."

"I did like you—before you deceived me. You pretended you were that."

"But I have grievances too—you said I was a queer little rat of a man."

Sally's laugh was gay but trembling. "I did say that, didn't I?"

"Yes, and you tried to underpay me, too."

"Oh, I didn't! You charged a lot more than the others."

Sir Richard shook his head firmly. "Not nearly as much as the Revenge was worth. I kept gangs of men scrubbing that boat till I nearly went into bankruptcy. And, what's more, you ought to keep your word, you know. You said you were going to marry Richard Leigh—Richard Grenville Cary Leigh is his whole name, you know. Will you keep your word?"

"But I—but you—but I didn't know," stammered Sally, feebly.

He went on eagerly. "You told me how he should wear his name—high and—and all that." He had no time for abstractions. "He can never do it alone—will you come and help him?"

Sally was palpably starching about for weapons to aid her losing fight. "Why do you like me? I'm not beautiful like Anne Ford." He laughed. "I'm not rich, you know, like lots of American girls. We're very poor"—she looked at him earnestly.

"I don't care if you're rich or poor," he said. "I don't know if you're beautiful—I only know you're you. It's all I want."

She shook a little at his vehemence, but she was a long fighter. "You don't know me very much," she went on, her soft voice breaking. "Maybe it's only a fancy—the moonlight and the sailing and all—maybe you only imagine you like me."

"Imagine I like you!"

And then, at the sight of his quick movement and of Sally's face I managed to get behind a curtain and put my fingers in my ears. No woman has a right to more than one woman's love-making. And as I stood there, a few minutes later, I felt myself pulled by two pairs of hands, and Sally and her lover were laughing at me.

**I felt myself pulled by two pairs of hands.**

"May I have her? I want her very much," he said, and I wondered if ever any one could say no to anything he asked. So, with a word about Sally's far-away mother and father, I told him, as an old woman might, that I had loved him from the first, and then I said a little of what Sally was to me.

"I like her very much," I said, in a shaky voice that tried to be casual. "Are you sure that you like her enough?" For all of his answer, he turned, not even touching her hands, and looked at her.

It was as if I caught again the fragrance of the box hedges in the southern sunshine of a garden where I had walked on a spring morning long ago. Love is as old-fashioned as the ocean, and us little changed in all the centuries. Its always yielding, never retreating arms lie about the lands that are built and carved and covered with men's progress; it keeps the air sweet and fresh above them, and from generation to generation its look and its depths are the same. That it is stronger than death does not say it all. I know that it is stronger than life. Death, with its crystal touch, may make a weak love strong; life, with its every-day wear and tear, must make any but a strong love weak.

I like to think that the look I saw in Richard Leigh's eyes as he turned toward my girl was the same look I shall see, not so very many years from now, when I close mine on this dear old world, and open them, by the shore of the ocean of eternity, on the face of Geoffrey Meade.

Made in United States
Orlando, FL
15 February 2022